SENATORIAL
PRIVILEGE

Forge Books by E. J. Gorman

The First Lady
The Marilyn Tapes

SENATORIAL PRIVILEGE

E. J. GORMAN

A TOM DOHERTY ASSOCIATES BOOK
NEW YORK

SENATORIAL PRIVILEGE

Copyright © 1997 by E. J. Gorman

This book is printed on acid-free paper.

A Forge Book
Published by Tom Doherty Associates, Inc.
175 Fifth Avenue
New York, NY 10010

Forge® is a registered trademark of Tom Doherty Associates, Inc.

Library of Congress Cataloging-in-Publication Data

Gorman, Edward.
    Senatorial privilege / E.J. Gorman. —1st ed.
        p.   cm.
    "A Tom Doherty Associates book."
    ISBN 0–312–85778–0
    I. Title.
    PS3557.O759S4   1997
    813'.54—dc21   97–13324

First edition: October 1997

Printed in the United States of America

0   9   8   7   6   5   4   3   2   1

To my editor, Greg Cox—
a strong, clear light in the dark, dark forest

ACKNOWLEDGMENTS

I would like to thank Amy Markon and Dori Butler for their considerable help with this novel.

SENATORIAL
PRIVILEGE

He was discreet about it. In this town, you had to worry about your rep, after all.

Over the twenty-six years he'd been here, there'd been two wives and a succession of mistresses. Wife number one, he'd divorced. Wife number two had died of a brain aneurysm. This was four days after she'd caught him having sex with his current mistress late one night in his office.

He was not only discreet, he was no braggart. A lot of his peers seemed to have sex not so much for the pleasures of the flesh but just so they could brag about it afterward. "I'll tell you one thing, that little gal was real surprised by the ride I gave her," one of them had said to him recently. "She just figured that with my white hair and all, I probably wouldn't be able to get a full-bore erection. But I wore her out. Absolutely wore her out."

Talk like this vaguely disgusted him. He wasn't a prude. He just didn't approve of sharing this kind of intimacy. . . . It somehow diminished the act itself . . . as if you were doing it for ulterior motives. But then, this was a town wall-to-wall with ulterior motives . . . the most treacherous city in the world, Winston Churchill had once called it.

"What're you thinking about?" she said.

"Winston Churchill."

She smiled. "That's nice. You're lying next to a completely
naked woman and you're thinking about Winston Churchill?"

He laughed. "I guess that *didn't* sound very flattering,
did it?"

He liked to treat his mistresses with the same generosity he
treated his home state. He was the prize champion when it
came to pork-barreling. His state received more federal dollars
than any other small state in the Union.

And his mistresses received more compliments, attention,
and gifts than any other mistresses in town, too. He never forgot birthdays, anniversaries, or PMS days. He'd been on a subcommittee that had looked into PMS and he took the subject
very seriously.

"Maybe you didn't like how I did you tonight," the mistress said coyly.

"Oh, come on, now. You're the best and you know it."

"Am I really? The best, I mean?"

"You know you are."

She lay on her side, and he was pressed up against her singularly lovely bottom. He was starting to get in the mood
again.

"That feels good," she said, as he pressed himself a little
harder to her.

"Yes, it certainly does."

He slid his hand between her arm and rib cage and began
playing with her nipple between his thumb and forefinger.

"Wow," she said.

"Wow is right," he laughed.

"You've really got stamina."

"Clean living."

"I bet."

"No, it's true," he said, pressing even harder against her backside.

Her hips had begun to move slowly and deliciously.

"That's your image, anyway," she teased. "The clean-living thing."

"Well, it's true," he said. "Compared to some of my colleagues, I'm an absolute saint."

"I wonder what they'd say if they knew about us?"

"Oh, they'd probably just smile a little. Maybe wink at each other."

"Not the press."

"No," he said. "The press would probably make a big thing of it."

"A big thing? Are you kidding? They'd make a scandal out of it. I mean, my father would spend every dime he had destroying you."

She liked to do that sometimes. Remind him of who really had the power in this relationship.

But right now, he was in no mood to worry about power.

His own hips had started to move in rhythm with hers. There was no other reality now except the sweet hot reality between her beautifully sleek legs.

"He really would," she said. "He'd go on TV and tell everybody how you were sleeping with his fifteen-year-old daughter."

"His *virginal* fifteen-year-old daughter."

She giggled, then parted her legs so that he could get up inside her.

"Right," she giggled. "His *virginal* fifteen-year-old daughter."

*   *   *

Later that night, he went back to his office and sat in his leather chair and took out a bottle of brandy from the bottom right drawer of his desk. Then he sat there and looked out the window at Washington, D.C. Sometimes, he actually got chills thinking of all the men who had been here before him. They hadn't been perfect men, either.

That's what he often said to himself when he started worrying about some of his extracurricular activities. True, he did seem to enjoy the company of teenage girls, but my God, who was without fault? Surely not George Washington, who'd cheated lavishly on the expense account the Continental Congress had given him. Surely not Jefferson, who'd kept slaves and likely sired a bunch of mixed-race children. And surely not his own personal icon, Jack Kennedy. My God, this was a man who had slept with movie stars throughout his sadly brief tenure as president.

It always made him feel better, thinking this way. Sure he was a senator and sure he had responsibilities and sure he probably shouldn't be sleeping with the fifteen-year-old daughter of the senator who sat right across the aisle from him.

But who in this life was without sin?

And in a town like Washington, who could afford to cast the first stone?

He sighed, sipped some brandy. He needed to get out of Washington for a while, back to his small-town roots. He saw himself as Jimmy Stewart, as Gary Cooper, a man from the plains who fought for right and justice.

He couldn't help it; he was just that kinda guy.

PART

1

ONE

1

"You think you could do it?"

"You mean pull the lever myself?"

"Uh-huh."

"You ask hard questions."

"You thought I was just going to be some high-school kid, huh?"

Amy McGuire smiled at the slight, sandy-haired seventeen-year-old in front of her. His name was Brian Wright and he was editor of the Roosevelt High School newspaper. He wore a white button-down shirt and blue, sharply creased slacks and black socks and cordovan penny loafers. And he wore a crew cut. He was a part of the fifties revival feeling in the air, and Amy liked it.

"You're right. I thought this was going to be a simple little interview."

"Well, it seems to me, Ms. McGuire, you being the district attorney and all, if you believe in capital punishment the way you say you do, you should be willing to pull the lever on the electric chair yourself."

Amy leaned back in her chair. She was a slender woman of average height and weight. She wore her dark hair short, which flattered the delicate bones of her face, and especially brought out the dazzling cornflower blue of her eyes. She wasn't beautiful, but most men found her extremely attractive.

Amy said, "If he killed a child, I could."

"How about if he killed somebody while he was sticking up a store?"

"Probably I could."

"How about drugs?"

"If he took drugs?"

"No, I wondered if you have ever taken drugs."

She laughed. "God, you're really asking me that? For a high school newspaper?"

"I liked your campaign. You seemed honest. So I thought I'd give you a little test and see just how honest you really were."

A lot of people had liked Amy's campaign. Small town like this, campaigns for district attorney were usually predictable. The Republican candidate always ran on a law-and-order platform and sounded as if he were actually trying to work up a lynch mob; and the Democratic candidate always talked about squishy soft issues like bad childhood and irresponsible parents, neither of which was much comfort to a sixty-seven-year-old who'd just been mugged by a twelve-year-old. Amy had run as an independent. Everybody at the country club and the union hall predicted disaster. She fooled them all.

She laughed. "You're not going to ask me about my sex life, are you?"

"Maybe later."

"Very funny."

"You prosecute drug cases. That seems like a fair question. I mean, asking you if you take drugs."

"I've smoked approximately ten joints in my life."

" 'Joints.' Cool. So how long ago did you smoke these ten joints?"

"When I was in college."

"And not since then?"

"Not since then."

"Solemn word?"

"Solemn word."

She glanced at her wristwatch, a piece of silver that complemented the gray suit and the frilly white blouse she wore. There was a good possibility that the verdict would come in today. She wanted to look her best.

When she looked back at him, he was smiling. Smirking, actually.

"All right," he said. "How about your sex life?"

"Very funny."

"It'd be pretty cool if we had that in the interview."

"Yes," she said, "especially if we had photos to go along with it."

"Photos!" He laughed. "That'd really be cool!"

They'd had their fun. She had to wrap up the interview and get back to work.

"You know, you haven't asked me any questions about how the district attorney's office helps people."

"Helps people?" Brian looked shocked.

"Yes, believe it or not, Brian, our office was set up so it could actually do some good."

Brian surprised her by seeming interested.

"Well, some of the people we bring charges against we help get in appropriate programs such as Alcoholics Anonymous and foster homes and spousal-abuse programs."

Brian was writing all this down quickly in his long reporter's-style notebook.

Telling him about the helpful ways of the DA's office took up the next fifteen minutes. Brian seemed particularly intrigued by the ways the office helped abused and neglected kids.

While she talked, Amy looked out the window at the hills surrounding the town of Crystal Falls. At twenty-seven thousand population, the place was still small enough to be one with the countryside. Deep forest was no more than seven or eight minutes away from the shopping district.

She wanted to be outside now. Weekend hiking was one of her real passions, and had been ever since her bitter divorce three years ago. She'd come to appreciate the solitary life. Hiking was especially fun at this time of year, when autumn blessed all the trees with fiery beauty.

"This was all Senator Cummings's idea," Amy said as she wound up her verbal tour of the office and all it did for people. "He'd heard of a DA's office in Virginia that was set up to help people, so he told my predecessor about it, and that's how it got started here."

"He really helped you, didn't he?" Brian said. "Senator Cummings, I mean."

"I wouldn't have been able to get through college and law school without him getting me the scholarships and the grants," Amy said. When she was about Brian's age, her parents had been killed in a car accident. Most people just automatically thought that the daughter of a prominent surgeon would be well taken care of with insurance. Not so. Her father was a kind and decent man but also a somewhat naïve one. A man at the country club had convinced her father, right before his death, that he should put all his available money in buying access land that the state government would need for its new leg of interstate. Unfortunately, this was at the time that the president and the Congress were cutting budgets for the infrastructure. That last leg of interstate never got built. Her father died with only a few thousand dollars to his name. Not even selling the family home helped much. There was a large unsettled tax bill. This meant that Amy had a particularly difficult time raising herself and her younger brother.

"Mr. Slocum, our American studies teacher, was talking about Senator Cummings the other day," Brian said. "Said he was probably the most popular senator our state's ever had. Six terms."

"And he'll probably run again next time," Amy said. "I sure hope so anyway."

"Mr. Slocum said that Crystal Falls probably wouldn't be half as big if it wasn't for Senator Cummings," Brian said. "He really brought the three biggest employers here himself?"

"He really did," Amy said, feeling a curious pride in the accomplishment, as if she'd played some role in it. This was because the Senator had always made her feel as if she were part of his family. "He's helped more people than any other person in this state."

Brian smiled. "You wouldn't be prejudiced, would you?"

"Probably a little bit," she said.

Brian stood up. "Well, I've got a test right after lunch so I'd better get back to school and do a little studying."

"You haven't read the material for the test yet?"

The boyish grin again. "What's the hurry? I've got two hours."

2

Twenty minutes after Brian left, when Amy was working with the material she'd need this afternoon for a pretrial conference, her phone rang and she picked up.

Midge, her secretary, said, "The courthouse just called, Amy. There's been a verdict."

"I'm on my way," Amy said, unable to keep the tension from her voice.

In many respects, this was the most important case she'd ever tried.

TWO

1

A long time ago, when Helen first moved to Washington, D.C., she dated a cop who'd spent a lot of time on the burglary detail in his early years.

He used to say pick a door, any door, I can get it open.

And, in truth, he had been able to open every single door she'd pointed to. Apartment doors, car doors, even doors to businesses. Of course, he locked them right back up again. But he'd made his point. With a few tools and a lot of practice, you could open just about any door you wanted to.

If only he'd been equally skilled in the sex department.

But by the time it was all over—and he'd at least had the decency to be brokenhearted—she'd picked up a number of his techniques. For both the boudoir *and* burglary.

She hadn't needed to use her burglary skills in many years.

But thank God she still remembered them.

There was a little task she needed to perform now that she was back home in small-town Iowa. Helen was the sister of

Senator David Cummings and, it had long been rumored, the real brains in the family. . . .

Today she was going to do a little breaking and entering. . . .

Wearing the disguise made her sweaty and uncomfortable.

Yesterday, she'd shopped at the Salvation Army, got herself some old, baggy clothes. Then at a theatrical rental place, she'd bought a reddish wig and some oversize reading glasses.

When she looked at herself in the mirror, she was startled to see how well the disguise worked.

She was no longer Helen. She was this new person . . . one who resembled a bag lady. . . .

She didn't have to go far, so she walked. Somebody was bound to recognize her if she had the car. . . .

Now Helen stood in the alley behind the house she was about to break into.

This was a lovely old neighborhood, the original wealthy section of the town back at the turn of the century. Lots of shade trees and refurbished Victorians and even a carriage house or two adjacent to the rear property lines.

If Helen had a time machine, that's the era she would set it for . . . turn of the century, straw boaters for the men and big picture hats for the women . . . and spending idyllic hours floating downriver while your suitor strummed his banjo and sang "Moonlight Bay."

Life seemed to have lost all its serenity and grace. If only she could have lived back then . . .

But right now there were other considerations.

Tightening her grip on her burglary tools, she hurried across the yard to the back door of the rambling old white Colonial.

She didn't have long.

In and out.

That's all there would be time for.

In and out.

She sure hoped she got lucky.

2

When Amy saw him, the first thing she did was look to the street. Maybe she could jaywalk and avoid talking to him.

But the traffic was too heavy. Even if she stood on the curb, he could come up and speak to her.

He'd called her three or four times in the past month, but she hadn't returned any of the calls.

Now she would have to talk to him.

"I hear there's a verdict," Sam Bowers said.

"Yes," she said. "That's why I'm in a hurry."

She had the perfect excuse to keep on walking, but he touched her arm and stopped her.

"You still carrying your gun?" he said.

She patted her purse. "I sure am." Lately, all law enforcement people had been getting death threats from political extremists. Sam had convinced Amy, and others in her office, to learn how to fire a pistol—and to carry the pistol at all times. Amy went to the police firing range twice a week.

"I don't suppose you want to hear this," he said, "but I've missed you. A lot."

"I've been very busy," she said.

He took a long moment to study her.

Sam was the assistant chief of police, a sun-browned man whose rangy body and angular, wise face evoked the old-fashioned western hero. A western hero who appreciated Benny Goodman and collected film noir videos. These days, Sam wore dark suits, white shirts, and conservative neckties. He believed that law enforcement was a profession, not just a job, and he wanted his clothes and demeanor to convey that atti-

tude. He was the first officer in the history of Crystal Falls to
hold a bachelor's degree in police science. Amy had always
found the law enforcement thing a little bit amusing. Back
when they'd gone to Crystal Falls High together, Sam Bowers
had been a major troublemaker. Nothing serious, but he'd
pulled an awful lot of pranks. He'd stayed that way, something
of a smart-ass, until his first wife died at the ridiculously young
age of twenty-six of melanoma. As Sam had said to Amy once,
it had been a terrible cost to pay for growing up.

"I wish you'd have dinner with me, Amy. I think there are
some things we should talk out."

Remembering the incident that broke off their six months
of dating, Amy felt anger heat her cheeks. "Unless you're willing to admit that Steve Arnette overreacted, there's nothing
to say."

"He didn't overreact, Amy. He was just doing his job. Remember, I don't like him either, but we've got to be fair about
this."

She smiled bitterly. "You really think we should have dinner, Sam? Look how angry I am already."

"You need to step back, be a little objective about it is
all, Amy."

He looked at her a long moment. "I really have missed you.
And I think you know that."

She sighed, her anger waning. "I've missed you, too, Sam. A
lot."

His smile was immediate, and boyish. "Then for God's
sake, Amy, let's drive to Iowa City some night next week and
have dinner."

"Sam," she said. "Please listen to me. I said I missed you.
But I didn't say that I wanted to see you again. You're not
going to change your mind about that night, and neither am I.
No matter what we do, that night's always going to come be-

tween us. You'll always believe Steve, and I'll always believe Richie. So it's better—"

She could see the pain in his chestnut-colored eyes. It was the same pain she felt now in her chest. She felt victimized by so many feelings—love, loss, anger, even the vestiges of lust. Sam was a good lover, kind and tender.

But to start it all over again . . .

"I need to go, Sam."

"Think about it, Amy, and I'll call you Saturday to see if you've changed your mind."

She felt an almost intolerable sadness as she spoke her final words. "Please don't call me anymore, Sam. It just makes it worse for both of us."

Then she hurried off toward the courthouse.

She was down the block, waiting at a red stoplight, when she felt someone come up quickly next to her.

Sam said, "There's a barn dance tonight. I'm going to be there. I hope to see you there, Amy. It won't be a date so there won't be any pressure." He smiled. "But I finally learned line dancing the way you wanted me to. Maybe I can do a little showing off for you."

She started to speak but he held up his hand.

"Don't say no. Just think about it, all right? You can come there when you want, and leave when you want. I promise not to put any pressure on you." He grinned. "But I have learned the tush-push."

She had to smile at that one. "I'll say one thing for you, Sam," she said, feeling sentimental. "You've sure got a cute tush."

"See, right there's something we could spend the whole night talking about," he said with a smile. "My tush." His gaze grew serious again. "We really had something, Amy."

That was one thing she'd always liked about Sam. No

macho bullshit about hiding his feelings. He wasn't ashamed to say what he felt.

"Please don't call me anymore, Sam."

He leaned away from her, as if her words had physically rocked him.

She walked quickly away from him, striding toward the courthouse.

She was just about to walk up the wide steps when she heard somebody call her name.

She looked to her right and saw Senator Cummings walking toward her. Even all buttoned up in a suit and tie, he managed to convey a Reaganesque and very casual manliness. He was a man who was comfortable with himself, and consequently comfortable with others.

"I take it you're hurrying to court."

She explained that there had just been a verdict.

"Well, I certainly won't keep you, Amy. I just wanted to say hello."

Though she was in a hurry, she wanted to thank him. "I got your roses for my birthday, Senator. They were beautiful."

"Probably not as beautiful as you," he said. "You're looking lovelier than ever, Amy."

She smiled. "You always say the right thing."

"That's because you haven't heard me without my speechwriters." Then, "By the way, how's that brother of yours doing?"

Amy was a firm believer in public relations where Richie was concerned. Always put your best foot forward. For one thing, even if she'd felt like saying something negative, she would never betray Richie that way. He needed all the support he could get in this town. Every bit of it.

"He's doing fine. He loves his job at the country club."

"Good," Senator Cummings said. "I knew he'd find himself someday. And by the way—you be sure and call the office one of these days and tell that sister of mine to schedule us all a dinner out at the house. As I remember, we had a darned good time the last time."

"We sure did," Amy said. And they actually had had a good time. Visiting the Cummingses was like visiting your aunt and uncle.

"I'd better get going," she said.

"I hope the verdict goes your way."

"Thanks," she said, and went up the steps two at a time.

Dean Koontz. Stephen King. Robert R. McCammon. Anne Rice. Susan Kelly was stocking up on all her favorites this morning as she stood in the dusty little world of Half-Price Books, Crystal Falls' only used-book store. When she died, she hoped that heaven had at least one used-book store. She loved these places.

She was a slight woman with dark hair cut to the shoulder, intelligent brown eyes, and a smile that was both innocent and knowing at the same time. She wore a man's red flannel shirt, jeans, and hiking boots.

"You got yourself a new 'do," Marie Sullivan said. Marie was a heavyset lady in her sixties who had apparently never heard about the dangers of smoking and obesity. Marie owned the bookstore so she got to smoke anytime she liked. And got to reach down beneath the counter of the checkout stand and sample one of the Russell Stover chocolates she always kept on hand. She usually wore a faded housedress and a festive little pink barrette in her short gray hair.

"Just cut some of it off," Susan said.

"Looks nice."

"Thanks."

Marie raised her favorite inevitable subject. "Too bad you have to waste it."

Susan smiled. "Uh-oh. I feel a speech coming on. Think I'll head for the back of the store."

"All I've got back there is romances, and I know you hate those." She reached beneath the counter for a chocolate.

"So you haven't found anybody yet, huh?"

Susan, having found what she wanted in the horror section, now moved to mysteries. The walls were lined with tightly packed shelves.

"Not yet."

"I tell you about my friend in Iowa City?"

"The guy who runs the triple-X store?"

"Yeah. But that doesn't mean he's not a nice guy."

"I think I'll pass."

She bought a Dick Francis and a Lawrence Sanders and a Joan Hess and a Nancy Pickard.

"I'd probably do a better job than you, picking your next husband."

"Meaning I haven't done so well?"

"Two husbands before you're thirty . . . you just don't seem to have much luck."

"I know," Susan said. "The brazen hussy of Crystal Falls. That's me." She laughed at her own joke. There'd been a time when her reputation had bothered her. The women of this valley saw her as a destructive force. . . . She'd married two of the most eligible men in this part of the state . . . and dumped them both. She was seen as a heartbreaker . . . and behind the closed curtains, women whispered about whom Susan would snare next. An upstanding married man? Maybe their *own* upstanding married man? That's what the women feared.

"I don't think Richie's ever gonna settle down," Marie said. "Not to be nosy or anything."

"Oh, of course not. Who could think you were being nosy?"

"I mean, if I *am* nosy it's only because I worry about you."

In a weird way, Susan supposed, that was true. For all her gossiping, Marie was essentially a decent woman. Hell, Susan liked to gossip just as much as anybody else, so she could hardly fault Marie.

"I guess you could always get Steve Arnette to marry you."

"I hate to remind you, Marie, but he's already married."

"Aw, hell, Susan. You know he'd dump that wife of his in a minute if you asked him to. The whole town knows it."

And therein lay Susan's conundrum. Richie McGuire, Steve Arnette, and Susan Kelly had all started kindergarten together. They'd been friends all the way through school. But around fourth grade, something ironic and terrible happened: Susan fell in love with Richie, and Steve fell in love with Susan. And it had never changed. Susan married two men to prove to herself that she no longer loved Richie, and Steve married a woman and had two children in order to prove that he didn't love Susan any longer.

Things hadn't changed any, either. She still chased after Richie, and Steve still chased after her.

Susan worked the big farm she'd inherited from her folks. She came to town three, four times a week, and every time she came she kind of cruised the streets looking for Richie. She was nearly thirty years old and she'd dumped two good husbands for the sake of her crazed, pathetic dream.

"Steve still has it in for Richie," Marie said. "You ask me, it was excessive force, the way he beat up Richie."

Richie had a drinking problem and a violent temper. Not a month went by without him getting into a fight of some sort. Three or four times, he'd beaten people badly enough to put them in the hospital briefly.

Steve Arnette was a cop who was also prone to violence. He

would probably have been dumped from the force if his cousin wasn't Senator David Cummings. Anyway, he'd tried to arrest Richie one night not long ago, and Richie had resisted. Steve had put a lot of damage on him. Richie, Susan had heard, was considering a lawsuit.

The front door of the bookstore opened, the bell above the doorframe tinkling.

Two women with armloads of romance novels came in and piled their wares on Marie's desk.

Marie fell into an easy conversation with the two about a famous romance writer who'd done a signing in a Cedar Rapids bookstore. According to everybody who'd been there, the author had been pretty drunk, and occasionally abusive. She even told three women in the signing line to shut up because she couldn't concentrate on autographing with the women jabbering away. Soon after, she had been whisked away by limo to the airport, where she was soon whisked away again, on to another triumph in Des Moines.

Susan checked out.

"Don't forget my friend in Iowa City," Marie said. Then to the two other women, "Trying to line her up, but she won't go."

But Susan could see that this pair was not as enamored of her as Marie was. This pair, in fact, judging by their steely gazes, did not approve of her at all. Crystal Falls' leading femme fatale. That's how they saw her—straight from *Melrose Place* and deep into southern Iowa.

Steve Arnette was leaning against her panel truck when she got outside.

"Hi," he said.

"I thought you weren't going to do this anymore, Steve. I thought we had an agreement."

"Last I heard," he said, "it was a free country."

Steve was blond and slender and handsome. He had always been a heartbreaker in his own right. But there was an air of petulance about him that had become more pronounced with age, something of the whiner and the self-pitier. This translated into his violence. He had a terrible reputation as a cop. He beat people up whenever he got the chance.

He looked good this morning, trim in his khaki uniform.

"How about if we go out some night?"

She pushed him gently but firmly from the door and climbed inside. She leaned out the window and said, "Steve, you've got a wife and two kids. You should be spending your time with them."

"Yeah," he said. "It's great hearing big moral speeches coming from you."

She turned on the ignition. "I have to go."

He reached in and seized her slender arm. "Maybe someday I'll kill that son of a bitch Richie. And then you won't have anybody to chase after anymore."

She put the truck in gear and drove away from the parking lot, trying not to think about how ugly and angry Steve had looked just then. He really did hate Richie—had hated him ever since that day on the playground when Susan had confided she loved Richie—and she feared that someday he'd make good on his threat.

Someday he might really kill Richie.

3

Helen realized that this was all pretty crazy, the disguise and sneaking up to the back of the house and everything, but right now she didn't have a hell of a lot of choice.

Not after what she'd learned last night, she didn't.

Brilliant white sheets hung on the clothesline, the soft

breeze carrying the smell of fresh laundry and reminding Helen of her girlhood.

She moved quickly, without looking around. She wanted to appear, to anybody who might be watching, as if she had legitimate business here.

She took out her handful of burglary tools and went to work.

4

The courthouse had been built during the worst of the depression years, back when the WPA was putting men to work. With its Grecian columns, majestic roof, and long, leaded windows, the courthouse had always been a hallowed place for Amy. Even as a little girl, she'd liked to come down here and walk around the marble halls, and glimpse the judges in their black robes. Even today, the courthouse was a special place for her, and sometimes in the middle of a trial she'd look around, and feel stunned to realize that the little girl had grown up to spend so many hours here.

Amy heard the echoes of her own footsteps as she hurried to the door reading Courtroom C.

The courtroom was formal and old-fashioned, with a wooden railing separating the public benches from the lawyers and the judge. At key spots on the walls hung reverential paintings of Washington, Jefferson, Lincoln, and FDR. Any president more current was bound to offend somebody. In a Republican district like this one, even the FDR portrait was probably pushing things.

The Sampson Food lawyers, two men and a woman, were already at their table, nervously fidgeting through their papers in an effort to look perfectly calm and self-confident. They all wore blue suits.

The jury was just now filing in. They were average people with a median age of around thirty-five or so. There was one black woman and one Hispanic man. Amy had fought hard to get them on the jury. They lived in the areas most affected by the Sampson landfills.

Just as Amy reached her desk, the bailiff, a white-haired man, walked out of the judge's chambers to the left and said, "Please rise, court is in session, the Honorable Douglas D. Hawthorne presiding."

Judge Hawthorne, a tall man with stooped shoulders and an eaglelike face, was the most prosaic of all the local judges. Strictly no-nonsense. He hated fireworks of all kinds, yours or his. The lawyer who took to playing Hamlet soon found himself appearing before a very unsympathetic judge.

Judge Hawthorne seated himself, looked around, banged his gavel on his massive and looming bench, and then said, "The jury has reached a verdict?"

"Yes, we have, Your Honor," said a fiftyish woman in a dark suit too heavy for this time of year.

The woman nodded, stood up, and glanced briefly at the single piece of paper in her hand.

The issue was quite simple, as Amy saw it, and had presented it.

In the course of the trial Amy had demonstrated that Sampson needed to be using dry landfills rather than wet ones. Wet landfills had a tendency to build up hazardous methane gas. Wet landfills also allowed large amounts of contaminated groundwater to leach into surrounding land. Amy supported these contentions with studies the state university had done on the health trends in the neighborhoods nearest the landfills.

Sampson had retaliated both in and out of court. The lawyers brought in paid experts who challenged all the scientific arguments in her case. They were better than average for paid experts. They might be able to persuade the jury with their humility and sincerity.

Outside of court, Sampson had used its own workers to spread the message that the expense of switching to dry landfills would cost money, and thus ultimately cost jobs. Amy didn't blame the workers for fighting her lawsuit. But she did blame Sampson management for lying to and exploiting their workers this way. Sampson could easily afford to switch to dry landfills. They could amortize the cost over four or five years and the cost would be negligible. And there was no reason that anybody would have to be let go. Amy had done her arithmetic carefully in advance.

Judge Hawthorne, glancing at his watch, which was something he often did, as if he had an important appointment somewhere else, said, "The jury foreman will please read the court the verdict."

5

As Helen discovered, the home was as beautiful inside as it was outside.

Many of the accoutrements she loved so much about Victoriana were here, and done in admirable taste—everything from shadow boxes to shellwork, from beaded pillows to flowers under glass, from Tiffany lamps to the white lacquered fireplace mantel. As she walked around the house, she could almost imagine H. G. Wells and Arthur Conan Doyle sipping sherry in the parlor.

She was very nervous for the first few minutes. After all, burglary wasn't exactly her calling in life.

Every time she heard a passing car on the street outside, her heartbeat increased perceptibly. She was even startled by a helicopter overhead, and wondered for a terrible moment if Chief Sam Bowers had somehow figured that she was in here.

Gradually, she calmed down.

There was nothing to worry about, really. Darcy was attending high school all day and Darcy's parents, the Crystal Falls version of the Beautiful People or whatever they were being called this year, were spending a month in Paris. The dears.

They were such pretentious people—they'd let everybody in Crystal Falls know that they would be here only as long as it took Dick to troubleshoot the factory back into prosperity. She still remembered the day that Dick Fuller's name appeared in *Fortune*. Every time Debbie Fuller mentioned the article, which was about every thirty seconds, she would patiently explain to the new listener exactly what *Fortune* magazine was, as if people in Crystal Falls had never heard of it.

Dick and Debbie Fuller were from Manhattan and devoutly believed that unless you lived on that hallowed isle you did not know anything about anything.

Helen wondered if they knew about their fifteen-year-old daughter Darcy.

Maybe they not only knew but approved. . . .

Somehow that wouldn't surprise her. . . .

She stood at the bottom of the long staircase that swept on up to the sunny second floor. She really couldn't get over all the details of this place . . . corner scroll brackets, balusters, corbels, spandrels, ceiling medallions. . . .

It really was like being marooned in a different time . . . one far more elegant than modern times. . . .

Helen sighed deeply and then climbed the stairs to the second floor.

If she'd been too nervous before, she was now too leisurely. She had to push herself to move faster. Quit being a sightseer.

In and out.

That's how she had to handle this.

In and out.

And that's exactly what had brought her here, too, the old in-and-out, as the pornographers called it.

Helen got to work.

6

"We find the defendant guilty on four of the six counts, Your Honor," the jury forewoman said, and then began reading the guilty charges one by one.

Amy allowed herself a moment of ridiculous glee. Amy McGuire, district attorney. It was like a corny TV show that played in her head sometimes. *Charlie's Angels* updated with herself as the new Farrah. Embarrassing, was what it was.

The fantasy didn't last long. Reality punched the off button on her little fantasy.

Even though she'd won all the most important charges, there was going to be an appeal. And the way the appeals courts had been behaving lately, you never knew how you were going to end up. In the meantime, of course, the people living around the wet landfills, the children especially, would keep right on getting sick. And Sampson Foods would continue to arrogantly do exactly what it wanted with its waste material.

She listened as the jury forewoman finished reading the verdict to the bench. Maybe it hadn't been an overwhelming victory but it at least said something about the community she lived in. The people here weren't going to be cowed by cynical threats from businesses long accustomed to doing just what they wanted.

After the foreman was finished, the judge had his say, thanking the lawyers for comporting themselves well in his court, and then thanking the jury members for their patience and their wisdom.

When Hawthorne returned to his chambers, Amy started neatly filling her briefcase with her papers. Ordinarily, she would have been accompanied by at least one other person from the office, but today everybody else was busy.

She was just turning to the back of the courtroom when she saw Sam Bowers standing there.

Or thought she did.

The man in the dark suit was about Sam's height and weight, and his face was tanned just about the same color as Sam's, but on closer inspection his face was haggard and his movements were jerky, without Sam's natural grace and composure.

She wished she hadn't seen Sam this morning.

For the past several months, she had managed to avoid him completely, which was no small feat given the fact that as Crystal Falls' two most important law officials, they should have been thrown together a great deal.

Damn Sam, anyway.

He was every bit as stubborn as she was, and that made for some real problems when you were trying to have a love affair.

7

Helen was tempted to stop in the master bedroom—she would like to have found something that would directly discredit the parents, but suddenly she was aware of time passing. She must have already been inside here, what? Ten minutes? Fifteen? Had to hurry . . .

Darcy's bedroom was the only place in the house that didn't continue the Victorian motif.

It was done in modern pinks—pink the walls, pink the curtains, pink the bedspread, pink the canopy bed, pink (for God's sake) the rug—and the walls were littered with magazine pages depicting a variety of "grunge" rockers. Helen was familiar with the term because she'd read about them recently in *Newsweek.* Most of them were junkies, few of them bathed

often, and a number of them had killed themselves. Rock music
had come a long way since the days of Frankie Avalon and
Connie Francis. . . .

She set about searching. . . .

Three minutes later, she found condoms and the slit-crotch
panties in the top drawer. Darcy was a lot older than her cal-
endar age of fifteen. Then she found the dildo.

She didn't touch it. Was actually afraid to touch it. So sleek.
So ominous. Just sitting there.

Like a dog that might leap at her at any moment.

The whole thought of something like this being inside her,
well—she shuddered.

She spent the next five minutes going through all of Darcy's
bureau drawers. And then she moved on to the closet.

Darcy must have had enough clothes to dress her entire
class at school. Fashionable, expensive, brand-name things, too,
no doubt thanks to all those trips that her parents were always
taking to San Francisco and London and New York, trips they
never tired of recounting when they sat at the country club and
held court.

There was an old saying in Congress, "An expert is somebody who lives fifty miles away and has a slide show."

At the Crystal Falls Country Club, the same rationale applied. A sophisticated person was somebody who'd been to
New York twice and lived to tell about it.

She wondered again if they knew what their daughter was
up to. . . .

For in her search, not only did Helen turn up K-Y jelly in
the large economy size, she also found three pairs of crotchless
panties, two bras with the nipple areas cut out, three vibrators,
some kind of penis cream called Hard Times, and a variety of
Polaroids showing Darcy in a variety of poses, all naked, all disgusting.

Helen felt the same way about the Polaroids she'd felt about the dildo.

Did not want to touch them.

Up in the far corner of the closet, she found the shoe box with more photos.

The youngest man in any of the Polaroids looked to be thirty-five or so.

Not a single high-school boy in the bunch.

Some of them Helen recognized, of course.

The assistant principal at the grade school. The owner of the Lincoln dealership. There was even a woman, the wife of the local Baptist minister.

Each and every one of them photographed with his or her very favorite sex toy, fifteen-year-old Darcy.

There seemed to be a photo of practically everybody in town—but not the person's photo she was looking for.

That was when the door opened downstairs.

"Shit," Helen whispered to herself. "Shit."

She froze, listening.

A woman. Singing. In Spanish.

And then the situation came very clear—Helen had carefully checked out the parents and the daughter.

What she hadn't checked out was the cleaning woman, probably an illegal.

Even though the golden couple was in France, the house still needed to be cleaned.

And so the cleaning woman was here.

Now what the hell was she going to do?

What if the cleaning woman came marching up here and found Helen in Darcy's bedroom?

How could Helen ever explain that?

Oh, this had been a very, very stupid idea.

The woman continued to hum as she moved around on the ground floor of the venerable Victorian.

In the living room, she turned on MTV. Rap music—coarse, vulgar, and threatening—boomed into life.

Helen tiptoed over to the window, pulled back the sheer pink curtains, and gazed down at the ground.

In the movies it was always so easy, climbing out of a second-story bedroom window.

The reality was quite different.

If she tried to climb out this window, she'd break her neck.

So now just what the hell was she going to do?

THREE

1

Lunch was a tuna sandwich with chips and a diet Coke.

Amy made a deal with herself.

She counted the chips. There were ten of them. And a pickle.

The pickle she didn't care about.

The temptation lay in the chips. Hadn't her bathroom scale read two pounds heavier this morning? Didn't all the women in her family start to put on serious weight when they reached her age?

She'd eat three.

That was a sensible compromise, wasn't it?

But after she'd eaten the third one, and after trying to fill herself up with the diet Coke, she glanced around the restaurant and then looked guiltily, and with great lust, at the fourth potato chip.

She had a beautiful rationalization.

How many times in her tenure as DA was she going to win a case as important as the Sampson case?

Not very often.

So didn't she deserve to celebrate a little? The rest of the lawyers who'd worked the case had gone off to the Embers for steak and a big birthday-style cake. She'd begged off. After getting back from the courthouse, and after running into Sam, she found a pink message slip on her desk.

She recognized the name instantly.

She also recognized why he had called her.

She spent five minutes on the phone with him, then hung up slowly, numbly.

Richie was back at it again.

He'd been sliding on the AA meetings—and, she'd suspected, starting to drink again, too.

Now she learned that the drinking wasn't the only thing he was sliding on. . . .

So given all this, didn't she deserve one teensy-tiny extra potato chip?

She thought about it all the time, all the existential aspects of the potato chip matter, all the metaphysical considerations, too, and then what she did was break the potato chip crisply in two.

She ate only half of the fourth potato chip and felt pretty darned good about herself.

2

It seemed that each decade produced its own very memorable scandal out at the Crystal Falls Country Club. Back in the fifties, a drunken man pulled out a .45 and shot his best friend in the groin. His best friend had been sleeping with the man's wife. In the sixties, the first Jewish member of the club found a swastika painted on the trunk of his shiny black

Chrysler. In the seventies, one of the club's board of directors had embezzled more than ten thousand dollars from the club's coffers. And in the eighties, a maid claimed that three drunken members, using their own drunken members, had raped her. The maid, now a much wealthier woman, soon left Crystal Falls.

The Crystal Falls Country Club was a sprawling, vaguely Moorish-style building tucked into some radiantly beautiful timberland out on the west edge of town. There were tennis courts, two swimming pools (one outdoor, one indoor), and a handsome golf course that big-city visitors invariably dubbed "a real surprise." What had they been expecting? Potholes on the greens? Cows wandering around? Caddies in bib overalls?

As she approached the club, Amy thought back to her own days as a member. Her father had been locally prominent, so that of course meant that the family spent an undue amount of time at the club. Amy had always resented this because it meant hanging around with the girls whose fathers were also members of the club. And Amy just happened to prefer the company of the lesser social stars—and for a very selfish reason. Going to movies and hanging around Orange Julius and giggling over *Playboy*—in other words, spending your long summer afternoons out at the mall—was a hell of a lot more fun than spending them at the club, where the same boring girls said the same boring stuff over and over again.

The club was always sending her invitations to join. Amy was, after all, the district attorney. And her father had been a prominent member. So why wouldn't she join? She was always putting them on hold, saying she "probably" would if she ever got time. Probably.

She drove her nice, sensible two-year-old blue Buick— which she had actually bought from a very nice old lady at church—up the winding asphalt that led to the entrance of the country club. She left her car in the parking lot and then walked over to the retaining wall, where you could get a look at most of the club's outdoor activities.

Below, in an almost eye-shocking valley of green, lay the tennis courts and the swimming pool and the first six holes of the golf course.

There was the *thwock* of tennis balls, the bright jagged screams of young swimmers, and the muffled voices of golfers yelling things to the group ahead.

It was a pleasant scene, one that almost made her wish she was a member here.

But this wasn't the real country club. No, for that you needed to go inside to the dark, mahogany-and-leather bar or the airy, bright restaurant that sat on a shelf above the same scene Amy was now seeing.

That's where the gossip went on, where reputations were made and lost, where people were branded this or branded that on the flimsiest of evidence. The very wealthiest always sat at the same six tables in the north corner, and it was sickening to watch the trek made by the less powerful people. A religious pilgrimage was what it had always looked like to Amy. Visiting the Vatican, and bowing and scraping and humbling oneself before the pope.

No, the country club might be fine in theory, but in practice . . .

No sign of Richie.

She decided to try down by the lockers.

Richie, who was her younger brother by four years, was called the tennis pro here. Actually, he did a little bit of everything, including bartending when the place was especially busy. This was his sixth job since getting out of the detox clinic Amy had paid for. Six jobs in nine months. She just prayed he could hang on to this one. All his life, Richie had been a star, and had been treated as such. In junior high, he set track records that were still unbeaten. In high school, he'd been the only sophomore ever to start as the varsity quarterback. His football luck continued on through college, where he'd been All–Big Ten three years running. His fortune appeared to carry right on into the pros, the Chicago Bears offering him a contract during his junior year. That's about when the drinking got out of hand. And shortly after—after having been a serious drinker since age fifteen—Richie did the inevitable. He piled up his car. Wrapped his yellow convertible around an oak tree out on the old river road by the dam. Richie smashed both legs. The girl with him was told that she would never walk again. And she wouldn't. Richie's athletic career was over. That was six years ago. He'd drifted back to town here—who the hell wanted a tapped-out former college football star?—and continued his downward spiral. Last year, Amy'd insisted that he check himself into St. Mary's Clinic, which was an aged convent that had been converted into a substance-abuse clinic that sat amid the bluffs on a beautiful hill overlooking the Dubuque section of the Mississippi.

At this time of day, the club was pretty quiet. The lunch hour was over and most of the members were back at work, or home overseeing their estates. Most of the golfers were retired; most of the screaming kids in the pool were preschoolers out here with their mothers. The tennis players at this time of day were almost all women.

That had been another one of her fears about Richie working out here. He was a great-looking kid, lots of curly, dark hair, a trim, hard body, and a killer smile.

Ever since he'd come back to town, he'd been seeing some of his old high school girlfriends. The trouble was, most of them were married to prominent local men. Richie had accumulated a rather formidable list of enemies. He had also accumulated a rather formidable list of traffic violations, including one charge of operating a motor vehicle while intoxicated. That was one of the two or three times that he'd fallen off the wagon since coming back from detox.

That she knew of.

She was sure he was drinking again, two, three nights a week. Maybe more.

But so far he'd been careful.

She hadn't been able to catch him. And he wasn't making it easy for her, either. She rarely saw him these days except for when he needed money. Once or twice a month, wearing his one and only suit and looking like a successful young executive, Richie would show up at her house.

When she saw him out there on the porch all duded up this way, she knew exactly why he was here.

Something's come up, and I just really need some money, Amy. I'm sorry to always be hitting on you like this.

It was never much—never more than a few hundred dollars—but it didn't need to be much to break her. She wasn't exactly getting rich as district attorney—her peers in law firms were making about twice as much as she was—and she had no savings to speak of. Keeping Richie in detox had taken everything she had. But she'd been desperately hopeful that it would be worth the money. Richie would never take a drink again. Ever. She'd been so sure of it. Now, in retrospect, she seemed so self-deluded and silly.

On the way to the outside door leading to the lockers—in an area that was deserted and silent now—Amy had to pass a garage where the golf carts were housed. The air smelled of car oil.

She was just walking past when she heard the sharp laugh.

She automatically turned to her left, to look into the heavy gloom of the garage.

At first, she didn't see anything but the somehow comic shape of the little tan-colored carts.

Then she saw two people in the back of the garage.

At this point, she would ordinarily have kept right on walking. What other people did wasn't any of her business.

But she recognized one of the people as her brother Richie. He was facing toward her.

The other person was a woman with her back to Amy. She had lovely and somehow familiar red hair.

They were embracing, Richie's hands covetous of the woman's shapely bottom.

And then, apparently sensing his sister there, Richie looked up and saw her.

Instantly, he eased away from the woman. Even from this distance, Amy could see a curious look of panic and guilt on Richie's face.

Which was very weird because Richie didn't have to hide anything from her.

Unless . . . unless this woman was married and the wife of somebody very prominent.

He knew how Amy felt about wedding vows. She believed in fidelity and didn't like the thought of her brother helping ruin marriages.

Then the woman turned around and looked out of the shadows at Amy.

And seeing her face, recognizing her for who she was, Amy realized that this situation was far worse than simple adultery.

This was no woman.

This was a girl.

High-school girl.

Fifteen years old.

Jailbait was the term they used to use.

And daughter of Crystal Falls' elite.

This was Darcy Fuller.

3

All Helen Cummings could think about was how bad she had things.

All she'd wanted to do was a little bit of B and E—and this to benefit somebody else—and what happens?

She gets trapped on the second floor of the house with the Mexican cleaning woman walking up the stairs now, whistling her ass off.

Helen felt inordinate sorrow for herself.

Certainly, there would be some who would look at her life—the huge Colonial house in Georgetown, the wonderful redbrick family manse here in Crystal Falls—as one of privilege.

But they didn't have any idea how difficult it was to maintain a lifestyle like this one . . . when you had a brother as difficult to handle as her own.

That's why she was in this house at this very moment. Taking care of another one of her brother's self-made crises.

This was a big one, a whopper of one.

And things might be even worse than either she or her brother realized. . . .

The bitch was coming up the stairs, the Mexican cleaning woman. . . .

In the old days, before first Bush and then Clinton really came down hard on illegals, Crystal Falls was a haven for illegals. In the summer and fall, the men and some of the women worked the fields detasseling corn or picking apples or helping with the winter planting. The children worked, too, but usually as cheap labor in stores or as domestics. Having an illegal as your maid was a status symbol, and a pretty expensive one. But these days, the illegals usually got discovered, and arrested.

Debbie Fuller was no doubt paying this illegal at least the minimum wage.

Helen glanced around.

The walk-in closet was the only possible hiding place.

The plastic scrub bucket hitting her thigh, and making this strange noise, the cleaning lady, still whistling, reached the top of the stairs.

There was a silence, as if she was trying to choose a room in which to start her cleaning.

Door number one, door number two, door number three, just like that game show that used to be on TV.

The bucket started banging against the cleaning woman's thigh as she began walking again.

Past door number one, past door number two—

My God, was she headed for Darcy's room?

There was just room enough to step into the closet and duck her head beneath a row of blouses and skirts and sweaters on hangers. Helen wished they were dresses. They would hide more of her.

She stood pressed flat against the back of the closet, her breath coming in gasps. She really had to lose twenty pounds and quit smoking if she was ever going to run for the empty seat. . . .

God, there it was again.

The Thought. That's how she thought of it, capital letters: The Thought.

And what a terrible thought it was.

Her brother dead . . . his Senate seat empty . . . the party turning to her in its hour of need . . .

Then she cursed herself. What kind of sister was she? The chemo was going to work and David would be fine again.

She was doing this for David, coming here. Not for herself. Absolutely not for herself.

The cleaning woman came into the room and set the bucket down. She was no longer whistling.

Helen froze in place.

She couldn't imagine any reason the cleaning woman would have to come into the closet—

So that's exactly what the cleaning woman did.

Went straight to the opposite end of the walk-in closet, rolled back the doors, and took down something that made the metal hangers ping when they touched.

"Forgive me, Blessed Mother, but the girl has so many blouses, surely she will not miss just this one. My daughter is so needy. She must have a good blouse for confirmation. Please forgive me, Blessed Mary."

Then she farted.

Helen was sort of astonished.

Here the cleaning woman—her name was probably Conchita; every Mexican cleaning woman she'd ever known had been named either Dolores or Conchita—here she'd just finished making a solemn prayer and now she was farting.

The coarseness of it sickened Helen.

Silence again.

Then the bucket was lifted up and started hitting Conchita's thigh as the woman walked out of the room.

She had to get out. No time for any more searching. The first possible moment, she had to get out.

Conchita walked out of the room and down the hall.

Helen heard the hollow sound of a toilet-seat lid touching the top of the toilet bowl itself. She heard this very clearly. The toilet was right next to Darcy's room.

Then Conchita cut another one and with such explosive force that Helen had to smile.

My Lord, was she actually going to sit here and listen to this illegal cut away on the crapper?

No way.

For one thing, this was probably the only chance she would have to escape.

She ducked down, beneath the line of blouses, and then on tiptoe began moving toward the door.

Had to be careful.

She was just thinking this when she stepped on a piece of bad flooring and a wood sound filled the air.

She froze again.

Had Conchita heard the wood moaning beneath Helen's weight?

Silence.

Helen started moving again, on tiptoes of course, but moving faster now.

No time to dawdle.

Had to get down those stairs and out of this house. Fast.

She had almost reached the top of the stairs when Conchita said, "Is that you, Puffy?"

Oh my God.

Conchita had heard her.

"Puffy? Are you being a bad kitty again?"

Still on her throne in there.

Had to try it. Had to move.

Tiptoes again.

She took the stairs one tortured step at a time. From the bathroom, nothing.

"Puffy?"

But this time she sounded doubtful it was Puffy.

"Hello?" she said.

And then the toilet was flushing suddenly.

Helen hastened down the rest of the steps. Hurry. Had to hurry.

She had just rounded the downstairs corner when Conchita reached the top step.

"Hello?" she said again.

Helen was in the kitchen now, eyeing the back door. Was she going to make it?

That was when the phone rang.

Conchita said, "Oh, shit, how can I do two things at once?"

Was she going to come down the stairs or was she going to answer the phone?

Helen hurried to the back door, opened it up, and then heard, from upstairs, Conchita saying, "Hello, this is the Fuller residence."

She was icy with sweat and terror, and she carried both with her as she reached the fresh air of the backyard.

God, that was a close call. So close.

She allowed herself a full minute of relaxing. Everything was fine now. True, she hadn't gotten what she'd come for. But at least Conchita hadn't caught her. Thank God for flatulence.

She took a moment to appreciate the orange butterflies, the red summer flowers, the blue sky. She wanted to be a girl again, lying on the banks of Prairie Creek, reading her Nancy Drews and petting Andy, her sweet old border collie. When she looked back on it, those had been the best days of her life.

She had just reached the alley when somebody said, "Say, wait a minute, will you?"

Panic.

Run or stay?

She looked around and as soon as she saw who was calling to her, she once again felt sick to her stomach.

The woman walking toward her . . .

What kind of terrible coincidence could this be?

The woman walking toward her was Lilly Swanson, one of her old schoolmates.

My God, even with the disguise on Helen was going to be recognized.

Lilly was one of the biggest gossips in town.

By sundown, Lilly would have told half of Crystal Falls that she'd seen Helen in this really weird disguise sneaking away from the Fuller home.

Run or stay?

Panic.

"I'm sorry to trouble you," Lilly said, coming ever closer. "But I wondered if you could help me with something?"

Then Lilly stood right next to her.

And was saying, "Say, you look sort of familiar. Do I know you?"

4

Darcy was smirking when she walked up to Amy, obviously taking pleasure in seeing the older woman upset.

When Darcy reached Amy, she said, "You've got a very nice brother there."

Then she turned around, her breasts straining against her white summery blouse, and said, "See you tonight, Richie."

Another smirk for the benefit of Amy, and then Darcy was gone.

Amy listened to the girl's footsteps quicken as they reached the stairway. Then the footsteps disappeared into the general hum of noise—distant lawn mower, dog, cars entering and leaving the parking lot.

Richie was wearing his tennis whites. He had a great tan and the whites made him look just that much better. He was a handsome kid, but it was a reckless kind of handsomeness, the reckless kind that had always gotten him into so much trouble, and given him the sense that the rules applied to everybody but him.

He stood with one Reeboked foot on the front bumper of a Jeep station wagon, his head hanging low.

He looked up at her suddenly and said, "I know you're pissed, Amy."

" 'Pissed' isn't the right word."

She walked away into the garage. The smells of car oil and

trapped heat were stronger. She could also smell dead grass on the blades of two Lawn-Boys standing in the corner.

"I take it you know how old that girl is, Richie."

"It isn't anything serious."

"It doesn't have to be anything serious for her father to bring charges. Or for you to get fired."

He shrugged. "She just comes around sometimes."

"During a school day?"

He looked at her directly. He was obviously miserable with hangover, his eyes red, his cheeks blanched, his mouth sullen. "I fucked up, all right? I'm sorry. I won't see her anymore."

"I just can't believe you."

He said, very quietly, "I'm tired of your sermons, Amy."

"Well, I'm tired of you being so irresponsible."

She took two steps forward and was then able to confirm her worst suspicions.

He smelled of whiskey.

"You want to come a little closer and get a real good whiff of it?"

"You're drinking again."

"I'd say that's my fucking business, not yours."

"You're my brother. So that makes it my business."

He shook his head wearily. "Even if I told you the truth, Amy, you wouldn't believe it."

"And what's the 'truth,' Richie?"

There was defiance in his blue eyes, the defiance of a sullen teenager.

"That I can handle it now."

"Booze?"

"Yeah," he said, "booze."

"It's not even two o'clock in the afternoon, Richie, and you smell like a bar already. That's 'handling it'?"

"You're not my fucking keeper," he said, and brought his foot down from the bumper.

"After they fire you here, then what?"

The look of defiance was still on his face. "I'm going to LA."

She almost laughed.

Every teenage boy and girl who wanted to escape some hard moments in Iowa always fled to LA. This had been going on since at least the twenties. Amy remembered seeing a photograph from 1921 or so, this huge billboard reading: There Is No California. Stay In Iowa.

Now Richie, half in the bag already today, was going to give it a try himself.

She felt anger and pity in equal amounts. She could see how ashamed he was. She could also see how much he was hurting. She wanted to slap him and hold him at the same time.

"Richie," she said. "You're not only kidding me, you're kidding yourself. You've got to get back to those AA meetings."

"Oh, yeah," he said, "I sure wouldn't want to miss those. A bunch of fucking whining bastards bitching about their lives all the time." He grinned coldly. "Believe it or not, big sister, those meetings actually drive some people to drink. Including me."

Then he took several steps forward and put his hands on her arms.

"Listen to me, Amy. Listen to me carefully. I've learned how to handle it now. I really have."

There was nothing to say.

Millions of alcoholics around the world sang this same pathetic song.

I'm not really an alcoholic. Not me. He is maybe. But not me. Not me.

"And, believe it or not, the bartender here told me that they're probably going to give me a raise, that they really like the work I've been doing here."

He had charm, he had poise, he had cunning—though not

nearly as much as he thought he had—but he had never been able to tell a lie worth a damn.

"I thought you were going to California," she said. "So why would you worry about a raise here?"

She knew instantly she shouldn't have been so catty. He deserved to be pushed around a little but not by her. No matter what, she loved him too much for that. Tough love was well and good in theory. It was a real bitch to pull off without making yourself feel terrible.

"I'll be all right, big sister, I really will be."

He took her to him and hugged her. That had been his name for her since he'd been able to speak. Big sister. Meant both fondly and just a bit ironically, the implication being that it was big sister, not little brother, who needed guidance and help.

She returned the embrace.

They'd always been close but never more so than after their parents died.

She used to worry desperately about him getting hit by cars, or coming down with some terrible disease, or getting himself paralyzed in a football accident.

"I'm going to be all right, Amy. I really am."

"I just worry about you."

He grinned. This was the good grin. The heartbreaker grin.

"Watch this," he said.

There was a white line that stretched from one garage wall to the other.

"This is my home sobriety test."

He pulled up his left leg and started hopping down the line on his right one.

"Now could anybody who'd had too much to drink do something like this?"

She couldn't help herself. She laughed. Sometimes he could be a little kid in a pleasant way, and this was definitely one of them.

He continued to hop down the line to midpoint, and then he turned around so he was facing her.

"OK, watch this," he said. "Blindfolded."

He then took his right hand and clamped it over his eyes.

And then started hopping toward her on one leg.

"Suitably impressed, big sister?" he said as he drew close to her.

"Suitably impressed," she laughed.

She felt guilty that she hadn't really screamed at him to make her point about AA meetings. She felt remiss in her duties as big sister. But the problem was . . . he had to help himself. There was nothing more she could do for him.

"You want to see me do it on my right leg?" he said.

"No thanks."

"So you've been charmed by my humble demonstration?"

How could she do anything but go along with this mood of the moment?

"Charmed," she said.

He was on two feet again. He walked over to her, took her by the arms again.

"Everything's going to be fine, sis."

"Darcy could get you into a lot of trouble, Richie. Prison trouble. The conviction rate on statutory rape charges is very high."

"I'm taking her out of my little black book immediately."

Then he had her by the arm and was gently walking her back toward the steps leading up to the parking lot.

"Dad's birthday is coming up," she said.

"Yeah. I was thinking about that last night. You get the flowers. I'll give you my half of the money on payday."

She'd never see his half, of course. But that didn't matter. The important thing was that he be there with her. They visited their parents' graves five or six times a year. They never missed birthdays.

When they reached the stairs, she decided to give it a final try. "Would you just try it again for me? Just once or twice?"

"AA?"

She nodded.

"You really believe in that stuff, don't you?"

"Yeah, I do."

"Then I'll go."

"Really?"

"Really. I'll go tonight, in fact."

She felt ridiculously optimistic at this moment, as if the weight of the world had been lifted from her shoulders.

He was going to go to AA again.

Things would be better.

Only when he was drinking would he even have considered playing around with somebody like Darcy Fuller.

Now he was going to be sober and judicious again.

Thank God for AA.

Back in the garage, the phone was ringing.

"I'd better get that, Amy."

She nodded and watched him trot back into the shadows and oil smell of the garage.

Everything was going to be fine.

For one long, wonderful moment she convinced herself of this.

5

"Yes, you do," Lilly Swanson said. "You look very familiar."

It wasn't easy, Helen keeping her face turned away from Lilly's.

Every time Lilly would get close, Helen would turn her face a few inches away.

Lilly was like a little kid who kept trying to get something that a big older kid was keeping just out of her reach.

"Say, I'll bet you're Debbie's cleaning woman, aren't you? Debbie said she was going to keep on having the house cleaned." Then, "Do you suppose you could do me a favor?"

Helen muttered, "If I can."

"Next time you clean there, would you look around and see if you can find a pair of sunglasses in there? They're Gaultiers and I hate to lose them. They're the kind Julia Roberts always wears." She paused with proper self-effacement. "A lot of people think I look a little like her."

Helen almost burst out laughing.

Yes, she thought, you'd look just like her if you were thirty years younger, lost seventy pounds, had dark hair, didn't have those outsize Norwegian features, and walked with slightly more grace than a moose.

Other than that, you two are dead ringers for each other.

"They have my initials inside the right stem," Lilly said. "In gold. Real gold."

"I'll look for them, ma'am; now I've got to be going."

"Say, are you all right?" Lilly said suspiciously.

"Yes, ma'am, I'm fine."

"Say, I thought that Debbie's cleaning woman was Mexican."

"I'm part Mexican, ma'am."

She almost said "señora" but decided that would be pushing things a little.

Lilly made her final attempt to see the cleaning woman's face.

But the cleaning woman kept turning away ever so slightly. . . .

"So will you look for my glasses?"

"Sí."

There, that sounded pretty good.

"And if you find them, I live right over there in that big brick place. Ours cost about twice as much as the Fullers'. But

don't tell Debbie that. I wouldn't want to hurt her feelings."
Then: "Or if you tell her, don't tell her who told you."

"Por favor," Helen said, suddenly realizing that she was not
exactly sure what por favor meant.

"See you," she said then, making her voice sound like
Charo's, her words therefore coming out "Chee you."

Then she was off, walking down the dusty alley, leaving a
very curious Lilly Swanson behind her.

So strange how that woman had kept turning away, Lilly
was thinking.

So strange.

FOUR

1

Sunlight streamed through venetian blinds and made bars of gold on Sam's desk. The room was small but well furnished with a mahogany desk and two deep leather armchairs. These were treasures he'd discovered while shopping for antiques with Amy last year.

He allowed himself a brief, luxurious fantasy. Tonight he'd run into Amy at the barn dance and by moonlight she'd fall back into his arms, and back into his life, forever. They were both stubborn people. Tonight he was going to take the initiative and say that he was sorry and that maybe he'd been wrong after all.

Maybe as early as this weekend they'd go up to Galena on the Mississippi and go antique hunting again. His sentimental memories of those days still snuck up and ambushed him every once in a while. He had just plopped himself down in his long-backed executive chair when his secretary buzzed him and said, "You said to let you know if Senator Cummings showed up. He just walked into the Chief's office and closed the door."

"The Senator ask to see Stander's file?"

"You really know this guy, don't you?"

Molly Reed was new to Crystal Falls. Its ways were still mysterious to her.

"Know him too well," he said. He thanked her and hung up.

So the Senator really was going to try and spring Ron Stander out of jail.

Angry, Sam stood up, grabbed the ancient smoking pipe that had belonged to his grandfather and that he still liked to toy with from time to time, and marched out of his office.

He hadn't been invited to the meeting between Chief Hadley and Senator Cummings but he was sure as hell going to attend anyway.

2

As Amy pulled into her driveway, the handyman Jimmy Wade paused the lawn mower he was pushing and waved to her. Amy waved back and then put the car in the garage.

The two-story white Colonial she lived in was technically more than she could afford. But the place had belonged to her dying aunt, who had made her a very good deal. Amy didn't have much extra money now but she did live in a very nice home.

She walked to the front yard to say hello to Jimmy.

As usual, when Jimmy saw her, he hung his head slightly and broke into a shy grin. Jimmy had been doing her yard work and home repairs ever since she'd moved in here a year and a half ago.

The lawn smelled sweetly of newly mown grass. Several birds sang in the trees. Long afternoon shadows were stretching across the yard. It was a quiet and melancholy time.

As she approached Jimmy, he let the lawn mower die and then reached into his pocket for something.

She'd assumed he was digging a tool out of his pocket.

She was surprised to see him produce a small gift-wrapped box. White wrapping paper with a little pink bow. The box had gotten roughed up while riding in Jimmy's pocket but that wasn't the sort of thing Jimmy would have thought about.

"Got something for you, Amy," Jimmy said, handing her the box and smiling shyly.

She accepted it with a smile of her own.

"They told me you won your case today, so I thought I'd get you something."

"That was very sweet of you, Jimmy. Thanks."

"You can open it up. I won't care."

Jimmy spoke with a certain halting quality to his words, as if he weren't quite going to get to the next phrase.

Jimmy was Amy's age. They'd gone through grade and high school together. These days, Jimmy was a huge, lumbering giant. The summer of high school graduation he'd been struck in the head while playing baseball. His injury had left him severely impaired. He had the personality of a ten-year-old. It was odd, seeing a big man like him, one who looked so purposeful, and with a full head of graying hair, talk like a young boy. You could never be sure what Jimmy understood—or didn't understand.

"Well, that sounds like a good idea," she said to his suggestion of opening up the package.

She eased the ribbon off and then started to neatly undo the paper.

"Mrs. Foster wrapped it up for me nice and pretty," Jimmy said, looming over her.

"She did a great job, Jimmy."

She opened the package and there it was.

"It's purty, don't you think?"

"I sure do."

"Hold it up to the sun."

She did just that.

"See how it sparkles?"

"It's lovely, Jimmy. It really is."

"I told Mrs. Foster you'd like it."

"Well, you were right."

"Will you put it in the front window with the other ones I brought you?"

"I sure will."

The shy grin again. "I dreamed about you again last night, Amy."

"Who'd I look like this time? Dracula?"

He grinned. "You only looked like Frankenstein that one time, Amy, and that was 'cause I seen that Frankenstein movie that one night."

Usually when men told you they'd had dreams about you, the idea was romance or sex or both.

"I dreamed you'n me got married."

His words stunned Amy. She didn't know what to say. The important thing was not to hurt his feelings. Jimmy could be very sensitive. Once, she'd said something cross to him and huge silver tears had appeared instantly in the corners of his eyes.

"That's very sweet, Jimmy."

"You was in a white dress. You looked real beautiful."

"And what were you wearing, Jimmy?"

"Me?"

"Uh-huh."

"Oh, you know, one of them black suits men wear to big fancy parties."

"Dinner jackets?"

"Yeah. Dinner jackets."

"Did we have a lot of guests at the wedding?"

"Amy?"

"Yes, Jimmy?"

"You're not makin' fun of me, are you?"

"Oh, no," Amy said, sliding her arm through his. He smelled of heat and sweat. "I'd never make fun of you, Jimmy."

"That's why I like you and Richie so much. You're always nice to me. Richie even said he'd take me up to the old line shack again someday." Back when electricity was brought to the rural areas, the power company built a line shack for their workers in the boonies. Jimmy loved it when Richie went up there with him.

"People shouldn't make fun of you."

"One day, Mrs. Watts said I was just this big dumb guy who was a burden to everybody since my mom died and couldn't take care of me no more."

"She shouldn't have said that, Jimmy."

"It made me cry."

"It would've made me cry, too."

"Honest?"

"Honest. Now tell me more about our wedding."

Jimmy smiled. "Well, they tied balloons to the bumper of our car. You know what kind of car it was?"

"What kind?"

"A new Cadillac. Right from the showroom over at Gruber's Cadillac-Oldsmobile."

"He let us borrow it. Mr. Gruber must've been in a very good mood. He's not usually that generous."

"No, he just give it to us."

"He did? Mr. Gruber?"

"Uh-huh. That was the best part of the dream. I was just walkin' down the street the way I do and I was walkin' past the showroom and Mr. Gruber come out and said, 'I hear you're marryin' Amy'n I want you to have this brand-new Cadillac.' "

Then Jimmy said, "Hey, watch this. Three out of three." He

picked up three small rocks from the ground, kicked back like a major league pitcher, and then let them fly, one at a time, at the nearby oak tree.

"Pretty good, huh?"

Before his accident, Jimmy had wanted to pitch in the local American Legion league. These days, he just threw rocks a lot to convince you—and himself—that he still had the talent. He must have spent half an hour a day throwing rocks at trees.

Inside, the phone was ringing.

"I guess I'd better go get that."

"You looked real, real purty, Amy. I wish I had a photo of it."

Every once in a while, Jimmy came up with intriguing if not downright poetic ideas.

Photographs of your dreams.

It really was a lovely idea.

Chaucer, her cat, was waiting for her right inside the kitchen door. He'd likely been there ever since he heard her pull in the driveway.

Chaucer was an overfed tabby who'd shown up at her back door one day covered with fleas and looking horribly lost and frightened. He'd appeared to be about three weeks old.

Amy advertised him in the lost-and-found section of the local paper. Nobody claimed him. Amy had herself a cat.

Amy reached down and grabbed him as she hurried to the yellow wall phone in the kitchen.

"Hello," Amy said somewhat breathlessly.

"Amy? This is Hugh Wylie."

"Oh, hello Hugh."

Hugh ran Flower Fashions downtown. Whenever she had to send flowers, she let Hugh handle her order. He had good taste and his prices were reasonable.

Chaucer seized the moment, nuzzling the speaking end of the phone with his pink nose, then meowing.

"I've got a cat here who apparently wants to say hello to you."

"Hello, Chaucer. How're you doing today?"

That was another thing about Hugh. He was one of those merchants who managed to remember everything. Customers appreciated it.

"I guess he's decided to be quiet for a while," Amy said, then gave Chaucer a little kiss on the forehead.

"First of all, Amy, congratulations on winning that case today."

"Well, thank you."

"It's time somebody stood up to Sampson." He paused. "Maybe the old days when the country club ran the town are on the way out."

"We can hope."

Hugh paused.

"I'm actually calling you about your brother Richie."

The moment she heard Richie's name, her heart rate quickened and she could feel her palms dampen.

Ever since high school, when she'd had to be both sister and parent to Richie, people had been calling her with "Richie" messages.

Seems like Richie got into a little car wreck.

Seems like Richie had himself a minor scrape in a tavern tonight.

Seems like Richie got my daughter pregnant.

One problem after another. Every one of which Amy inevitably got herself involved in.

It got so that Richie just automatically turned his failures and grief over to her, as if she were a secretary who was an expert at handling delicate situations for her boss.

She'd hoped that his last stay in the detox clinic would change all that.

But things hadn't changed.

She thought of how he'd smelled just a short time ago. Middle of the day and he'd reeked of whiskey.

And now she was getting another "Richie" call.

"Did something happen?" she said.

"Oh, no, nothing like that, Amy. I just wanted to make sure that it was all right if he put things on your charge account here."

What else could she say? "Oh, sure, Hugh. That's fine."

"Oh, good. I just got back in the store and Ida said that Richie had called and ordered a dozen yellow roses sent out and to put them on your account."

Was he sending her roses because she'd won the case today? She'd be happy to get a thoughtful gift from him, even if she had to pay for it herself.

"Who'd he send the flowers to?" she said. "I'm just curious."

"Let me check the slip. Just a second."

While she waited for Hugh to return, she let Chaucer clean her face for her.

Chaucer was an expert at face cleaning. With that long pink tongue of his, he could handle almost any job.

She smiled ticklishly at the feel of his rough-surfaced tongue dragging across her cheek.

Then Hugh was back.

"Let's see. Oh. The Fullers."

"Dick and Debbie?"

"Uh-huh. But that's kind of strange."

"What is?"

"Well, Dick and Debbie are in Europe. And—" He paused, obviously reaching the same conclusion that Amy had reached as soon as he'd read the Fullers' name.

"Well," he said. "I guess it really isn't any of my business who he's sending flowers to. Long as you say it's OK for him to use your account."

"It's fine, Hugh. But I appreciate you checking with me." Then: "So this order just came in?"

"Just about fifteen minutes ago, I guess."

Which meant that Richie had called the flowers in after Amy had left him at the country club.

"As I said, Hugh, I really appreciate you checking with me."

"No problem. And next time if you're not home, I'll just check with Chaucer."

"He'd like that, Hugh."

She hung up with a sour stomach and a racing mind. She was an old-time, world-class trouble borrower, a natural-born worrier.

All she could think of was Richie involved with Darcy Fuller.

He'd minimized their relationship, made it sound as if it were nothing more than a little harmless country club flirtation.

Now she knew better.

This time, Richie could well be in some very serious trouble. At the very least, he would lose his job at the country club. At the worst, he could go to prison for several years.

The glow of the day—the glow of winning against Sampson—faded completely now.

She slumped against the wall, putting her head back and closing her eyes.

All the money she'd spent on that last detox clinic.

All the hopes she'd had.

Gone, now. Gone completely.

3

David Conners Cummings had won the genetic lottery bigtime. He was tall but not too tall; rugged but not too rugged; handsome but not too handsome. Mentally, he'd won a lesser prize in the gene pool—nobody would ever accuse him of

being a genius. But he had an aura. He really did. Even people
predisposed to disliking him—Senator Cummings's political
foes, for example—admitted to being charmed by him after
just a few minutes in his presence. Now, at sixty-six, he was
even more impressive physically than ever. His hair had turned
snow white, adding to the hawklike visage the stamp of nobil-
ity. A lot of Roman senators would have sold every one of their
slaves to have Cummings's looks.

Sam Bowers didn't want to be intimidated by Cummings
but he was.

Sam had knocked on the Chief's door and then peeked in
and said, "Mind if I join you?"

Senator Cummings didn't give the Chief time to speak. He
said, "I was hoping you'd join us, Sam. We could use your wisdom on this matter."

He certainly knew how to butter your bread.

The Chief's office had recently been redone by his wife,
who had been taking classes in interior decorating out at the
community college.

It was now this weird amalgam of new and old—antiques
and heirlooms mixed in with steel office furniture. The Chief
kept telling everybody how much he liked it. Obviously, the
person he was trying hardest to sell was himself.

"Sit down, Sam," Senator Cummings said, indicating the
comfortable armchair next to his.

Today the Senator was dressed in a white turtleneck, a tan
suede jacket, jeans, and penny loafers. No socks. He looked
like one of those guys you see on aftershave commercials at
Christmastime.

Sam sat down.

"We're talking about the Stander kid," the Chief said.

"He isn't a kid," Sam said.

He wanted to make his feelings plain. He just had.

"Well, he just turned eighteen, Sam," Cummings said calmly. "I don't think that makes him a geezer."

He winked at the Chief.

Sam resented the wink. It implied that the Senator and the Chief could handle this brain-addled upstart if they just let him talk himself out.

Sam said, "This is his second drunken driving charge. He almost ran into a station wagon last night."

" 'Almost' being the operative word here, Sam," the Senator said. "The fact is that he didn't run into it. Whether by the grace of God or whatever, not one person in that station wagon was hurt."

"They had to go into the ditch to avoid him."

"The Senator's right, Sam. Outside of a little damage to the station wagon, nothing serious happened."

"Earle clocked Stander at eighty miles an hour and said he was so drunk he couldn't get out of the car by himself." Earle was the best of the three cops who worked the night shift. Sam swore by Earle's word. Earle had been damned upset by what he'd seen last night. Thus Sam was damned upset.

As he spoke, Cummings took his pipe from his pocket, tamped some tobacco down into it, and then lit up.

"He's not a bad kid, Sam," Cummings said.

"As I said, Senator. He's not a kid. He's eighteen."

Cummings glanced at the Chief again. This time he didn't wink. He could obviously sense that Sam was in no mood for humor. He looked at Sam and said, "All right, then. He's not a bad young man. Just a little rambunctious."

Cummings stared at him a moment and then said, "His mother isn't doing all that well since her operation, Sam."

"I'm sorry to hear that," Sam said. "She's a nice woman. She really is. But that doesn't have any bearing on this. He should stay in jail until he can raise bail."

"What good'll that do, Sam?" the Chief said. He was a freckled, ruddy-faced man with a fleshy face and huge hands and a body not meant for suits and neckties. He'd grown up a farm boy, and he would die a farm boy. Sam liked him but he didn't respect him. Like most people in this town, the Chief always did what Senator Cummings wanted him to. As the Chief had said to Sam once, "This town was damned near bankrupt when David Cummings went to Washington. By the end of his first term, it was one of the most prosperous towns in the Midwest. Why shouldn't we go along with him?"

Cummings said, "You don't think you're being a little harsh?"

"No."

"Sam, damn it," the Chief said in his familiar whine. He'd found this an effective method of dealing with his officers. They hated his whine, and would stay in line just so they wouldn't have to hear it again. "Ron's mother is a friend of mine."

"I like to think she's a friend of mine, too, Chief," Sam said.

Cummings sighed. Stared at his well-manicured hands for a long time. Then he looked up and said, "Doc Klever gives her three, four months at the outside."

"Goddamn it, Senator, don't do this to me," Sam said.

The Chief looked at Cummings to see if he was offended by Sam's words. He didn't appear to be.

"Do what to you, Sam?" Cummings said quietly.

"Make me feel like an incredible shit because I want to obey the law."

The Senator stared at him a thoughtful moment longer and then said to the Chief, without taking his eyes from Sam, "He's teaching us a lesson here, Chief. And we should take it to heart. He's telling us that none of us is above the law. Not one of us."

Cummings turned away from Sam and then reached inside his tan leather jacket and took out a checkbook.

He showed it first to Sam and then to the Chief. He looked like a magician showing a prop to the audience.

"You know what our good friend Sam here has done, Chief?"

The Chief just watched Sam.

"Forced me to be creative."

He set the blue checkbook down on the Chief's desk, picked up a pen, and started writing.

Finished with the check, he tore it off and handed it over to the Chief.

"I believe you said two thousand dollars."

"Two thousand dollars?" the Chief said.

"His bail."

"Hell, Senator, you're not going to put up his bail, are you?"

"What else can I do, Chief? The Stander family doesn't have a pot to piss in. Where're they going to get that kind of money?"

Cummings stood up and then offered Sam his hand.

"Thanks for keeping me on the right side of honest, Sam. I'm sorry I got carried away there, wanting to get Ron out of jail without doing it legally."

He took his hand back and glanced over at the Chief.

"The fact is, I'm going upstairs right now and have a talk with the boy. Oops, sorry, Sam. Have a talk with the 'young man.' " The Senator offered him a nice Hollywood smile. "I'm going to rag on his ass for a while. Remind him about his mother and remind him about the wreck he almost caused last night."

He leaned down and picked up his stylish western fedora. It was white and went well with his ivory-colored turtleneck. Cummings had a number of these fedoras in various colors. He looked just as good in every single one of them.

He walked to the door, opened it slightly.

"I'm supposed to check in with my office in a little bit. Guess I'd better head on over there." He nodded to Sam. "I knew we could work it out, Sam. When you come right down to it, we're both reasonable men and we both love this town of ours very much."

Then he put his western fedora on and walked out the door.

"Now there's a classy guy," the Chief said.

"Yeah, or a sociopath."

"What the hell's that supposed to mean?"

"People that charming always scare the hell out of me."

"You know the kind of people who scare the hell out of me?" the Chief said.

"No. What kind?"

"People who barge in on meetings they weren't invited to."

"I guess I should apologize, Chief."

The Chief shook his head. "I don't give a damn about apologies, Sam. But what I do give a damn about is helping that man who just left here. The things he's done for people in this town are just amazing. Rich, poor, black, white—hell, he was the one who got all those illegals in the hospital when they came down with influenza a few years back."

"We owe him a lot," Sam said. "I was never disputing that, Chief."

"You could have been a little more respectful."

"I was just trying to make my point."

"Oh, you made it all right, Sam. You made it real good."

Sam walked to the door, put his hand on the knob.

"Sam?"

He turned around, faced the Chief.

"Yeah?"

"One thing."

"All right."

"Never make the people in this town choose between you and the Senator. Because you know what?"

"What?"

"They'll choose the Senator every time. And that goes for me, too."

"I guess maybe I should remember that," Sam said.

The Chief watched him coolly. "Yeah, I think that'd be a real good thing for you to remember."

Sam walked out into the hall.

FIVE

1

Darcy Fuller watched as the gas station attendant kept peering through the windshield of the Triumph sports car for a better look at Darcy's breasts.

She wore a red tank top under a sheer white blouse, the tank top only emphasizing the size of her breasts. The miniskirt she wore rode halfway up her thighs. The only way the attendant could get a look at those would be to lean into her convertible, and he was way too timid for that.

A real stud would have looked at her frankly, almost daring her to say something.

But this kid, all pimples and horn-rimmed glasses, looked like the dweeb of all dweebs.

He wanted to look but was scared to look.

The DX station was crowded in the late afternoon. A couple of suburban women with big vans were pumping their own gas, trying to prove how liberated and self-reliant they were. A couple of grade-school boys using the air hose to fill up their

bicycle tires. And one of the town's old Mexican men was looking over a new radial tire. The air smelled of oil and gas. The
three bays were filled with cars, two up on hoists. Every few
minutes a metal tool would clang to the floor. Beautiful fall day
like this. Black and Gold posters everywhere. The Iowa
Hawkeyes incited great loyalty and excitement. This senior
boy who thought he was really hot shit had got his father's box
seats and wanted to take Darcy with him. But he was a dweeb,
too, nice looking and slick in his way, but real prim and proper.
No fun at all.

Two guys from school pulled in in their open Jeep. When
they saw her they nudged each other and grinned.

She wasn't being immodest when she said that most of the
boys at Crystal Falls High wanted to bop her. She was the Sexy
New Girl. Next year there'd be another Sexy New Girl and
she'd be Old Stuff, if her family hadn't moved by then. But
not now. Now she was hot.

A tow truck came in tugging an old car. A towel delivery
truck carried several bundles into the station. A candy truck
pulled in right behind it. A guy in a uniform went inside carrying a clipboard.

She was watching all this—she had to do something while
the attendant was glomming her boobs—and that's how she
happened to see the silver Lincoln Towncar pull onto the far
end of the drive.

She smiled to herself.

She always did when she saw him like this.

It was like being in one of those old spy movies she'd seen
on TV.

When we see each other, don't let on that you know me.

That was one of his big rules: secrecy. He was absolute
about it, too.

Don't let anybody know you know me.

She wondered what he'd do if she just walked up to him, slid her arms around his waist, and kissed him.

Guy would probably start screaming.

Guy would just freak out.

Guy would just probably fall down dead right on the spot.

The dweeb said, "I'm going to check your oil."

Should I spread my legs? she wanted to say.

But the dweeb was like the guy in the silver car. He'd probably freak out, too.

Then she had her idea.

She picked up her cell phone, punched the number she knew by heart, and listened to three rings.

"Hello."

"Guess where I am?" she said.

"Jeez, I told you about these cell phones."

"You're about fifty feet away."

"I am?"

"Look out your window."

She saw him look out on the drive for the first time. He looked startled.

She didn't wave. Didn't let on in any way that she knew him.

"We'll talk later," he said. And rang off.

She smiled.

Cell phones scared the shit out of him. Too easy for other people to listen in.

"Oil's fine," said the dweeb, hungrily gaping at her breasts from above.

She handed him the credit card. He nodded thanks and then took off at a half trot back to the cash register.

She watched the door of the silver Towncar open, watched the handsome man step out.

The way he walked, the way he held himself, reminded her

of her father. But then, wasn't that why she treated men the way she did? To pay back her father?

A few months ago there'd been this article in *Cosmopolitan* about women who enjoyed teasing men and then destroying them in some fashion.

The article, written by a woman with a serious name like Sonia or Judith (and with Ph.D. after the last name), insisted that teases and femme fatales were simply visiting all their pent-up rage on men. Their fathers hadn't shown them sufficient attention or love, so these women were going to take it out on the other men in their lives.

At first, Darcy thought the article was pretty lame. But the longer she read, the more she believed.

Especially the part about how femme fatales liked to ruin the lives of their lovers.

That was one reason Daddy had been so eager to get out of Buffalo and come out here. When she was fourteen, she'd had an affair with Daddy's new vice president, a married man in his forties. She'd capped off the affair by secretly videotaping the veep and herself in bed and then sending the pictures to the veep's wife.

Daddy had kept threatening to go to the district attorney, but he didn't want a scandal any more than the veep did.

She so enjoyed seeing Daddy (and dear Mommy, for that matter) get upset about the veep that she almost told him about the much briefer affair she'd had with his golfing partner. . . . They hadn't actually slept together . . . but damned near. Wouldn't that upset Daddy even more?

That one she decided to keep to herself. Maybe someday when she was a little older, someday when she needed a handy weapon to hurt Daddy with, maybe then she'd pull that story out and use it on him. But for now . . .

She'd hated the idea of coming to Crystal Falls, afraid that she'd have nothing to do. But she was an inventive girl and soon found plenty to do.

They were shaking his hand, the handsome man who'd just stepped out of the silver car.

He was a celebrity to them, the handsome man.

He was a man who carried with him the aura of fabled, far-off lands, of treasures untold, of power unimaginable. He was Senator David Conners Cummings and, best of all, he was their friend. Was there a man or woman or boy or girl he hadn't helped in this entire community?

And they were well aware of this. And so they acted both grateful and a little starstruck when they were around him. As now.

He walked inside.

She kept thinking about last night, how he'd looked when she'd told him about the photos.

For my scrapbook, David, she'd said. That's the only reason I took them, she'd said. For my scrapbook, honest, she'd said.

But he knew better.

She saw the panic in his eyes.

Good Lord, somebody having photos of the two of them making love—

Good Lord.

She looked over at the silver car. She'd always wanted him to take her for a ride in it, but he'd been too afraid.

Couldn't afford to be seen with her. Under any circumstances whatsoever.

The dweeb was back.

"Here you go," he said, handing her the credit-card holder for her signature.

She signed her name.

When she handed the holder back, she caught him looking right at her breasts.

"You should see my nipples," she said.

It was cute and even a little bit sexy, the way the dweeb blushed.

"Why, I didn't—"

"It's all right," she said, a peculiar gentleness in her voice. In an odd way, she really had been touched by the way the dweeb had blushed. This was one of the few times she found herself wondering what having a nice, normal relationship would be like.

But then Senator Cummings was back on the drive, and she lost interest in the dweeb and nice, normal relationships.

The Senator allowed himself a single glance in her direction—quick and nervous—and then he was in his big silver car and sweeping out of the gas station.

The dweeb took the credit-card holder back from Darcy and said, "You, uh, you aren't gonna complain to Red, are you?"

"Who's Red?"

"Guy that owns this place."

She smiled up at him. "What would I complain about?"

"Well, you know—"

And damned if he wasn't blushing again. Standing right there on the drive on this fine, sunny autumn afternoon, and blushing his little dweeb ass off.

"You mean complain about you staring at my breasts all the time."

He wanted to cut and run.

He was sweet. She couldn't get over it. Whoever would've thought she'd find a dweeb appealing in any way?

In her gentlest voice, she said, "No, I won't say anything to Red."

"I appreciate it."

"You're sweet, you know that?"

His cheeks were starting to go crimson again.

She leaned forward and turned on the ignition.

"You really are sweet," she said again, right before she peeled out of the station.

But then half a block away, she forgot all about the dweeb.

All she could think about was the neat little plan that had just now come to her.

She figured, this time in the afternoon, he'd probably be going home.

She didn't have much trouble finding him. Just pulled up behind him at a stoplight.

And tapped her horn with the heel of her hand.

He looked back in his rearview and saw her there. His blood pressure was probably soaring.

He didn't honk back, didn't wave, didn't let on in any way at all that he knew her.

When the light changed, he pulled away from the stoplight and started down the street toward home.

She started down the avenue, too.

And that was how it went for the next twenty minutes. She just stayed right on him.

Finally, when he was about halfway home, her cell phone rang and he said, angrily, "Just what the hell do you think you're doing?"

"Just going for a ride."

"This isn't funny."

"Chill out. Wow."

He broke the connection.

She thought of maybe giving him a break, of only following him for a block more, and then falling away.

But she was having too much fun.

She followed him all the way home, and then, just to really scare the shit out of him, she pulled into his driveway and honked the horn.

His neighbor, a gray-haired lady filling her side-yard bird feeder, looked out to see who was honking.

The red Triumph wasn't a car she was likely to forget.

The Senator got out of his car and virtually ran into the screened-in back porch.

But by then, Darcy was bored.

She'd had as much fun as she could possibly get out of this situation.

2

"I just had to show you this outfit," Sally Frazier said to Amy. "Isn't it fun?"

Sally was a private-practice lawyer who specialized in divorce and estate law. In a town like Crystal Falls, a lawyer had to offer a range of services to survive.

Sally had pulled into the drive just as Amy was getting into her jeans and T-shirt for the night. Tuna fish sandwich, salad, and a small slice of cheesecake were to be the evening's repast.

Sally was a short, slight woman with a tight cap of auburn curls. She was more cute than pretty—the dreaded word "perky" was frequently applied to her—and she had a tendency to pile on the pounds . . . and then lose them by some kind of deal with the devil. Every Crystal Falls woman over twenty-five envied her. Yes, she could pack the pounds on . . . and shed them with ease.

The outfit was a "cow-gal" special with western shirt, vest, skirt, and boots, each with ample supplies of fringe. The white cowboy hat, which contrasted nicely with the velvet blue of the outfit, was perched at a cute angle on her head. She looked darling.

"If he doesn't like this, I give up," Sally said. The past month, she'd been dating a recently divorced man she'd met at the Friday night barn dance. They'd had several dates and the guy hadn't so much as tried to kiss her. Sally had speculated on this. The guy was everything from impotent to gay to a murderer who got himself worked up into an ax-wielding frenzy whenever he had sex. Sally read an awful lot of serial-killer novels.

"Well, you think this'll do the trick?"

"It should," Amy said.

"I've never heard of a case before where the woman has to give the guy Spanish fly, have you?"

Amy laughed. "Boy, there's a phrase I haven't heard since high school."

"Dick Hamer tried to convince me he'd put some Spanish fly in my Pepsi one night."

"Dick Hamer? I only vaguely remember him."

"He was in training to be a serial rapist. I used to go to the drive-in with him. That's how I got interested in wrestling."

This was pure Sally, joke after joke. She was fun but Amy found herself occasionally needing a rest from Sally and her humor.

"So how about you, toots?" Sally said. "You going to break down and go to the dance the way Sam wants you to?"

Amy had told her about seeing Sam earlier.

"I don't think so," Amy said.

"You want me to talk you into it, don't you, kiddo?"

Amy smiled. "Maybe I do."

"He's a hell of a nice guy."

"Yes, he is."

"And pretty sexy, too."

"I couldn't disagree with that."

"And, kiddo, best of all, he wants to marry you. He told me that himself."

"He did?"

"Uh-huh."

"When?"

"A week or so ago in the Pizza Hut. The eunuch and I were in there getting a pizza. Sam came over and sat down. So of course we talked about you and he said he wanted to marry you. He's serious, kiddo. He really is."

"It's just—"

Sally shook her head. "Don't tell me it's just Richie." She took Amy's hand and held it for a moment. "Toots, you know there's a possibility that Sam's version of things is the truth."

Amy withdrew her hand, saying, "I'd rather not talk about it."

"See. See how uptight you get? All I did was mention that night and you turn into a hermit."

A knock on the back door. Through the red-and-white checked curtains, Amy could see Jimmy.

She walked over to the door and opened it.

"I'm all done, Amy."

"Good, Jimmy. I appreciate it. Step inside and I'll go get your money."

She always paid him in cash, a crisp new twenty, a crisp new five. He accepted checks, but when you gave him cash, he seemed incredibly proud of himself, as if he'd just been handed a major award.

"You know Sally, don't you, Jimmy?" Amy said as she reached in the cupboard for where she always kept Jimmy's money in an envelope.

The two said hello to each other.

"Oh, and you could do me a favor," Amy said, taking a loaf of bread from the counter. "You could drop this off at Richie's place."

"Sure," Jimmy said. "I like going to Richie's place."

Amy smiled at Jimmy's sweet innocence. In some ways, it wasn't sad at all. In some ways, it was enviable.

Amy baked bread twice a week. It was good, no chemicals or preservatives, made in a bread maker Sam had bought for her last Christmas.

She wrapped the loaf in GLAD wrap and then carried it

over to Jimmy. Richie lived in a rented A-frame out near Hartson's Woods. Jimmy lived right down the road in an old shack.
A lot of people offered to take Jimmy in but he always de-
clined. He loved his old shack. It was close to Bevins Creek,
where he liked to fish.

"Here's for your usual great job," Amy said, handing him
the new bills.

As usual, a very pleased smile broke on his face. It really
was like some kind of honors ceremony. He folded the money
very neatly in half and then stuck it in his shirt pocket.

"I'll remember about the bread," he said.

"Thanks."

"And don't worry," he joked, smiling like a little kid. "I
won't eat none of it, either."

Amy laughed. "I wasn't really worried about that, Jimmy."

"I was just joking, Amy."

She leaned forward and kissed him on the cheek. "I knew
you were joking, Jimmy."

He looked self-conscious now and she was sorry if she'd
made him uncomfortable.

"Thanks again, Jimmy."

Jimmy nodded and left.

"You sure are nice to him," Sally said.

"He makes it easy."

"Yeah, he is pretty sweet." Then she glanced at the gold
watch on her slender suntanned wrist. "Oh, God, I told the
eunuch I'd pick him up for dinner."

"You're picking him up? I thought he had that really nice
Corvette."

"Yeah, didn't I tell you?"

"Tell me?"

"He only took me out in his Corvette for the first couple of
dates. He then informed me that he didn't want to risk some-

body slamming into him so would it be all right if we took my car on dates?"

"Maybe you're right," Amy smiled. "Maybe he is a serial killer."

Sally walked over to the kitchen door. "I'm expecting to see you there tonight, kiddo."

"I'll probably stay home."

"He loves you," Sally said softly. Then, "And he's willing to take his car on dates. What more could you ask for?"

Amy laughed. Even though she got tired of Sally occasionally—which didn't stop them from being best friends—Sally almost never failed to lift her spirits.

"Well, I'll think about it."

Sally winked at her. "See you tonight, kiddo."

Then she was gone.

3

She was waiting for him when he got home.

She sat in the living room, in the rocker that had belonged to her grandfather, the only male she had ever truly loved, and she thought of how she was going to approach this whole thing.

She could just confront him, of course. That would be the simplest, tidiest way. And he would tell her how he'd fucked everything up—sounding like a frightened little boy—and she would then tell him how he should go about unfucking it up.

But confronting him that way wasn't all that much fun. Over too fast.

Probably be better if she tried stony silence. That always drove him crazy. Absolutely bonkers.

Yes, she thought, listening to him beneath her in the garage that was directly beneath the living-room floor. Yes, stony silence it would be.

She sat listening to the grandfather clock ticking away eternity. That had belonged to her grandfather, too. Sometimes she just liked to sit here and listen to it tick. It was like communicating with her grandfather beyond the grave or something. Not that she believed that bullshit. David did, of course, because David didn't have the nerve to confront the fact that when he died he would be no more exalted or longer-lived than roadkill. End. Fini. He was always trying to convince her of the afterlife. He knew that she was smarter than he was, and he knew that if she believed in it, then he could believe in it, too. Right now, since he couldn't convince her whenever they had one of their Afterlife Talks, he still had nagging doubts.

All this had started with his illness eighteen months ago. The diagnosis. The surgery. The chemo. After that, David engaged her in more and more Afterlife Talks, and was frantic to get her to believe.

The house was a sprawling ranch-style made of redwood and native stone. It sat at the end of a long, curving, lonely road and was protected by enough security equipment to guard a sheikh. These days, with so many wackos running loose, a man like David couldn't afford to take any chances. The place had a quiet elegance, wall-to-wall bookshelves on the north wall of the sweeping living room, an antique marble fireplace, and a large dining room done in country French.

She heard him come quietly up the interior steps leading from garage to kitchen. Heard him opening the kitchen door. Heard him coming into the living room. Felt him standing by the fireplace, watching her.

She feigned great interest in the paperback she was reading and looked up only after a full minute or so.

"Oh, hello, David."

"We need to talk."

"I'm just not in the mood for talking. Sorry. I'll go fix us some dinner."

"I said," David said, "I need to talk. You know what I've been up to, don't you?"

She looked at him and smiled. "Do I?"

"Don't go bitch on me, Helen."

"What a perfectly lovely thing to say to your sister. Your own flesh and blood. The woman who raised you. The woman who's stood by you all your life. 'Don't go bitch on me, Helen.' Perfectly fucking lovely."

Academy Award performance here. Really grinding it into him. Really making him pay.

She set her paperback down, stood up, and said, "I'm afraid it's leftover night. Some of that beef-and-vegetable stew from the other night. Fresh rolls, though. You really liked the rolls."

The clock ticked. Grandfather. God, if only David had turned out to be half the man their grandfather had been.

"You're deliberately ignoring me."

There now. Great stuff. She loved it when panic hit him. Served only to remind him who was the real boss in this household.

"I'm not ignoring you, David. I'm simply doing what your doctors told me to do. Keep feeding you lots of good, healthy food. Is there something wrong with that?"

She smiled and walked out of the living room and into the kitchen.

He followed her. Good puppy.

She stared at the big double-door olive green freezer-refrigerator.

Everything she needed, except the rolls, was in Tupperware bowls of various sizes.

She opened the bowls, beef in one, vegetables in the other, rice in the third, and then carried them over to the microwave, which sat above the long, wide counter by the sink. Thank God for the microwave.

She put everything into microwave-safe bowls and then locked them in and set all the buttons.

"Helen," David said.

She didn't answer.

She went into the dining room, opened a drawer in the china cabinets, and took out place settings for two.

"Helen," he said as she started to set the table. "Helen, we have to talk."

Definitely Academy Award here.

Poor David was going crazy.

And she was unflappable. As if he weren't even here.

"Helen," he said. "Helen. Goddamn it."

She looked up at him and smiled sweetly. "And here I've gone through life thinking my name was Helen Cummings. And now I suddenly realize that it's Helen Goddamn it."

He clamped a hand on her thin wrist.

"You know what I've been up to, don't you?"

She was the perfect picture of innocence. "I don't spy on my own brother."

"You heard me arguing with her the other night, didn't you, out in the drive?"

She set down a knife and fork on the place setting.

She had heard, of course. Darcy had pulled up in the drive around midnight and knocked on the back door. David had been up, watching Tom Snyder interview a Senate colleague of David's.

Helen had been awake reading.

At first, she couldn't get a good look at the girl standing on the dark drive with her brother. David had kissed her several times, and then the girl had leaned her face back into the moonlight.

Darcy Fuller.

That little bitch who'd been out here with her parents for a party over the Memorial Day weekend. Helen had the impression that it had been going on since then.

He never learned. Six or seven times in his long senatorial career, her brother had gotten involved with teenage girls. Six or seven times, Helen had had to work her magic to extricate him from what could have been a career-crushing dilemma. Thank God, most parents cared more about money than they did their children.

Now there was a new problem.

David had hooked himself up with the most devious little bitch Helen had ever known.

This one was a sickie, a real sickie.

Not enough that she was having sex with a United States senator. She had to have photographs of it, too.

"I guess I still don't know what you're talking about, David."

She was about to plump an elegant blue cloth napkin down on the table when he took her wrist again. This time, there was some pain.

"You heard everything, didn't you? The other night? Through your bedroom window?"

She sighed. "They all look alike, don't they, David?" She spoke softly. Wearily. "You're probably not even aware of it. If you put them all together in a line, you'd see what I'm talking about. Now let go of my fucking wrist, you understand me?"

He let go of her wrist.

"I keep trying to figure out what it's all about, this thing with teenage girls. Is it because of Mary Claire Riley, the girl who dumped you in tenth grade? Is that what you're doing? Trying to win her back through these girls? I don't know what else to think, David. They're very sexy, I have to give you that, but they're so stupid. That's what I can't understand. How you can spend so much time with people who are so stupid?" Then she smiled. "But it's not their minds that attract you, is it?"

"She has pictures of me."

"I know. I went over to her house today."

"You what?" Panic again. Poor David. Crumbled so easily. Wept and wept and wept when he was given his cancer diagnosis. Begged her and begged her and begged her to believe in an afterlife.

He was going to die and she was going to fill out his term and then she was going to run for her own Senate seat. She had the party connections. She had the voter appeal. She had the skills and the knowledge.

Up until a few nights ago, it had all looked so simple. David would die and she would step into his office.

But she hadn't counted on Darcy and her photos. Darcy and her photos could destroy David before he had a chance to die. And if that happened, if the voters were to learn of David's penchant for young girls, then the Senate seat would be gone for good.

She had to get the photos and the negatives.

"Go get us a nice bottle of wine from the cellar," Helen said.

"I want you to tell me what you were doing out at Darcy's today."

"You go pick us out a nice bottle of wine—red, of course, something with real body—and I'll put dinner on the table and then we can have a nice, leisurely conversation."

Among the many things David didn't understand was wine. Without Helen's guidance, he'd serve everybody their pint of Mogen David grape.

"I can't believe you went out there."

"Just go get the wine, David."

He started to argue. She pointed toward the door leading to the kitchen. "Go on, David. Go on."

He started to argue again but then stopped himself.

When Helen was in this particular kind of mood, there was no hope of dissuading her. No hope at all.

"Maybe you should've sent Steve Arnette instead of going yourself," David said later.

Helen shook her head. "I don't want to use Steve unless we absolutely have to. He's a little crazy."

Steve Arnette was their younger cousin whom they'd gotten a job on the police force. He was always in some kind of trouble with Chief Hadley. Lately, he was in trouble for roughing up Richie McGuire. Excessive force. Arnette did them discreet favors sometimes. But because Steve was the son of the neurotic Cathy Beth, Helen's least favorite niece, using him for a job was always a last resort.

"You're sure Lilly Swanson didn't recognize you?"

"Positive."

"God, if she did—"

"She didn't."

"So you didn't find the photos?"

"No."

"She's probably got them hidden someplace."

"You need to see her one more time, David."

"I don't want to go near her. After she told me she had those photos—"

"You have to find out how much she wants."

"I don't think you understand her, Helen."

"Meaning what exactly?"

He sipped his wine. He'd chosen well and Helen had been sure to compliment him. Positive reinforcement.

"Meaning she doesn't care about money. Hell, her father's rich."

"Then what does she care about?"

"Power."

"What kind of power?"

He thought a moment. God, he looked positively presidential when he was thinking, the sleek, fabulously masculine face, the sweep of white hair. . . .

"She likes to see me scared. That's the only way I can explain it. When she told me about the photos . . . she saw how scared I was and she loved it. Couldn't quit smiling."

"They're all such a pleasure, your little nymphets." She paused. "Maybe you should've stayed married."

His fork had been halfway to his mouth. His hand froze in position. "You drove them both away, Helen. You. Not me."

"That's a nice thing to say."

"But true."

"We had our little disagreements, your wives and I, I don't deny that, but—"

"Little disagreements? God, Helen, you really are blind to yourself. You pushed those women out of my life. They didn't have a prayer up against somebody like you. You even alienated my own daughter from me."

"If I'm such a terrible person, why are you and I still together, David?"

He spoke without rancor. "Because you're the smart one. And you always have been."

They didn't speak for a time, finishing their meal.

Then he said, "I don't mean to sound unappreciative, Helen. I really don't."

"That's all right."

"I wouldn't even have been elected to the state legislature if you hadn't been there."

"Let's not get maudlin."

"I don't know why I do it. The young girls, I mean."

"You picked a doozy this time."

"You really think she'll take money?"

"I guess we'll find out," Helen said. "If she calls you tonight, make sure to make it clear that you want the photos back and that you're willing to pay for them. If you get the negatives."

"And what if that doesn't work?"

"Then I'll talk to her."

He looked up from the last of his food. "What'll you say to her?"

"That she's destroying a good man. That she's destroying somebody this country needs. And that if this thing ever goes public, she'll be destroying herself in the process. Girls who get involved in these scandals, they carry it with them the rest of their lives."

"I'm not sure it'll work with her."

"It might not work with her but I'm sure it'll work with her parents."

"Her parents?" He seemed startled. "You'd go to her parents?"

"As a last resort."

"That seems like a real risk."

She reached across the table and touched his hand. In the flickering candlelight, he looked more handsome than ever.

"You've got our backs against the wall, David," she said. "You've made it necessary to take a real risk."

"I'm just so damned scared," he said.

He looked as if he were going to be sick to his stomach.

"Just so damned scared," he said.

SIX

1

She was going to go, she wasn't going to go.

That's how Amy spent the hours between seven and eight o'clock, sitting in the living-room recliner, watching the two guests on *Crossfire* argue about a new drug law that the White House had proposed, a law Amy was against. Much as she hated drug dealers, and the ruins they'd brought to America, she hated the loss of liberty more, especially in the area of wiretaps.

And as she watched she thought . . . I should go, what could it hurt? . . . and then . . . I shouldn't go, Sam'd just think I want to get started up again.

The phone rang . . . and she admitted that she was excited.

Maybe it was Sam, getting a last pitch in about tonight.

See you there in about an hour? he'd say.

And she'd say what she really felt . . . all right, Sam. I'll be there. And maybe I'll even say let's try it again. But this time you'd better realize how much my brother means to me. No more treating him like some kind of criminal. He's had his problems . . . but he isn't hard-core. He's basically a nice guy. And I know he can stop his drinking. I know it.

"Hello," she said, trying to keep any hint of excitement from her voice.

"It's me," Sally Frazier said.

"I thought you had a date."

"I do. The eunuch's in the men's room right now. Probably trying to find his pee-pee."

Amy laughed. "God, you're terrible."

"I know I am. But I've got the night planned out pretty well and maybe the eunuch will come around."

"Oh?" Amy said, knowing she was about to be set up for a joke.

"Yes. I brought an anatomy chart along. I'm going to give the eunuch a little chalk talk."

"I'm sure he'll enjoy it."

"What I'm really calling about, kiddo, is you."

"That's what I figured."

"I really think you should come tonight and see Sam. One of us has to have a decent relationship. And at least Sam knows how to unzip his pants by himself."

"I'm going to surprise you."

"You are? And say yes?"

"I'll be there a little later." That's the way she'd been leaning, so she might as well commit to it.

"That's fantastic, Amy. You're doing the right thing. You really are."

I hope so, Amy thought. I sure hope so.

2

Three miles west of Amy's house, in a small bar located on the highway leading to Dubuque, Richie McGuire ordered his third scotch in less than an hour.

"Gonna ride the tiger tonight, eh, my friend?" the bartender said.

Richie grinned. "Yeah, and he better not buck me off, either."

The bartender fixed him a new drink and set it down in front of him. The place was busy with a Friday night crowd. It was the considered opinion of the bartender that Friday nights were different from any other night in the bar business. There was a certain desperation, even violence, to Friday night crowds. They were frantically trying to put the workweek behind them, grimly trying to forget that they were spending their lives in jobs that meant nothing to them, working for bosses they despised. So drinking became not so much a pleasure as a purgative. Now, just before seven o'clock, you could feel it already. Mousy little men fancied themselves bar studs, and swaggered around appropriately; spouses, wives and husbands alike, phoned home with lies for their mates ("Be home by eight, I promise"); and the brawlers were getting that first glint of rage in their eyes. Oh, yeah, Friday night was a very special night, especially if you were a bartender and had to oversee the playground full of drunken kiddies.

"How you think the Hawks're gonna do this year?" the bartender asked Richie with genuine interest.

Richie was the only thing resembling a celebrity in the entire town of Crystal Falls. He'd Been There. Maybe not for long, maybe not at the very top, but nonetheless he'd Been There, and his opinion was valued greatly.

"Their line's gonna give them some problems."

"Yeah?"

"Uh-huh. They've never really replaced Becker and Anderson."

"They were good."

"They," Richie said, with no fear of contradiction, "were great."

Somebody down the bar called for another round. The second bartender was already busy.

"Guess I better get that," the bartender said, and then took a swipe at the bar top with his beer rag. "The line, huh? I'll have to remember that." He'd be quoting it for a long time to customers inclined to talk about football. That's what Richie McGuire told me, he'd say. Right, Richie McGuire. Straight from the horse's mouth. The bartender would even overlook the fact that Richie still had a tab in the bottom of the cash register drawer for $203.43, past due going on a year now.

Richie knew he had to be careful. Was knocking them back way too soon.

He was thinking about Darcy and how much he needed the country club job. It wasn't anywhere near the best-paying gig he'd ever had, but the idea of moving among the town's elite made him feel good about himself. He had the fantasy that someday one of the really rich country club members was going to pluck him up and make him a star again. Not in sports, obviously, but in business. Hire him for some really important job. Then Richie'd be up there again. Nice clothes, nice car, the respect of everybody in town. It'd be like hearing Saturday afternoon football cheers again.

He should never have started playing around with Darcy. Must've been out of his mind.

Who was going to hire him if they found out he was screwing around with the fifteen-year-old daughter of an important club member? He'd be DOA, that story ever got around.

She was reckless as hell, Darcy was. It almost seemed as if she wanted to get in as much trouble as possible, and pull somebody else in with her.

He had to smile. She didn't even have a real license to drive her sweet little sports car around. Hell, she was too young to have a driver's license. Had a learner's permit was all. But she didn't care. If she got caught, so what? Yeah, he had to smile. He'd been a lot like that when he was her age.

He hadn't actually been to bed with her. That was the only thing in his favor.

He'd played around, necked some, a few harmless little feels, but no actual going to bed.

And there wasn't going to be any, either. Next time she contacted him, he was going to end it.

Next time she—

A curious quiet came over the bar then. At first, lost in his own thoughts, Richie wasn't aware of it. He was thinking about how good he looked in his tennis whites. That was a funny thing for a guy to think about himself, but it was true. When he was in his tennis whites, he felt special. No mistaking him for a workingman or a low-level businessman or anything like that. The whites marked him as special, apart from the crowd.

Then he became aware of the silence, and he looked up and saw the bartender's odd expression and heard the bartender say, "You better not be in here, miss. Legal age is twenty-one."

And he knew instantly whom the bartender was talking to.

The little bitch had come in here looking for him.

He spun around on his barstool and looked at her.

Another micromini, this one buff blue, and a sheer blue blouse. And no bra. She had her hair fixed in an elegant tangle on top of her head. She looked both young and fresh, and old and cunning.

The guys were all smiling a lot. The gals were all frowning. Here they'd been the center of attention—bar like this, the guys inevitably outnumbered the gals—and now she'd taken all the spotlight for herself.

"Wondered if you wanted to go for a ride, Richie."

The guys, excited, thinking about how much they'd like to

go for a ride with her, started poking each other and grinning even wider.

All Richie could think about, now that he was forlornly drunk, was how she was going to screw up his country club gig. He must've been out of his mind to ever get involved with her.

Without even thinking about it, he crossed the room to her.

And then he was grabbing her by the arm. And shaking her hard. And screaming into her face.

"You get the hell out of here and leave me alone! You understand that! You don't belong in here!"

He had no idea how hard he was shaking her. He was suddenly so drunk that he had lost control of himself.

But a guy he didn't know stepped up and grabbed his arm and said, "Hey, Richie, you're hurting her, man."

Richie was still shouting. "She doesn't belong in here!"

And Richie lunged for her again. He had no intention of hurting her. He just wanted to make his point emphatically.

The guy, obviously interpreting Richie's lunge as a very violent act, put himself in front of Darcy.

Richie ran into the guy's chest.

For the first time, Richie realized how big the guy was. Six-five, maybe 270, 280, with hard blue eyes and a fist-broken nose.

He obviously was not intimidated in the least by the town hero.

"Lay off her, man."

"Richie's right," the bartender said. "She don't belong in here."

"That doesn't give him any right to push her around," the man said. "She's just a kid."

Richie was sobering up again. That was the kind of drunk he was, phasing in and out of his booze.

For the first time, he saw the scene clearly, saw what he'd done, and felt embarrassed. He'd way overreacted. He should have taken her aside and told her nice and quiet that she didn't belong here. And, in fact, didn't belong anywhere Richie was. He was way too old for her in every sense of the word.

Calm, rational, adult.

That's how he should have handled it.

Instead, looking around, he now saw what a scene he'd created.

"I'm sorry, Darcy," he said. "I didn't handle that very well."

Darcy startled him then. She had a terrible temper and a foul mouth.

But you could never underestimate Darcy's cunning.

She started crying. And if you didn't know her, you'd swear that her tears were the real thing. The sweet, innocent tears of a fifteen-year-old girl.

"I guess I just thought you meant all those things you said to me, Richie," she said.

Now, after such magnificent emoting, she even had the women on her side.

How could you take advantage of a little lost kid like this? the stares said now.

Bad enough that you're screwing around with an underage girl. Do you have to break her heart on top of it?

Little bitch.

She was some piece of work, she was.

But she wasn't done. Oh, no.

She just started shaking her head miserably and saying, "I guess I shouldn't have let you do any of that stuff to me. I was real stupid."

The bartender said, "Richie? Why'n't you take her over in the corner booth and talk to her, huh? I mean, I got a business to run. Boss comes in and sees this, he'll kick my ass."

She'd done it beautifully, conveyed to the crowd the sense that Richie had not only slept with her but made her the kind of promises young lovers have been making to each other for thousands of years.

"All right, Richie?" the bartender said.

What choice did he have but to play through this charade?

He looked at the bartender, looked at the crowd, sighed, then said, gently, "Let's go over to that booth, Darcy."

He led her through the hushed crowd. Now, without the jukebox playing, the place was eerily silent.

He got her seated on one side of the booth, then sat down across from her.

The jukebox boomed back to life. You had to shout to be heard.

Darcy looked at him and smiled. "I put on a pretty good show, didn't you think?"

"You little slut," he said, all his rage back again. "You little slut."

Darcy, who was tucked into the booth so that nobody could see her, just smiled her cute little ass off.

3

The old Hartford barn had been built in 1912. At the time, it was the showplace of the entire valley. Not only were the house and the barn and the outbuildings all state-of-the-art; Hugh Hartford hired a chemist full-time. Hartford wanted his milk cows to be the most productive in the entire state, and that included the farmers on the Wisconsin border to the east. Those boys had long been reputed to have the best dairy cows outside of experimental laboratory farms. Six weeks after the Hartford house was built, it caught fire and killed Hartford, his wife, and their three children. Nobody could afford to rebuild the place and restore it to its former self, so it stood empty until a Crystal Falls man had the idea to put on dances every Friday night in the barn. World War II, Korea, Vietnam, hippies, yuppies, boomers, and X'ers . . . all the generations came and went . . . and society changed so much a fella could hardly recognize it sometimes . . . but by God every Friday night there was a dance out at the Hartford place.

Amy could hear the music when she was still half a mile away. As usual on warm nights, all the doors and windows of the white two-story barn were open and the recorded country music poured out into the night and the countryside. Also as usual, the parking lot was so crowded that cars had to park alongside the road, stretching back a quarter of a mile on a night like tonight.

She parked and walked up to the barn, passing all sorts of couples, young, old, heavy, thin . . . all having one thing in common . . . western clothes. Amy wore a simple red checkered western shirt with white piping, jeans, and cordovan cowboy boots. Everybody she passed smiled and said hello. This was a nice place, the old barn, and it brought out the best in most folks. Wedding receptions, anniversary parties, square-dance clubs . . . the good old Hartford barn was the right place for just about every kind of festivity. It had been refurbished half a dozen times over the stretch of the century . . . and would be refurbished again to make sure that it lasted well into the next century.

There was a crowd around the front door, mostly men having their smokes and drinking their beer. A year ago, the owners of the barn had posted No Smoking signs inside. There'd been the predictable fuss, but by now the old dogs had taught themselves some new tricks. They went outside when they wanted a smoke.

The speakers inside blared a very bouncy, upbeat song. Those were the fun ones to dance to.

"I don't believe it," a familiar voice said behind her.

She turned and saw Sally standing there.

The man with Sally was tall and trim and very handsome in

a slightly empty sort of way. He looked uncomfortable in his western getup, which included a fancy red kerchief and just about the fanciest cowboy boots Amy had ever seen. They had everything except electric lights on them.

"This is Hal," Sally said.

Hal leaned forward to put his hand around Amy's. He surprised her by having a steely grip.

"I've heard a lot about you," he said.

Amy smiled. "Don't believe everything she tells you."

Hal smiled, too. "Don't worry. I don't."

"He's inside," Sally said.

"Oh," Amy said, trying to sound nonchalant. "That's nice."

"God, what a faker she is," Sally said with a laugh. "As soon as I mentioned Sam, her heart started hammering away. But she has to play it nice and cool."

"She loves drama," Amy said.

"Yes," Hal said, "I've noticed that."

"Well, don't just stand there, Amy."

"How about giving me a minute to relax?" Amy said.

"She's scared," Sally smirked. "Scared, scared, scared. Just like a seventh-grade mixer. Afraid to go up and ask the cute boy to dance."

"I think I could use a little more apple cider," Hal said. "Anybody else?"

Both the women said no.

When Hal was gone, Sally said, "Guess what?"

"What?"

"He French-kissed me tonight."

"Great."

"Then he slid his hands down on my bottom while he was still kissing me."

Amy laughed. "This is going to get pornographic, isn't it?"

"I certainly hope so. Maybe tonight I'm going to get lucky."

"I'll say some prayers."

"Hey, I hope I didn't embarrass you. Pushing you so hard about Sam. In front of Hal and everything, I mean."

"No. Nothing to worry about."

"I do push too hard sometimes, don't I?"

Amy smiled. "You? Push too hard? Boy, who could believe a thing like that?"

Amy looked at the doorway, past the men in their cowboy hats, with their beer bellies and contraband cigarettes and cigars.

"You really saw him in there, huh?" Amy said.

"I not only saw him in there. He came up to me and asked if I thought you were coming here tonight."

"And you said what?"

"I said I sure hoped you were."

"And he said what?"

"You know, kiddo, this really is like seventh grade."

"C'mon, he said what?"

"He said, 'God, I hope she shows up. I sure want to see her.' He's one of those guys who isn't afraid to show a little emotion. I like that. And you should like it, too."

By this time, Amy's heart really was hammering. "I do like it. Very much."

"Then go get him. Grab his hand and throw him to the floor and take advantage of him right there."

Amy shook her head. "Boy, you really have a lurid imagination."

"I take that as a compliment."

Amy smiled. "I know you do."

Hal came back. "This is the best cider I've ever had. I wish they sold it by the quart so you could take some home."

"Guess what?" Sally said.

"What?"

"Amy's ready to go inside."

"Wow," Hal said. "So they're going to meet up after all."

"Yeah, and she's psyched, too. Aren't you, Amy?"

But Amy didn't have much to say at the moment. All she could do was watch the doorway.

Sam stood there in his western clothes, looking not only handsome but cordial, too. He was wearing that slightly sad smile of his Amy liked so much.

4

"I want you to leave me alone, you understand that?"

"You ever think maybe I'm in love with you?"

"Bullshit."

"It could happen. I'm a normal teenage girl."

"Yeah, right. Fifteen going on thirty-five."

"What's that supposed to mean?"

"It means that you're not a normal teenage girl."

"Thanks a lot."

Ping-Pong was what they were playing, Richie and Darcy.

He'd wanted her to leave fifteen minutes ago but she was still here, sitting across from him in the booth.

The bartender found every excuse possible to come over and see if they wanted anything. He couldn't take his eyes off Darcy. She was sexy and gorgeous all right.

"Look," Richie said, trying to sound reasonable, maybe even a little bit paternal, "I've got to get my life together. What we did—I shouldn't ever have gotten involved with you, Darcy. I'll take the responsibility for that. I really will. But you should be with people your own age."

"You're dumping me."

"God, Darcy. You can't look at it that way."

"Why can't I?"

"Because it's not the way things are."

"Oh? And how are things?"

She still sat in the corner, hunched up and angry. Richie sighed. "You should be with people your own age."

"I hate people my own age."

"You know what I mean."

"No, I don't know what you mean, Richie. Tell me."

He knew she was enjoying herself, playing the sensitive young girl. She was about as sensitive as a prison guard.

"Your whole life is ahead of you, Darcy."

"Maybe I want you in my life."

"Look, can we cut the bullshit?"

"You think this is bullshit, Richie? You think this is bullshit?"

"How come you never said any of these things before?"

"Maybe I was afraid, too."

"Right."

The bartender was back. "I hate to say this, folks, but the kid has to go. I got the liquor license on the line here."

Then she was crying.

Richie looked over at her in disbelief.

It was almost like a joke. She was just running a number on him. A gag.

Any moment now, she was going to look up and smile at Richie and the bartender.

"Knock off the bullshit," Richie said.

"Hey, Richie," the bartender said, glowering at him. He nodded to Darcy, who now had her head down and was pretending to weep very, very hard. "Poor kid."

"This is all bullshit."

"Doesn't look like bullshit to me, Richie." He shook his head, then said: "Take her outside, Richie. Now." Then, to Darcy: "I'm sorry, miss. But I just can't afford to have you in here. Nothing personal."

Richie could see that the bartender was still intimidated by Darcy's tears.

"Here, miss."

The bartender helped her out of the booth.

She kept up her tears.

The bartender treated her very gently, as if she were aged and infirm.

He got her on her feet and then nodded for Richie to come over and help her.

The jukebox was dead. Everybody was watching. Just standing there, drink in hand, gawking. This was something worth seeing. Richie and some beautiful little jailbait snatch like this one.

The bartender had just turned away, and was walking back to his station, when Darcy let go.

She looked up at Richie with her tear-streaked face and said, in a voice loud enough for everybody to hear, "What if I'm pregnant, Richie? What if I'm pregnant?"

A nightmare. That's what this was.

Richie was standing there and hearing it loud and clear—"What if I'm pregnant, Richie? What if I'm pregnant?"—but he still couldn't quite believe her.

Why would she do this to him? Why would she want to destroy him so utterly?

Dumping her. Of course. What she'd just said a few moments ago. That she was being dumped. That's how she saw this. Her ego. Nobody dumped her. She was the one who did the dumping.

And she wasn't finished.

"I'm twelve days late with my period, Richie! You know what that means?"

Talk about eating it up. The men and women in the bar just couldn't believe their luck. Not often in a tacky little sports bar like this one—they really went all out on the decorations, the cheap bastards, a lone Hawkeye football schedule posted between the doors marked Gents and Gals, big deal—not often in a place like this did you get a floor show.

But Richie and the jailbait were really putting on a wild one here.

And Richie upped the ante.

He lunged at her. Grabbed her by the shoulders and started shaking her.

"Hey!" the bartender exploded. He turned on Richie and the girl.

And jumped on Richie, yanking him away from Darcy. "You tryin' to strangle her? She's just a kid, you crazy son of a bitch!"

And you could tell, just by watching their faces, that that's what the customers thought, too.

That Richie had jumped on her and started to strangle her. It all happened so fast.

All he'd been trying to do was shake her, get her to admit that she was just playing to her audience. . . .

The nightmare feeling again.

Almost dreamlike, this whole thing. Here he was, pretty drunk, standing here in the middle of the floor with this underage girl, and everybody thinking he'd tried to strangle her.

Jesus, Mary, and Joseph, how had he ever gotten himself into a situation like this.

Way beyond his control. Way beyond. He could feel his entire life collapsing around him.

By morning, the story would be all over town.

You hear about Richie McGuire? This teenage chick comes into the bar where he's drinking and tells him right in front of everybody that maybe she's pregnant and it's obviously his kid and everything—and you know what the son of a bitch does? Tries to strangle her. No, I'm not shittin' you. Tries to strangle her and right in front of everybody, too. Right, Richie McGuire. Man, that son of a bitch's been a loose cannon ever since he got dumped by the Bears.

"I'll walk you out to your car," the bartender said, taking her gently by the shoulder.

She had one last dramatic moment in her.

She walked over to Richie, everybody positively bedazzled by every moment of this wonderful soap opera, and stood on her tiptoes and kissed Richie on the cheek and said, "I'll always love you, Richie."

And then, because she was at an angle where nobody except Richie could see her face, she grinned at him, letting him know for sure that this was all a joke, and that she was embarrassing him as a way of punishing him for "dumping" her.

Then one more time: "I'll always love you, Richie. I mean it."

She started crying again.

The bartender led her gently away, leaving Richie to stand in the middle of the bar, right underneath the Bud Tiffany-style lamp, to be scowled at and scorned by everybody in the place.

"You don't check IDs anymore, huh, Richie?" somebody said. And everybody laughed.

"I'd sure like a crack at changing her diapers," somebody else said, followed by more laughter.

"She's got some nice pom-poms," said a third wag. "She must be a cheerleader."

Richie walked numbly back to the bar. There was a half-finished drink there. It wasn't even his. He didn't care. He hoisted it up and threw it back and then he reached behind the bar and picked up a bottle of J & B scotch that the bartender had been using.

Richie poured his own. Generously.

The place was quiet. At least the jokes had stopped.

Richie gunned half the drink in a single gulp.

He was trying to convince himself that it had all really happened. He'd just stopped in here for a few quiet drinks, convinced that his little flirtation with Darcy was going to end quietly and quickly.

And now this.

The bartender was back. "You buy this place or something while I was gone, Richie? That why you're pouring your own?"

"I'll pay for it."

"That means you'll put it on that fucking tab you haven't paid anything on for a year?"

The jukebox was still silent. Everybody was hearing this discussion.

"You know I'll pay it off."

"Oh, right, Richie. Just like I know the sun'll come up in the north tomorrow."

Then: "She's a nice young girl, Richie, whether you think so or not."

Richie looked at him and smiled He couldn't help it. This guy was so fucking stupid. He'd bought her act completely. No questions asked.

"What's so funny, Richie?"

"You. That's what's so funny."

"Oh, yeah?"

"Yeah. Because you believed her. This was all for your benefit, all of you."

He looked around at the bar patrons. Nobody was smiling. Nobody even looked halfway friendly.

"God, I can't believe this. You really bought that bullshit act she was putting on?"

Silence.

"I really need another drink," he said to the bartender.

"You're cut off, Richie. You and your tab."

"Hey, I—"

"You tried to strangle her, Richie. Maybe you're so drunk you can't even appreciate what you did. But you tried to strangle her. Can you understand that?"

He wasn't yelling. He wasn't angry. In fact, he sounded a little sad about it all.

Up until a few minutes ago, Richie had been somebody he liked having around his place. Maybe Richie hadn't made it in the pros but he'd made All–Big Ten three years running, and how many guys ever did that?

No more.

The Richie days were over. At least in this place.

"Tell you what," the bartender said. "I'm going to buy you your last drink in this place and then I want you to haul ass out of here."

Richie started to protest but the bartender said: "I could've called the cops, Richie, you jumping on her that way. Underage kid and all."

He shook his head.

Poured out a drink, a stingy little drink, and pushed it across to Richie.

"Drink up and get out," he said. "I got a daughter her same age and when I think of her gettin' involved with some older guy like you—just drink up, Richie, and get the fuck out."

Richie glanced around at the other patrons.

They were just watching him. Stony-faced. She'd finished him with that pregnancy bit. Absolutely finished him.

He looked at the bartender and pushed the drink back at him. "I don't take charity."

"Yeah," the bartender said. "You got a lot of pride. Pushing fifteen-year-old girls around."

Richie stepped away from the bar.

His legs were wobbly, both from drinking and from the anxiety of the past twenty minutes. He felt weak, ready to collapse. And he could still not quite convince himself that his world had all come tumbling down so fast.

Couldn't this be a nightmare?

The crowd parted for him. Nobody said anything. They just watched him walk too carefully—the way a drunk does when he fears his walk will give him away—straight to the entrance and then out into the night.

He stood out there in the parking lot listening to the big trucks on the nearby interstate and smelling the smoky scent of autumn.

And started crying. Couldn't help it. Rarely cried. But that's what he did now. Silent tears streaking down his cheeks, and his lower lip trembled like a little kid's.

It had all gone so wrong, so fucking wrong.

So wrong.

Still crying, he staggered to his car, inserted the key into the ignition, and pulled out of the parking lot.

5

This was the third time Jimmy had come down the hill to leave the bread off with Richie. He lived on the hill right above Richie's place. It only took him a few minutes to get down there.

Now it was raining.

He could have, of course, left the bread off the first or second time he'd come down here. But that way he wouldn't have been able to go into Richie's house and see all his neat trophies and the framed photographs of Richie in his football uniform.

Someday Jimmy wanted to be just like Richie, walk around town and have people smile at him, have people think he was real neat, the big cool brother that every boy wanted to have.

Richie's place was more like a cottage than a house, a little one-story place with a shake roof and leaded windows and vines that crawled like hungry snakes over all four walls.

In the rain, the place was dark. And frightening. Darkened houses scared Jimmy. On TV, people were always finding dead bodies in darkened houses, and Jimmy was afraid that someday the same thing would happen to him.

The rain didn't bother him. For one thing, he was wearing his black slicker with matching rubber boots and rain cap. Amy had given him the whole outfit last Christmas. He loved Christmas and he loved Amy. He could tell that other people ran out of patience with him. Not Amy. Amy never ran out of patience. He was going to give her pieces of quartz that beamed in the sun. He figured that if he gave her enough pieces of quartz, she would marry him. Then he would live in her house and she would make him dinner all the time, and sometimes they would kiss. And other things. Sometimes when he saw Amy, his groin got hot and almost painful. Then he'd sneak off and do the dirty thing by himself. But someday he'd put his dirty thing inside Amy . . . the way that man and woman did in the pictures some boys had shown him once.

He started looking in the darkened windows.

He couldn't see much.

He saw no bodies. At least he could feel grateful for that.

But he also felt deserted. A lot of times when Amy had him drop things off here, Richie would answer the door.

Where is Richie now? he wondered.

Richie always had a lot to do, a lot of places to go. And a lot of girls around him all the time, too.

One time he'd peeked in the window and seen Richie and this girl naked. They'd been doing what the couple in those photographs had been doing. It had made Jimmy sad and he didn't know why, as if Richie had betrayed him in some way. Jimmy didn't understand that feeling. He had many feelings he didn't understand. Someday when he married Amy, he could tell her about these feelings. Amy was smart. She could explain them all to him.

Jimmy stood in the rain looking at the woods in back of Richie's place. They weren't deep woods, maybe a quarter mile deep at most. They weren't like the nearby state park, where the woods seemed to go on for miles and miles. But they were fun to play in and they were the best place of all to find the quartz that he frequently brought Amy.

The rain in the leafy trees made a hissing noise now. A hissing noise like a snake. Snakes terrified Jimmy. Even garter snakes. There were downtown kids who'd wait for Jimmy sometimes and throw garter snakes on him. And he'd start crying and screaming. And they'd laugh and laugh and laugh. He had nightmares about snakes, about big boa constrictors wrapped around his legs and working their way slowly, surely up around his hips and chest and—

He shuddered, even thinking about it.

He looked at the front door of the cottage. He could just leave the bread between the inside door and the outside door. It would be safe in there.

But then he wouldn't see Richie.

He listened again to the rain hiss in the leaves.

Snakes.

He had the sudden urge to get back to his own little place up on the hill.

He'd come back when Richie was here. He always had to walk down the hill, though. Couldn't just look down the hill. There was a windbreak of large oaks on the west side of his house and they blocked his view.

Hissing. Hissing.

He'd go back home and then try it again in a while.

Richie would invite him in. He was sure of it.

Sure of it.

6

Amy was one of those people who didn't have much rhythm. She remembered taking tap lessons as a little girl. At recitals, the instructor always kept her way in the back, behind the other, taller girls. Trying to hide her.

That was one reason Amy liked line dancing so much. Hippos could line dance and look OK doing it. Hippos and Amy McGuire.

In the past forty minutes, Amy and Sam had danced virtually every dance. No talk of romance, no talk about brothers who caused dissension, no talk of what this dancing meant in terms of their future relationship.

They just danced to one song after another, out on the floor in the midst of people of every kind, short, tall, skinny, fat, young, old. People having fun. Fun you didn't have to be ashamed of in the morning.

The only occasional reminder of a less than perfect world was the deep roll of thunder across the sky. Rain had been falling steadily the past twenty minutes.

After a song by the Mavericks, Sam said, "Could I buy you a beer?"

"That sounds nice. I'm getting thirsty."

"Why don't you grab a table and I'll find you."

"Great."

Sam wore a deep blue western-style shirt with white piping and white buttons. His white Stetson gave him the look of a somewhat melancholy cowboy star of the fifties.

She found them a table and sat down, watching Sally and her boyfriend out on the dance floor. They seemed to be having a great time.

As she sat there, Amy tried hard not to think about what a good time she was having.

That would just make it all the harder if their night ended badly.

She felt good about being Sam's partner, in all respects of that word, but what if it didn't work out?

When Sam was still several feet away, carrying two bottles of Schlitz with glasses on them, she saw a frown trouble his face. She wondered what was wrong.

Sam sat the glasses down and said, "Damn."

"What's wrong?"

"My flip phone."

"Somebody's calling you?"

"Sure sounds like it."

He reached in his back pocket and extracted the phone. "Yes?" he said.

He had to plug his other ear with a finger. The noise level was pretty high in here.

Sam didn't say anything for a time. Just listened. He said, "Well, give him my best. I'm happy for him. I'll see you in fifteen minutes."

Sam clicked off, put the phone in his back pocket again.

"Trouble?" she said as Sam sat down.

"Gil Harmon? His wife had two miscarriages the last couple of years. Now she's in the hospital again. In labor. This one's going to happen. Gil wants to be with her, and I don't blame him. But unfortunately, that means I have to cover for him tonight."

"Gosh," she laughed, trying to make the moment light. "And here I thought we'd enter the dance contest later tonight."

He smiled. "You're not half as bad a dancer as you think you are."

"Now there's a compliment."

He smiled. "I've really enjoyed this."

"So have I."

"Maybe sometime—"

"—we could do it again," she finished for him.

"I just want to say one thing."

Don't ruin it, Sam, she thought. Let's have good memories of tonight.

Baby steps. That's what they were taking tonight. Baby steps. Later on, they'd worry about walking and running again.

"I'm willing to reopen the investigation into what happened to Richie that night."

There. He'd done it. Changed the mood.

"Let's talk about that some other time, Sam. Right now I just want to sit here and think about what a great time I had tonight."

He reached over and took her hand. "This has been great, Amy."

Then he stood up, walked over to her, drew her face up to his, and kissed her tenderly on the lips.

She felt thrilled and sentimental at the same time. She really did love Sam, and probably always would.

"All right if I call you tomorrow?" he said.

"I'd like that."

"Good. Now I'd better get going." He smiled. "I haven't had a night patrol in years. Break up a lot of teenage groping in the park."

She smiled, the smile concealing the disappointment she felt now that the night was ending.

7

She was angry.

After leaving the bar, Darcy had felt a certain elation. She'd done a very good job of humiliating Richie in front of his friends.

They'd never quite look at him the same again.

That bit about being pregnant had been perfect.

When a man in his twenties gets a fifteen-year-old girl pregnant . . .

And especially when he treats her as badly as she had made it seem that Richie was treating her . . .

She'd felt pretty cool.

But now that she was about halfway home, she felt empty and lonely.

She hadn't cultivated any real friends in Crystal Falls, so she had no girlfriends to call. Nor were there any boys her age who interested her. . . .

And then she remembered her good friend the Senator. And smiled . . .

She still felt like raising a little hell. What could be more fun than dropping in on the Senator?

Tell him she was still trying to decide what to do with the photos she had of him.

Watch him beg and writhe.

He really had no dignity.

And that made him fun to watch.

She drove up to the next corner and then flipped a U-turn, heading toward the county road that would take her to the Senator's home in the deep woods.

Oh, yes, this was going to be a lot of fun.

8

The last time the Senator had been up for reelection, a good friend of Richie McGuire's had asked the college star if he'd appear at a Fourth of July picnic for the Senator, kind of a public-relations deal.

Helen had thought this was going to be a slam dunk. How could Richie refuse? Hadn't his sister gone through law school with funds the Senator had gotten for her?

But Richie had indeed turned him down. Said that he, Richie, was more inclined to vote for the Senator's opponent. The man Richie had told all this to said that Richie had been pretty drunk when he said this. Drunk, and arrogant, letting the All–Big Ten thing really go to his head, not understanding, apparently, how fleeting sports prominence was.

The day following this phone call, Amy McGuire had personally come over to the Senator's local office and told the Senator, who was home for one of his weekends, how embarrassed she was that her brother had acted that way.

The Senator had been a lot more forgiving than Helen had, and clearly Amy knew it. She kept playing to Helen, trying to put sympathy in her eyes, but Helen felt no sympathy at all. She wasn't particularly enamored of sports figures, anyway. She was especially not enamored of this particular sports star.

She knew, Helen did, that someday she would be able to return the favor. If you just waited long enough, she knew, your enemies always did something you could take advantage of. . . .

She thought of all this as she sat talking on the phone in the den. David was in the living room, watching a Clint Eastwood movie he'd rented.

Doris said, "Then you know what he did?"

"What?"

"Tried to strangle her."

"You're kidding."

"Right in the middle of the bar. And everybody standing around."

Looked like Richie McGuire wasn't anybody she'd have to worry about repaying. Looked like Richie was going to do just fine on his own.

"Then what happened?"

"She left," Doris said.

"Richie was drunk, of course."

Doris sighed. "Of course. Richie's always drunk."

Then, "That's absolutely what happened and Al was right there to see it."

Al was Al Robertson, one of the local bank presidents and a longtime supporter of the Senator's. Helen had gone to school with his wife, Doris.

"He used to be a pretty nice kid," Doris said. "When he was growing up, I mean. Amy did her best raising him, but I think he was one of those kids who needed a stronger hand. His father was a very stern man."

"Yes, I remember."

"His father would've made sure that Richie turned out all right."

"I think you're right."

Doris said, "Oh, God."

"What?"

"I've got some cookies in the oven. They're probably char black by now. I'd better go."

"Thanks for the info," Helen said. "You're a lot more reliable than TV."

Doris laughed. "In other words, I'm a great gossip."

"In other words," Helen said, "you're a great gossip."

Helen hung up feeling a glow of satisfaction. It was always nice to see an old enemy come to a bad end.

But as she picked up her paperback again, she wondered suddenly if Richie's situation could possibly have some bearing on the Senator's situation.

What if the police got involved and started asking Darcy all kinds of questions about her love life?

What if she talked about her relationship with the Senator? . . .

As the thunder rumbled across the sky, she looked up at the ceiling.

Ever since she was a little girl, she'd liked being in a nice, warm, snug house while it rained. It made her feel so secure, as if she were safe from harm of all kinds.

But now that she was older she knew that harm came in all forms. Sometimes completely unexpected forms.

The form of a fifteen-year-old girl, for instance.

9

In the old days, when it was still all right to put all kinds of bad shit in your lungs, a lot of reporters said that Senator David Cummings looked like the Marlboro Man. But when smoking went out of fashion, they said he looked like Clint Eastwood. He didn't, of course; he was actually better looking than Eastwood, and even more rugged. The trouble was, and he could admit this to himself only upon occasion, he wasn't as smart as Clint. Nor as passionate. There was a hollowness to David Cummings that even he noticed when he stared into the mirror.

He got the looks; his identical twin sister, Helen, got the brains. And the passion.

And that's how they'd always played it. All the years growing up, Helen had the smart ideas and she used her brother as the tool to make those ideas come true.

That's why he'd run for student senate in high school. Then run for student assembly president in college. And then for state assembly. And then for Congress. And finally for the Senate itself. Because Helen told him exactly what to do and how to do it. In those days, women didn't have the opportunities they had these days, and so Helen didn't have much choice but to live through her brother David.

The funny thing was, almost everybody knew about their relationship. You didn't have to talk to David very long to realize that he wasn't exactly a wizard. But charming? Good-looking? Gallant? That was David.

In Washington, David had a huge office. He needed it. He

had one-half the office space for himself and his staff; Helen used the other half of the office for herself and her staff. Even Helen's staff was smarter than David's. She had a better eye for hiring.

But not even Helen and all her wiles could get much respect for David in Washington, D.C.

He was known as the most pro–pork barrel man in the whole Senate. Again, this was Helen's idea. She reasoned, and correctly, that the only people you really had to care about were your constituents back home.

So that was all they worried about.

Republicans and Democrats came and went; presidents found favor, and then were toppled; wars broke out, and came to bloody ends. Balanced budgets, supply-side economics, and back to balanced budgets. And through it all there was one constant: Senator David Cummings, now in his twenty-sixth year in Congress, and ready to run for another six.

For his home state, he built expressways that nobody really needed; set up defense contracts for manufacturers not really up to the job; created science centers that received hundreds of millions of dollars for work that was at best specious; and, in addition, blessed his state, and especially the area in and around Crystal Falls, with hospitals, highways, swimming pools, parks, floor control projects, historic-preservation projects, airports, schools, and museums, and spent nine million dollars on an advertising campaign for the slaughter hogs produced by local farmers. At the first sign of a serious rise in unemployment, Cummings's state was flooded with new make-work projects that put people to work immediately.

Citizens Against Government Waste gave him the award for Most Wasteful Senator three years running. Common Cause called him a "disgrace." The *New York Times* said that not since Boss Tweed had a politician pandered as much to his constituency. And pointed out that Cummings had named more than fifty buildings and highways for himself.

And Helen didn't give a damn.

Through seniority and gall, David had become one of the most senior players in all of the Senate. Which meant that his colleagues went along with his largesse or they suffered the consequences. And Helen was great at thinking up consequences. She was a positive master at it. Just ask the congressman whose dalliance with a Hollywood starlet became front-page news. Or the congressman whose gay boyfriend was revealed to be a French spy. Or the black senator whose husband was shown to be embezzling funds from her office. For Helen, retribution was always swift and deadly and served as a warning to others. This is what happened to this senator; it could just as easily happen to you.

Everything had been going fine until the diagnosis several months ago. . . .

A knock. Or was it?

David, sitting in the leather recliner, was caught up in the video of *Thunderbolt and Lightfoot*, Jeff Bridges being just as good as Clint himself in this particular movie. . . . David couldn't be sure if it was somebody knocking or not.

Hadn't heard a car drive up. Hadn't seen any headlights wash across the front window the way they did, hadn't heard any voices . . . just this small knocking sound.

Put down his drink. Picked himself up from his recliner. Walked across the large living room.

On the way, he glanced out the window. And saw it.

Sitting right in the drive. Brazen as its owner. Darcy's little red sports car.

Oh, God, was Helen going to chew his ass out. She'd blame

him for Darcy coming here. She wouldn't believe that he'd been innocent.

He opened the door.

She smiled, fetchingly as always, half innocence, half sexuality, and said, "Is this the orphanage? I'm just a lost little waif looking for shelter."

"Did you bring the photos?"

That was her only legitimate reason to be here as far as he was concerned. The photos. And the negatives.

"Gee, I thought you liked me, David. I just stop by to be friendly and you jump me about the photos."

"I want them, Darcy. Now."

For the thousandth time, he cursed himself for being stupid enough to get involved with her. Her mother—how it all started—was one of the local leaders in David's reelection campaign. Her mother had hosted several fund-raising events for him, one of them in her own home. This was where he'd met Darcy.

Being involved with underage girls was some kind of weird vampire thing was all he could conclude. He sucked their youth from them and that gave him the power he needed to go on. One day he wanted to drop off a pair of nice senatorial cuff links for Darcy's father. Darcy answered the door. Her parents weren't home. She invited David in for a cup of coffee. He knew he shouldn't but he did. And that's how it started. Before he left that day, he'd made love twice to a fifteen-year-old girl. The thing was, he hadn't thought about his cancer that entire afternoon. She made him forget things. Not until last week had he learned that she kept a camera in her bedroom closet. She knew how to operate it automatically. A kid at school had rigged it up for her. She photographed all her lovers, she'd giggled when she'd first shown David the photos. The difference was, David had said, not all her lovers were United States senators up for reelection.

Now, standing in his doorway, she said, "I don't know what you're so worried about."

"If you're not going to do anything with them, why do you want to keep them?"

"Because it's fun."

He could see the pleasure she took in all this. Took him a few times with her to understand how much she liked having power over him. Now that he understood it, now that he knew she had those photos, it scared the shit out of him.

"You going to invite me in?"

"I don't think that'd be a good idea, Darcy."

"Bet your sister wouldn't like it, huh?"

"I just don't think it'd be a good idea. I don't think we should see each other anymore."

"You still mad about this afternoon?"

"This afternoon?"

"When you pulled into that gas station and I got you on the phone."

"Oh. No. I'm not mad about that anymore. But I still think you should leave."

She looked at him and smiled. "I thought maybe we could talk about the photos."

He could see she was playing a game.

She wanted anything she couldn't get.

Right now, that meant she wanted to be inside his house. Just to prove to herself that she could do it.

"You're just playing games."

"No, I'm not. I just want to spend a little time with you."

"And then you'll give me the photos?"

She thought a moment. "Yes."

"You have them with you?"

She tapped her fashionable little arm-slung purse. "Right here."

"And the negatives?"

She tapped the purse again. "Right here."

"You'd better not be lying to me."

She gave him a mock pout. "I thought you trusted me."

"Yeah, right, Darcy." Then, "You really have the photos with you?"

"I really do."

"And you're going to give them to me?"

"If you invite me in."

"What made you change your mind?"

The mock pout again. "Maybe I just don't like to see you so unhappy."

Bitch, he thought. Little bitch.

She was great at power games. No doubt about it. Helen could put her to good use in the Senate.

But what choice did he have?

How could he turn her away when there was the possibility, however slim, that maybe he really was going to get the photos?

He looked out at the yard behind her. The brown grass was already sodden with rain. Almost every night, raccoons and opossums came up on the lawn and ate the food he left out for them. He loved animals. That was one reason he hated the rain. The animals stayed in. He hoped they were warm and dry wherever they were.

"I'm going to be very, very pissed if you're lying to me, Darcy."

"Lying to you?"

"About having the photos."

"Oh."

"So are you telling me the truth? You really have the photos with you?"

A tiny, enigmatic smile, crushingly sexual. He could taste her, feel her. Whatever else Darcy was, she was a wonderful lover.

"I have the photos."

"And the negatives?"

"And the negatives."

"And you're going to give them to me?"

The smile again. "If you let me come in. And if you're nice to me."

He stood back from the door. "Come in, then."

The moment he said it, he knew that he'd made a mistake.

But by then, of course, it was too late.

Darcy was already inside.

SEVEN

1

There was a time he couldn't wait to pull a night shift like this. He was so young and night shifts were just so damned interesting. Night was when everything happened.

But then the birthdays started adding up, thirty and then the unthinkable thirty-five, and night shifts didn't sound so interesting anymore.

For one thing, Sam Bowers knew, he had a hard time staying awake. Even when he was pouring coffee down all the time. For another, the night was a lot more dangerous than when he'd started back on the force. Mostly, this was because of drugs. Most people thought of the cities as the only place where there was a big problem. But drugs had come to rural America in a big way. Drugs made the existing criminal population a lot more dangerous. And drugs created their own class of criminals, dealers and pushers. These guys, blinded by greed, were perfectly willing to kill anybody who stood in their way. Anybody. Not a month went by without somebody being found dead in a grassy ditch beside some gravel county road. Drug deal gone bad. Always.

And one other thing about the night shift: it got in the way of your love life.

Here he'd been having a great time with Amy, the woman he loved, the woman he wanted to marry, the woman he hoped would bear his children; here he was having a great time with Amy, and his phone goes off, and fifteen minutes later he's manning a patrol car, the chill autumn rain cutting down knife-like, the roads slick and hazardous, the number of cars on the road very heavy, this being Friday night and all.

Right now, he sat in the shadow of a large oak tree, watching a section of the main drag. This was about a mile from the highway, where the teenagers really liked to take their cars flat out. He figured if he could inhibit them a little bit right here, maybe they wouldn't be so reckless when they hit the highway. A good friend of his had died during an illegal drag race. The kid was sixteen.

So Sam Bowers sat in his car and watched the street and listened to the rain thrum on the metal roof of the car, sounding vaguely like steel drums.

And thought about Amy.

That's all he'd been doing since he'd fallen in love with her a year and a half ago.

Thought about Amy.

2

Amy did the electric slide, the tush-push, and the macarena.

She danced with old men, young men, bald men, hairy men, smiling men, frowning men, men who hit on her, men who seemed charmed by her not at all.

In the middle of it all, Sally Frazier, looking slightly disheveled but beamingly happy, rushed up to her and said, "Guess what he did out in the car?"

"What?"

"Put his hand inside my bra."

Unfortunately, Sally, who had a tendency to speak very loudly, had attracted the attention of two older ladies who did not seem especially pleased with her good fortune.

"I just came in here to use the ladies'," Sally gushed, paying no attention to the disapproving women. "I'll let you know what else happens."

Then she was off.

Amy tried a few more dances but then finally admitted the truth: the one and only reason she'd come out here was to see Sam. And Sam was gone.

And so, a few minutes later, Amy was gone, too.

3

Helen had dozed off reading one of her old Faith Baldwin novels. She had a sweet tooth as far as her reading went. She loved romances of the old-fashioned kind. And hated the romances today, where the heroines were little more than sluts and the men were thugs.

The scream woke her.

She wasn't sure it was a scream. Might even have been part of a nightmare she had. She'd had a run of nightmares lately, inexplicably.

But somehow the echoes of the scream lay on the silence that filled the aerie.

A scream. Yes. Definitely.

And a woman screaming?

A woman? What would a woman be doing— Then she had a terrible thought: Is Darcy here?

She collected herself.

David. Her brother. He'd brought in a woman while she was asleep. And for some reason, the woman was screaming.

My God, she thought. He's going to ruin my plans yet. A year at the outside, Dr. Reinhardt, the oncologist, had told her secretly. Maximum.

But what good would a vacated seat do her if it had been left in scandal?

Who was screaming and why?

She got up from the chair, pulled her robe around her, and started quickly down the hall.

Damn David, anyway. She'd been taking care of him all his life. Now it was his turn to take care of her. The least he could do was die and leave her his Senate seat. It was her turn for the spotlight, her turn.

He sat there on the edge of the chair with his head in his hands and made sickly whimpering noises. He wasn't exactly crying but he wasn't exactly not crying, either.

Every few moments, he'd looked over at Darcy on the floor. She'd made him very angry—said he was never going to get the photos back and that she was going to tell her father what he'd done to her—and he'd shoved her.

A blind moment of fear and panic.

Saw it all going down the tank.

Respected Senator in Tryst with Underage Girl.

What was it that Lyndon Johnson had once said? "The two worst things that can happen to a politician are to wake up with a live boy or a dead girl."

Well, Darcy was dead, no doubt about it. He'd tried all her pulse points, and nothing. She'd cracked her head on the edge of the TV when he'd shoved her backward.

A complete accident.
A harmless little shove . . .
And now this.
This.

"My God," Helen said, "what the hell happened?"

"I don't know," her brother said, still sitting on the edge of the chair. "She got hurt."

"Obviously she got hurt, you stupid bastard. But that doesn't tell me what happened."

"I guess I pushed her."

"You guess?"

"Well, I pushed her. Just a little. Not enough to hurt her. She just fell backward and hit the edge of the TV set. The edge is pretty sharp and . . ."

He was babbling now.

Worthless. One worthless son of a bitch, her brother David.

As she looked at the girl lying on the floor of the living room, Helen realized that she'd always assumed her brother would do something like this. Couldn't leave the little girls alone, could he? No matter how many times he'd almost been burned, he'd always gone back and found another one. . . .

She said nothing. Scuffed across the room in her slippers and knelt by the dead girl, knees cracking as she knelt.

Looked her over.

"Did you touch her after she fell over?"

"What?" He sounded groggy, drugged.

"I said did you touch her?"

"I guess so."

"Don't touch her anymore, you understand me? The police lab'll be looking for all kinds of evidence."

She stood up and went over to him and cracked him hard across the face.

"You stupid bastard."

"I didn't mean to knock her over."

"You didn't mean, you didn't mean. You've been telling me that all your life and I'm sick of hearing it. You didn't mean. You killed her."

"I didn't mean—"

He stopped himself. Then smiled. "God, I almost said it again, didn't I?" Then, in an almost imploring tone, he said: "What're we going to do, Helen? What're we going to do?"

By this time, Helen was far across the room at the dry bar, pouring several inches of scotch into a glass.

What she wanted to do was stand here and scream names at him. God knew, that's what he had coming.

But she had to think clearly, concentrate on the problem at hand. That was her role in the little dance they always did, she and her brother.

He got them into trouble, she got them out.

"Maybe we should—" he started to say.

"Shut up."

"What?"

"I said to shut up."

"You don't have to talk to me that way."

"I should talk to you that way a lot more often. Then maybe you wouldn't do so many stupid things."

"God, first cancer and now this. I don't deserve it, I really don't."

He started crying then.

Sat there like a big overgrown baby and blubbered.

She supposed she should go over to him and try to make him feel better.

But she sure didn't feel like it.

She wanted to slap him some more.

The dream of her own Senate seat had been about to come true when . . .

And then, as she was sipping her scotch, leaning on the bar, looking out the window, trying to will out of existence the dead girl on the floor . . .

. . . she remembered the conversation she'd been having right before she'd picked up her Faith Baldwin book and started to doze off.

Praise God, praise God.

There might be a way out of this after all.

Just then David revved up the blubbering. She shook her head. He made her sick. She could barely stand the sight of him.

But she had to pull him through just this one more time. For her sake, not his.

"I get cancer and now this," David said every few moments between sobs. "Cancer and now this."

She went over and stood above the dead girl and felt a wave of optimism.

With a lot of careful planning, she could get them out of this situation. She was sure of it.

Then she stalked over to David and slapped him across the face again and told him to shut the hell up.

She had a lot to think through and she didn't need him wailing in the background.

PART

2

EIGHT

1

The rain was a bitch.

It had already flooded out two small bridges, filled up a few dozen basements, knocked down three power lines, and washed out a lot of the fall planting local farmers had done in the past two weeks.

Away from town, the rain had also turned a lot of the county roads into treacherous mud puddles resembling, in places, quicksand.

David did the driving. Helen did the scouting. She was looking for signs of any other vehicles.

All they needed was to get pulled over for speeding or something. A nosy cop could look in the trunk and destroy their lives.

Excuse me, Miss Cummings.

Yes?

Well, I just took a look in your trunk and darned if there doesn't seem to be a dead girl in there.

A dead girl? Don't be preposterous.

No, ma'am. I mean I know how nice and respectable you and the Senator are, but there really does seem to be a young lady in your trunk. You want to walk back there and take a look at her?

At which point, David would go totally to hell and admit everything.

He'd be sobbing when they brought him into the police station.

He'd be screaming his guilt for all to hear.

And Helen, who had waited so long and so patiently to become a senator, would see all her dreams dashed.

She said, "Watch your speed."

"I'm doing thirty miles an hour exactly."

"Doesn't look like it from here."

"You're looking at the speedometer from an angle."

"Just watch your speed."

They were nearing the City Limits sign out by Bevins Creek. From there, it would be a short drive to the place Helen had in mind.

Nice, short drive on an old road hardly used anymore.

Perfect place for a corpse to be in a trunk.

David said, "I really did like her."

"Yeah. I can see why."

"You're being sarcastic."

"David, she was trying to blackmail you."

"But she could be sweet."

"Right."

"She could."

"I'll take your word for it."

"Her parents are going to take this real hard. They really loved her."

"Right now, I can't worry about her parents."

"She had a nice little dog, too."

He started crying again. Was just driving along and his eyes overflowed with tears.

"I didn't mean to kill her. I really didn't."

"I know."

"When I saw her fall—and I heard the noise her head made, you know, cracking against the TV set—I knew right away she was dead."

"Don't think about it, David."

"I really didn't mean to kill her."

"You're speeding again, David, and don't tell me it's the angle I'm looking at the speedometer."

He erupted, as he did upon occasion when his sister's bossiness really got to him.

He took his hand off the wheel and began banging the steering wheel. And he began shouting.

"Just shut your fucking mouth, Helen! And keep it shut! You fucking understand me!"

He put his face, his crazed face, close to hers, and when he shouted he sprayed spittle all over her.

She knew enough to leave him alone now.

"I didn't mean to aggravate you," she said quietly.

"I say she's a nice girl, you tell me she isn't."

"David, please—"

"Maybe she was trying to blackmail me. But that doesn't mean she wasn't a nice girl at least some of the time."

"David, listen to me—"

"You've never liked a single fucking girl I've been with my whole life."

"David, she was—"

"Neither one of my two wives. Not any of the four women who lived with me. Not one of them, Helen. And you know what?"

She didn't say anything, just stared straight ahead.

"Now we've got a dead girl in the trunk of our nice new

Lincoln Towncar, and you still can't say anything nice about her."

She was watching the road ahead, something David wasn't paying much attention to, when she saw Hartson Bridge. Or what was left of it.

The bridge itself had vanished beneath several feet of muddy water. All you could see was the steel top of the bridge where people liked to sit when they fished.

The creek had overflowed its banks and was flooding the entire area with muddy brown water.

"Oh, shit," Helen said.

"Maybe we can make it."

"No way."

"This is a big car."

"No way, I said. What if we got stuck out there. We'd have to call for help and there we'd be with a dead girl in the trunk and everybody snooping around."

"I'm sorry I yelled at you, Helen."

"Yeah, well right now I'm a lot more worried about how we get out to the woods."

He looked at her and his anger was gone completely. Now he was a helpless little boy again.

"What're we going to do, Helen? What're we going to do?"

2

When she got home, Amy fixed herself a cup of instant hot chocolate and carried it to the living room, where she turned on Jay Leno. Much as she liked her western boots, it was a whole lot more comfortable to sit around in her cotton pajamas and her slippers. Every few minutes, she'd hit the mute button on the remote and listen to the wind whip the rain through the trees.

Then she'd stare at the phone on the end table and think about calling Richie.

She'd never gotten over that need to call him when a storm came up. Make sure he was all right. Just as she had when she was raising him her last two years of high school.

Sometimes, Richie resented this kind of oversight. Other times, he seemed amused by it in a sentimental way. You never could tell how Richie was going to react to things. A lot of it depended on if he'd been drinking.

She decided against calling him.

He was a big boy now. Too big, in some ways, she thought, recalling this afternoon and seeing fifteen-year-old Darcy in his arms.

Richie still held the belief that he was invincible. Oh, he might take a few knocks, but nothing could really hurt him. Which wasn't true, of course. The world was a perilous place for even the toughest of people. And given Richie's fondness for the bottle, he was anything but tough.

After a bathroom run, Amy came back to the living room and sat on the couch again.

And picked up the phone.

She just had this feeling was all.

She dialed his number.

She was being foolish.

No, she wasn't. She was just being cautious, and there was nothing wrong with being cautious.

Her self-debate proved pointless.

Richie didn't answer his phone anyway. He was one of those people who hated answering machines.

Leno's second guest was Steve Martin. She'd always liked Martin. He was one of the few handsome actors perfectly willing to make an utter ass out of himself.

After Martin came a country singer she'd never heard of.

She used the song time to try Richie again.

She punched mute as she dialed.

Rain lashed the roof, howled in the eaves.

There was still no answer.

She wondered where he was, whom he was with, what he was doing.

She loved him so much.

Conan O'Brien came on next. She always liked the first of the show, when it was just Conan and his sidekick, Andy, better than the guests.

She watched the opening segment and then tried Richie's number again.

No answer.

What was she so nervous about?

Richie was probably dazzling some sweet—but legal— young thing he'd met in a bar somewhere. He was still numero uno with the ladies of this town.

And wouldn't he be embarrassed when he got inside his cottage door, his lady all primed for a night of amore, and here his sister was calling him up and checking on him like he was a little kid or something?

She sighed, put the receiver down.

Richie was fine.

She just had these terrible feelings sometimes.

Sort of like . . . premonitions, she supposed.

But she was being crazy.

Richie was putting the moves on some lady right now. And he was probably drinking, too. But at least he was all right. That, she was sure of.

Wasn't she?

A few minutes later, she picked up her new Patricia Cornwell novel and went to bed.

She hoped she had a romantic dream about Sam tonight. Those were her favorite dreams of all.

3

"I can't see."

"Turn on the defroster."

"It's goddamned seventy degrees out and I should turn on the defroster?"

"It may be goddamned seventy degrees out, David, but there's steam all over the window."

"It's not steam."

"Well," Helen said, "whatever the hell it is."

"You never were worth a shit at science."

"Well, you were never worth a shit at staying out of trouble, so I guess we're even."

"I think I can smell her."

"Oh, God, now who's the one who doesn't know anything about science."

"I just said—"

"I know what you just said. A, she hasn't been dead for even an hour yet, and B, she's in the trunk. So you couldn't smell her even if you wanted to."

"Yeah, that's what I want to do, Helen. I *want* to smell her."

Helen reached up and smeared her hand across the window, cutting a swatch of clear glass on the windshield.

"A fifty-thousand-dollar car and you can't see out of the window."

"It was forty-five thousand."

"If I were you, David, I'd just keep my mouth shut."

"I just thought—"

"Did you hear me? About keeping your mouth shut?"

They drove.

They were going up a very steep hill. The thing was, after getting rained out at Hartson Bridge, she replanned their whole trip. They swung west. This way, they'd come in from the east. It meant extra miles. But what choice did they have?

What she didn't plan on was the condition of the county roads. By now, so soaked, so sodden, they were little better than mud puddles.

Even a big-ass car like this one was sluicing through the mud and fishtailing all over the place.

A couple of times, he'd almost gotten them stuck.

She supposed she should have driven, but she wasn't up for taking on his ego any more than she had to.

He would take very personally her suggestion that maybe, just maybe, he was a shitty driver.

They drove.

"You can't possibly see through all that steam on the window."

"I told you," he said, "it isn't steam."

"You're going to get us stuck."

"Not if you shut up."

"Oh, yeah, like I'm going to *talk* us into going into the ditch."

They drove.

He couldn't see shit.

A couple of times, the big Lincoln slid over to the side of the road and its rear tires sank into the mud.

He gave it a lot of gas fast and that seemed to do the trick.

He didn't get stuck.

He said, "I'm going to turn on the defroster."

"Finally."

"Now you can relax."

"Right, we're riding around with a dead girl in the trunk and I can relax."

After a while, he said, "There's Carlyle Woods."

"Thanks for pointing that out."

"I'm going to feel better when we get rid of her," he said. Then, "That sounds pretty cold-blooded, doesn't it?"

And that's when it happened.

When he was telling her about how cold-blooded he felt.

The rear right wheel reached a large pothole and sank half a foot into deep mud.

One moment he was driving along, and then he wasn't driving at all.

He was trying to fight his way out of the hole.

The middle of nowhere. Late at night. The rain slicing down in silver sheets. The windshield fogged over even with the defroster working. A dead girl in the trunk.

My God.

"Shit," he said.

"Shit is right."

"We just have to stay calm."

"Go forward a little bit."

"What the hell you think I'm *trying* to do?"

"Try it again, then."

He tried it again, the big engine throbbing, pushing, but the right rear wheel sunk deep in the muddy hole.

"Shit," he said again.

"Try reverse."

"What?"

"You heard me. Try reverse."

"That won't do any good."

"Try it," she said.

He put his hand on the gearshift and brought it down to R.

The gear whined a little. The car moved scarcely at all. He got even less traction in R than he'd gotten in D.

"Not that way," she said.

"Not that way what?"

"You're doing it like an old lady."

"What're you?" he said. "An Indy 500 driver?"

"The thing is to get it rocking. Put it into reverse and then slam it into drive."

"I'm sure that'll be real good on the transmission."

"Right now," she said, "I couldn't give a damn about the transmission. Right now I just want to get rid of your girlfriend."

"This is some goddamned luck I'm having. First my cancer—"

"And now a dead girl."

He glowered at her.

"Don't give me that kind of look, David," she said. "You were the one who killed her, not me."

"I didn't kill her."

"You pushed her."

"I may have pushed her but I didn't kill her. I want you to get that straight."

"Try reverse again."

"Oh, yeah, that'll do a lot of good."

"You want to just sit here, then?"

And that's when he thought he heard—through the slashing rain, through the hammering of his heart, through the rumble and roar of thunder—something moving through the night.

He glanced up, the good manly lines of his face slick with sweat, and gazed into the rearview mirror.

And said, "Oh, no. Oh, shit."

4

The county people had a deal with Chief Hadley. The Crystal Falls officers would swing out by the state park every night and check things out. The county had had major financial troubles last year and had downsized the sheriff's department by four patrol officers. While the state park was technically within their jurisdiction, it was a bitch to reach the way the new patrol maps had been drawn. A county car had to swing way the hell over here just to take a drive through the park. It was actually much easier for a Crystal Falls car to do this, so the Chief said that his own people would handle the park.

Sam Bowers had just finished tooling through the park. He hadn't seen any signs of life. Nobody was going to be out here on a night like this.

But when he was near the west end of the park, way up on a hill, he could see down into the river valley, and that's where he saw the silver Lincoln Towncar.

He was sure it belonged to Senator Cummings.

But what would Cummings be doing out on a night like this?

Sam dug his binoculars out from the glove compartment and had himself a look.

Helen, the Senator's sister, was sitting shotgun. The Senator was behind the wheel. They were arguing, which was no surprise. Everybody knew about their arguing. She was the brains of the outfit and the Senator resented it. And so they argued. A few times, they couldn't control themselves and had arguments right out in public.

They were sure arguing now, both of them gesturing wildly as they shouted back and forth within the confines of the sleek new car.

Then he watched as the Senator shifted gears and gave the big car some gas.

The Towncar rocked a little but went nowhere.

They were stuck.

What the hell were they doing out on this county road at night?

He put the binoculars away, then swung down the steep, angling asphalt road and drove out of the park, which was eerily empty in the downpour.

He was an animal lover and missed the sight of the raccoons, opossums, bunnies, and owls who lined the park roads every night.

He couldn't get the image of the angry Cummingses out of his mind. Even by their standard, this looked to be an exceptionally violent argument.

And again the question: What the hell were they doing out on a county road so late at night?

As he left the park and cut over to the county road a quarter of a mile away, he thought he'd soon have his answer.

The county road was a mudhole.

Along with cutbacks in personnel, the county hadn't had enough road-use taxes for needed repairs. Those taxes had ended up in a medical contingency fund. So some of the roads were in pretty bad shape. This particular one, Sam knew, had needed grading and fresh gravel for more than two years.

After climbing two very muddy hills, Sam got them in his sight.

They were still sitting there in the silver Lincoln, the Senator jamming the gears back and forth in an attempt to wedge the car free.

For one thing, he'd been driving way the hell over on the side of the road, which is how he'd gotten stuck.

For a second thing, no amount of rocking the car back and forth was going to do any good.

Sam thought about the chains in the trunk. He'd probably be able to tug the Lincoln out of its hole. He just hoped that the regular shift guys had thought to leave the chains in the trunk where they were supposed to be.

He turned on the red emergency lights, no siren, and climbed the hill up to the Cummingses' vehicle.

5

"Oh, my God," Helen said when she turned around and saw the police car coming up the hill, emergency lights staining the rain a bloodred color.

"Now what do we fucking do?" David said.

He sounded as if he were about to cry again.

"Get control of yourself, David. For God's sake."

"He's going to ask us what we're doing out here and what're we going to tell him?"

Helen did what she usually did whenever David gave in to panic. Became the strong one. "We're going to tell him that we were out driving around and got caught in the rain."

"Why were we driving around?"

"Because, David, we *wanted* to drive around."

"What if he doesn't buy it?"

"David, you're a United States senator. If you want to drive around, that's your business."

"What if he wants to see in the trunk?"

"Why would he want to see in the trunk?"

"Oh, God, he's right behind us."

And so he was.

Sam Bowers was climbing out of the official Chevrolet with the heavy-duty engine in it.

He was shrugging into his black rubber raincoat and walking toward the silver Lincoln.

He spent a long minute in the downpour sizing up the situation, getting down on his haunches for a better look at the muddy hole.

Then he was walking around the car and checking the other rear wheel.

Finally, he was walking back to the stuck wheel and looking at it again.

"Oh, God," David said, "he's coming up here."

"Of course he's coming up here. What the hell did you think he was going to do?"

Sam was knocking on David's window.

David touched the electric window button. "Hi, Sam."

"Evening, Senator. Helen."

"You've got some night for it, Sam."

He leaned in closer and smiled. "Doesn't look much better for you two."

"Oh, you know how my brother is. Heavy foot and all. I told him to slow down."

David Cummings smiled with great pain, obviously wanting to start in on his sister, but not wanting to be unseemly and do it in front of Sam. "*After* we got stuck, that's when she told me to slow down, Sam."

Now it was Sam's smile that was pained. Long as he'd been a cop, he'd never figured out what expression to wear when people were cutting each other up with small verbal knives.

"I've got a chain in my trunk," Sam said. "I think I can pull you out of there."

"We'd really appreciate it, Sam," Helen said.

"I'll pull my car up the hill," Sam said, "and then dig out the chain."

"That'd be great," David said.

"Thanks, Sam," Helen said.

Sam gave her a little salute and then started back toward his car.

"No problem," David said.

"It's not over yet."

"He didn't even ask what we were doing out here."

"Oh, shit."

"What?"

"Look."

"What the hell's he doing?" David said, starting to turn around.

"Don't turn around, you idiot. He'll know something's wrong for sure."

"What the hell's he doing?"

"Probably looking at our bumper," Helen said, "trying to figure out the best place to put the chain on."

"God, if that trunk ever came open . . ."

They both sat staring straight ahead, trying very hard to look as if they were just two regular people who'd run into a little bad luck.

The only thing was, David's whole left side was trembling. He vaguely recalled that that might be the sign of a stroke.

Sam got down on his haunches and examined the bumper. The underside looked as if it would support the chain and the pulling force needed to extricate the car from the hole.

Then he stood up and went over to the stuck wheel and examined it some more.

Sand would help. Pour a quarter of a bag or so in the hole, that would help him get traction.

A lot of people in this area kept a bag of sand with them all year round. Usually, in the trunk.

Sam went up to the Senator's window and knocked again.

"Hi," the Senator said.

It was strange but he had this kind of sickly smile on his face. Like he was real nervous about something.

"I was wondering if you had any sand in your trunk?"

"In our trunk."

"Right, your trunk."

The Senator looked at his sister and said, "He wants to know if we have any sand in our trunk."

Sam leaned down so he could see Helen. "That'd really help, Helen."

"In the trunk," the Senator said. "He said the trunk."

"I heard what he said, David. I'm not deaf."

"You think you've got any?" Sam said.

Rain hissed. Inside his heavy rain gear, Sam was sweaty. He felt greasy. A shower would be nice.

Helen made a peeved face. "You're not going to believe this, Sam, but the last time we were home, I had our yard man take the sandbag from the trunk. We had to haul around a bunch of posters and things so I figured we could use the room."

"Isn't that always the way?" the Senator said.

"Well, just thought I'd give it a try."

"Sorry, Sam," Helen said.

"Yes, *very* sorry, Sam," said the Senator.

"My God," David said. "That was so damned close."

"Close? What the hell're you talking about? He just asked if we had any sand in the trunk."

"The trunk—that's exactly my point. You know what we have in the trunk."

"You overreacted. As usual."

"You didn't look so calm."

"A hell of a lot calmer than you did."

There was about ten feet of chain in the trunk. There was also just the right hook Sam needed to attach to the Lincoln's rear bumper.

He carried the chain and the hook up to the Lincoln and got it set up and then he went back and drove his car up the hill so that it was directly behind the Lincoln.

He was really sweating.

On the way back to his car, he slipped and fell to one knee in the mudhole.

The rain blinded him.

This was a hell of a night.

He stood erect and then started the process of attaching the free end of the chain to his patrol car.

After he finished that, he walked back up to the Lincoln. The Senator rolled the window down.

"It'd probably be a good idea if you two could be out of the car when I'm trying to pull it." He nodded to their fashionable trench coats. "I think you'd survive all right."

"You mean get—outside, Sam?"

"Yes, ma'am, that's what I mean."

She sounded as if he'd asked her to crawl on her hands and knees through a couple of miles of sheep dung. She almost looked nervous about something.

"C'mon, we'll be fine," David said.

His sister didn't look too sure about that.

Sam spent the next few minutes making sure that the cars were lined up properly.

Then he climbed behind the wheel of his patrol car and began the slow process of pulling the car out of the mud.

The Senator and his sister stood off to the side and watched. They looked a little bit lost, and more than a little bit helpless.

Factotums made sure that U.S. senators never had to bother themselves with the details of an ordinary life.

It was a nice life, Sam thought. Having people do for you instead of you having to do for yourself.

He was a still a little bit pissed the Senator had helped the young man with his bail this morning.

He felt the big Lincoln begin to stir in the mud, roll a few inches up the tracks the tire had left.

Sam's engine strained; the Lincoln rolled a little more forward.

Progress. A few more pulls and the Lincoln would come free.

Sam gave his car more gas.

That was when the Lincoln's trunk lid popped open.

David stared at the trunk lid in disbelief.

Since the hood of Sam's car faced the back of the Lincoln, Sam had a clear look at the trunk.

Apparently, David hadn't slammed the trunk hard enough when he'd set Darcy in there.

Now the trunk was open.

The Senator let out an animal yelp and began wading through thick mud to reach the trunk before Sam could see the body inside.

Sam wondered what the Senator was so excited about. A little rain in a trunk wasn't going to hurt anything.

But both the Senator and his sister looked startled, then alarmed, when the trunk popped open.

Now the Senator was trotting ass over appetite to get to the trunk lid and close it.

He was a few inches from the rear taillight of the Lincoln when he fell facedown into the mud.

Sam started to get out of the car to see if he could help the Senator, but Helen was next to her brother in moments.

Sam noted a curious fact: before she bent down to help her brother, Helen clomped through the mud and slammed the trunk lid down.

Then she turned back to her brother, who was struggling to his feet. His face and hands were covered in mud. He held them up to the rain, which started the process of cleaning him up.

Sam went back to pulling the Lincoln out of its hole, noting one more curious fact before he finally freed the rear wheel: Helen was just standing there watching Sam's police car tug the Lincoln free, when she suddenly stomped through the mud again and checked on the trunk, pushing down on it to make sure that it was fixed good and tight.

If it hadn't been raining so hard, if Sam wasn't already late making his in-town rounds, he might have thought a little harder about the strange behavior he was seeing.

But there wasn't time.

"We sure appreciate this, Sam," Helen said, still standing in the rain.

"We sure do," the Senator agreed.

Sam waved at them from inside his dry, warm car and then headed back to town.

NINE

1

Twenty minutes later, the Lincoln pulled off the county road and drove up on a wide swath of grass that led up to a densely wooded area.

The rain continued, a frenzy.

The Senator and his sister moved without speaking. They knew what they had to do and they had to do it quickly.

The Senator opened the lid of the Lincoln and reached down inside. Then Helen reached down inside.

For such a slight girl, Darcy sure seemed to weigh a lot.

They grappled awkwardly at removing her from the trunk. There was still no evidence of blood anywhere.

Once they had the body free of the car, they began moving quickly.

They carried Darcy into the woods, following a narrow dirt path that wound around several huge oaks, and then a stand of firs and scrub pines.

They only spoke once, and that was when the girl started to slip from Helen's hands.

The Senator reached under the body and held it up so it wouldn't hit the ground.

Helen got her grip once again, and they continued their trek.

The woods seemed deeper and darker than the Senator remembered, something out of the Brothers Grimm perhaps. A lonely owl hooted somewhere. The Senator felt the eyes of unseen creatures watching him, watching.

The forest smelled of pine and mint and earth and autumn-dead leaves.

Every once in a while, the Senator and his sister would run into a low-hanging bough or a tree stump. They'd curse under their breath but keep moving.

Had to keep moving.

Eight minutes after they started into the forest, they reached the clearing above Richie McGuire's little cottage.

This was where they were going to leave her.

They surveyed the entire area.

No lights in the cottage, meaning Richie had already drunk himself into oblivion. His yellow Mustang sat in the front yard.

No cars on the road in front of Richie's. No sight of anybody wandering around in the area.

But then who'd be wandering around on a night like this?

They carried the body out of the woods and set it atop the clearing and then began covering it frantically with sodden leaves until the girl looked like a natural mound instead of a girl at all.

"We need some more leaves," Helen said.

"I'm soaked."

"You may not mind going to the gas chamber but I do. Now let's put some more leaves on her."

They worked quickly, doubling the amount of leaves that disguised the girl.

Helen was just picking up another handful of leaves when she saw movement down on the side of the cottage.

Believe it or not, somebody was hiding in the shadows down there, watching Helen and the Senator covering up Darcy.

Helen told David to look down on the east side of the cabin.

At first, David couldn't see what she was talking about. But finally, his eyes adjusting to the rain and the gloom, he said, "It's that damned Jimmy."

"That crazy guy?"

"Not crazy. Brain-damaged."

"Whatever," Helen said. Then, "I'm going down there."

"You're what?"

"He saw us, didn't he?"

"He'll tell Richie."

"He won't tell Richie anything once I get done talking to him."

"God, are you sure?"

"Let's get in the car and drive over to his place."

"You know where it is?"

"Right down the road."

"What if he tells Richie?" David said.

"Richie's already out for the night. You know how he drinks."

"There he goes!" David said.

And sure enough, there was the shadowy figure of Jimmy running across the small valley that upsloped to a windbreak, on the other side of which was his little shack.

"Let's get in the car," Helen said.

2

Sam was about halfway back to town when the two-way came to life.

"Sam, you know the Fuller girl? Over," Maude, the dispatcher, said.

"Sure. Over."

"Well, her folks are out of town for a while. Darcy's supposed to call the neighbor lady every night at eleven and tell her everything's all right. Over."

"And she hasn't called? Over."

"Not so far. Over," Maude said.

"Well, given what I know about Darcy, I wouldn't worry too much. She likes to have her fun. If she hasn't called in by midnight, I'll start looking around for her. Over."

"Thanks. How'd it go with the Senator and his sister, by the way? Over."

"Fine. Over."

"Well, stay dry. Over."

They signed off.

Sam got himself comfortable behind the wheel and started thinking about Amy.

Maybe things were finally going to be all right between them. Maybe the worst was behind them.

He hoped so.

He'd never been brokenhearted before, and it was a bitch. He'd lost ten pounds in three months, and even started sucking on an occasional cigarette, after having given them up eight years ago. And no woman, not even the most beautiful, seemed to interest him at all. There was Amy and only Amy.

Yes, tonight had indeed been promising. He just hoped she'd go out with him on a night when he didn't get called into work.

In fact, soon as he reached town, he'd take a run by her house. He did that most nights, anyway, in his private vehicle. Just seeing her house made him feel better.

3

The place was a one-room shack that sat on the edge of a creek that was now overflowing with rainwater.

When the Lincoln turned from the road to the short road leading to the shack, David cut the lights and coasted all the way up to the door.

"You sure you can handle him?"

Helen, in the darkness, smiled. "You think you can do a better job, brother dear?"

He didn't say anything, just put his hands on the wheel and his head on his hands.

"I can't believe it," he said. "We finally get her out of the car and then Jimmy's watching us."

"I said I can handle it. You wait here."

She got out of the car. The ground beneath her hiking boots was wet but not muddy.

She clipped on her flashlight and followed its beam up to the door of the shack. Ten years ago, one of the local siding companies had trained a young crew by having it side Jimmy's place. The siding was long faded now. Its dark brown color looked sodden in the rain.

The front yard was a mess of rakes, hoes, empty pop bottles, comic books, orange rinds, and dog shit.

She knocked once, loudly, on the screen door. The ancient door jiggled under the weight of her hand.

"I know you're in there, Jimmy."

"Go away, Miss Helen."

"I want to talk to you."

"You're gonna put me in that place again, aren't you?"

"Not if you're a good boy."

Rain fell. Thunder rumbled. Lightning revealed clearly the squalor of the front lawn.

"Jimmy."

"I don't want to go there again."

"You won't if you help me."

"Help you? Help you do what, Miss Helen?"

"Help me help the president of the United States."

"Ah, you're just saying that."

"Isn't my brother a senator?"

"Uh, yeah."

"Well then, it stands to reason he'd know the president of the United States, doesn't it?"

"Uh, I guess so, Miss Helen."

"Open the fucking door, Jimmy. I'm getting soaked out here."

He just had to say it one more time. "I don't want to go back to that place again, Miss Helen. I really don't."

"Open up, Jimmy, or I'll put you in that place right away tonight."

Thunder again. Lightning.

In the gloom, she saw David roll down the window and stick his head out into the rain.

She shone her flashlight on his face.

He ducked back inside the car, like a startled lizard.

When she was a senator, she was going to show people the power the job really held. She wouldn't be a nervous wimp like her brother.

Jimmy opened up.

She pulled the screen door back and went inside.

The stench was the first thing she noticed, of course. Burned greasy food. Spoiled food. Dirty clothes. A sweat-soaked mattress. Dust and filth. And dog shit. Dog shit, every-where.

She wanted to vomit.

Jimmy didn't turn on his kerosene lantern. She used her flashlight instead, playing it around the dumpy room. She paused at the wall next to his bed, surveying the magazine pages he had Scotch-taped there.

Heather Locklear. Courteney Cox. Pamela Anderson. The current crop of sexpots.

She supposed what he did was lie down on his bed and jerk off while he was looking up at the photos.

Somehow, the idea of Jimmy masturbating both tickled and disgusted her.

He was a pretty disgusting character, actually. He used to do yard work for her. She caught him one day peeking in the bathroom window when she was getting out of the shower. Most people would probably think this was harmless. Helen was frightened by it because in some profound way Jimmy scared her. The thought of him seeing her naked really gave her the creeps.

She didn't turn him over to the police but she did call a friend at the nearby psychiatric hospital and had her take Jimmy for one week and put the fear of God in him. He got the shock treatments, he got the straitjacket, he got the violent ward, where people screamed all night just the way stir-crazy animals did at the zoo.

He came home not only chastened but terrified. For long months after his release, Jimmy had told everybody about all the terrors of the place. The other patients frightened him.

He told Helen he didn't want to work for her anymore. He also told her that he would never peek in anybody's bathroom window again, either. Sacred honor.

"You saw what happened, didn't you?"

"Huh?"

"C'mon, Jimmy. We saw you watching us."

"I didn't go nowhere tonight."

That got her smiling. "Oh, no? Then why are your hair and your clothes soaking wet?"

"Oh."

"You saw us."

"You're going to send me back to that place again, aren't you?"

"You know what we were doing?"

"What?"

"We were carrying out a job for our boss. And you know who our boss is?"

"Who?"

"The president of the United States."

"Wow. Like in Washington and everything?"

"Exactly."

"Was the girl dead?"

"Yes, she was. And you know why?"

"Huh-uh."

"Because she was a spy."

"Wow. Really?"

He was buying it. Jimmy wasn't smart enough to fake enthusiasm. "She was a spy and she took some secret documents and we had to get them back from her."

"I think I saw this on TV one night. On some spy show."

"You probably did, Jimmy. Anyway, she had an accident when we were taking the documents from her."

"An accident?"

"She fell and hit her head."

"God. That must've hurt."

"I'm sure it did."

"I fell and hit my head once."

"I know you did, Jimmy."

"It hurt real bad."

She reached out and touched his shoulder tenderly.

"But you can't tell anybody any of this—not anybody, Jimmy, you understand?"

"Sure. I understand."

"Because if you do—"

There was a long silence. He said, "I don't want to go back there, Miss Helen. You promise me I won't have to go back there."

"If you keep our secret, Jimmy, you won't have any problem. You won't have to go back there ever again."

"Honest, Miss Helen?"

"Honest."

" 'Cause that place scares me."

"It scares me, too, Jimmy."

"So I won't tell nobody about tonight."

"I believe you, Jimmy."

Thunder again. Lightning. Jimmy appeared ghostlike in the silver flaring of the sky.

Despite the chilly temperature, the shack smelled hot and filthy. She needed to get out of here.

"I'll be seeing you, Jimmy."

"Yes, ma'am."

"You just remember what I told you. No matter what happens—you don't know anything about anything."

"You don't have to worry about me, Miss Helen. No, sir."

"Good boy."

At the door, she paused. "If you think you just have to tell somebody, Jimmy. . . ."

"Yes, ma'am."

"You come over and talk to me. Understand?"

He nodded.

Raindrops plopped from the sky, tree leaves, the shack overhang, a myriad of hissing and popping noises in the quiet night.

She looked at him a moment longer, and then started to leave.

But he was near her now, grasping her sleeve. In the shadows, his eyes glistened with tears and his voice trembled.

"You won't ever let them put me in that place again, will you, Miss Helen?"

She patted his hand. "Not if you're a good boy and do just what I tell you, Jimmy."

He started crying now. "I'm afraid, Miss Helen. I'm afraid they're going to put me back in there."

"You just be a good boy, Jimmy, and you won't have anything to worry about."

Then she was gone.

4

In the morning light, there was evidence that last night's storm had been a lot stronger than a lot of folks had realized.

Large branches had been ripped from trees and flung into the streets. Several electrical wires had been severed, and power wasn't restored on the east side of town until 7 A.M. The damage at the Hawkeye Mobile Home Court was especially bad. Three trailers had been severely wind-damaged.

Amy heard all this on her office radio as she sat at her desk preparing for another pretrial hearing this afternoon. She was tired and, as her secretary had politely pointed out, maybe just a wee bit on the owly side this morning. Amy had smiled: "Me? Owly? Who'd believe that?" As everybody in the office knew, Amy was subject to mild mood swings. She was never an outright bitch, but there were days when she was a whole lot pleasanter than others.

She marked the page she was reading with a yellow sticky, then reached over and picked up her receiver.

For the tenth time since waking this morning, she tried Richie's number.

Six, seven, eight rings.

And no answer.

This didn't signify that he wasn't there.

Oh, no, on the contrary. It signified that he was most likely there and sleeping off another hangover. Two mornings a week, he reported to the country club around noon. Perfect hours for a guy who wanted to tie one on the night before.

Ten, eleven, twelve rings.

She realized she was getting obsessive.

She had a bad feeling, the same bad feeling she'd had last night. She felt angry with Richie for making such a botch of his life—but at the same time she felt protective, almost maternal, about him.

Maybe she hadn't raised him properly.

Maybe she just hadn't had the wisdom or the courage to crack down on him when he was fourteen. Maybe if their parents had been around, Richie would have turned out to be a nice, normal kid with no undue problems.

Maybe.

Her intercom buzzed.

"Yes?"

"Bob Medlow would like to see you. He says it won't take long."

Amy had a pretty good idea why the young lawyer had stopped in to see her this morning. This wasn't a good time, not with a pretrial hanging over her . . . and Richie sleeping off a drunk.

But she sighed and said, "All right. Tell him to come in."

If nothing else, Medlow was as good as his word. If he said a few minutes, then that's all it would take.

This morning he wore a tan silk suit, his sun-bleached hair

complementing the suit very well. His slender body and tortoiseshell spectacles gave him a dramatically earnest look. Local juries seemed to love his carefully contrived appearance. He was the most successful trial lawyer in the county and he'd turned thirty only last month.

"The coffee's improving around here," he said, setting his cup down on her desk.

She smiled. "You sound like a restaurant critic."

"Four-star coffee at the DA's office. That'd be a pretty interesting headline, don't you think?"

He sat down, set his briefcase next to his chair, then leaned forward, picked up his coffee cup, and took a long sip.

"It really is good," he said.

"We're thinking of opening up a lunch counter."

"Who would think that behind such a sweet face would lurk such a smart-ass? I certainly wouldn't."

She laughed. She actually liked Medlow. She'd never been involved in a Medlow trial and she wasn't necessarily looking forward to it.

"You've sure got the gift of gab, as my Irish aunt used to say, Bob."

"Well, if I didn't, I sure wouldn't be winning all those cases." He laughed. "My modesty is becoming, isn't it?"

He leaned forward, ever the dramatic actor, and said in little more than a stage whisper, "Do you see what I have here?"

She saw a plain manila file folder.

"If I guess correctly, do I win a refrigerator?"

"No. But if you guess correctly, you'll save the taxpayers a whole lot of money. And give a good, honest policeman back his good name."

"I knew this was going to be about Steve Arnette."

"He's a good man, Amy."

"No he isn't, and you know it. He's a bully and a sadist and there's no way he should be a cop."

"You're pretty cynical for your age, young lady." He smiled as he spoke, but she paid more attention to his eyes than his words. He looked as if he were preparing to say something pretty dramatic. "Let me make this clear, Amy. I am in no way calling your brother Richie a liar."

"That's nice of you, Bob."

"What I am saying, and what I've said from the beginning, is that Richie was very drunk that night and doesn't remember how things happened."

"And your client Steve Arnette is of course giving us the one true account of the evening?"

"No, and as you well know, we don't have to rely just on Steve's version of things."

"His partner, Haymes?"

"His partner, Dutch Haymes. Twelve years on the force. Father of five. Good, devout Lutheran. He was there, too, and he goes along with Steve's version of the altercation."

What had happened was all pretty simple. Outside a local nightspot three months ago, Richie had been staggering across the parking lot when Arnette and Haymes pulled in. Arnette and Haymes said they wanted to give Richie a sobriety test. But somehow, a few minutes later, the three of them ended up behind the building in the alley. No witnesses. Richie got his nose and two ribs broken. Arnette and Haymes swore that Richie resisted arrest and swung at both of them. They didn't, they insisted, have any choice but to use force.

Amy suspected that Sam knew Richie was telling the truth when he said that the two cops had simply attacked him.

But with no witness, how could he go against his own men?

So Sam bought the company line. Amy went ahead and took Richie's deposition and started the process of bringing charges. Arnette hired Bob Medlow to defend him. A lot of her former supporters now disliked Amy. They felt she was using her office to protect her brother.

Things got so heated between Amy and Sam that Amy broke off their informal engagement. She hadn't seen him for a long time, not until last night.

Bob Medlow said, "I hear you were at the barn dance last night."

"So that's what this is about."

"Can this be? Is the lady clairvoyant?"

"In this case, I think I *am* clairvoyant. You heard that Sam and I were together for a while last night, so now you're thinking that I'm going to drop the charges."

"You are clairvoyant."

"I'm not."

He looked genuinely dismayed. The playfulness was gone from his voice. "You're really going on with this bullshit, Amy?" Then, "I'm sorry. That was very unprofessional." He leaned forward again, with his usual urgency and drama. "You know what the boys and girls in Des Moines are saying about you, Amy. That you've got a great political career ahead of you—if you handle things right. Defending your brother like this, especially with his reputation—it looks bad, Amy."

"I know how it looks, Bob."

"And most people in town—well, frankly, they believe Arnette and Haymes." He made a sad face. "I'm sure that hurts your feelings, but it's the truth." Then: "Richie doesn't always tell the truth, Amy. I mean, let's put that on the table, too."

Richie did tell lies, no doubt about it. When he was twelve years old, he accidentally burned down the family garage. He made up a story about seeing a hobo fleeing the fiery scene.

When he was sixteen, he got angry at his girlfriend and smashed all the windows in the car he was using—which just happened to be his sister's. Richie insisted that a rival football team, angry over losing to Richie and his friends, had done the damage.

And then when he was nineteen, he was accused in a paternity suit. He denied ever sleeping with the girl. A lie detector and a blood test said otherwise.

There were many, many other lies, too, of course. Richie was just one of those people who seemed to prefer lies to truth, and she was skeptical about many of his claims to innocence.

But the incident with Arnette and Haymes was different.

Amy said, "Have you looked into your client's history?"

"I have."

"Then you've seen that eighteen citizens over a ten-year period have filed brutality reports against him."

"And the Chief," Medlow said, "cleared him of all but one of those charges."

"Yes, and that one, poor Arnette was suspended for three days—with pay—while Mike Forbes still limps around today because of how Arnette injured him."

He leaned back, making a big display of ruminating, elbows on the arms of the chair, fingers steepled in front of his mouth, a contemplative look in his brown eyes.

"I'll tell you what."

She smiled. "Whenever you say that, Bob, I know you're going to offer me one hell of a deal."

He smiled back. "You know me too well."

"And actually I like you. But don't ask me why."

"Probably because I'm cute."

"Probably."

He got dramatic about being contemplative. He started making faces, weary faces, as if the weight of the cosmos were on his shoulders. Amy wondered if he'd minored in drama.

"I'll tell you what, Amy."

"This should be good."

"Let's just say that we quietly agree that neither of our clients is exactly an angel. Would you go that far?"

"I'd go that far."

"That's step one. Step two is admitting, again in a very quiet way, that neither of our clients is known to tell the truth very often."

"Richie isn't psychotic or sociopathic, if that's what you're implying."

"I hate those five-dollar words. Too damned clinical. Let's just say that both of our clients are bullshit artists of the first tier and let it go at that."

"And you're getting at what here?"

"I'm getting at the fact that we quietly withdraw your brother's complaint—"

"No way."

"I didn't interrupt you. Please don't interrupt me."

"You didn't interrupt me," Amy said, "because you've been doing all the talking. Bob, I'm busier than hell. Will you get to the point?"

"What if my client agrees to pick up Richie's medical bills, which I believe amount to something like twelve hundred dollars? That's a lot of money for Richie to come up with."

About that, she couldn't argue. She'd already gotten two calls from one of the nuns at the hospital asking if she could please mention discreetly to Richie that his bill was now ninety days old. "If he can't pay the whole thing, Amy, could you ask him to call us and we'll set up some sort of pay schedule." Richie didn't have any insurance.

"I can see interest in your eye," Medlow said brightly. "You're starting to see things my way. Your aura is changing colors, too. That's a very good sign."

"My aura? I'm surprised you don't wear a mood ring and ask me what my astrological sign is."

"I already know. Pisces. I figured that out last year at your birthday party at the bar association."

She sighed and sat back.

"You're probably right," she said. "Probably neither one of

them is telling the exact truth. They're both hotheads, so they both probably played a role in getting the fight started."

"There you go."

"But."

He smiled. "Here we go."

"But if we drop the charges, Arnette is going to think he can keep right on doing what he's doing. And nobody's going to stop him."

"This one scared him, Amy."

"Yeah, I'll bet."

"Your friend Sam took him out behind the jail one night after they'd both had more than their share of the hard stuff—and beat, you should pardon my French, the living shit out of my client Arnette."

"You're kidding? What brought that on?"

"Seems your man friend and the Chief almost came to blows themselves. I guess Sam has always felt that Arnette is a bad cop and should be fired. He was extra pissed about this particular dustup because it came between you and him. So I guess one night Arnette and Haymes were in the back of the station and Arnette was bragging about how he'd beaten the crap out of this homeless guy—and Sam just lost it. Sam's a by-the-book lawman."

"He sure is."

She wanted to call Sam and tell him thanks for his faith in Richie, even if Sam hadn't been able to tell her.

"Sam told me that he figured that both Arnette and Richie played a part," Medlow said. "But that Arnette way overreacted. And used his nightstick on your brother—who was unarmed."

"I wish he would have told me all this."

Medlow shook his head. "He couldn't. We're talking the thin blue line here. Sam had to stick up for his department, even if that meant defending a prick like Arnette."

She laughed. "A prick? I wish I had that on tape."

"As you well know, Counselor, we can't be crazy about every single client we have."

"He's a psycho."

"Yeah, I'm afraid he is. But my job is to get you to drop the matter."

"I can't make that decision."

"Oh?"

"It'll be up to Richie."

"You can urge him to do it."

"That I *can* do."

"Will you?"

She thought a moment and then said, "Yeah, yeah I will. Because he needs the money more than he needs a victory in court. But you've got to promise me one thing."

"If I can."

"You have a talk with the Chief. You tell him what a shit that Arnette is."

"Deal."

He reached across the desk and they shook hands.

She really did like Medlow, and he actually was kind of cute.

She said, "Now get the hell out of here."

He grinned. "Yes'm, boss lady."

5

Two hunters found the body.

The duck season had opened the previous weekend, and any section of timber that wasn't posted became a hunting ground.

The covering of leaves was what first startled the men. Furious flies buzzed around the mound of leaves. Several crows perched nearby, obviously studying the flies carefully. There might be food involved here. They had eaten earlier when a squirrel had been struck and killed by a truck hauling steel rods to Dubuque. But the thing concealed beneath the leaves promised to be an even better meal.

The crows watched the furious black flies in the sunny autumn morning.

As the first hunter later told police, he knew immediately that the shape beneath the leaves was that of a human being. Just couldn't be anything else.

Both hunters had seen enough TV to know that they shouldn't touch or move anything at the crime scene.

One of the hunters knelt down next to the body and parted a few crinkly yellow leaves.

He saw one dead blue eye staring up at him. The eye belonged to a white girl. Other than that, he couldn't tell anything else about her.

The discovery hit both men pretty hard. They both had teenage daughters of their own.

Several years ago in Crystal Falls, an escaped convict had stalked a fourteen-year-old girl through the woods, beaten and raped her, and then put a double-barreled shotgun up her and pulled both triggers.

The people of the town had never forgotten this and never would.

One of the hunters went down the hill to the cottage belonging to Richie McGuire.

The hunter could see McGuire sleeping in there, but no matter how hard he pounded, the hunter couldn't raise Richie.

He finally tried the doorknob, but the place was locked.

Richie was still sprawled across his bed, asleep.

The hunter knew Richie. Most everybody did. Richie was obviously sleeping off a particularly bad drunk.

At the time, the hunter later told police, he didn't make any connection between Richie and the dead girl.

The second hunter went back up the hill. He thought that
this was a hell of a day to be dead. Iowa didn't get much pret-
tier than during an Indian summer like this, the leaves burning
brown and yellow and russet red and burnished gold; the blue
sky vibrant with arcing hawks and pheasants; the air itself
melancholy with the smoky smell of the surrounding hills
where leaves were being burned; and the temperature a just-
right seventy-six degrees.

It was a hell of a day to be dead, all right.

The second hunter guarded the body this time. The first
hunter trooped back to the Bronco and drove down the hill to
the nearest farmhouse.

By the time he got back to the body, the hunter found that
several other hunters had appeared. A circle of men with shotguns stood in a semicircle around the corpse.

"I'll bet I can tell you who it is," one of them said.

"Who?" said the first hunter.

"Fuller's daughter, that rich prick from New York."

"Yeah?"

"His daughter."

"What makes you think it's her?" the first hunter said.

The man turned and gestured down the hill. "You know
who lives there?"

"Sure. Richie McGuire."

"Right. And guess who was seeing the McGuire girl."

"Oh, bullshit. Richie wouldn't be crazy enough to do that.
That's just gossip."

"Is it?" the man said. "Guess you didn't hear what happened over to Riley's Pub last night."

"I did," another hunter said. "Chick came right into the
tavern and accused Richie of knocking her up. And then Richie
tried to strangle her."

The first hunter said, "You get hold of the police?"

Just as the second hunter was about to speak, the sound of the siren could be heard heading out of town.

"Wonder if Richie's down there now," somebody said.

"Oh, he's down there all right," said the second hunter. "I pounded on his door a good five minutes. Saw him sleeping in there but I couldn't wake him up."

"Sleeping one off," said another hunter.

"Hell, yes, sleeping one off," said the first hunter. "That's all he ever does anymore."

"You really think he could kill somebody?" said the second hunter.

The first hunter snorted and looked at the other men for support. "That temper of his? You kidding?"

The second hunter stared down the hill again. He looked sad, as if his mind was filled with a terrible memory. "Man, ten years ago Richie had it by the balls."

"He sure did," the first hunter said, and now even his voice was touched with a certain sentimentality. A small town like this needed heroes. And at one point, Richie McGuire had been the biggest hero this town had ever known.

TEN

1

The Chief knew enough to defer to Sam Bowers.

This was the kind of crazy shit that Sam had gone to college to learn.

In the old days, before there had even been a State Bureau of Investigation, before the legislature required all chiefs to take additional schooling each summer, before you practically had to know chemistry to conduct a murder investigation . . . in the old days, you drove out to the crime scene, you and your men scoured the area, you drove back to town and started asking questions, and then in a day or so, you nabbed your man. Small-town murders were generally pretty easy to solve. They almost always involved one of two things—sex or money. Every once in a while, you'd get a really wild one (a case that involved both sex *and* money, like when that Philips gal and the farmhand murdered her husband so they could inherit the farm and then get married to each other), but for the most part, you just started asking questions and soon enough you'd get your answer.

The way the Chief figured it, he could wrap this puppy up in less than eight hours if Sam Bowers hadn't already called in the state boys.

The Chief had already heard what happened at Riley's Pub last night. Given where the body was found, it didn't exactly take a Nobel Prize winner to look down the hill at Richie McGuire's cottage and figure out who the killer was.

But, no, he'd had to defer to Sam because if he didn't the state boys would be all over his ass for not cooperating. Sam and the state boys (and girls; two of the people who were on their way here from Des Moines were gals).

Sam had a checklist. He carried the checklist on his clipboard. And he carried his clipboard with him at all times when he was working a crime scene.

And as he worked, he checked off the appropriate task as it was completed:

- Photograph crime scene
- Measure crime scene
- Collect and catalog evidence
- Draw crime scene
- Go over crime scene with crime lab
- Process crime scene
- Limit no. of evidence gatherers
- Keep accurate records of process
- Cellophane envelopes for small objects not organic in nature
- Paper envelopes used for organic evidence

And so on. Thirty-nine things to check off before his crime-scene investigation was complete. A lot of the locals seemed to find his approach amusing, but he didn't care. He assumed that he would someday take over the department. He wanted everything in place by the time that moment came.

He spent the first forty-five minutes going over the area right around the body. He was assisted by a crime lab tech who'd arrived from Cedar Rapids.

By this time, at least forty people—gawkers—stood on the edge of the timberland, watching.

There wasn't really much to see. Evidence collection was a pretty boring thing to watch.

From time to time, his gaze would inevitably stray downhill to Richie's cabin.

At least a dozen people had come up to him this late morning and told him about the relationship between Richie and the dead girl.

He knew why he was putting off going down there.

His first waking thought this morning had been of Amy. How they were going to get back together. How they would soon enough be getting married and putting the whole business with Richie behind them.

Now he was going to have to ask Richie about the Fuller girl and he was afraid of how Amy was going to take this.

Are you accusing my brother of murder? she'd say.

The relationship that had looked so good last night was starting to look bad again. In fact, worse than it had ever been.

What if Richie really did kill the girl?

Would Amy blame Sam just for doing his job?

He went back to consulting with the crime-lab tech and kept looking down the hill.

2

Panic.

That was always the first thing Richie felt on hangover mornings.

Panic and familiar questions.

Where did I go last night? Who did I see? Did I get into any trouble.

Heat.

Hangovers always left him with a feverish feeling and with a terrible, almost unslakable thirst.

After swinging his legs off his single bed, he sat up straight for a time on the edge of the mattress, head in his hands.

The old and terrifying questions.

His mind dark.

He could remember getting to Riley's Pub after work at the country club.

He could remember starting to get drunk and talking to the bartender and . . .

And then what?

If he couldn't remember anything . . . didn't that mean that nothing remarkable had happened?

Right. That was it.

He couldn't remember anything bad . . . because nothing bad had happened.

Simple enough.

But he knew better.

Jesus, Mary, and Joseph did he know better.

Like a couple of months ago when he'd been bopping that banker's wife out in the country-club darkness . . . the woman couldn't wait to get him inside her . . . such a stupid risk . . . his whole life in Crystal Falls could have ended right there.

But he didn't remember any of it for some thirty-six hours afterward.

Then he was sitting in Riley's Pub and the door opened up and here came the banker and his wife . . . and then Richie flashed on the whole stupid chance he'd taken in the parking lot the other night.

So he didn't always remember things right away.

He examined himself.

Given his temper and his tendency to fight, he always examined himself for cuts and bruises. If things had really gotten out of hand, he would see it on his body.

He checked himself out.

No bruises or cuts on his fists. No bruises or cuts on his legs or feet. He felt his face and head. No lumps or bumps.

So—no fight.

He thus eliminated one of his biggest worries on mornings like these. Hadn't he really torn into somebody?

Answer: No he hadn't.

Feeling a little better about himself, he stood up, creaky as an old man, and staggered to the old Kelvinator refrigerator in the corner.

Inside, he found the elixir: Diet Pepsi. When he was really dehydrated, as now, he could gun two or three of them just standing at the refrigerator.

Popping the tab on a can, he staggered over to the closed bathroom. He went in and took a piss.

All the time he was pissing, he was also gunning Diet Pepsi. In and out.

When he was finished in the john, he walked shakily back to the bed.

Boy, he was really in rough shape this morning. Legs really wobbly.

He sat on the edge of the bed, drinking his can of pop.

All he heard at first, in the late morning silence, was the

birds. Wrens, jays, robins. Singing their assess off in the beautiful day.

Only gradually did he come to hear the undertone of human voices.

His first reaction was that he was having an auditory hallucination. God knew, he'd had hallucinations before. You couldn't put them away the way he did without damaging your brain a little.

But as he sat there, he slowly began to realize that these voices weren't echoes of the previous night—as they sometimes were. These voices were real. Here and now.

But where would voices be coming from? He lived in the boonies.

He stood up and wobbled over to the back window and looked up the hill.

A large group of people. Maybe fifty or so.

And several cops.

Cops? What the hell was going on?

He felt very vulnerable standing here in his Jockey shorts, body feverish, head pounding, mouth dehydrated. Vulnerable and young—and yet, at the same time, very old, too. As if his life had all been lived. And it had not been a good one. Not a good life at all.

He looked up the hill and for the first time felt a stirring of terror in his belly and chest.

Cops could mean only one thing: trouble.

And trouble so close to his cottage . . .

He leaned forward, pushing his head to the relatively cool glass of the window. The coolness felt like a balm.

He wished he could remember last night. . . .

The cops right up there on the hill . . .

. . . and him not able to remember last night.

Without quite knowing why, Richie McGuire started trembling.

3

Amy's secretary, Midge, was the one who broke the news.

Amy was looking over some of the paperwork one of her new assistant DAs had set on her desk. The young woman was a Mexican-American and very nervous about this, her first real job since graduating from the University of Iowa Law School this spring. She had nothing to worry about. The way she'd scoped out the forthcoming trial was impressive. Amy certainly hadn't been doing work of this quality her first year out of law school.

Midge knocked.

Amy said, "This isn't more pictures of your granddaughter, is it?"

Ordinarily, Midge would've laughed at Amy's joke. Midge's daughter had just given birth to a beautiful little six-pound girl named Shannon. Every day, it seemed, Midge had more new photos of the infant. The office joke was that there was no place to escape to.

But Midge didn't have photos this morning.

She just opened the door and said, "I just got some news that I think you'd better know about."

Midge was a fiftyish lady whose hair was still naturally red and whose green eyes were usually merry. Whenever anybody in the office got depressed, they went to see Midge. She got their engines started again.

But Midge wasn't starting any engines this morning.

Amy had rarely seen the woman look this somber.

Midge walked into Amy's office and said, "I just got a call from the police department. The body of a teenage girl was found this morning."

"Oh, God," Amy said, thinking of the girl's parents. As a substitute parent herself, she used to worry constantly about Richie. Still did, in fact.

"Who was she?" Amy said.

"The Fuller girl. Darcy."

"My God. She was just—"

"Fifteen," Midge said.

"Where did they find her?"

Midge touched long, slender fingers to the front of her blue jumper and white blouse outfit. There was some shift in her gaze, as if she was reluctant to answer the question.

"Up in those woods off Swanson Road."

"Why, that's where my brother lives."

"Right."

At the mention of Richie, Midge's face tightened and she averted her eyes momentarily.

"Was this near Richie's cottage?"

"I—I suppose so."

"You suppose so? Midge, there's something you're not telling me, isn't there?"

Midge sighed. "I didn't want to tell you this but you'll obviously find it out anyway."

"Find out what?"

"The body was found right up the hill from Richie's."

"But that doesn't mean anything."

"No, of course it doesn't."

But Midge's mood hadn't changed. She still looked self-conscious and uncomfortable talking about this.

"I want to know everything," Amy said. "What else did the police say?"

"Just that they'd sent a crime-scene team out there and Sam insisted on calling in the State Bureau of Investigation."

"So Sam's in charge?"

For the first time, Midge offered a tiny smile. "You know how the Chief is. He said something like, 'I let Sam take over so he can do all that scientific crap he does and impress all the gawkers.'"

Amy wanted to smile. She could picture the grouchy and intolerant Chief saying exactly that. But there was no humor in her now.

On the hill above the cottage. Richie's cottage. It didn't have to mean anything, but of course it did mean something. Given Richie's reputation for carousing, it meant a lot. Midge knew this. That's why she'd been so reluctant to speak.

"Somebody from the office should be out there," Amy said.

"Yeah, probably," Midge said.

"Maybe I'll go."

Midge looked at her. "I could ask Dick."

"You mean you think I shouldn't go? Because of—"

"Maybe it'd look better if somebody else from the office took it."

She said it gently. The way a good friend would. Midge was a lot more than a secretary. Inside that attractive head of hers was a lot of hard common sense.

"I really want to go, Midge."

"I know."

"But it's probably better if Don goes, right?"

"Right."

"He didn't do it. I'm sure of it."

"I'm sure of it, too, Amy."

"He's not a bad guy."

"I know."

"He's had some bad luck."

"Yes, he has."

"And I wasn't exactly a great parent."

"You know better than that, Amy. The way you loved him . . . protected him . . . very few kids get a parent like that. You made him your whole life."

Amy looked at her directly. "You've never liked him, have you, Midge?"

"I can't say I'm crazy about him."

"Why?"

"All the grief he's brought you. It's hard to stand by and watch sometimes."

"He really didn't kill that girl."

"I don't think he did but—"

"But what?"

Midge sighed. "He was over at Riley's Pub last night and she came in. Darcy, I mean. There was a scene."

Midge described what the police department had told her fifteen minutes ago.

Amy listened in silence.

"But that doesn't necessarily mean anything," Midge said. "Lots of people get in little dustups when they've been drinking."

"She left without him?"

"That's my understanding."

"He probably didn't even see her the rest of the night."

"Right."

But Amy realized what she was doing. Trying to convince not Midge but herself of Richie's innocence.

Amy stood up slowly and walked over to the window and looked down on the town of Crystal Falls. She loved and hated the old place. She loved its sense of history and the plainspoken goodness of most of its people. But she hated the whispers and the gossips, the people whose sole pleasure was to rejoice in the pain of others. But every town had people like that. Crystal Falls wasn't any better or any worse than anyplace else. She let her gaze linger a moment on the city square, the bandstand and the Civil War memorial and the park benches where the old men played checkers eight hours of a sunny day.

"A lot of people are going to jump to a lot of conclusions," Amy said quietly, not turning around to face Midge.

"Yeah, they are."

"They're going to condemn him before they even have any of the facts."

"That's why I think you'd better put Don in charge of this one, Amy."

Amy turned around and faced Midge.

"I want to prove to people I can do my job, Midge. If the evidence warrants—"

She stopped. Took a deep, slow breath.

"If the evidence warrants," Midge said, "you could charge him with murder?"

"Yes, if I had to."

"If the evidence warrants, you could see that he was prosecuted to the full extent of the law?"

Amy hesitated at first, then: "I think so."

"If that's your best answer, Amy, maybe you'd better talk to Don."

Grimly, sadly, Amy nodded her head in silent agreement.

4

Sam Bowers knocked twice, got no answer, then knocked twice again.

The only other time he'd ever been out to Richie McGuire's cottage was when he'd dropped off a sweater that Amy had knitted for her brother. The two men had never gotten along especially well. Richie saw small-town lawmen as fools and Sam saw Richie as a glory-hog who couldn't admit to himself that his glory was long and forever gone.

Sam knuckled out a third series of knocks. Then he walked over to the window right of the door and peered inside.

The one-room place looked like a college dorm room of the male variety. Dirty socks, shirts, and pants were draped over various pieces of furniture while the surfaces of tables were covered with crusty pizza cardboard boxes, empty beer cans, and a few glistening red packs of Trojans. There were dirty dishes in the sink, dirty dishes on the small kitchen counter, and even dirty dishes stacked on top of the small and ancient refrigerator. Sam was no neat freak himself, but living like this was inexcusable.

A toilet flushed.

Moments later, Richie emerged from the closet-sized bathroom buckling up his trousers. He wore no shirt, no socks. He had a hairy barrel chest and for all his drinking, he looked to be an exceptionally strong and reasonably well kept young man.

He'd obviously heard Sam's knocks.

He came to the door and opened up.

"Hey, what the hell's going on up on the hill?" Richie said, sounding almost like an innocently inquisitive kid. But the anxiety in the bright blue eyes belied his tone of innocence. He looked scared.

"Mind if I come in?"

"Not at all," Richie said, some of the old swagger suddenly in his voice. "As soon as you tell me what the hell's going on up on the hill."

"Body was found."

"Body?"

"Yeah," Sam said, looking directly at him. "Fifteen-year-old girl named Darcy Fuller. I think you know her."

"Oh, my God. Darcy? What the hell happened?"

Sam used Richie's moment of shock—one he might well be faking—to push on inside.

He started scanning the place with his practiced cop's eyes.

"You just getting up now?"

"Yeah. But I want to know more about Darcy."

"You remember much about last night?"

"What the hell's that supposed to mean?"

Sam nodded to an empty fifth of J&B scotch sitting on the floor next to the rumpled single bed.

"It means it looks like you tied one on last night."

"You think I had something to do with Darcy dying?"

"I'm not assuming anything, Richie—except that you were probably pretty drunk last night. At least that's what I hear from the people at Riley's Pub."

Sam could see Richie struggling to remember. Sam had only been that drunk once or twice in his whole life. It was a scary feeling, waking up and not being able to remember anything. And then, even when people told you what you'd done, not being quite able to remember even then. The dark terrors. No doubt about it. Especially with a dead girl found not more than fifty yards from your place.

"How'd she die?"

"We're not sure."

"Then maybe it wasn't murder."

Sam could hear the hopefulness in Richie's voice. Richie had to know that he was going to be the number one suspect in this thing.

"Maybe not," Sam said.

"I'm going to make some instant coffee. You want some?"

"No, thanks."

Sam watched as Richie ran some tap water into a battered little pan and set the pan on his two-surface hot plate.

"I need a caffeine fix," Richie said, grinning nervously. "I'm a coffee junkie. Mainline the stuff."

Sam studied him a long moment. For the first time since he'd ever met Richie, he felt a little sympathy for him. The guy had a serious drinking problem and the problem was destroying him. Over seventy percent of America's prison population was behind bars because of crimes committed while drunk or on drugs.

"I'm not accusing you of anything, Richie."

"Yeah. I can tell that. You come fucking breaking in here and give me the evil eye and then tell me you're not accusing me of anything. Well, fuck you is what I say, Sam. You think that badge makes you king shit. But I'll tell you something, man. I didn't kill that girl so I don't have to be afraid of you. I don't have to be afraid of you at all."

The Greeks called it catharsis, a cleansing of the soul.

Richie, through his angry speech, had just cleansed part of his soul.

He lifted the pan, said, "Shit!"

He'd burned himself on the handle of the blackened metal pan his hot water was in.

He reached over and grabbed a piece of newspaper and folded it up and used it to insulate his hand from the handle.

He poured steaming water into what appeared to be a dirty cup. His hand was trembling badly.

When the cup was full, he set the pan back on the hot plate, then picked up his drink.

He carried his cup back to his bed and sat on the edge.

Sam nodded his head. "Believe it or not, Richie, I want to help you."

Richie gave him a twisted smile. "Say, that's right. I forgot the angel you're playing here. If you arrest me for murder, my big sister will like you even less than she does now."

"I need to know your itinerary for the whole evening, Richie."

Richie sipped his coffee, winced when the scalding liquid burned his lips.

Richie said, "How'd she die?"

"I told you. We don't know yet."

"You know *when* she died?"

"Not yet."

"You don't know how and you don't know when but you're all ready to throw my ass in jail."

"Nobody's getting thrown in jail, Richie. Right now, I just need you to calm down and answer some questions."

Richie stared at him. "There's only one question that matters, Sam, and you know it. And you don't even have to ask it. I'll answer it right now. I didn't kill her." His right hand made a fist. "I didn't fucking kill her."

"You had some sort of run-in with her at Riley's Pub last night."

Richie shook his head miserably. "She was putting on a show for them."

"Who's 'them'?"

"The customers."

"Why would she do that?"

"She was into all kinds of power shit. You know, proving to you that she was smarter and tougher than you were."

"She accused you of getting her pregnant?"

Richie smirked. "If she was pregnant, then it would've been a virgin birth, man. I never fucked her. I'll admit I kissed her some and we did some messing around, but I never fucked her. Man. I'm not crazy."

"State law says you could be charged even for kissing her. Her father could certainly press the point if he wanted to."

"Well, I guess I didn't know that. I just made very sure that I never fucked her. All right?"

"Where'd you go after Riley's?"

"Home."

"Can you prove that?"

"How would I prove it?"

"You call anybody from here?"

"No."

"Anybody stop over?"

"No."

"Anybody see you pulling in last night?"

"Who'd see me? Nobody lives around here—except Jimmy."

"You see Jimmy last night?"

"No."

"You're bullshitting me, aren't you, Richie?"

"What the hell's that supposed to mean?"

"You don't remember anything at all about last night, do you?"

"I remember I didn't kill her, if that's what you mean."

"What route did you take home from Riley's?"

"Up over the bridge."

"Which bridge?"

"Hartson Creek Bridge."

"Bullshit."

"You're saying I *didn't* take Hartson Bridge home?"

"The rain washed it out around eight o'clock last night. According to the people in Riley's, you didn't leave until around eight-thirty."

Richie sighed. He looked miserable, scared and frantic. "What the hell's the big deal about the bridge, anyway?"

"The big deal is that you don't remember anything at all about last night. You don't even remember the route you took getting home."

"And that means I killed her?"

"That means you may have killed her and not even know it."

"Nobody forgets stuff like that."

"There're a lot of guys in prison who don't remember doing what put them there, Richie."

The bluster left Richie for a moment. He looked like a plain scared kid. "I thought you said you wanted to help me."

"The only way I can help you, Richie, is if I know the truth."

Richie stared up at Sam with a sad, baffled expression on his face. He was still trying to put last night together again in his mind.

"The truth is, Sam," he said quietly, "I didn't kill her. I really didn't."

There was a knock on the door.

Sam went over to open it.

Amy stood there.

She looked just as sad and frantic as her brother.

"Hi, Sam," she said. "I thought maybe I'd stop by and see how things were going."

He knew in that moment that he was going to lose her again, and all because of her brother—lose her forever this time.

5

They came with broken bones and broken dreams, hopes and fears, dreams and nightmares.

For many, this was a place of last resort. If the man and his staff couldn't help you, then you might well be beyond the help of anybody.

There was the woman trying to secure help for the operation her blind son needed. There was the man who felt he was being unduly hounded by the IRS. There was the farmer who believed that the bank was not being cooperative in giving him a loan for farm equipment. There was the grandmother who insisted that her nephew had been sentenced to prison even though he was innocent. There was the owner of a small business who was trying to get some business from the federal government.

They were sick, poor, desperate, bitter, angry. They were white, black, brown, yellow, red. Some were rich, most were poor. They were of all ages and creeds, and both sexes. A lot of them didn't even belong to the proper political party.

But day after day, they filled Senator Cummings's home office here in Crystal Falls.

Upon occasion, the waiting area resembled a doctor's office, especially in the cold and flu months of January and February, the waiting area crawling with germs from sneezing, hacking, sniffling, snuffling citizens.

Senator Cummings tried to come back for at least three days a month. This was his home base and needed to be protected. There were more votes in this part of the state than any other. Cummings didn't bring home staffers. Usually he and Helen came home alone.

They longed to see him and hear him and touch him, just the way people had longed to see and hear and touch Jesus of Nazareth, Lenin, FDR, and Elvis—longed to give him their problems and have him resolve them.

This particular morning was no different.

Just ask the fidgety little woman with the crippled grandson. Or the unemployed Vietnam veteran whose health insurance is running out. Or the twitching man with the nervous disorder who was injured in the workplace but can't get his workers' compensation.

You can see the hope in their eyes.

A United States senator is an important man. He can pick up the telephone and kiss a few asses or make a few threats and your problem is taken care of.

And that was particularly true about *this* United States senator.

There was virtually no one in this valley who had not been helped in some way large or small by this man. As he liked to tell you whenever he helped you, that's why he wanted to be a senator in the first place: so he could improve the lot of the common man . . . the man who wasn't rich, who didn't have important connections, the man who needed a powerful friend from time to time.

So they reelected him.

They knew he was vain, they knew that his sister was actually the brains, they knew that he liked to bottle and liked to lady even more, they knew that he would not be remembered for any great contribution to a better national government. . . . They knew all these things and they didn't give a damn about them.

When you need a meal, when your kid is sick, when you can't find a job . . . it doesn't matter if the guy isn't exactly Thomas Jefferson. Just as long as he can deliver.

And delivering was what Senator Cummings had long been known for. Not that there wasn't the occasional excess. But one had to keep it in perspective. They were doing the will of the people, the men and women of the Congress, and so they could not be expected to live ordinary lives. As one senator had drunkenly explained at a dinner recently, the little people wanted their leaders to live enviable lives. The limo, the lobbyist Learjet, the junket to the South Seas . . . this was evidence that the men and women of the Congress were a special breed. . . . The drunken senator had even argued that perhaps divine intervention played a role in elections . . . that God himself had chosen a small handful of the nation's people to inspire and lead the millions . . . and to live and to indulge themselves in a few harmless and well-earned luxuries once their hard daily work was done. Helen had said that she thought this particular senator was a "psychotic bullshit artist," but David had been quite taken with his words . . . with his notion that God had personally selected every man and woman in the Congress . . . and that every junket, every under-the-table bribe, every girlfriend (or boyfriend) put on the payroll, every piece of inside-trader stock market information was only something that this august body deserved. So even though Helen hadn't bought the senator's speech, David found himself secretly admiring the man for taking what some of the little people might take to be an unpopular stand.

He got to his office a little late this fine fall morning. There were already sixteen people waiting to see him. Sixteen people . . . and one dog and one cat. You could bring animals—hell, he'd always come out and pet them and talk a little baby talk to them—as long as they didn't bite, bark, or leave tiny brown nuggets on any of the furnishings.

Sixteen people. But that was just the beginning. By eleven o'clock, more than twenty people were waiting for him.

Other men might sink under such an onslaught. Not our boy. There was nothing he liked more than helping people, than getting on the phone and kicking some bureaucrat's ass around the block because he had failed to help this fine citizen who was sitting across from the Senator at this very moment.

What it was was the gratitude he saw in their eyes. It was almost as good as coming. Almost.

Tears made him feel especially good. The weary sobs of the widow he'd helped get fuel oil for the brutal winter. The silent tears of the grateful teenager he'd helped get an abortion. The misty eyes of the factory worker he'd helped get a new job.

He fed on tears. Tears told him he was doing his job, tears told him he was special man indeed.

Tears were his reward.

"Helen on line two."

"Thanks, Evelyn."

This was between constituent visits.

Had to take a pit stop every once in a while.

Wander down the hall and empty the bladder, which was getting increasingly tough to do given his prostate problems.

Then refill the old coffee cup.

And then just sit in the executive chair and stare out of the window at the fiery autumn hills where he and Helen used to play. Every once in a while, he'd remember the time he and Helen . . . Well, they hadn't actually come close to *doing* it. . . . But they had been necking pretty heavily. And groping each other pretty eagerly.

The funny thing was, even after all those years, he felt a real stirring of desire every time he thought about that long-ago time.

The even funnier thing was . . . when he looked at Helen today? Well, when he looked at her today, he couldn't even imagine kissing her. Let alone groping her.

But when he looked back in his mind's eye . . . saw that day under the shadowed overhang of that small cave . . . it still got him hot.

And then for the first time in his life, he realized what might explain his desire for teenage girls: was he constantly trying to recreate that day with Helen . . . when they'd been fifteen (him) and fourteen (her) respectively?

He wondered if his sister still thought of that day from time to time.

He picked up the receiver. "Hi."

"Hi. You hear the news?"

"Guess not."

"Some hunters found the body."

"When?"

"Hour or so ago, I guess."

"So the police are out there?"

"Yes."

"Any word," he said, "on Richie?"

"Not yet."

"Matter of time, probably."

"Right. Everything's going just fine."

"You saved me, Helen. You really did. I just went all to pieces and you saved me."

"We're in this together."

He checked his watch. "I'd better get going, Helen. There're a lot of people waiting to see me."

She said, after a pause, "You've got your appointment tomorrow morning."

"Right."

She knew he hated to talk about it, think about it . . . why was she always bringing it up? Didn't she know the anxiety it caused him? And didn't she know that anxiety meant stress and stress meant a weakened immune system response?

It was almost as if she *wanted* him to get all wrought up and scared.

"I'm sure everything'll be fine."

"I'd just as soon not talk about it."

"I don't know what you're worried about. You know the doctors say that everything is moving along just fine."

"You never know when they're telling the truth."

His heart rate had increased.

She really must take pleasure in this. It was like some kind of torture.

But then he felt guilty.

After all his sister had done for him, and he had thoughts about her like this?

"Maybe you should join that support group, David."

"No thanks."

There was a cancer support group meeting twice weekly—nights—at the hospital.

That was the last thing he wanted to do: sit around in a room and listen to terrified people trying to rationalize the fact that they were desperately ill.

It would only serve to remind him of how scared he was, how hopeless he sometimes felt.

Thinking this, he smiled bitterly.

He was always helping people. Now he found himself in a position where *he* needed help.

He wished he had his own version of Senator Cummings to go to.

"Thanks, Helen. For everything."

"My pleasure," she said. Then, "Now you don't sit around and worry about your medical appointment tomorrow. I'm sure that everything's going to be just fine."

But of course, soon as she said it, he *did* start worrying.

Started worrying a *lot*.

What if he walked in there tomorrow and the oncologist said, "I'm afraid we've got a little bad news here, Senator."

But that wasn't his only problem, obviously. Twice this morning he'd found himself wanting to pick up the phone and tell Chief Hadley about Darcy. He just didn't know if he could handle all this stress—his medical problems and now the death of Darcy. He hoped he could hold on while Helen fixed every-thing.

ELEVEN

1

"So you didn't see Darcy after you left the tavern?"

"No."

"You're sure?"

"I'm positive."

"And you came straight home?"

Richie said, "Yes."

Sam looked at Amy. Then back at Richie. "What route did you take home?"

"Amberson Avenue."

"What time was this?"

"Probably nine-fifteen or so."

"Probably?"

Richie sighed. "I wasn't paying a hell of a lot of attention to the time."

"Then what were you paying a hell of a lot of attention to?"

"My driving."

"I see." Then, "I want to establish one thing here, Amy."

"All right," she said.

She had been sitting in a chair at the wobbly kitchen table. Sam sat in front of her, in another chair. Richie sat on the bed. He looked terrible. She wanted to go over and sit next to him and put her arm around him. Comfort him the way she'd comforted him so many times before.

"I want to establish that Richie doesn't have any idea what route he took home last night. He was too drunk to remember this morning."

Amy said, "Is that true, Richie?"

He looked angrily at Sam. "He's showing off, Amy. He wants to show you what a badass he is."

Sam sighed. "Amy, I've been through this with him. First he told me he took the route out by the old bridge. Now he tells me he took Amberson Avenue. He doesn't know. He was too drunk to know."

He had turned around in his chair, facing her.

"Amy, I can't really ask him questions with you here."

"I *want* you here, Amy," Richie said. "Don't let him try any bullshit like that."

Amy said, "I'd like to talk to Richie alone for a minute, Sam. I'd appreciate it."

"I'm in charge here, Amy."

"I realize that."

"And you talking to him alone . . . are you talking to him as the DA or as his sister?"

"I just want to talk to him is all."

"I really shouldn't let you do this, Amy."

"Just a few minutes, Sam. Then I'll leave and go back to my office."

"The Chief isn't going to like this."

"I'd really appreciate it, Sam."

Sam stood up.

"You're going to get both of our asses in a sling, Amy."

"I won't be long. I promise."

Sam walked over to the door. "I really wasn't hard-assing him, Amy."

"I know that."

"If anything, I was trying to help him. Once the state boys get here, they'll really start in on him. I thought it might help for him to at least have his story straight."

"I appreciate that, Sam. I really do."

He opened the door and looked outside. The beauty of the late morning rode inside on the scented breeze. "Hell of a morning for something like this."

"Yes," Amy said, half whispering. "Hell of a morning."

Sam glanced at Richie, then at Amy. He stepped outside then, closing the door quietly behind him.

"That son of a bitch," Richie said.

"He's trying to help you."

"Oh, yeah, that's what he's doing. Trying to help me all right."

"Believe it or not, Richie, he is."

"You being in love with him wouldn't be coloring your opinion, would it?"

"You're my brother, Richie. You're my first concern. Always. And you know it."

He put his face in his hands. Shook his head back and forth.

"Is he right, Richie? Don't you remember last night?"

He lifted his face, looked at her. "Not much of it, no."

"Do you remember being at Riley's Pub?"

"It's not real clear but I remember most of it, I guess."

"You remember Darcy being there?"

He sighed, stared at his hands. "I remember trying to take her by the shoulders and shake her."

"Why did you want to do that?"

"She was hinting that I'd gotten her pregnant. I hadn't. I couldn't've. I'd never slept with her."

"You're sure of that?"

"What the hell does that mean? Am I sure of it? Don't you believe me?"

"Maybe you slept together when you were drunk and don't remember."

He shook his head. "I was never that drunk around her. I mostly saw her during the day. Out at the club."

"Did she ever come out here?"

"A couple of times."

"Inside?"

"Yes."

"And sat down?"

"Yes."

"Then Sam'll probably find her fingerprints in here."

"Oh, great, that's just what I need."

Amy paused, choosing her next question carefully. "You really think you were just trying to shake her last night?"

"Yes. I'm positive."

"Some people are saying that you were trying to choke her."

He sighed. "I can see where it would've looked that way." He raised his gaze to hers. "Honest to God, Amy, all I wanted to do was shake her, stop her from letting everybody think that we'd been to bed together. God, why did I even spend any time with her?"

"But you weren't trying to choke her?"

"No. That's one thing I *do* remember. They started shouting at me, like I was really going to hurt her or something. I remember wanting to explain myself so they'd know I wasn't going to choke her or anything. But I was so drunk, I couldn't talk real clearly."

"Do you remember anything after that?"

"Not real clearly."

"Don't lie anymore."

"What the hell's that supposed to mean?"

"You lied to Sam a while ago. About taking the bridge home. That's the kind of thing they can catch you in. And it makes you sound as if you're lying about everything. So you don't remember coming home?"

"Not exactly." He looked at her hopefully. "But I didn't find any blood on me or my clothes this morning."

"From what I could gather, there wasn't any blood on her, either."

"Oh."

"So the last thing you remember is waking up this morning?"

"Pretty much."

"How did this place look?"

"What?"

"Did it look like you might have had a struggle with somebody in here?"

"No," Richie said. "Not at all."

"Did you see anything of hers in here? Tube of lipstick or a comb or anything like that?"

"No. Nothing."

She didn't say anything for a time. She walked over to the window by the kitchen area and looked up the hill. Sam was up there talking to Doc Klever, the medical examiner. Doc had delivered about eighty percent of the town's current young generation. Moses had personally made him a doc, went some of the local humor. Good, competent man who still made house calls and late-night calls. He was a sweetie in every regard.

"I'm in trouble, aren't I?" he said.

She turned back from the window. "Maybe."

"Oh, Amy, don't bullshit me."

"Right now, things don't look good, Richie. But Sam and his people are getting started on their investigation."

"I know he's your boyfriend, Amy, but do you really think he knows what he's doing?"

She came over and sat down next to him on the couch. The air was sour with the smells of sweaty sleep. She took his hand. "I know you're scared, Richie. I'd be scared, too. But Sam's a good law officer and a very honest one."

"He hates me."

"He doesn't hate you."

"Yeah, then why did he take Steve Arnette's side the night Arnette beat me up?"

"Because Haymes took Arnette's side. Sam doesn't trust Arnette but he does trust Haymes. And Haymes said you started the fight, and were resisting arrest. There were no other witnesses. That didn't give Sam much room to maneuver. He had to take Haymes's word for it."

"Haymes'd naturally take Arnette's side. Arnette's dating his sister now."

She shook her head. "Small towns. Somebody's dating somebody's sister so they say one thing. Or they're not dating somebody's sister so they say another. It'd be funny if it wasn't so pathetic."

Richie put his face in his hands again. "What'm I gonna do, Amy?"

"I'm going to get you a lawyer."

His head jerked up. "You think this is serious enough that I need a lawyer?"

"I think it'd be a good idea, Richie. And I think the best criminal-defense lawyer around here is Tom O'Brien."

"But he's Bob Medlow's partner. And Medlow represents Arnette."

"Different trials, Richie. And he really is the best around. I think you should take a quick shower and go see him after Sam finishes up here."

"I didn't kill her, Amy."

"I know."

"You really believe me?"

"I really believe you."

"I'm going to change, Amy. I really am. I don't want to live like this anymore."

Maybe this is what it takes, Amy thought. Maybe you really do need to hit rock bottom before you see any reason to change.

"I'll call Tom when I get back to the office."

"I still feel weird," he said, "having him being partners with Medlow."

"It's fine," Amy said. "It really is."

She was about to walk back to the window by the kitchen when she noticed the large brown lunch bag on the counter. She hadn't seen it before.

"Here's the bread I had Jimmy drop off for you," she said.

"The what?"

"The loaf of bread. Wheat bread. I was making myself a loaf so I decided to make an extra one for you. I asked Jimmy to drop it off here."

"Oh."

"You remember seeing Jimmy yesterday?"

"No."

"Or seeing this on your doorstep?"

"Huh-uh. But you sound like it's a big deal or something."

"I'm just curious about what time Jimmy dropped it off."

"Why?"

"Because if it was last night, maybe he saw you get home—or saw something, anyway."

Richie nodded. "He doesn't usually leave things for me. He waits till I'm home so he has an excuse to come in. He likes to look at my football pictures and then listen to me tell him about my glory days." Richie sounded sad, sentimental. "*Some*body's got to listen to me brag."

"I'm going to drive up the hill and see if he's home. It's worth a chance, anyway."

Richie got up and padded over to the sink—his naked feet slap slap slapping the floor—and stuck his head under the faucet and let cold clear well water pour down his head and face. When he was done, he toweled his head off and then went over to the refrigerator.

When he got the door opened and put his hand inside, Amy, ever the watchful sister, said, "I wouldn't start drinking with Sam around."

He offered her a weary smile. "Diet Pepsi."

"I'm sorry. I shouldn't have said that."

"You're trying to protect me, Amy." His voice was sad again. "The way you've been trying to protect me ever since Mom and Dad died."

"I've probably overprotected you."

He came over and kissed her tenderly on the cheek. His face was dry but still cold from the water.

He glanced out the window. "He's coming back."

"He'll want to talk to you."

"Yeah."

"Just don't lose your temper. And don't lie. That's the worst thing you can do. If you don't know the answer to a question, just say you don't know."

"You know what I want to know?"

"What?"

"Where Darcy went after she left Riley's."

"Yes. That's what I want to know, too. And that's what I'm going to find out."

"You? No offense, but do you know how to investigate a case?"

She tapped him on the head and gave him a sisterly smile. "Remember when I worked for the DA's office in Des Moines for three years? Remember what my title was?"

He smiled. He looked as if there might actually be a tiny bit of genuine pleasure in that smile. "Say, that's right. I forgot. You were an investigator."

"Right."

"God, I'd really appreciate the help, Amy."

A knock. Sam.

She went to the door.

"Thanks for letting me talk to him, Sam."

"No problem."

She looked back at her brother. "Remember what I told you."

He nodded. He was putting on a white short-sleeved shirt. He looked a lot better than he had fifteen minutes ago.

Amy said, "I'll talk to you later, Sam."

2

Susan Kelly pulled her truck into the alley next to the Fitzsimmons Hardware loading dock and then went inside. There hadn't been a parking space on the street. Jimmy was with her. He worked on the farm a couple of afternoons a week. "I'll be right back," she said. She was in a hurry. Jimmy always poked along in stores and slowed her down.

Susan loved hardware stores, associated them with her father. He'd always taken her to town in his truck. She liked the smell of sawn lumber, the orderly rows of hammers and pliers and screwdrivers and a hundred other items arranged along the wall. She liked the talk, too, the men who stood around the cash register and talked with the owner. She'd never felt welcome in barbershops—strictly a male province—but this was the next best thing . . . listening to men talk politics and baseball and town gossip.

There were two men talking to Mike Fitzsimmons now.

One of them was smoking a pipe. She loved the scent of the burning tobacco.

She took out her list and started filling her shopping cart. She bought Fiberglas insulation, a caulking gun, a doorknob, and a rake. She did most of the fix-up work around the farm.

She pushed her cart to the front. She had several other stops to make before going back home. She was worried about the new colt. It wasn't taking well to its food and seemed mysteriously sluggish. She invested a lot of love in her animals. She didn't want to get back to the farm and find that the colt had died. She felt guilty about coming into town at all . . . but there were some supplies she just had to get.

She was several feet from the register in the front of the store when a white-haired man named Morris Dodd came through the entrance door and walked right up to the register and said, in a breathless way that interrupted the conversation, "You hear about the dead girl?"

Now, no matter what the men had been discussing—in this case, the chances of the Hawkeye football team going to the Rose Bowl this year—nothing, repeat nothing was more riveting than the subject of dead girls. One could only hope that this dead girl was also *naked* when they found her. There probably wasn't a single subject in the entire world as interesting as a dead girl who was naked.

"What dead girl?" Fitzsimmons said.

"That snotty new one. That Darcy Fuller."

"She's dead?"

"Yeah. And guess where they found her."

"Where?"

"Up behind Richie McGuire's little cottage."

Fitzsimmons whistled. "Well, sounds like that son of a bitch finally went and did it."

"He sure did," said one of the other men.

"That temper of his and all his drinking," Fitzsimmons said. Then, "They find Richie yet?"

Dodd nodded. "He was down in his cottage. Sleepin' off a drunk."

Not until this moment did the men notice that Susan Kelly was in the store. They all knew her history with Richie. How she'd screwed up her life for him. And how Steve Arnette was still sniffing after her even though he had a wife and child. This was a small town.

"Sounds like your old friend's got himself in a little trouble." Fitzsimmons said.

"Richie wouldn't kill anybody," she said. She couldn't keep the anger out of her voice. So few facts . . . and they'd already convicted him and sent him to prison.

"He's got a pretty bad temper," Fitzsimmons said. "You've got to admit that."

She put her items on the counter.

Fitzsimmons started ringing them up. He could obviously see that she was mad.

"I guess we are kind of jumping to conclusions," he said, a note of apology in his voice.

But at the moment, Susan was having no part of any apology.

She just continued to silently glare at the men.

3

One of the fundamentalist ladies in town had started some rumors about Jimmy a few years back.

The woman had it on good authority—who this authority was, she never did say—that Jimmy was both a Satanist and a pedophile.

She did her best to get all of Crystal Falls riled up about this.

Fortunately, most of the people were too smart to get caught up in such lynch-law justice. They knew Jimmy, and knew what had happened to make his mind work so slowly, and they continued to welcome him as a regular part of daily life.

Eventually, the fundamentalist lady found a new target: she said that the new Catholic priest was not only a Satanist, he was also an alien, and recruited people for abduction.

But hilarious as some of her accusations were, Jimmy had heard them and had taken to hiding out in the cellar of his shack. A century ago, people had stored fruits and vegetables in their cellars. Whenever Jimmy felt bad, or scared, he climbed down the rickety ladder to the cellar.

Amy wondered if he might be down there now.

She'd been knocking on the shack door for the past five minutes and had received no answer. What was strange was that Jimmy's ancient red Schwinn bicycle, complete with mud flaps and a tiny American flag that sat atop the light, was laid against the side of the shack. Jimmy never went anywhere of any distance without his Schwinn.

She knocked again, and nothing.

And then she heard the sound of something scraped against the faded linoleum floor inside.

Amy walked over to the lone front window and peeked inside.

At first, she didn't see anything untoward, but then, looking more closely, she saw the white tips of fingers on the floor, sticking out from behind the overstuffed chair.

Jimmy was hiding.

"Jimmy," she said, "it's Amy. I know you're in there. I need to talk to you, Jimmy. I really do."

"I'm not feeling so good," he called back.

"What's wrong with you?"

The flu, she answered to herself.

Jimmy always said that when he didn't want to tell you something.

I've got the flu and my throat is kinda scratchy, he always said.

He said, "I've got the flu, Amy, and my throat is kinda scratchy."

She had to smile.

Oh, God, Jimmy. You poor guy.

"I wouldn't want you to catch it, Amy," he said. That was how he usually finished. Not wanting you to catch his ravaging flu.

"You know what, Jimmy?"

"What?"

She continued to peek in the window.

Jimmy was still crouched behind the chair, half shouting over the top of it.

"I've got the flu, too."

"You do?"

"Uh-huh."

"Oh."

"So you can't give it to me because I've already got it."

"You didn't have it yesterday when I was mowing your lawn."

"Oh, I had it, all right. I just didn't tell you."

"Oh."

"So if you've got the flu and I've got the flu, I guess you can open the door and let me in."

If Jimmy could fib, so could she, though she felt guilty deceiving him. It was like lying to a child.

He stood up slowly, as if he were having difficulty moving. He looked around the dusty room at a pile of wrinkled shirts. He quickly grabbed a blue turtleneck sweater and pulled it over his head.

He walked slowly over to the door and opened it up.

"Hi, Amy."

"Hi, Jimmy. You want to go up and see the horses?"

"Sure."

To the west was pastureland where the nearby horse ranch grazed its animals.

A colt chestnut mare followed its mother around by the eastern edge of the white fencing. The tiny animal walked on heartbreakingly wobbly legs.

They leaned on the fence and watched her. This was a very nice ranch, the outbuildings clean and new in the sparkling sunlight.

"You remember last night, Jimmy?"

"Last night?"

"Yes. The storm and the rain."

"Oh, sure, Amy. I remember that."

"Did you stay home last night?"

"Uh-huh."

"Did you hear anything?"

"Hear anything?"

She hadn't been looking at him, had been watching the colt. Now she angled her face toward his.

"You know, somebody in trouble. A scream or something like that."

"Gosh, no, Amy."

He seemed nervous. Very nervous, in fact. She wondered why. And he'd been hiding behind the chair. That was something he did only rarely.

She sensed something wrong.

"Jimmy?"

"Yes."

"We're friends, right?"

"Why, sure."

"You trust me?"

"Why, I sure do, Amy."

"And I trust you."

He smiled. "You're not going to ask me about that cookie the other day, are you?"

"Cookie?"

"You put those two cookies out for the ground squirrel who lives under your back porch."

"Oh. I'd forgotten about that."

"You know what I did?"

His cheeks were red. He averted his eyes.

"I'll bet it wasn't very bad, Jimmy, whatever you did."

"When you went back inside?"

"Yes."

"After setting those two cookies on the bottom step of the back porch?"

"Right."

"Well, I picked up one of those cookies and ate it myself."

She laughed. "I'll bet that made the ground squirrel mad."

"I shouldn't've done that, Amy, and I'm real sorry."

She touched his arm. "It's all right, Jimmy. It really is."

"You sure?"

"I'm positive."

He sighed deeply. "Wow, I'm just glad you're not mad."

"But that isn't what I came to talk to you about, Jimmy."

"It isn't?"

"We need to talk about last night."

She saw it in his face, sensed it in his entire body, a tension that put a sickly expression in his eyes. "Last night?"

So he does know something, Amy thought. He wouldn't have reacted that way if he didn't.

"Yes," she said. "Last night. I'd like to ask you a few questions, Jimmy."

She was so surprised by what he did next, she didn't even react until there was nothing she could do.

One moment, Jimmy was standing next to her at the fence watching the horses—and the next, he was running down the hill back to his cabin.

Even from all the way up here, she could hear his front door slam shut.

By now, he'd be hiding again, and there'd be no coaxing him out this time.

Leaving her to wonder just exactly what he did know about last night, and the death of Darcy Fuller.

TWELVE

1

Amy made the decision on the drive back to town.

Once she was in her office, and had dealt with the blizzard of minor problems that awaited her, she buzzed Dick Wilson and asked him to come in. He said yes but he needed a few minutes. He'd just now walked in the office for the day. He'd been in court.

Wilson was a tall man with curly dark hair and a somber face. He was especially good as a prosecutor. It was assumed by the local political observers that once Amy gave up the DA's office, Dick Wilson would step in, even though he was still considered by many to be an Outsider. Which translated to somebody who hadn't grown up here. Wilson had had the temerity to grow up in Cedar Rapids, to never have spent more than a single day on a farm, and to drive a weird-looking SAAB. He also played classical music on his SAAB tape deck. His wife, a willowy beauty, had set up Crystal Falls' first ballet school. He was one strange dude, Dick Wilson.

He wore the vest and trousers of his three-piece blue serge suit. His tie was power yellow instead of power red. He'd once explained to Amy that he preferred yellow because it hid mustard stains better.

Just as he was about to set his bottom on a chair across from Amy's desk, her phone buzzed and she spent the next five minutes trying to pacify a crotchety old judge who insisted that one of her prosecutors was failing to be properly respectful to him. On and on it went. Amy knew that Dick had plenty to do and felt guilty about making him sit there and listen to her talk.

Finally, she wrote out a sign that read:

I'M SORRY

Dick Wilson, ever the smart-ass, then wrote out his own sign and raised it for her to see.

UP YOURS

That was pure Dick Wilson.

When she finally hung up, Wilson said, "What's his problem this time?"

"He said that he caught Brenda smirking after he gave one of his rulings."

"She must've forgotten to genuflect in front of him this morning."

Being with Dick almost made her forget the scene she'd just left, the dead girl on the hill, and Amy's confused and disheveled brother in the cabin below. Dick obviously didn't know about any of this yet.

"So," Dick Wilson said, "is this finally the morning?"

"The morning?"

"Yeah, that we have sex on your desk there."

She laughed and shook her head. She probably should give

him her speech about sexual harassment, but there was an innocence about him that made him funny instead of threatening.

"I guess I'd better tell you where I've just been," she said.

He immediately picked up on her mood and dropped his joking.

When she finished relating the events of last night and this morning, he said, "Leaving Richie right in the middle."

"Exactly."

"Sam won't move unless he gets some very good proof."

"I know."

"But you're in the middle, too."

"Yes, I am, Dick. And that's why I asked you to come in here."

Her phone buzzed again. "Damn," she said under her breath. Then she leaned forward and spoke on the intercom. "Unless it's the president of the United States, I don't want to talk to him."

"It's Jimmy."

"Oh. I'll take it."

Maybe Jimmy was ready to explain why he'd run away this morning. Maybe he was ready to explain that he knew something about Darcy Fuller's death.

She saw line two flashing. "Thanks."

She punched line two and said, "Hello, Jimmy?"

But there was just a dial tone.

Sighing, she spoke into the intercom again. "Jimmy wasn't there."

"He must've hung up."

Got scared, Amy thought. Called her and then got scared. She put the phone down.

She said, "I want you to take over this case, work with Sam."

"Wow. You sure?"

"Positive. He's my little brother, Dick."

"I know. But Amy, you're a professional."

"I'm not *that* professional, Dick. I'm not sure anybody is. When Sam was asking him questions this morning, I almost interrupted several times. You know, trying to protect Richie." She shook her head. "I just couldn't handle it, Dick."

"I've got to ask you something, Amy."

"All right."

"What if I do take over the case and I start to believe that Richie killed her?"

"Then you bring charges against him."

"And head up the prosecution?"

"And head up the prosecution."

He leaned forward. "You sure you don't want to think about this a little longer?"

"I've thought about it enough, Dick."

"Well, I guess I can't say no. I just hope this doesn't affect our friendship, Amy."

"All you have to worry about is the case, Dick. Handle it the way you normally would. You can't afford to worry about my feelings. And you know I'm right."

He sighed. "Yeah, I guess you are."

"You should probably give Sam a call and get things started."

"Yeah, I probably should."

Then he stared at her a moment. "I'm sorry about all this, Amy."

"Thanks."

"I'm sure Richie didn't do it."

"I hope not."

She felt guilty saying that—as if she had betrayed Richie—but she had to be realistic. Richie was the prime suspect. . . .

Her phone buzzed again. "I'd better take this."

He stood up. "You're sure about this?"

"Very sure."

"You can always change your mind."

"Thanks, Dick. But I won't be changing my mind. It's better for this office if you handle it. That way people won't start whispering. If I handle it—"

The phone buzzed again.

She waved good-bye to him and then picked up.

It was the Rotary Club wanting to know if she'd be the luncheon speaker a month from now.

2

Jimmy wanted to cry.

He felt scared and confused.

Sometimes he had nightmares of being trapped in a vast midnight forest, the way Hansel and Gretel had been. He felt scared and confused at these times, too.

Sometimes, he woke up from his nightmares with hot tears streaking down his cheeks.

Scared and confused.

He looked at the phone next to his cot.

He'd called Amy's office three times since running away from her this morning.

Twice, he'd hung up when the woman at the desk had answered. The third time he'd asked for Amy.

He was really going to do it, really talk to her, really tell her the truth about last night.

But then the woman said one moment please.

And he got scared again.

Couldn't help it.

And hung up.

And now it was as if his legs and arms wouldn't work. Felt so bad. Really bad. Should have told her the truth.

And then he saw the wren in the window and he felt better.

He talked to birds sometimes and they talked back to him.

He used to tell people about this but they'd laugh at him and say, "So you're talking to the birds again, huh, Jimmy?"

And then they'd wink at each other.

And Jimmy would know they were making fun of him again. He hated it when they made fun. He'd get real mad, like he wanted to hurt them or something; and then he'd get sad. Sad was the worst part.

He'd ride his bike home. He'd always take the alleys until he got out into the countryside. By taking the alleys, he made sure that nobody saw him. Sometimes he didn't want to be seen at all. Sometimes people watching you, the way they smirked and whispered and pointed, sometimes that hurt even more than people hitting you or throwing things at you.

Maybe that was why he liked Amy so much, why he wanted to marry her.

Because she'd never once made fun of him in any way. Never once. And she was so pretty, so very pretty. And she smelled good. Like flowers. And she had a nice shape. He thought of her breasts and legs sometimes and then the heat would start in his groin and he'd feel uncomfortable. God, how he wanted to marry Amy.

The phone rang.

He stared at it a long time.

Six, seven, eight rings.

What if it was Amy? What if she was calling and said that she wanted to know the truth about last night?

"Hello," he said.

"Jimmy?"

"Yes. This is Jimmy."

"This is your friend Helen."

"Hi, Helen."

"I just wanted to see how you're doing."

"I'm doing fine."

"Do you remember our talk last night?"

"Uh-huh."

"And our secret?"

"Uh-huh."

"And what would happen if you told anybody our secret?"

"I remember, Helen."

"You know what I saw this morning, Jimmy?"

"What?"

"That place where they sent you that time."

Jimmy felt his stomach get all twisted up, the surface of his skin get sticky with sweat.

"I don't want to go back there, Helen."

"I know you don't, Jimmy. That's why I'm trying to help you. So they won't ever send you back there again."

"I won't tell nobody."

"You promise?"

But of course he'd already tried to call Amy.

"I promise."

"I just wouldn't want to see them put you back there, Jimmy. Because I'm your friend."

"Don't worry."

She paused. "Do you want a nice surprise, Jimmy?"

"I love surprises."

"I know you do. Well, you wait until two o'clock this afternoon."

"Two o'clock?"

"That's right. Are you going to be there?"

"Two o'clock?"

"That's right, Jimmy. Two o'clock."

"What's gonna happen?"

"Well, it wouldn't be a surprise if I told you now, would it, Jimmy?"

"I guess not."

"You be there at two o'clock."

"OK."

"And remember about not telling anybody our secret."

"I'll remember."

When he went back to the window to see if the wren was around, he found the bird gone. He'd been going to tell the wren about the surprise.

Two o'clock.

Helen really was a good friend of his.

Good friends gave you surprises.

Amy was always giving him surprises.

Amy was an even better friend than Helen: Amy would never ever think of putting Jimmy back in that place again, the way Helen would.

This time, when he felt sad again, sad being something that Jimmy was very familiar with, it was because the wren was gone.

He loved talking to the birds and having them talk back to him.

They really did have conversations, even if people did think it was funny when he told them about these words he exchanged with the birds who perched on his windowsills.

Jimmy went over to the window and looked out.

He saw robins and jays and at least two fiery red cardinals. But no wren.

Maybe the wren was off somewhere getting a surprise of his own.

Stood to reason—if folks like Jimmy got surprises, why shouldn't birds get surprises, too?

Jimmy went outside, then, to sit on the stump of a fallen tree.

Every few minutes he'd pull his railroad watch out of his pocket and take a look at it.

Two o'clock was two hours away.

And two hours, when you were waiting for something real good, two hours could be a real long time.

Then the wren came back and sat on the grass next to Jimmy and pecked at the grass.

Jimmy told the wren all about the surprise at two o'clock.

The wren was very happy for Jimmy. Birds were always happy when human beings got nice things.

3

Somebody had once told Steve Arnette that he looked a little like Robert Mitchum, and Arnette had never forgotten the compliment.

Now he never missed a Mitchum movie. He was always trying to pick up a mannerism or two from the movie star. The hardest one to pick up was the sleepy-eyed look that Mitchum was so famous for. For Mitchum, it was natural to look this way. Arnette had to do some squinting to get the sleepy-eyed look down. And sometimes he looked sort of weird, squinting like that all the time.

Arnette's father had been the town drunk. He'd also been feared. But he'd also been jailed a great deal. A lot of people secretly felt that Steve Arnette was paying back the people who'd treated his father so badly. The only reason Steve had ever survived in this town was because of his cousins, David and Helen Cummings. They'd gotten him the police job. They'd sweet-talked Hadley into keeping him on whenever Steve got a little gung ho arresting somebody. He was the perennial second stringer. All his life he'd played second string to Richie McGuire. Richie was the football hero, the most popular student, and the winner of Susan Kelly's heart. Steve was good but never good *enough*. The woman he'd married . . . a little hausfrau . . . she repelled him so much he felt guilty about it. She was good-hearted, she'd faithfully borne him two children, she was always telling him how much she loved him. . . . God, if only he had the money to leave this town . . . and could somehow persuade Susan to go along with him. Steve Arnette didn't understand that his father had been a dangerous bully. Steve Arnette saw his father as the victim.

Arnette had a fresh-pressed khaki uniform on. He was also wearing his mirror sunglasses.

As if Arnette weren't ominous enough . . . he was doubly scary when you couldn't see his eyes.

He hadn't been summoned to the crime scene . . . in fact he would've been a whole hell of a lot more valuable watching for speeders . . . but Arnette had driven out here so he could strut around for the gawkers, especially the younger women, a lot of whom found him curiously appealing.

A couple of the state boys had arrived and were going over the area where the body had been found. They used a variety of tools and spoke in a language Steve Arnette had never heard before.

Arnette stood downslope, just to the left of the state boys, and said, "You guys need any help, just let me know."

He said this loud enough for Eileen Conroy to hear. Eileen had just about the sweetest pair of tits in town, and Arnette had had designs on her for years. She might outwardly look like the happily married mother of three. But Arnette knew all about women and their secret desires. That's why he had to laugh about all this abusive spouse bullshit. He slapped his own wife around good and hard sometimes and he bet that she secretly thanked him for it. Maybe she didn't ever come right out and *say* she was grateful for the black eyes and bruised ribs, but he knew what she was thinking. Women needed a little help knowing their limitations, knowing what they should and shouldn't be doing. And Arnette, being the sweetheart he was, was only too happy to show them the true path to happiness and fulfillment.

The state boys looked at each other and smiled briefly. In

every little town they went to there was an Arnette, snappy
fresh uniform, mirror shades, bully swagger. Every single town.

"Thanks for the offer," one of the state boys said. "But
we're doing just fine."

"I'll be around if you need me," Arnette said, still playing
to Eileen Conroy and her fabulous tits.

Benny Drew, an old fart who farmed not far from here,
stepped away from the gawkers and walked over to Arnette.
Why couldn't Eileen Conroy come and talk to him? He didn't
need any old farts.

"You think he did it?" Drew said.

"Who you talkin' about, Pops?"

"The McGuire kid."

"Oh."

"You think he did it?"

Arnette smiled and looked at the scarecrowlike figure of
the farmer. He always wore the same ratty old cardigan when
he came to town and his dentures always clicked when he
talked. They were clicking now.

"Hell, yes, he did it."

"That why Sam Bowers's keepin' in the cabin down there?"

Arnette was about to speak but one of the state boys said,
"Maybe we shouldn't be talking about the case, Officer Arnette."

The way he talked, the state boy, he sounded like some fag
high-school teacher. In eleventh grade, Arnette had had a fag
civics teacher. Arnette was the only one who *knew* that the guy
was a fag. The rest of the students were too dumb to pick up on
the obvious. Anyway, that was how the fag civics teacher had
talked, just like the state guy. Very precise. Even a little lispy.
Like Vincent Price, a little.

"They givin' you orders now, Arnette?" the old fart said.

And you could hear the glee in his voice. It was not often
that a citizen of Crystal Falls got to see Arnette embarrassed in

any way. Benny Drew would tell this story far and wide and chortle about it with each telling.

"I got to go down and see Bowers," Arnette said. He was glad he was wearing his shades. He wouldn't have wanted the old fart to see his eyes right now.

The state faggot had embarrassed him and there wasn't a damned thing he could do about it. His cheeks were burning. He could feel them. It was like when he'd been a boy, when people would make jokes to him about his father. His cheeks burned a lot back then. And sometimes, even when he was in his late teens, he'd go home and close his bedroom door and cry just like a little kid. Every time he'd go somewhere, he'd know he was being judged. There goes Bill Arnette's kid. Just like him. He fought a lot of them, Steve did, trying to win himself some respect. But you couldn't fight everybody. And you couldn't win respect with your fists. You could win fear and you could win subservience. But you couldn't win respect. The worst day was the day they buried his father following the heart attack. Steve and his mom sat in the backseat of the hearse and looked out the window. Folks knew who was being buried. And they smirked. And told little jokes to each other. He wanted to get a gun and kill every fucking one of them, every fucking one. They couldn't even pay his father any respect in death. He remembered all this when, five years later, he put on the police uniform. He would spend the rest of his life paying them back for the way they'd treated his father.

He took a last longing glance at Eileen Conroy's breasts and then strutted down the hill to the cottage.

"Your sister told you about getting a lawyer," Sam Bowers said.

"Yeah."

"Probably be a good idea."

"I didn't kill Darcy."

"I didn't say you did."

"Then why would I need a lawyer?"

"That's just the way the law works, Richie."

"You think I killed her, don't you?"

"I think it's a possibility."

"A possibility. Shit, you've got me convicted and living on death row."

"You need a lawyer, Richie. That's all I'm saying."

Richie stood up, walked over to the window, and stared dully out at the gorgeous day.

"I'm really in deep shit this time, aren't I, Sam?"

"I'm afraid you are."

"I didn't sleep with her and I didn't kill her."

"I want to believe you, Richie. I hope what you say is true."

Richie turned back from the window. "For Amy's sake, huh?"

"For Amy's sake and for yours. You and I haven't always gotten along, Richie, but I've always thought you were basically a decent guy with a drinking problem. I want to see this whole thing cleared up for Amy's sake *and* yours."

Richie sighed. "I appreciate you saying that."

He glanced out the window and saw Arnette making his way down the hill.

"Great, here's what I need." Then, "Arnette."

"I'll handle him. Don't worry."

Sam walked over to the door and opened it. "What're you doing here, Steve?"

"Thought I'd see if you needed any help."

"Well, I don't. You should be in town, anyway."

"Let you have all the glory, huh, Sam?"

"I'd watch your mouth, Steve."

Arnette smiled. "You're kind of between a rock and a hard place, aren't you, Sam?"

"That's my business."

Sam could feel Richie walking up behind him.

"Amy's not gonna like it if you arrest her brother for murder." Then, "I always knew we'd nail that fucking punk."

Sam had no warning. And before he could even throw a shoulder into Richie, the younger man had bolted through the door and had jumped on Arnette, throwing him to the ground.

The two men were then rolling around on the grass and throwing punches at each other. These were clearly two men who despised each other. They fought with no semblance of honor. They bit, scratched, gouged.

Then Richie was on his knees. He had enough leverage now to put some pretty heavy punches on Arnette. He must have hit the other man a dozen times. He knocked off Arnette's mirror sunglasses.

Sam got Richie by the hair and yanked him to his feet. "Now you get in that cabin and stay there. You understand me?"

He gave Richie a hard shove through the door.

"The son of a bitch jumped me," Arnette said.

The way his left eye was puffing up and starting to discolor . . . Richie had also, it appeared, given Arnette a black eye.

Given Arnette's macho ego, he was going to have a hard time explaining away a black eye given him by Richie McGuire.

"You saw it," Arnette said. "He jumped me and you're my witness."

"I'm your witness, Steve, that's right. But now I want you to get back to town."

"That son of a bitch." Arnette was so angry, he couldn't get a grip on his temper.

"You already said that."

"This time you're going to stick up for me, not him, Sam."

"You're right. I am. But now we've both got to get back to work."

"That fucking son of a bitch."

"I'll see you back at the station, Steve."

But Arnette could not be quelled. He glared at the cottage and said, "I'm going to kill that fucker someday, man. I really am."

Sam knew there was only one way to end this conversation. He bent down and picked up Arnette's twisted mirror sunglasses.

He handed them to the other man silently, and then turned and went into the cottage.

"Real smart," he said to Richie.

"I can't stand that son of a bitch."

"Well, in case you haven't noticed, he doesn't like you a whole hell of a lot, either."

Sam went over to the coat rack and grabbed one of Richie's college letter jackets.

He threw it to Richie and said, "Let's go."

"Where?"

"You're riding into town. By now, Amy's arranged for a lawyer. You need to sit down and talk to him."

"This whole fucking town is going to railroad me."

"Now you sound as paranoid as Arnette."

"Well, it's true, isn't it?"

"No, it's not true, Richie. The Chief and I want a real investigation done. We'll find the real killer. That I don't have any doubt about. But in the meantime, you need to talk to a lawyer. And you need to stay out of trouble. Jumping Arnette that way was a stupid thing to do."

"Yeah, well maybe it made me feel better."

The juvenile belligerence of Richie's voice irritated Sam. He said, "Put your jacket on and let's get the hell out of here."

4

"I'm very sorry, Amy," Mrs. Gallagher said at the lunch counter that afternoon. "You did so much for that boy and now look. I just want you to know that we're all behind you, Amy, one hundred percent."

There'd been a Woolworth in Crystal Falls until the late seventies. The lunch counter there had been *the* place to eat when you were going through your young years. Nothing had been more thrilling to Amy, back in her high school days, than to sit at the Woolworth lunch counter and have a ham sandwich and a vanilla shake. Her grandfather used to sit at this counter. Her parents, back when they were first dating, also sat at this counter. And for her birthday, her mother always brought her here, mostly because that's where Amy pleaded with her to go. The shake always left her with an ice-cream mustache.

She wore such a mustache as she listened to Mrs. Gallagher.

Woolworth no longer owned this store; a chain named Bargains, Inc. did. But the lunch counter was the same. So Amy usually ate her lunch here.

Mrs. Gallagher was an old family friend, a stout, gray-haired lady who always seemed to have a shawl wrapped around her, even in summertime.

She had a shawl wrapped around her now.

"I just want you to know that what that brother of yours did is no reflection on you," she said. "And I'm speaking for a lot of people when I say that."

"But Mrs. Gallagher—"

The older woman glanced at the red Coca-Cola wall clock and said, "Gosh, I didn't realize what time it was. I've got bridge club in another twenty minutes." She patted Amy's hand, then stepped down from her counter stool.

"We'll all be praying for you, Amy," she said. She made a

clucking sound. "You did so much for him. I just can't believe he'd do something like this to you."

Then she was gone, taking the heavy scent of her cologne with her.

She's already convicted him, Amy thought.

She knew that Mrs. Gallagher, who really was a decent person, was speaking for a lot of people. They believed that Richie—whom they'd long suspected would come to a bad end—had killed Darcy. Period. They didn't even need an investigation or a trial to convince them. It was already a closed matter.

Usually, Amy was a pretty quick eater. Since she was always trying to lose six or seven pounds, she allowed herself the luxury of food only at breakfast, lunch, and dinner. No snacks. So she should be wolfing her sandwich and shake down as usual.

But she had no appetite. Mrs. Gallagher's summary judgment of Richie was still in her ears.

The town of Crystal Falls had already sentenced her younger brother to prison for murder.

THIRTEEN

1

The way the townspeople waved at Helen Cummings, you knew that they revered her almost as much as they did her brother.

David Cummings couldn't always make it back here more than six or seven times a year. There were key Senate votes he had to stay in Washington for, or party functions, or lobbyists to listen to.

But Helen . . . Helen was the one you knew you could always turn to.

She walked along the sunny street, on her way to the small frame house where Chief Hadley lived. It was a pleasant, tree-lined area. You didn't hear many children, however. Most of the houses here were filled with retirees. They'd raised their own tribes. Now, when you did hear kids, it was grandchildren come to visit Grandma and Grandpa.

As long as she'd known him, Chet Hadley had driven a blue Dodge. With blackwalls. And no fancy chrome. Hadley had a cousin over in Cedar Rapids who could get him a good deal on such a beast, so whenever the new models came in for the year, Hadley scooted over to Cedar Rapids (or CR, as most people around here called it) and got himself a new car. Only within the last few years had he broken down and gotten a car with air-conditioning in it. He still didn't have a cassette player.

It was lunchtime, so the Dodge was in the narrow driveway. Chief Hadley was a man of habits. Unless there was some sort of crisis, he was always home at twelve exactly for lunch. And he always went back to the office at five of one. Before she knocked, Helen knew she'd hear the sounds of Paul Harvey on the radio inside. Hadley never missed Paul Harvey, either. He considered Rush Limbaugh, a man who'd taken a lot of his show from Harvey's, to be nothing more than a loudmouth upstart. Harvey was still his man.

Beth Hadley answered the door. She wore, as usual, a flowered housedress, an apron, heavy black oxfords, and a somewhat anxious smile. She was greatly intimidated by the Senator and his sister.

"I just wondered if I could sneak in and talk to your husband a few minutes."

"Why, sure, Helen. He'd be glad to see you. C'mon in."

The house was like the Dodges Hadley bought, nothing fancy. There was a flower-patterned couch, a few Ethan Allen end tables and lamps, and a large Zenith TV console. The house was dust-free and spotless. Beth was a relentless housekeeper. The local wisdom was that since the Chief and she couldn't have children—her being the problem, not him—she'd taken the maternal instincts out on her house.

A toilet flushed upstairs.

Beth smiled with a certain embarrassment, obviously wishing that her husband hadn't chosen this exact moment to flush. Bodily functions didn't need to be advertised.

"He'll be right down."

"Thanks, Beth."

"Would you like coffee or anything?"

"No, thanks."

"Well, for gosh sakes, you can at least sit down."

And with that, Beth flew across the room and brushed off a couch cushion, as if it had been covered with dust.

Helen thanked her and sat down.

"It's awful about that Fuller girl, isn't it?"

"It sure is," Helen said.

"At least they got the right man, anyway," Beth said. "Chet still can't think about the Baxter thing without getting upset. He doesn't want another one of those."

Five years ago, a man named Mike Baxter worked nights at a convenience store. Graveyard shift. Somebody came in around two o'clock and shot him three times. No killer, no murderer, was ever discovered. These were the scariest kinds of murders to lawmen and private citizens alike. The idea of somebody just driving around out there, and then just stopping in and killing somebody . . .

"That's all he could talk about at lunch," Beth said. "How this wasn't going to be like the Baxter case."

Steps on the staircase. The sight of a pair of brown Hush Puppies oxfords. The cuffs of dark pants. Slowly, Chief Hadley came into sight. With his fluffy white hair and puffy cheeks, he looked more and more like Santa Claus. The sloping belly didn't hurt the effect, either.

"Well, Helen," Hadley said, obviously both surprised and pleased to see her.

Fifteen years ago, Chet's brother had been about to lose his farm. This was back in the eighties, when so many family farms were being shut down by banks. Chet had gone to Helen and Helen had made a couple of calls to a good friend of hers who was close to the president, and that friend then promptly called somebody in the Department of Agriculture . . . and Chet's brother kept his farm.

Chet Hadley had a special affection for Helen and David Cummings, and God help anybody who gave them grief of any kind.

"You like some coffee, Helen?"

"No, thanks, Chet. Beth already offered me some."

"You like a Pepsi or something?"

"I'm fine, Chet. Really."

Beth said, "Well, this sounds like business, so I'm going to go back to cleaning my oven. Nice to see you, Helen."

"Nice to see you, too, Beth."

Beth nodded and left the room.

"You've got a good woman there, Chet."

He smiled. "And believe me, I know it. Thick and thin that woman's been with me. Thick and thin." He sat down in an ancient rocking chair that he always told her had belonged to his grandfather.

"I ever tell you where I got this chair?" he said now.

Helen almost smiled. "No, Chet, I don't believe you did."

"My Grandpa Flaherty brought it over here all the way from Ireland."

"It's beautiful."

"And," Hadley said, "comfortable."

He rocked forward and backward as if to demonstrate just how comfortable it really was.

He said, "So how can I help you, Helen?"

"I'm just concerned about the Fullers."

He nodded somberly, his little potbelly pressing against the khaki shirt of his uniform. He wore a Stetson outdoors. He was of that generation of midwestern men that preferred western-style clothes.

"Oh, that's right. You know them, don't you?"

"Yes, I do."

"I phoned them personally this morning," Hadley said. "Took a while but I finally tracked them down in a hotel in London. They're on their way back."

"You think you might've arrested young McGuire by the time they get back?"

He thought a moment. "Boy, I don't know about that, Helen. Something like this, we want the cooperation of the district attorney's office. They may not be ready to arrest *anybody* yet."

"Especially with McGuire's sister being in charge of the investigation."

"Amy? Oh, she's a straight shooter, Helen."

"Oh, I know she is, Chet. I just mean that since her brother's involved and all—"

"She's already taken care of that."

"She has?"

"Yep. Put her deputy in charge of the case about an hour ago."

"Well, that's good to hear."

But of course it wasn't. Helen had come here to talk Chet into arresting Richie McGuire immediately. She was going to use Amy as her excuse, tell Chet how he had to bypass her and arrest Richie on his own.

But Helen was nothing if not resourceful.

"They'd feel a lot better stepping off that plane tomorrow," she said, "knowing that the man who'd murdered their daughter was behind bars."

"I suppose they would."

"I don't have to tell you what the Fullers mean to this community, Chet."

"No, you don't."

"He controls a lot of jobs around here. And if he ever took a dislike to us—"

"Mexico," Hadley said.

She nodded somberly.

Nobody had to tell any small-town official about how fast jobs could disappear to Mexico. Up near Dubuque last year, a plastics manufacturer closed up shop and took 950 jobs across the border. He gave his workers and the town ninety days' notice.

"You really think he might do that?"

"Put yourself in his position, Chet. Man moved his family out here and turns around this whole plant so that it's profitable again, and employing more people than ever. And then what happens? His daughter is murdered by some drunken ex–football star. How's that going to make you feel about the town?"

"Not very good."

"Not very good is right. And there's one more thing. And I want to be careful not to hurt your feelings here, Chet."

"You mean the Baxter case?"

"Yes, the Baxter case. Nobody's blaming you. In big cities, murders go unsolved all the time. But you can bet that that's what Fuller is thinking about as he's crossing the Atlantic. Living here the last year, I'm sure he heard about it."

"The Baxter case."

She nodded. "The Baxter case and how nobody's ever been charged in it."

Hadley was starting to look uncomfortable.

"But there's a way out of this, Chet."

"Oh?"

"What if he steps off the plane and the first thing he hears is that you've already got the guilty man in jail?"

"I guess that'd probably make him feel good, wouldn't it?"

"He can't bring his daughter back, Chet. But at least he can get justice."

"And that's how he'll look at it, isn't it?"

"That's exactly how he'll look at it, Chet."

"What if this deputy of Amy's says he doesn't want to arrest him yet?"

"Then you just remind him about the Baxter case and how people around here feel about that."

"You know him? This Dick Wilson?"

"No I don't, Chet."

"He seems reasonable enough, I guess. But Richie is his boss's sister. He'll be sure to take that into account."

"Then that's when you'll just have to put your foot down, Chet."

"Put my foot down."

"That's right, Chet. Put your foot down."

She could see he was wavering. This was one hell of a spot to put a lawman in, and she knew it. But the sooner Richie McGuire was put behind bars, the better it would be for David.

"How's your brother's farm coming these days, Chet?"

She had never been much of a believer in subtlety.

"He's doing real well. Thanks to you."

"I like to do favors for people I like." She looked straight at him when she said this: "I think most people do, Chet, don't you?"

"It'll take some doing, Helen."

"I know, Chet. But I like to think that I can count on you."

He sighed, then smiled. "I'm not being a very good friend to you, am I, Helen?"

"You're a cautious man, Chet. And there's nothing wrong with caution."

"He's the killer. Richie, I mean. I don't have any doubt about it."

"Then you shouldn't feel bad about locking him up. And neither should this Dick Wilson."

"Amy'll be another matter."

"As you said, Chet, Amy has put this Dick Wilson in charge. He's the only one you have to worry about."

"Even the state boys agree with us."

"Oh?"

He nodded. "I had a talk with one of them just before I left the office. He says he doesn't have any conclusive proof yet but from everything he knows, it sure sounds like Richie's our boy."

"I'd mention that to Dick Wilson."

He smiled again. "I'm going to handle this for you, Helen."

"I'll really be appreciative, Chet. I plan to be at the airport tomorrow to meet the Fullers, and I'll sure be glad to tell them that the killer's in custody."

Helen stood up. "I probably should be going, Chet."

"How's that brother of yours?" Hadley said as he walked her over to the screen door.

"Just fine."

"He's in our prayers."

"He's a tough customer, Chet. He's going to beat this thing."

He wasn't, of course, he wasn't going to beat this thing at all, she thought.

Chet didn't know it, but he was right now in the presence of the next senator from Iowa.

"You tell him hello for us."

"I sure will, Chet."

"And you never have taken us up on our invitation to dinner."

Oh, Lord, she thought, enduring a three-hour dinner over here would be just about unbearable. Washington had spoiled her. She liked dining out at the best restaurants, and rubbing elbows with interesting and important people. Just two weeks ago, she'd been at a Georgetown brunch where the guest of honor was Kevin Costner.

Dinner at Beth and Chet Hadley's just wasn't going to cut it.

"That sounds wonderful," Helen said. "Let's set something up for sure."

She walked down to her car and drove away.

2

Amy was interviewing a witness in a manslaughter case when the call came. This was an hour after Helen Cummings left Chief Hadley's house.

She excused herself from the room where she and the woman had been talking. She wanted to take the call in her private office.

"This is Richard Fuller, Amy."

She noted the fact that he called himself Richard instead of Dick. Even though they knew each other from various civic functions, Fuller wanted her to know that this was a different circumstance. "Richard" spoke to his authority in Crystal Falls.

"I'm very sorry about your daughter. Please give your wife my sympathy."

"I appreciate that, Amy. But sympathy isn't going to do a hell of a lot for either of us right now."

"No, I suppose it isn't."

"I don't want another Baxter case here, Amy."

"You don't have to worry about that, Dick."

A pause. "I'm told that your brother was seeing my daughter."

"He knew her, if that's what you mean."

" 'Knew' her. That's a nice euphemism."

"He didn't sleep with her."

"Oh?"

"I asked him that directly and he said they hadn't actually gone to bed."

"There's some fancy dancing. What the hell does 'hadn't actually gone to bed' mean exactly?"

"He didn't sleep with her."

"Or so he says."

"I believe him."

"Of course you believe him, Amy. He's your brother."

Dick Fuller obviously needed somebody to take his anger and loss out on. Amy was handy. She doubted that Dick would ever ask the much harder questions of himself—what kind of father had he been? What had he *really* known about his daughter?

"I've taken myself off the case, Dick. I don't want there to be any suspicion that this case isn't being investigated properly."

"I already knew that."

"Oh?"

"I—I spoke to Chief Hadley a little while ago."

"I see."

Another pause. "He seems to think that you have quite a bit of influence over your deputy DA, this Dick Wilson."

"He's running the case, Dick. I didn't even ask him to report to me. I want him to be independent in every way."

She felt hurt and angry that Chief Hadley had questioned her integrity. She'd worked so damned hard to remove herself from the case . . . and that still didn't seem to be enough.

"He'll be completely independent of me, Dick. And that's a promise." Then: "My brother's a suspect. But the investigation is just starting, Dick. We don't know where it'll lead. Your daughter may have had other friends."

"What the hell's that supposed to mean?"

"It means just what I said, Dick. We'll have to talk to all her friends, see if she was seeing somebody you didn't know anything about. That's just good investigative procedure."

"Anything to take suspicion off your brother, is that it, Amy?"

"That isn't it at all. And I think if you were a little more rational right now, Dick, you'd understand what I'm saying."

"A man your brother's age starts hanging around a girl my daughter's age . . . there's going to be trouble. And that's exactly what happened."

"I'm sorry, Dick."

"I hope he realizes he can be prosecuted for even being with her . . . whether they actually slept together or not."

"I made him aware of that, yes."

A long pause. "I wish you could hear my wife crying, Amy. I don't think I've ever seen a person this distraught."

Amy thought of the day her parents were killed. She knew exactly what Dick Fuller was talking about.

"I really am sorry about Darcy, Dick."

He sighed. "I appreciate that. I——" He sounded calmer now. "I just don't want another Baxter case here, Amy. No matter where it leads."

"I understand that. And I'm going to make sure that the killer is apprehended very soon."

"Even if the killer is your brother?"

"Even if the killer is my brother."

Another pause. "You may not know this, but Chief Hadley is going to arrest him in an hour or so."

"Arrest him? On what basis?"

She knew she was hurting herself with Dick. She sounded frantic, angry. Hardly the objective prosecutor she'd just claimed to be.

"He thinks there's enough evidence," Dick Fuller said. "He also thinks there's a chance your brother may try to run. I guess he did that one weekend when he was arrested for reckless driving."

That particular incident had taken place just as Amy was finishing up her B.A.

Richie had set a scoring record that weekend in the high

school playoffs. He and his friends celebrated all of Saturday night and all of Sunday. About 2 A.M. on Monday morning, Richie's car left the river road. The borrowed convertible plunged deep into the chilly black waters of the river. While Richie had his supporters—nobody had been injured, and the local Ford dealer promised to fix up the convertible for just cost—many townspeople demanded that he be punished. He could easily have killed somebody. Chief Hadley called Amy and told her he was going to arrest her brother. Richie had been standing next to her when the call came. He slipped out the back door and ran up into the timbered hills, where he hid out until later that night, only surrendering when Amy assured him that he wouldn't have to spend any time in jail. A year before, a friend of Richie's had gotten into some driving trouble over in Rock Island. Admittedly, the kid had a big mouth. They put him in a cell with six other prisoners. By dawn, Richie's friend was dead. Richie had a terror of jail that was almost obsessive. He frequently had nightmares about being put behind bars.

"The Chief feels it's necessary."

"I see."

"I know you're in a bind here, Amy. I'd be a little more— sympathetic, I suppose—if it wasn't my daughter we were talking about."

"I understand, Dick. I really do."

She was seeing Richie's cottage. Chief Hadley's car pulling up to the front door. The Chief getting out. Richie peering out the front window like a scared little kid. He'd be so scared, so scared. . . .

"I guess I'd better go now, Amy. I just wanted to be able to tell my wife that you wouldn't stand in the way."

"You have my word, Dick."

"That's all I need, Amy."

"I'm sorry, Dick. I really am."

"I'm sorry for both of us, Amy. I lost a daughter. You may lose a brother."

For several long minutes, Amy sat in cold silence, staring at the phone and thinking of Richie.

3

"We've arrested people on a hell of a lot less than this, Sam," Chief Hadley was saying.

"Maybe you have, Chief. I haven't."

Hadley made a sour face. "Now don't go and get all high and mighty on me, Sam. I know you think I'm an old hack who doesn't know his ass from a hole in the ground, but the fact is, there's already one hell of a case against Richie McGuire. And the last time we tried to arrest him, he ran away."

"That was a long time ago."

"Still and all, Sam. There're certain patterns to Richie's life. I don't want to risk him getting away." Then he said the magic words: "Nobody wants another Baxter case, Sam."

They were in the Chief's office and had been for fifteen minutes.

When the Chief had first told him about arresting Richie, Sam couldn't believe it. Richie was certainly a high-priority suspect right now—but arresting him?

Sam's first impulse was to wonder who'd gotten to the Chief. Hadley had a lot of cronies in this town and Sam sensed that one of them had convinced Hadley to arrest Richie.

Hadley would never question the person's secret motive. If Hadley owed him a favor, or thought he did, Hadley would do the person's bidding. No questions asked.

Hadley's phone rang.

"Hold calls," Hadley said to his intercom.

A male officer responded, "It's the Mayor, Chief."

"Oh, hell," Hadley said.

A police chief always took a mayor's phone call. That was just good small-town protocol.

"Tell him just a minute," Hadley said.

He looked up at Sam, who was now standing.

"You've got to keep your feelings for Amy out of this, Sam."

"I'd feel this way even if Amy wasn't involved. We're just arresting him way too soon."

"I'll tell you one thing," Hadley said. "I have a gut feeling the son of a bitch'll run away if I give him half a chance. That's what convinced me, Sam. I don't want to have to chase the bastard all over nine or ten states—when we just could've arrested him in the first place."

He nodded to the phone.

"I better not keep the Mayor waiting any longer, Sam."

Sam was walking back to his office when he saw Steve Arnette leaning against the red Coca-Cola machine.

"Looks like Amy's little brother's going to spend the night upstairs, huh?" he said.

So Hadley had told somebody else in the station and that somebody else had told somebody else and—

"We'll just have to see what happens," Sam said, not wanting the confrontation that the other two cops sitting at a lunch table wanted to see.

"The asshole's guilty, Sam," one of the other cops said. "Who the hell else would've done it?"

"He's been in our face too damned long," his partner said. "Always something with that bastard. Somebody always getting him out of trouble." He shook his head. "This one, nobody's going to get him out of."

Arnette smiled. "I just wish the Chief would let me go arrest the sumbitch. I'd have myself a real good time, I'll tell you that."

"Boy, that sun is bright as hell in here, isn't it?" Sam said.

"What the hell you talking about, Sam?" one of the cops at the table said. "There aren't any windows in this room."

"Gosh," Sam said, "then why would Arnette be wearing his sunglasses in here? Must be that black eye Richie gave him this morning."

And with that, Arnette's considerable ego deflated right in front of his cronies, and Sam walked to his office.

He had been seated less than thirty seconds when his intercom buzzed and he was told it was Amy on line two.

He felt the usual thrill over picking up the phone and hearing her voice. This had to be true love, he reasoned. He'd gone with his share of women and none of them had ever affected him this way. He even found himself scribbling her name over and over again as he sat at his desk sometimes. Like a lovestruck sixth grader.

He thought all these things before he actually heard her voice.

When she spoke, all romance was banished. She sounded grim.

"I assume you know that Chief Hadley's going to arrest Richie."

"I just left Hadley's office. I'm sorry, Amy."

"Richie has a thing about jail."

"I know. He told me about it on the way into town."

"I know I'm meddling here, Sam. And I know I promised not to, but—do you think the Chief would let you arrest Richie?"

"Boy, I don't know."

"He'd feel safer if you were the one with the warrant and everything, Sam."

"The Chief's still doing all the paperwork, I guess. I suppose he might consider letting me do it."

"Just convince him that Richie'll be much more inclined just to surrender himself if you do the arresting."

"I don't see why he'd object to that."

"I'm meddling, I know."

He sighed. "This is a terrible thing for everybody, Amy."

"I just talked to Dick Fuller. They're devastated, of course. Unfortunately, he's already got Richie tried and convicted. And so does most of the town."

"I'll go in and ask him."

"Thanks, Sam."

"Why don't I pick up a pizza and swing by your place for dinner. You probably won't feel much like cooking."

"That sounds good, Sam. That's nice of you."

Nice of me? he wanted to say. Nice of me? I get to spend some unexpected time with the woman I love and it's *nice* of me?

Then he felt a terrible guilt. He was definitely taking advantage of a horrible situation. A girl was dead; a man might well find himself in the worst kind of trouble with the law.

And Sam was taking advantage of it.

"I'll let you know how I come out with the Chief," he said.

"Thanks, Sam. I really appreciate it."

The Chief was finishing up the warrant paperwork when Sam knocked on his door.

"I've been thinking," Sam said.

Hadley smiled. "Whenever you say that, I know you're going to try and con me."

"Why don't I arrest Richie McGuire?"

"You? Why you?"

Sam shrugged. "As you say yourself, I know his sister very well. And I know Richie pretty good, too."

"I was figuring on doing it myself."

"He'd probably be a lot more peaceful if I was there."

"All right," the Chief said. "Then why don't we *both* do it."

That was the best he was going to get out of this, Sam knew.

As he'd expected, the Chief didn't want to give up such a high-visibility arrest.

The Chief wanted them to know that he was ever vigilant. Arresting Richie would be great public relations.

"All right," Sam said. "We'll both do it."

"There's just one thing."

"Oh?"

"I'm not taking any shit from him. You know how Richie can be. He acts up at all, I'm going to use my club on him."

"He'll be all right."

"You have any idea where he is right now?"

"I dropped him off at the lawyer's. I can check. I'll bet he's still there."

"You check, Sam. Then we'll go get him."

Sam called the Medlow-O'Brien law offices and asked if Richie McGuire was still in with Tom O'Brien. The receptionist said yes, he still was.

Sam told the receptionist that he and the Chief were on their way over.

4

What Richie McGuire really wanted to do was sit there and cry like a little kid. At this point, he was so overwrought that he noticed his right hand twitching every once in a while. Twitching.

Being a charter member of the Cosmic Macho Football

Club, however, he had to sit there and pretend that he had everything under control.

"So you left Riley's at about—"

"About nine."

"And went straight home?"

"Straight home."

Just don't ask how I got there, he thought.

Tom O'Brien was the kind of guy Richie usually disliked on sight. He was one of those yuppies with the six pounds of mousse on his red hair and deep reserves of arrogance swelling his chest. He'd have a BMW and once a month or so he'd watch XXX videos with his wife and he'd speak up every once in a while at school board meetings just to let people know that he was, after all, a Concerned Parent. He'd say all the right things, do all the right things, and he'd kill his mother for a dollar if he needed to. Richie saw his type six days a week at the country club. There was a certain amount of amusement in their eyes whenever somebody told them about Richie's football achievements. Who gives a rat's ass about some college football star? their gaze always said.

Tom O'Brien sat here now in his three-piece suit and said, "You kill her, Richie?"

"What?"

"Did you kill her?"

"What the fuck is this all about?"

"I just need to know."

Richie frowned, shook his head. "Of course I didn't fucking kill her, man. What kind of guy do you think I am?"

"Technically, I shouldn't ask you that question. Most lawyers don't want to know if their clients are guilty or not. But I figure it helps me. Knowing, I mean. If they're innocent, I handle it one way. If they're not, I handle it another way."

"Well, I'm innocent."

"Great. So what did you do when you got home?"

"Went to bed."

"Right away?"

"Right away."

"No phone calls."

"No."

"Any snacks?"

"No."

"You don't remember shit about any of this, do you, Richie?"

"Some of it, I do."

"You remember actually getting home?"

"Yeah. Because I had to break one of the panes in the front door."

"Oh?"

Richie held up his right hand and showed O'Brien the long scratches on his knuckles.

"The police see those?"

"Yeah."

"They ask you about them?"

"Uh-huh. Sam did."

"Sam's a good man."

"I'm glad you like him so much."

"You're a real hothead. You'll want to watch that, Richie. You pull shit like this in front of a jury, you're dead."

At the word "jury," Richie felt molten acid work its way up his stomach to his throat.

"I'm hoping this won't get as far as a jury."

"So am I, Richie. But that's generally good advice whether you go to court or not. Your temper, I mean."

"I didn't kill her."

"Yeah, you said that."

Richie wanted to hit him. Plant his fist right in the middle of that smug, patrician face.

"Your biggest trouble is you don't have any alibi."

"Amy said you were gonna be this big help. You aren't helping me for shit."

Richie looked around the large office. Everywhere you looked—walls, desk, table, atop the glass-and-mahogany bookcases behind O'Brien—everywhere you looked, O'Brien had pictures of his kids.

Little towheaded boy, little towheaded girl. Richie wanted to be his kid. You'd have it made, being his kid. He'd spoil you rotten, you'd live in one of those big-ass new houses out at the big-ass yuppie enclave that was turning Crystal Falls into a bedroom community, and you'd have all the goodies you ever wanted. Plus, the kind of social circles you ran in, you'd be bopping all those sweet little rich girls who had a treasure chest of jewels and diamonds between their legs.

O'Brien sighed. "Your sister's a damned nice woman, Richie."

"Yeah, she is."

"So I agreed to help her."

"You want a medal?"

"No, but what I do want is you to help me. I can't do this by myself. You've got a big problem here, Richie, and you giving me all this macho bullshit isn't helping me at all."

"I didn't kill her."

O'Brien leaned forward. "Richie, personally, I don't give a shit if you killed her or not. That's not the issue here."

"It isn't?"

For the first time, Richie began to suspect that for all his slick, sleek ways, O'Brien was not a candy-ass after all. There was a hard, almost cold intelligence at work here.

"No. The issue is can we prove you *didn't* kill her."

"I said I didn't."

"Richie, for God's sake, listen to me. It's not enough that

you say it. We have to have some proof. Can you remember talking to anybody on the phone last night?"

"No."

"Can you remember watching TV at all?"

"TV?"

"Yeah. If you got home around nine, maybe you stayed up and watched the news."

Richie shook his head. "I'm not much of a news watcher."

"So you drove straight home—"

"And went to bed."

"Did Sam ask you which route you took to get home?"

"Yeah."

"And you said—"

"I said I took the old bridge."

"Which was," O'Brien said, "washed out at the time."

Richie felt his cheeks burn. This was like sitting in the principal's office and having him humiliate and degrade you for a full period.

"You have any idea which way you took home?"

Richie shrugged. "There are only two other choices. I obviously took one of those."

"Your knuckles."

"Yeah?"

"Sam check out the windowpane you said you smashed?"

"Yeah, he did."

"He say anything about it?"

"Just wrote something in his little notebook."

O'Brien sighed again. "The Fullers are two of the most important people in this town, Richie."

"Tell me about it."

"They're going to want this case resolved very quickly, and that means they'll grab at the first guy who looks right for it."

Richie watched his hand. The trembling was back. "And I look right for it?"

"You didn't invite her to Riley's last night?"

"Hell, no. It was a complete surprise."

"She always follow you around like that?"

"We played a lot of games."

"You ever heard of the term 'jailbait'?"

"I didn't sleep with her."

"You ever kiss her?"

"Yes."

"Do anything more?"

"Felt her up a little."

O'Brien didn't look happy. "Anybody ever see you making out?"

"Not that I know of."

"How about the country club? They know what was going on between you two?"

"No."

"You're sure?"

"I'm sure. We were very careful."

He almost gagged on his own words. They were lies. They'd taken all kinds of reckless chances.

Richie said, "It doesn't look so good, huh?"

"We just need to get our defense together. We just need to have you remember a whole hell of a lot more about last night. Does it usually come back to you?"

"Most of it."

"Close your eyes."

"Huh?"

"Close your eyes and concentrate."

Richie did as he was told. "Do you have any recollection at all of seeing Darcy after you left Riley's last night."

"No."

"Don't say it so quickly. Think as hard as you can."

There was . . . something.

Something that whispered to him . . . but he couldn't quite

hear the words. Just the faint hissing of the whispers themselves.

Something . . .

"Shit," Richie said.

"Well, keep at it. That's the important thing." He shot his sleeve and looked at his watch. "I'm due in court in ten minutes."

"Then that's it? That's all the time I get?"

Richie knew that he sounded like a small, helpless child who'd just been deserted, but he couldn't help it.

"Richie, I'm sorry. I know you're scared. But I've got to go. Call me later this afternoon and we'll talk some more."

Richie reached out his hand.

Looking surprised, O'Brien joined his hand with Richie's and they shook.

"I'm sorry I was such a prick to you," Richie said. "I—it's just the way I am sometimes."

"You don't owe me any apologies, Richie. I'd probably be just as angry as you are if I woke up and found myself in this mess."

"I really have to rely on you helping me, Tom. You're my only hope."

Richie could hear the tears in his voice, feel them in his eyes. He'd never cried in front of anybody before. Not even Amy. Ever.

"I'm going to do all I can, Richie. I really am."

Richie wanted more reassuring words than those—he wanted a *guarantee* that he wasn't going to be charged with the murder—but this was the world of adults and there were no guarantees.

"C'mon, Richie. I'll walk out with you."

O'Brien held the door for him and then together they walked down the hall and outside.

They had just reached the sidewalk when they saw Sam Bowers pull up in his official car. Sam had to make the arrest alone because at the last minute Hadley was called to the district attorney's office for a deposition.

"Need to talk to you a minute, Richie," Sam said as he started to climb out of the Ford.

Richie had never heard Sam's voice this distant before. There was a cold, professional quality to it that made Richie's hand start twitching again.

5

Helen called her brother from home.

"How'd it go?" he said.

"Hadley's going to help us."

"We just need to get this wrapped up fast."

He is such a child, Helen thought. No patience.

"How're things going at the office?" she said.

"Oh, fine. You don't think Hadley'll change his mind, do you?"

"Of course not."

"A lot of people like him in this town. Richie, I mean."

"A lot of people *used* to like him. Not so much anymore. He's sort of frittered that all away, I think."

"It's all everybody's talking about," David said. "Everybody who comes in here brings it up. And they all think he killed her."

"Then I don't know what you're so nervous about." Then, "Maybe you're just worried about your doctor's appointment tomorrow?"

"God, Helen, I asked you not to bring that up."

"I was just saying—"

"Sometimes I think you *want* me to worry. I wasn't thinking about my doctor's appointment at all. But now I am, of course. Thanks a hell of a lot."

"I'm sure you're going to be fine. And even if you *had* to be operated on again—"

"God, Helen, just be quiet, will you? Nobody said that there's any recurrence at all. Everybody at the hospital seemed very positive the last time."

"Well, they're *paid* to be positive—or to *look* positive, any-way—but in your case, I'm sure they *felt* positive."

"God, I can't believe you sometimes. My own sister."

"I just wanted to let you know how it went with Hadley."

"I appreciate that."

"And I don't like being chewed out every time I call."

"Then quit talking about my appointment tomorrow. See, now *I'm* bringing it up again."

She could see the faces of the senators on the floor when she assumed her rightful place . . . Ted Kennedy, Trent Lott, Alphonse D'Amato . . . they'd all be happy to see her as a col-league . . . knowing that she'd been running her brother's sen-atorship for years, anyway.

"I'll let you know if I hear any more," she said.

"Great. Now I'd better get back to my appointments." Then, "You know what I just almost did?"

"What?"

"I almost stole one of our new secretary's ham sandwiches."

"You're kidding."

"Huh-uh. Ham's about the worst thing you can eat when you're trying to kick cancer."

"Right."

"So I almost picked one of them up and stuffed it into my face. Can you believe that?"

"Oh, I'm sure one or two ham sandwiches wouldn't hurt you. Not even three."

"You know, sometimes I think you don't *want* me to get well, you know that?"

"That's a nice thing to say."

"Well, it's true."

"I just want you to enjoy yourself, David. You went through a rough time with the chemo and all—you have to enjoy yourself a little bit."

"Oh, shit."

"What?"

"I'm such an ingrate. Here I am accusing you of wanting to make me sick . . . and all you're worried about is me being happy. I don't know why I say the shit I do sometimes, Helen. I'm very sorry."

"Oh, that's all right. I don't expect you to be appreciative of every single little thing I do for you, David. You don't have the time. You've got to look at the bigger picture."

"That's what I'm good at, isn't it? The bigger picture?"

Oh, yes, David, you're practically a fucking *whiz* on the big picture. A regular whiz and no doubt about it.

"Well, I'll talk to you in a while," she said.

"Thanks for everything," David said, contrite as only David could be.

"My pleasure," she said.

And hung up.

6

One time Richie had smashed old man Ryerson's window with his baseball. He had to sneak over in the Ryersons' yard to see if he could find his ball. He couldn't.

Which meant that the baseball was somewhere inside.

Which meant he'd had to sneak in the back door—old man Ryerson, who was retired and slept a lot, always left his back porch screen door open. Richie would have to sneak in there and get his ball back.

So he creaked open the door . . .

. . . and tiptoed into the kitchen . . .

. . . and tiptoed into the dining room, where he knew he'd find the ball on the floor . . .

. . . and there, by God, it was, his brand-new hardball sitting right on the floor amid shining shards of broken glass . . .

. . . his brand-new baseball.

He thought he'd heard something and—

—spun around.

And behind him he saw Tuxedo, old man Ryerson's nasty-tempered black-and-white tomcat.

Tuxedo hissed at him.

Richie gulped. Tuxedo couldn't hurt him. And he couldn't bark. So now was the time to grab his ball and get out of the house as fast as he could.

He started to tiptoe across the glass, his seventy-five pounds crackling the glass shards as he passed over them.

"What the hell you think you're doing, Richie?" old man Ryerson said out of nowhere.

Richie spun around.

This time Tuxedo had a companion . . . old man Ryerson himself.

"Oh, God," Richie said.

"Oh, God, is right," old man Ryerson said. "It's time that sister of yours gave you a damned good spanking."

Then old man Ryerson, who was a lot stronger than his gnarled body led you to believe, stepped forward and took Richie's ear in between his thumb and forefinger . . . giving it a good hard twist . . . and then marched him out the back door and over to Richie's house, where he demanded that Amy come and take care of this damned little brother of hers. . . .

Amy wasn't here right now to rescue him.

And he wasn't in trouble over a smashed window . . . he was in trouble over murder.

Sam reached in his pocket and said, "I have a warrant here for your arrest."

O'Brien spoke up. "What the hell are you talking about, Sam? Arresting him on what grounds?"

For the first time, Richie sensed that Sam was uncomfortable about this whole thing.

"The Chief feels there's enough evidence," Sam said, "to bring Richie in."

"I didn't kill her, Sam," Richie said. "I honest to God didn't."

O'Brien, cooler now, elected a more professional approach. "You want my opinion, Sam, he didn't have anything to do with this."

"The Chief makes the final decisions, Tom. You know that."

Richie's attention had already started to drift. . . .

Without quite being conscious of what he was doing, he was assessing the various avenues of escape open to him. . . .

There weren't many . . . and none of them were very good.

Here you were standing on the sidewalk on a sunny autumn day . . . each of the businesses on this particular street shaded by awnings . . . the sidewalk itself crowded with businesspeople and shoppers . . . and just where the hell would a guy escape to, anyway?

"This is a formal charge?" O'Brien said.

"Yes."

"I see that warrant?"

"Sure."

Sam handed O'Brien the warrant.

The lawyer skimmed it, shook his head.

"Hadley doesn't have shit," O'Brien said.

"He doesn't seem to feel that way."

"Circumstantial. And not good circumstantial."

Could run down to the end of this block and then run over and hide in the antique rail depot that was just now being restored . . .

But then what? Then where?

"I want to take him with me now, Tom," Sam was saying.

"I still can't believe this."

"The Chief's expecting me back in just a few minutes."

"I know this isn't your idea, Sam. And I also know you don't like this."

"What I like or don't like, doesn't matter."

. . . if he ran across the street now, he could get in the alley . . . maybe up one of those fire escapes . . . a roof . . . maybe hide up there till nightfall and then . . .

But, hell, as many men as they'd have looking for him, they'd find him for sure up there on the roof. . . .

"You mind if I come along?" O'Brien said.

"Fine by me."

"I just want you to tell me the truth, Sam. You don't agree with this, do you?"

"I already said my piece, Tom. The Chief asked me to bring Richie in and that's what I'm doing."

"You think Amy's going to like this?"

"Amy's not in charge of this case."

Sam knew why O'Brien was arguing so hard. Much of the town already believed Richie to be the killer. Bring him in, put him behind bars, formally charge him with murder . . . and for most people, including most police officers . . . the case would be closed.

Richie might as well plead guilty and get it over with. . . .

And that was when Richie saw the familiar black panel truck that Susan Kelly drove. He remembered that this was the day she came to town for groceries. She always parked her truck in back of U-Save and then went inside. . . .

. . . the truck would be parked . . .

. . . if he could just get away . . .

"May as well get it over with, Tom," Sam said.

O'Brien shook his head. "Guess you're right. Richie, I hate to say this but—"

And that was as far as he got.

Before either Sam or O'Brien could speak another word, Richie bolted from them.

He ran straight into traffic.

Car brakes screamed. Horns were honked. Several people swore.

But all Richie cared about was getting to the other side of the street, finding the alley, and using it as a chute that would ultimately dump him in the safety of Susan's truck. . . .

But then what?

No time for that now.

Run. Had to run.

He finally reached the alley. Saw, blessedly, that it was empty.

And ran . . .

. . . shouts behind him now.

His old injuries started to hurt. Was already beginning to hobble a bit.

Thought bitterly of the drunken night he piled up the convertible and ended his football career . . .

. . . so many things he'd fucked up in his life . . .

. . . run and keep on running . . .

. . . so many things that should've been good for him . . . jobs . . . women . . . and he'd fucked them all up . . .

. . . run and keep on running . . .

. . . Sam was against him. He could see that. Sam had a lot of influence on Amy . . .

. . . would Amy turn against him, too? Would Sam convince even her that Richie was a killer? . . .

. . . run and keep on running . . .

Came to the head of the alley.

Sirens sounding now.

Saw the familiar black panel truck. Susan was just now pulling up behind the supermarket in the middle of the next alley. . . . If he could just get there in time . . .

He pushed harder, faster, but almost immediately his hip and leg began hurting pretty badly . . . it was like trying to run with a charley horse . . .

. . . but he had to run . . . had no choice . . .

. . . knew that once they got him in jail, he'd never see freedom again . . . that was how cops worked . . . and even Amy admitted it . . . they decided on their man to the exclusion of all other suspects . . .

. . . run . . .

He could hear Sam shouting his name now.

Somewhere behind him . . . close behind him.

Could Sam actually shoot him?

But then there wasn't time to think about anything except taking advantage of the slight break in traffic flow.

He hobbled across the street and into the next alley.

7

Amy said, "What's all the commotion?"

When Midge looked up from her computer keyboard, Amy saw that something was terribly wrong.

"I—," Midge started to say, and then stopped herself. "I didn't want to be the one to tell you, Amy."

"Tell me what?"

"Richie escaped."

"Oh, my God."

"That's why we're hearing all the sirens suddenly. Sam went over to O'Brien's to serve them with an arrest warrant . . . and Richie took off."

"He didn't do it, Midge. I know he didn't."

"Well, I hate to say it, but this certainly isn't going to help him look innocent."

"No," Amy said. "It sure isn't."

She drifted silently back into her office, closed the door.

She went over to her desk, sat down, swiveled around in her chair, and looked out the window.

The town always looked so peaceful.

But right now there'd be a manhunt going on. A lot of angry people wanted to get their hands on her brother Richie.

Poor Richie.

But what if he'd actually killed her?

She'd seen this same naïveté in some of the people in the courtroom.

Despite all kinds of evidence to the contrary . . . they just couldn't believe that their loved one could ever be capable of doing such a thing. . . .

Maybe she was just as naïve as they were. . . .

Maybe Richie really had . . .

But no. Had to stop thinking that way.

Richie had acted foolishly, no doubt about it—first, by getting involved with the Fuller girl at all, and then by running away.

But did that mean he was a killer?

No, no matter how hard she thought about it, she couldn't see Richie killing anybody . . . not even when he was drunk.

"Oh, Richie," she said out loud, so many years of fear and misery in her voice, a decade and a half of worrying that Richie

would someday get into a kind of trouble that she couldn't get
him out of.

"Oh, Richie," she said again.

And this time it was like a prayer.

8

The panel truck would be locked.

The closer he came to it, the more he was convinced that
when he actually got there, when he actually put his hand on
the back door handle, he would find that the truck was locked
. . . and then he would be screwed for sure.

Sirens.

Shouts.

Five yards from the panel truck . . .

Stumbling now, totally exhausted . . .

Stink of sweat . . . no time for a shower this morning . . .

Stumbling ahead . . .

The back door handle starting to grow large and larger in
his vision . . .

Please, oh please.

Stumbling . . .

Hand reaching out for the door. Taking the silver handle in
his right hand . . . turning it to the left and . . . *locked!*

Falling to his knees now.

Please, oh please.

Wanting to cry . . . still in disbelief that any of this is actually happening to him.

Please, oh please.

And then turning the handle to the right and . . .

The handle turns!

Yanks the door open!

Sirens louder now.

Footsteps slapping somewhere nearby.

Once again—shouts.
Only one place to go.
Inside . . .
The womb-dark interior of the truck.
Hiding . . .
He climbs inside and there in the front of the truck sits
Jimmy, who smiles and says, "Hey, hi, Richie!"

PART

3

FOURTEEN

1

It didn't take long for the news of Richie's escape to reach all corners of the county.

They came by truck, car, motorcycle, even tractor, came right to the town square where Chief Hadley was hastily organizing a posse.

Thirty years ago, the local newspaper editor had written a piece about manhunts, and his words very much applied to what was happening this afternoon.

> Unless you've been in a war, you haven't really had the opportunity to feel the constraints of civilization be removed. Unless, that is, you were involved in the recent manhunt that took place here in the county. A full day and night of the manhunt yielded two dead cows, one dead collie, a dozen or more smashed windows, and several drunken brawls. And what of the criminal being sought? Why, he escaped to our sister state of Missouri,

where he was quietly apprehended by a rookie deputy. Before the local lawmen responsible for our well-being organize another manhunt, they'd better make sure that the posse they collect is comprised of reasonable, sane, and most importantly *sober* members of this community. The posse wrought far more damage than the man they were chasing. After all, all he'd done was rob a bank. He didn't get trigger-happy and kill cows and dogs. These are some things that the city council should discuss at the next open meeting.

Not that anybody remembered these words. Or would have heeded them even if they had.

It was just too damned exciting a place, the Crystal Falls town square, to remember those kind of cautionary words at this moment . . .

. . . because at this moment men with rifles and shotguns and hunting dogs filled the sidewalk in front of the bandstand and the venerable Civil War memorial that time and pigeon shit had given a bronzed patina. . . .

A number of the men were Steve Arnette's drinking buddies. These were the most impressively got up. They wore camouflage outfits and spoke to each other in paramilitary parlance. Their leader, a chunky man with a bandito mustache and a Pat Buchanan bumper sticker on his Range Rover, kept patting his shotgun and saying, "I see that sumbitch first, he's gonna be one sorry mother, let me tell ya. Poor little innocent gal like that." He carried a Steyr-Aug rifle, which cost more than most people around here earned in a month.

"Yeah," one of the others said, "Richie never did think his shit would draw flies."

This was one contingent of the posse.

The second largest group was the younger farmers. Their clothes ran to green John Deere caps, flannel shirts, Sears jeans, and black boots, which were long enough to get you through snowdrifts but not so long that they'd sweat your feet the way cowboy boots did.

These were the men with the hunting dogs sitting in the bed of their Chevrolets and Fords. The dogs ran to Labs and Springers and German shorthairs. Bloodhounds were pretty much left to the South.

There was a third group, too, the retirees. These were the older folk you saw in the library and the Wal-Mart and the Recreation Hall. People looking for something to do. They had convinced their wives that they were desperately needed on this particular mission, and so the missuses gave them permission. One of the guys tried to sneak his old army pistol out of the house. But his wife put out a flat palm and he obediently placed the pistol on it.

Then there were the lawmen, Sam and Chief Hadley and the other officers. All in uniform, all heavily armed.

Sam was surprised that Steve Arnette wasn't here. If ever there was an event made for a bully like Arnette, it was a manhunt.

Chief Hadley instructed the men in the ways of the law. Steve Arnette's buddies mostly smirked when Hadley talked. They wanted to kick some ass, and all Hadley wanted to do was talk about legal crap.

The farmers, however, were very attentive, noting every word the Chief had to say. A few of them were old enough to remember the last manhunt. They didn't want to see a repeat of that.

The Chief then said, "Anybody here got a flask of booze on him?"

The farmers all shook their heads.

Two of Arnette's buddies looked guilty.

"You guys got flasks?"

"It's our constitutional right to carry flasks," one of the men said sullenly.

"Give it to me," Chief Hadley said.

"I can carry a goddamned flask if I want to," the man said.

"All right," Hadley said, his toughness surprising some of the men who thought of him as a fussy old fart. "You get to keep your flask—and I get to kick your ass out of this group here."

"That's bullshit," the man said.

"Ah, hell, Harry, give him the friggin' flask," said his friend.

"Shit," Harry said.

"You, too, Ralph," Hadley said.

"Me, too? What're we gonna use for booze?" he said.

"There won't be any booze," Hadley said. "That's the point, you dumb bastard. Now hand over those flasks."

They handed them over.

They didn't look happy.

Hadley then went over to the old guys and told them all to make sure they were wearing bright shirts and jackets. Didn't want somebody mistaking them for a cow in the bushes . . . and opening fire.

When he said that, a few of the men looked a little nervous, as if real danger was something they hadn't considered before.

Sam was watching all this, and talking to the other lawmen, when he saw Amy crossing the town square.

Even from here, he could see that she planned to go along on the manhunt. She wore jeans, a buff blue sweater, and a red windbreaker.

The closer she got, the sadder she looked.

She'd had to deal with the unthinkable. First her brother had been accused of murder. Now, he'd escaped.

As a smart prosecutor, Amy knew all about manhunts. They'd hunt her brother like an animal. There'd be dogs, and state helicopters overhead, and reckless men walking the farm fields and forests. At least a few of them would be eager to be the man who brought down the killer.

Sam was sure Amy had heard a lot of the gossip already making the rounds. That Richie was armed and in a psychotic state. That he had a hostage. That he had seriously wounded a woman who saw him running away. That he had stolen two shotguns from a hardware store. He'd also been sighted in six or seven different places. Nothing coined misinformation faster than an escaping killer.

Small town like this, it didn't take long for such fables to be accepted as fact.

Sam looked up at the fiery trees of autumn, and the perfectly blue sky, and the crisp white dignity of the three different church spires the town was so proud of.

Nice, peaceful place.

Until this morning, anyway.

Amy came over, slightly out of breath, and said, "I'm going with you."

"All right."

She looked at the men in military uniforms.

"I should've figured they'd want in on this," she said. She'd had several run-ins with the local far right, many of them questioning the county government's right to levy and collect taxes.

"They'll be all right."

"You going to guarantee that, Sam?"

Her anger narrowed her eyes, pinched her lovely mouth.

"It'll be all right," he said. "We'll find him and bring him in."

Her eyes scanned the posse.

"Somebody's going to try and shoot him. Just look at them."

No denying, Sam thought, some of these men were the sort who'd do just that.

"You think the Chief can control them?"

"He's doing a good job of it now," Sam said, and told her about the flask incident.

He was just about to say more—just about to praise a man he didn't, in reality, have a whole lot of respect for—when they saw Bobby Sunshine running across the town square.

Bobby was one of the local disc jockeys. He worked the morning shift. He tried real hard to be a Howard Stern type of "shock jock," but that was hard to do in a place like Crystal Falls, where people still believed in (and for the most part, practiced) civility. One morning, he'd made fun of the new "Buttermilk Queen," a local community-college girl selected by a local dairy to be their spokesperson. He never made fun of anybody on the air again. Several merchants dropped their advertising and one of the Buttermilk Queen's cousins punched Bobby out in the Pizza Hut parking lot.

God only knew what was making Bobby—with his punk haircut, his earring, his nose ring, and his lavender slacks—so excited at the moment.

Bobby went around Sam and ran over to where the vehicles were parked, and where Chief Hadley was still telling everybody to hand over his flask if he had one.

"I've got some news!" Bobby said. The name and the attire might lead you to believe that Bobby was just starting out in this business. But actually Bobby Sunshine had been at this business ever since the sixties, when he'd been known as Frank Flowerpower . . . and the seventies, when he'd been known as Disco Donny . . . and the eighties, when he'd been known as Gary Groovy. He looked young at first glance, but you didn't get that kind of ring under the eye until you'd shot most of your body and all of your soul.

"Listen, everybody!" Bobby Sunshine shouted after climbing up in the bed of a truck.

"Hey, it's that radio guy!" somebody said.

"Yeah, that queer!" somebody else said.

"He isn't a queer!" said a third. "He damn near raped my niece on their first date!"

"Listen!" Bobby pleaded. "The station just got a call from Darcy Fuller's dad. He's offering a fifteen-thousand-dollar reward for anybody who brings in Richie McGuire!"

While all the men were cheering—and filling their heads with fantasies of what fifteen thousand dollars would do for them—Chief Hadley and Sam were exchanging worried glances.

The offer of the reward made the situation even more dangerous. Now the men would have to contend not only with their own normal macho impulses—who wouldn't want to shoot and kill a man when you could get away with it?—but also their greed.

Who the hell couldn't use fifteen thousand dollars, even if you did have to pay forty percent to Uncle Sammy?

That still left a guy with a nice piece of change.

"He wanted me to be sure you all understood this, about the reward and all," Bobby Sunshine said to the crowd, his fancy yellow shirt billowing out from his slender body like a sail. "He said he'll pay cash and he won't ask any questions."

"All right," Chief Hadley said. "You've had your say, Bobby. Now get the hell down from there."

Bobby said, "Start listening to KROC. We're going to have bulletins about Richie McGuire every fifteen minutes!"

Then he jumped down from the truck before Hadley got up there and threw him off.

"God, that's all we need," Amy said.

Sam shook his head. "It sure doesn't help any, I have to say that."

"Now you know what I've told you men," Chief Hadley was saying. "I expect responsible behavior out there. And I expect constant communication. If you get any leads, any kind of leads at all, I expect to be informed immediately. You understand me? Immediately. And I'm not going to listen to any bullshit excuses, either. I don't want any cowboy crap out there. You got that?"

Only a few of them even gave him a perfunctory nod. They were too eager to get into their vehicles and head out.

This wasn't only a manhunt now. This was also a treasure hunt, with fifteen thousand dollars as the prize.

"All right, you know the quadrants you've been assigned to," Chief Hadley said. "Now let's get out there and find him."

Sam smiled to himself. Hadley sounded like a coach.

"I guess we may as well go, too," Sam said.

Amy nodded.

They walked over to Sam's police cruiser and got inside. Just as Sam was about to back out of his parking space, Chief Hadley leaned in the window and said, "I guess I don't blame Fuller for offering that reward. But it sure as hell isn't going to make our job any easier."

"No, it sure isn't," Sam said.

Chief Hadley looked at Amy. "You got any ideas of where he might be, Amy, I'd sure appreciate you telling us."

"I will, Chief."

"I'd appreciate it. Sooner we get him behind bars, the safer everybody is."

She nodded.

"Well, you're headed east, Sam, and I'm headed west. Maybe I'll see you around suppertime."

With that, Chief Hadley stood erect, straightened his white Stetson on his white head, and then turned around and walked over to his police vehicle.

"You don't, do you?" Sam said.

"I don't what?"

"Have any idea where he might be."

"None." She looked at him. "I want to find him, Sam, even more than you and Chief Hadley do. I'm terrified that one of Arnette's buddies will get to him first." She shook her head. "Fifteen thousand dollars, no questions asked. That's another way of saying dead or alive, isn't it?"

"Yeah," Sam said. "That's how I interpret it, anyway."

He put his car in reverse and backed into the street.

2

As he parked his car on the long driveway, Officer Steve Arnette felt familiar anger. It always pissed him off when he had to come out here and see his second cousins David and Helen Cummings.

All the time he was growing up, Arnette had had to wear David's hand-me-downs. All the time he was growing up, he had had to accept their charity.... They were always bailing his old man out of jail and always bringing groceries over so that Arnette and his brothers would have something to eat. And these days ... whenever Arnette got a little excessive in his law enforcement, and whenever Hadley wanted to fire his ass, he just asked cousin Helen to call the Chief and do a little politicking of her own.

But as useful as they were, as useful as they'd always been, Arnette resented them. All the time they were handing out their charity, their entire demeanor (especially Helen's eyes) was saying that you were a lesser being for accepting it.

Arnette rang the bell and waited for someone to appear. He was eager to join the manhunt. Helen had called him right before the Chief started the searchers out of town. He wondered what the hell she wanted. She never called him unless there was a little "thing" he could do for her. Usually the little "thing" involved helping her get cousin David out of some jam he was in. Like the time he'd brought the black hooker home with him from Des Moines. This was a blackmail situation. The hooker, who had finally figured out who David was, could demand money for not going to the press. Cousin Helen asked Arnette to "scare her a little." Which he'd gladly done. Arnette was a past master at inflicting pain that left no physical signs. Between his fist and the dildo he used, the black hooker was not about to say anything. Ever.

Helen answered the door. She looked tired and oddly nervous. Helen usually looked fresh and completely in command. Even when he was a little boy, Arnette had sensed that Helen ran her relationship with David. David was impressive to look at but was none too swift in the brains department.

"Hi, Steve," Helen said. "C'mon in."

As usual, he felt like an intruder. Everything in here was valuable, from the somewhat severe modern furnishings—he hated chrome and glass, which always reminded him of those fag hairdressers he liked to hassle—to all the antiques.

Unworthy, he supposed. That was how he always felt here. That was how they always wanted him to feel.

"Pepsi?"

"No, thanks."

"Coffee?"

"I'll tell you, Helen, I'm in a little bit of a hurry."

His tone surprised both of them.

He was used to talking to Helen in the tone of a supplicant. Anything Helen wanted, Helen got, and he had to oblige her whether he wanted to or not.

But just now he hadn't sounded happy at all. He'd sounded irritated that he'd had to come out here.

They looked at each other as his words echoed in their ears.

"Oh," she said. "I see."

"I just meant," he said quickly, "the manhunt and all. You know, with Richie McGuire. That's why I'm in a kind of a hurry. But anything you need, Helen—"

She smiled.

He'd slipped back into his supplicant tone.

For one shining moment, he'd been a free man, capable of speaking his mind to his cousin.

But then, seeing her displeasure, he'd reverted to type—to sniveling, ass-kissing type.

"Let's sit down in the living room," she said.

The centerpiece of the living room was the grand piano that

sat in front of a large window overlooking a valley gorgeous with the colors of autumn. In the sunshine, the valley had an almost unreal look, like a painting in an old book. How could anything real be this beautiful?

"You know how hard David works to bring business to Crystal Falls, Steve."

Arnette nodded.

"He'd planned to bring some prospective businessmen here next week, in fact." She sat on the edge of a love seat, her hands folded neatly on her chocolate brown skirt. She still had damned good legs. For the thousandth time, Arnette found himself wondering why she'd never married.

"Well, now this thing with the McGuire boy has ruined his plans."

"Oh?"

"Of course. He doesn't want to bring anybody in here with a manhunt going on."

"We'll have caught him by then."

She nodded. "I'm sure you will—if everything goes all right. If he doesn't get to Mexico or someplace."

"We'll get him, Helen. Don't you worry."

"But that's just the trouble. Even if you do get him—"

Just then, the grandfather clock in the corner chimed. Arnette listened, momentarily lulled, like an infant who is being rocked.

You could really escape from the world in a place like this. He'd always envied the rich their houses. The heavily wooded areas where they were hidden away. The deep plush carpeting. The expensive appointments. All the books and CDs and paintings. The refrigerator that was always packed with the best of foods. The dry bar where only the best of liquors and wines could be found.

Oh, yes, a place like this was a real escape. You didn't hear all the traffic the way you did at his house, you didn't have a couple of bratty kids crying all the time, you didn't have to fork over $657.83 a month on a house you hated so much you'd almost torched it twice . . . with the wife and the two kids still in it.

"Are you listening to me, Steve?"

This was like a teacher catching you when you'd put your head down on the desk and started going to sleep.

"Oh, sure, right," he said, bringing himself back from the fantasy of living in a place like this.

Someday, he'd have a house just like this one—and a new, young wife—and he damned well wouldn't feel unworthy. He'd feel just as cocky and arrogant as cousin Helen did.

"What I'm saying," Helen said, "is that we really need to have this thing wrapped up before these gentlemen get here next week."

"I guess I'm not sure what you mean 'wrapped up,' Helen."

For the first time since he'd arrived, Arnette found himself interested in why Helen had summoned him here today.

"Wrapped up?" What the hell was she talking about?

"I take it you know about the reward."

"I sure do," Arnette said. "I heard it on the radio. That's going to make a lot of those guys pretty damned trigger-happy."

Helen paused a moment, then said, "What if I offered you the same deal?"

"What same deal? You mean, the fifteen thousand dollars?"

"That's just what I mean, Steve."

"Wow," he said. "So if I spot him first—"

When he was a little kid, he'd always gone around imagining that he was going to win all these contests he heard about on TV. Why, just win one of them, and his life would be changed forever. New house for him and his brothers. No more worries about running out of grocery money. And no more worries about the old man, either. When people had money like that, they were just automatically happy and things took care of themselves. If he could just win that damned contest, the old man would miraculously give up the bottle and they would have the same kind of happy life he'd always secretly longed for.

"I know there's bad blood between you two," Helen said.

"Yeah."

"Started with Susan Kelly, didn't it? Back in high school?"

"Yeah."

That was another thing he'd always dreamed about, right along with winning one of those contests . . . winning Susan Kelly, too. He still felt she was the only woman he'd ever really loved . . . which sometimes made him feel oddly guilty about his wife. But she'd borne his children and stayed by him all these years, so even if he hated her . . .

If only he'd won one of those contests . . . and then won Susan Kelly, too.

"She thought she was going to get herself the son of a prominent surgeon," she said. "All she got was a drunk."

"He's a drunk, all right."

"She should've chosen you, Steve."

"Ah, hell."

"No, really. I'm being serious here. Now there's nothing wrong with that wife of yours . . . I'm not saying that . . . but Susan and you would've made a very nice couple."

He smiled. "I'll tell her what you said."

Helen watched him carefully a moment before she spoke. "You're still a young man, Steve."

"Twenty-eight isn't so young."

"Oh, hell, Steve, be serious. You could start your life all over again."

He shrugged. "I suppose."

"Let's say that Richie got killed in this manhunt."

His eyes narrowed. He watched her. Listened.

"For the sake of argument, I mean. Say that Richie was killed and you got my fifteen thousand and you got Fuller's fifteen thousand. You think you couldn't start your life all over?"

Suddenly, he realized what she was talking about.

He said, "Believe me, Helen, I sure wouldn't mind killing the son of a bitch. But—"

He shook his head.

"But what, Steve?"

"But if I did, they'd be all over me."

"Who would?"

"Hell, everybody would, Helen. Everybody knows we hate each other. And he's even got a lawsuit going against me."

"You could make it look good, Steve. You could make it look as if you didn't have any choice but to kill him."

His eyes searched her face. He wanted to understand her interest in all this.

"You'd have thirty thousand dollars," she said. "And it would be over."

"What's your interest in this? Because of David bringing those businessmen here?"

"Of course. Why the hell else would I be interested?"

"I don't know. That's what I'm trying to find out."

For a few minutes there, they'd actually been speaking as equals.

But her superior ways were back. "I don't like your tone, Steve."

"I just meant—"

"I just don't see how you can turn thirty thousand dollars down so quickly."

She was obsessive on the subject.

"Listen, Helen. First of all, I don't know if I can even find him. Second of all, if I bring him in alive, I'd still get Fuller's reward."

"If you bring him in dead, you'll get a bonus."

"A bonus?"

"Twenty-five instead of fifteen from me. I just—" She sat there, looking oddly flushed, agitated. "This is a black mark on this community. We need to get beyond it as soon as possible. If he was dead—"

"If he was dead, the story would die with him."

"That's it exactly."

He became aware of the creaking leather of his Sam Browne belt. What she was offering him was forty grand all told.

What she was also offering him—at least potentially—was starting his life over.

Maybe the dreams of Susan Kelly weren't dead yet.

"David and I could take care of any problems with Chief Hadley or the Mayor," she said quietly. "I think you know that, don't you?"

"Well, I guess it's something to think about, Helen."

He looked at his watch and stood up.

She walked him to the door.

He almost hated leaving this house. Much as he resented it, the place was a form of sanctuary.

"It's a lot of money, Steve."

"It certainly is."

"And we could handle any of the fallout."

He smiled at her. There was no supplicant tone in his voice now. "I sure wish I knew why you wanted him dead so bad."

"Are you trying to tell me that *you* don't want him dead, too?"

With that, he nodded good-bye and left.

David stood in the kitchen listening to everything his sister said to Steve Arnette. The whole thing was getting far too complicated. A part of him wanted to pick up the phone and call Chief Hadley and get it over with.

But then Helen was walking back inside. She looked at him and said, "Are you all right?"

"Fine," he said, feeling miserable. "Just fine."

3

Some of the searchers, especially the old-timers, thought, To hell with the manhunt, I'll just enjoy the day.

In creeks and ponds the reflections of the fiery trees could be seen, like the impressionist paintings of the masters. In the hills, up where the county's two riding stables lay, you could see Appaloosas and mustangs and palominos run the meadows. And nestled down in the valleys were the well-kept farms where dogs and cats and raccoons exerted their privilege as family pets to laze in the sunshine of the yard. And in the sky, hawks dove down the air currents, putting on an acrobatic show for anybody who wanted to see.

Who gave a damn about some drunken killer when God put this feast before your eyes?

Not all the searchers were so philosophically inclined, of course. Arnette's buddies seemed to see Richie McGuire behind every tree, barn, and shack they passed. Their trucks and vans were always jerking to a stop, and somebody dressed in camouflage was always leaping from the vehicle to the ground, rifle ready. They probably would have looked more impressive if they hadn't been quite so chunky, or if they'd shaved recently, or if they didn't bark a strange military code back and forth.

The rednecks just wanted to kill somebody. They drove up and down the dusty gravel roads and walked across the farm fields and climbed the narrow trails up to the timberline. All they talked about was what they were going to do with Richie McGuire when they caught him. He'd always been such an arrogant prick to their kind—had never had time for them in high school, had even less time for them afterward—that it was going to be fun to bring that bastard in. And if he gave them any trouble . . .

There were about twenty professional lawmen from nearby counties. They did the least talking and the most looking. They picked out the best nonprofessionals they could find and organized them into special units and gave each unit a walkie-talkie. Two of these units swung west, to search the area over by the old cattle auction barns . . . and the other two units swung north, up by the land that had been ceded to the Indians following an 1883 treaty. But by 1904, the Indians had figured out that the white man had done them in again . . . so they petitioned the federal government to move them to their tribal lands in South Dakota. The reservation, including several very interesting totems, had been rebuilt and preserved inside a theme park called Tomahawk Village, which came complete with a carnival midway and a variety of tent shows built around "Indian" themes. There were a lot of places to hide in Tomahawk Village . . . and so the searchers got busy.

"You all right?" Sam said.

"Just a little headache, I guess."

"There's some Tylenol in the glove compartment."

"Thanks," Amy said.

"Can you take them without water?"

"Sure."

"That's a trick I never mastered. If I take them dry that way, they have a hard time sliding down my throat and they start to disintegrate. And then they leave this aftertaste."

She smiled sadly. All she could think about was Richie. But she had to carry on her normal human functions, too. So she made a joke. "Sounds like you've got a real medical problem."

"You really are a smart-ass, you know that?"

They'd checked out the area over by the deserted high

school, and then they'd checked the area out around Richie's cottage. Now they were driving out the river road. A lot of houseboats had been docked here for the winter. Any one of them would be perfect for hiding in.

He looked at her. "He's going to be all right."

"Not with a fifteen-thousand-dollar reward, he isn't," Amy said.

"There's always the chance that he'll give himself up."

She shook her head. "I don't think so."

"Why not?"

"He's very paranoid. Always thinks somebody's trying to get him. This plays right into that. He figures that if the law gets him, there'll be a quick trial and he'll go to prison the rest of his life."

He hesitated before he spoke. "I'm going to ask you something that may piss you off."

"I know what you're going to ask, Sam. And it doesn't piss me off."

"He's your brother."

"It's a possibility we at least have to consider," Amy said. "But I don't think he killed her."

Sam smiled. "Neither do I."

He gave the police car a little more gas as they drove down the long row of houseboats.

It'd be so nice to be on one of those boats today, Amy thought. Do a little fishing off the top, sit up there in a lawn chair and read a paperback while you're waiting for a tug on your fishing line.

It'd be so nice.

The Kelly farm consisted of four hundred acres put variously into corn, alfalfa, and soybeans. There were three hundred head of cattle. There were also six outbuildings, including a new blue silo, and a two-story white frame house that had been painted the year before. Generations of her people had prospered here because as far back as the thirties they'd known about contour plowing, crop rotation, and other methods of soil conservation.

Susan pulled the truck up the driveway. She wanted to get as close to the back door as possible. Cut the distance he had to run.

As they'd driven out the county road, Susan had heard the sirens from town. The manhunt was already on.

Susan cut the engine and said to Jimmy, "Go unlock the back door."

"OK."

"Thanks."

When she handed Jimmy her keys, she could see how proud he was to be given an important task like this one. You gave Jimmy just a few basic things to do, and he had a little self-respect.

She walked to the back of the truck and swung open the door.

Richie knelt behind a stack of empty cardboard boxes.

"Hurry," she said.

He hurried.

Jimmy worked the keys just fine and proudly held the door open for them.

They got inside and closed the door.

Susan had redecorated her kitchen a few years back. It was a country-style kitchen with exposed brick walls and open shelving. There was a stained-glass window she'd picked up from an auction. The quarry-style floor completed the feel of rustic living—which was in striking contrast to all the new appliances she had.

The first thing Richie said was, "I could use a drink right now."

Susan looked at him in disbelief.

Booze had gotten him into this trouble—she had discussed the murder with him on the way out here—and yet now all he could think of . . . when he needed to be especially sharp and sober . . . was having a drink.

"I don't think that's a good idea," she said.

Richie was instantly angry. "I didn't ask for your approval, Susan. I asked for a drink."

"Oh, don't fight, you guys," Jimmy said, sounding like a frightened child. "Please don't fight." His two favorite places were Amy's and Susan's—he spent a lot of time in both places and wanted them to be peaceful.

Susan put a hand out and touched Jimmy's shoulders. "It's all right, Jimmy."

"All he wants is a drink, Susan."

She nodded. "Yeah, I suppose one won't hurt him, will it?"

"He's a real nice guy, Susan. He really is."

Susan smiled. "Yeah, I guess he is, isn't he? At least sometimes."

"Sorry I got mad," Richie said.

"We're all a little stressed," she said. And then went over to one of the cupboards and took down a bottle of Old Grand-Dad. "This all right?"

"Fine."

"You want ice?"

"No, thanks."

She took down a glass, poured him about two inches.

He took it. She tried not to notice how hard his hand was twitching.

She said, "They're going to come here, you know."

He nodded. "The big thing was, you got me out of town. Which I really appreciate."

She looked at him. Her eyes were hard. "You thought I was going to turn you over, didn't you, Richie?"

"No, I wasn't saying—"

"Oh, hell," she said. "Never mind." She felt that bitter mix of love and betrayal she always felt when she was around Richie. How could she love him any more . . . and have him appreciate her feelings any less?

She walked out of the room, went into the living room, and turned on the thirty-five-inch Zenith TV console.

She channel-surfed, looking for any mention of Richie and his escape.

"Anything on the tube?" he asked from the kitchen.

"Nothing I can find," she said, snapping the set off.

She went back to the kitchen. "Where'll you go?"

"The old line shack," he said. "It has that root cellar in it."

"That's a neat place," Jimmy said. "I used to play in there till Dink Farnsworth told me there was monsters down there."

"That sounds like something Dink would say," Susan said. People were always trying to get poor Jimmy riled up. It was a nasty little game they played to make themselves feel superior. Jimmy was the one who should feel superior. He had a good heart and a pure mind.

"Not many people know about the root cellar," Richie said, sounding as if he was trying to convince not only Susan but himself as well.

"Then what do you do?"

"Wait till night. Then sneak out."

"To where?"

"Chicago, probably, or maybe head down the Mississippi."

"They'll catch you, Richie."

He flared again. "What the hell am I supposed to do? Go to prison for a murder I didn't commit?"

"You could always turn yourself in."

"Oh, yeah, I'd get a real fair shake in this town, wouldn't I?"

He sat at the table, head down. He looked confused and

weary and scared. She felt desperate for him. But she needed to keep a cool head. One of them had to, anyway.

"How about if I talk to Sam?" she said.

"About what?"

"About you giving yourself up and him keeping the investigation open."

"Fuller thinks he's got his killer. If Fuller's happy, the rest of the town'll be happy, too."

"I could always talk to Helen Cummings," Susan said. "She's got a lot of clout. If she said there was going to be a thorough investigation, there'd be one."

She could see that he was at least thinking this over.

"This posse and all, Richie, there'll be some people who'll use any excuse to shoot you. Not to mention that reward Fuller put up."

Again, she sensed him weakening.

"You'd be safe, Richie. I don't like to think of you all alone and running."

She more than sensed it—she saw it in his eyes as he raised his head and looked at her.

He wanted her to call the law and say come get him.

When you had men with guns and hunting dogs after you, running was a scary proposition.

Then she saw him pull back, give in to his paranoia about how everybody meant him harm.

"They wouldn't do jack shit about the investigation," he said, "and you know it."

"You going to run?"

"You shouldn't run, Richie," Jimmy said. "You could get hurt bad if you do."

"You going to run?" Susan said again.

He sighed. "I don't have a hell of a lot of choice, do I?" Then, "And I'm going to need that old .45 of yours, Susan."

"Oh, no," she said, picturing Richie firing blindly in a moment of panic. "Oh, no. No way."

Richie got up so angrily that his chair flew into the wall behind him. "You gonna send me out there without a gun, Susan? You really gonna pull that shit on me?"

Susan put her head down and sighed deeply. This was all so crazy—so crazy.

4

Helen was thinking that all the money her brother paid L.L. Bean every month was finally being put to some good use.

The bridge spanned the river at its widest point locally. Right now, three TV mobile vans were parked single file along the bridge.

Senator David Cummings, looking handsome as all hell in his L.L. Bean hunting clothes, stood on the bridge with a Remington shotgun cradled in his arms and looked pensively at the camera. Helen, who had insisted, stood next to him. She also wore fashionable hunting clothes.

David was saying, "That's the nice thing about a community like ours, everybody pulls together."

"So you're joining in on the manhunt?"

"Absolutely," David said. "The Fullers are important members of this community. And darned nice folks, I might add. So we're determined to bring the killer to justice any way we need to."

"Does that mean violence?"

"We hope not," Helen interjected. "But if it does—"

"I can't tell you how much we all loved little Amy in this community," David said.

Looking good, Helen thought. Until he screwed up the girl's name. Looking forceful. Looking determined. She always judged her brother's performances. Like a critic.

Oh, yes, the voters were going to mourn him . . . and feel that only one person could ever replace him . . . and that person was . . .

"Miss Cummings, do you know how to shoot that pistol you're carrying?"

"I certainly do."

"You think you could actually shoot a man?"

She made a face. "You have to look at what he did. Took the life of a beautiful young girl whom this community really cared for. I guess if I kept that in my mind . . . I think I could shoot."

Careful. Had to be careful. Had to remain the staid, handsome older woman.

Didn't want to look like one of those harsh bull dykes the NRA was always pushing in front of the cameras.

The three reporters kept spewing out questions.

"And you, Senator? Could you shoot somebody if it came down to it?"

Senator David Cummings had learned how to shrug from watching Ronald Reagan shrug. Reagan was the past master of the shrug. No one had ever shrugged so eloquently.

Shucks, the shrug said, I'm just your average guy without any big, philosophical questions running around my head.

I just do what all decent folks would, I guess.

"If it came down to protecting my community," David said, shrugging at just the right moment, "I guess I could kill a man if I had to."

"This Richie McGuire's been in a lot of trouble in the past, hasn't he?"

"I'm afraid he has been," David said. "Some people don't think he ever got over the disappointment of seeing his football career go down the tubes."

"His football career?"

"He was going to play for the Bears," Davis said. "Then he wrapped his car around a tree and—"

"Was he drunk?"

"Well, that's what he was charged with," Helen said. "Operating a motor vehicle while intoxicated."

One of the camera operators suddenly went Hollywood.

Got down in this crouch and started circling the Senator and his sister.

Shot steep angles up, then climbed on top of the bridge ledge and shot them steep angles down.

Dramatic.

Helen was worried about her right side.

Her right side had never been for shit.

How could her left side be so beautiful and her right side be so . . . unbeautiful?

"You have confidence in Chief Hadley?"

"Perfect confidence," David said. "He's an old and trusted friend."

"He certainly is," Helen said.

David looked up. One of the state patrol helicopters had suddenly materialized.

The cameraman who'd just gone Hollywood swung his lens up to the sky.

This was all dramatic as hell.

Now if somebody would only get killed.

Talk about your powerful opening shots.

You're sitting at home eating dinner in front of the TV set and what do you see? You see some local bastard—somebody you actually saw at the supermarket and the DX station all the time—you see him get gunned down by the posse.

Man, talk about drama.

It was the kind of thing both the reporter and the camera operator would put on their respective sample video reels when they started looking for work again . . . better work . . . bigger cities. Murders were what could get you there. Sex, murder, tragedy, and the fall of the powerful. Every night before they went to bed, TV consultants got down on their knees and prayed to the dark god of ratings that they would soon be blessed with a story that would include *all* of these elements.

"Senator Cummings, you helped Amy McGuire—Richie's sister—through law school, didn't you?"

Helen spoke. "My brother has helped dozens of people through law school. Amy was just one of them."

"Then you know Richie pretty well?"

Helen again: "In a small town like this one, everybody knows everybody."

"You really think you could kill him if you had to, Senator?"

"I just hope he gives himself up," David said. "Before that becomes necessary." But as he was speaking, he was wondering if his cousin Steve Arnette had caught up with Richie yet.

Richie wouldn't be alive very long after Steve found him. Steve hated Richie.

Helen glanced at her watch. "Well, we want to catch up with Chief Hadley now."

"You're in contact with him?"

Helen held up her walkie-talkie. "Constant contact." She looked at David. "Now if you'll excuse us—"

"Just a little bit more of both of you with your guns."

"Like this?" David said, bringing the rifle up to his shoulder, aiming it.

"Perfect."

David pretended to be squeezing off some shots.

"Now you, Miss Cummings."

Helen didn't hoke it up as much as David had. She just brought her shotgun up and held it at an angle to her face.

She didn't point it at anybody.

"Fantastic."

David and Helen thanked the reporters and camera crews—

you always wanted to be nice to them because then they'd be nice to you.

They were just piling into their Range Rover when they heard the shots.

One, two, three of them, the echoes floating up the wide river between the lovely, fiery autumnal trees that lined the banks.

"God," David said, "you think Steve may have got him already?"

"I sure as hell hope so," Helen said, and gave the ignition key a savage twist.

FIFTEEN

1

Amy was sort of ashamed of herself.

She wasn't much of a churchgoer—in fact, she rarely went more than two or three times a year—but now she was praying silently and fervently that Richie would be all right. That he wouldn't be hurt . . . and that he wouldn't hurt anybody. Fear had always made Richie do terrible things that he later regretted.

"You all right?" Sam said.

She was a little embarrassed to say what she'd been doing. Oddly enough, admitting that you prayed was a pretty intimate thing. . . . In a weird way, it was easier to talk about sex than religion.

But that was stupid. She believed in God, so why not simply say it?

"I was praying," she said.

He looked at her. "I do a little bit of that myself from time to time."

"You do?"

"Sure. A lot of people, they get to be older, they don't believe in it anymore. But I guess I still do."

"I'm just so worried about him, Sam."

He nodded. "We need to find him, no doubt about it. You know what I've been thinking?"

"What?"

"Susan Kelly. Do you think she'd help him?"

She thought a moment. She knew that Susan had tried several times to get on with her life. The way Susan had talked the last few years, she wanted to get Richie out of her life forever.

"I'm not sure," Amy said. "She's pretty bitter."

"She may be bitter but I think she's still in love with him."

"I feel so damned sorry for her," Amy said. "Richie should've married her a long time ago. She was one of the few decent women he ever went with. She didn't care about him being a football star or a cool guy or any of that stuff."

"We're not very far away. Why don't we give her place a try?"

Amy sighed. "I guess we might as well."

2

What Susan ended up doing was preparing a knapsack full of basics for him. The food consisted of two meat-loaf sandwiches, three apples, five granola bars, a dozen Oreos, and a dozen sliced carrots. She also put in Band-Aids, iodine, and a hunting cap with ears. The temperatures would be sliding down into the forties tonight.

The last thing she put in was a box of bullets for the gun she'd given him.

All the time she was filling the knapsack, Richie stood by the window, staring out at the farm fields.

It was pretty obvious what he was trying to do: remember last night . . .

Jimmy sat in the living room looking through magazines. Earlier, Richie had snapped at him. Jimmy could be tiresome sometimes. No fault of his own. She had suggested looking through magazines in the living room.

Jimmy hadn't wanted to go. Richie was his hero. Always had been. He clearly felt sad that he'd irritated him. But he'd trudged off to the living room anyway. . . .

"Damn!" Richie said, and made a fist.

"You remember something?"

He turned and looked at her. He seemed weary and forlorn. She wondered how he was ever going to summon the energy to stay ahead of the posse.

"Almost," he said. "I started to focus in on something and then it just"—he shook his head—"it just faded away."

"You'll remember, Richie."

"Yeah, but will I remember before they start shooting?"

"You could always turn yourself in."

His anger came quickly. "We've been down that road, haven't we?"

She cinched up the knapsack, carried it over to him.

He took it and said, "I'm sorry I snapped at you."

"Never mind that right now."

He reached over and took her hand. "Man, I've treated you like shit my whole life, haven't I?"

She smiled sadly. "Pretty much. But it's not all your fault. I could've found somebody else anytime I wanted to."

"You really thought I was worth the wait?"

She laughed. "Oh, sometimes I suppose I had a few doubts. Like the night you stood me up for my twenty-third birthday dinner. I was real pissed that night, Richie. In fact, it was a good thing you *didn't* show up because I probably would've tried to shoot you or something."

"God, I'm sorry. I really am."

She slipped her hand out of his. "Like I said, Richie. I'm just as responsible for it as you are."

"After this is all over, if I can stay out of prison, I—"

She shook her head. "No promises, Richie. This isn't the time. You're likely to say something pretty stupid right now—and I'll probably be stupid enough to believe you."

"A guy can change, can't he?"

"Let's see what you're like when Sam finds the real killer."

"You mean if I ask you to marry me, you'll say no?"

She touched her fingers tenderly to his face. "You're a romantic son of a bitch, I have to give you that. You've got the whole county after you and you still have time to think about marriage."

Then, "Why don't you go in and see Jimmy?"

"Yeah," he said. "I probably should do that, shouldn't I?"

He had almost made it out of the kitchen when he suddenly turned back and walked over to her.

She couldn't ever remember being kissed like this before. At this moment, he needed her so desperately she was a bit overwhelmed. She'd always dreamed of Richie in her arms this way. But now that the moment was here . . . a part of her wanted to tear his clothes off and make love right here on the kitchen table . . . and another part wanted to run away. She'd never felt this *needed* by anybody before, and it was a bit spooky. . . .

"Wow," she said.

" 'Wow' good or 'Wow' bad?"

" 'Wow' I'm not sure. I mean, you were pretty overwhelming just then."

"Good. And that's just a preview of coming attractions, too. We'll save the good stuff for later."

He grinned and he was a reckless boy again for just a millisecond—no men, no dogs, no helicopters chasing him—and she remembered him then in high school, the golden boy in the convertible, with the movie-star looks and the odd moments of tenderness . . . mixed in with the odd moments of anger and violence.

"You'd better go see Jimmy," she said. "He was pretty hurt."

"Ah, shit," Richie said. "I hurt people's feelings even when I don't mean to."

He walked into the living room.

"Hey, Jimmy."

Jimmy looked up from his magazine. "Hi, Richie. You feelin' better?"

"It's not me I'm worried about, tiger. It's you."

"How come you're worried about me?" Jimmy said.

The innocence of the question made Richie feel even worse. He was always lashing out at people who cared about him.

He sat down on the couch next to Jimmy.

"You watch over Susan for me, will you do that?"

"You goin' someplace, Richie?"

"Yeah. Just for a few days."

"Where you goin'?"

Better not let Jimmy know where he was headed. Jimmy might accidentally let something slip.

"Don't worry," he said. "I won't be gone long."

"It's because of Chief Hadley, isn't it? And all those men?"

Richie sighed. "Yeah, yeah, it is, Jimmy."

"They want to hurt you, don't they, Richie?"

"Some of them do, anyway."

"That Steve Arnette . . . he really hates you. I think he hates me, too. Just the way he looks at me sometimes."

"Don't worry about Steve Arnette, Jimmy. He won't hurt either one of us."

Sometimes Jimmy got afraid of people, and you had to reassure him that things were going to be all right.

"He won't hurt us, Richie? He really won't?"

"He isn't as tough as he thinks he is."

"He's pretty mean sometimes. He took my bike away once and wouldn't give it back to me for three days."

"He ever tries anything like that again, you tell me, all right?"

"You think you can whip him, Richie?"

"I know I can." Then: "Listen, Jimmy, I'm sorry I snapped at you in the kitchen there."

"Oh, that's all right, Richie. You were just nervous and stuff."

"No, it isn't all right. You're one of my best friends, Jimmy."

Jimmy's eyes instantly reflected the pride he felt. How could I ever treat this poor guy like shit? Richie thought.

Richie put out his hand.

"You want to shake hands, Richie?"

Richie laughed. "Yeah."

Jimmy said, "How come?"

"Oh, it's just something people do when they make a pact."

"What's a pact?"

"You know, when they agree to do something."

"Oh. Are we making a pact?"

"We sure are. We're making a pact that we're going to be good friends forever."

Jimmy smiled. And put his hand in Richie's.

Susan came to the door of the living room. "There's a lot of dust about a mile down the road, Richie. Could be somebody coming here."

Richie tensed.

A few times the past half hour, he'd been able to forget the posse. Now the reality was back.

He felt sick and scared.

As he got up from the couch, he said, "Jimmy, you didn't happen to see anything at my cabin when you left the bread off, did you?"

By now, Susan was standing next to Richie. They both saw the strange expression on Jimmy's face. He wasn't good at concealing things.

He said, "Huh-uh, Richie. I didn't see anything. Honest, I didn't."

Richie looked at Susan again. *Was* Jimmy holding something back? He sure did look and sound strange all of a sudden.

"You'd better go," Susan said.

He knew she was right.

He wanted to stay here and find out what the hell was making Jimmy act so oddly. . . .

But he had to run. Run.

"I'm glad we shook hands," Jimmy said.

"Yeah," Richie said. "So'm I, Jimmy."

The slightly dazed expression was back in Richie's eyes and voice.

Now there was only one thing he could concentrate on: escape.

In the kitchen, she helped him heft the knapsack straps over his shoulders.

Then she handed him the gun.

"I love you, Richie," she said.

This time, their embrace was not the wildly passionate kiss of a few minutes earlier.

This was a kiss that spoke of care and tenderness, of solace and succor, the kind of cherishing kiss a man gives a woman on the night of their twentieth wedding anniversary, the kiss of a man who loves a woman not just sexually but mentally and spiritually as well.

She was so moved, her eyes filled with tears. A lone silver tear ran down her cheek.

Richie went to the door and then lit out, running across the barnyard to the woods behind the farmhouse.

He reached the woods a few minutes later and then immediately climbed an oak tree on the edge of the forest.

He wanted to see if the vehicle on the road turned into Susan's.

It did.

The police car swung into the driveway and stopped.

A familiar figure emerged from the car and walked up to the back door of the farmhouse.

Richie shuddered.

What the hell was Steve Arnette doing here?

And given Jimmy's fear of Arnette, would he blurt out that Richie had just been here and fled into the woods?

Richie couldn't wait around to find out.

He scrambled down the tree and set off through the deep forest.

3

Arnette pulled his cruiser right up to the back door. When he climbed out, he was carrying a Remington shotgun.

Susan was waiting for him on the back stairs, Jimmy standing next to her.

"I take it you heard about what happened to Richie?" Arnette said. He couldn't quite keep the pleasure out of his voice.

"I heard."

"There's only one person in this town who'd hide him," Arnette said.

"He isn't here, Steve."

"Has he been here?"

"No."

He looked at Jimmy. "Has he been here, Jimmy?"

Jimmy looked at Susan for a long moment, then at Arnette. "Huh-uh, he hasn't been here."

"You've got him trained pretty well," Arnette said to Susan.

"He's telling the truth," she said. "Richie hasn't been here."

"There's a reward for him, Susan. Somebody's probably going to pick him off."

"And you wouldn't, I suppose?"

Arnette stared down at the shotgun dangling from his fingers. He smelled of heat and cigarettes.

"Maybe we could make a deal," he said.

"What kind of deal?"

"You tell me where I can find him. I promise to bring him in safely."

"He didn't kill that girl, Steve."

"Maybe he didn't. But if he didn't, running sure as hell's not going to do him any good."

"He's scared. You know how paranoid Richie gets."

"He's real scared," Jimmy said. "I ain't ever seen him this scared."

"You're worried about him, huh, Jimmy?"

Then, "He's got good reason to *be* scared, Susan, don't you see that?" Arnette said. "Bunch of drunk guys out walking the fields—first sight they see of him, they'll kill him."

"And you won't?"

"Not if we make a deal."

Ever since he mentioned his "deal," Susan kept thinking that maybe Steve had changed. Maybe he'd forgotten his bitterness toward Richie and herself. But then she looked at how he stood there—even when he was just talking, there was an animal tension in his body . . . an animal tension that told her Steve hadn't changed at all. His first opportunity to kill Richie . . . he'd take it.

A breeze came off the cornfields to the west. For a moment, Susan closed her eyes and wished herself away from this. She wanted to be a girl again, riding her favorite roan up in the hills.

"You'd better go," she said. "You and that gun of yours've got a lot of work to do today."

When he looked at her just then, the angle of his head, she saw the sorrow he felt, and knew that even now he was still in love with her. She wanted to touch him, then, nothing romantic or sexual, just touch him because, of course, she knew just how he felt. . . . It was the same way she'd felt about Richie all these years.

But then the sorrow was gone and his old anger was back again.

"You want to help Richie, Jimmy?" he said.

Then, "You hear me, Jimmy?"

"Richie's my friend," Jimmy said.

"I know he's your friend. That's why you should want to help him."

"Susan'd get mad if I said anything."

"I told you to leave him alone," Susan said.

Arnette shook his head. "Listen, Susan, I'm not joking. I'd promise you I wouldn't hurt him."

"You'd kill him first chance you got, and you know it."

"Even if I gave you my word?"

"Your word," she said. "Your word. You beat him up the night you arrested him and everybody knows it. So now you're going to bring him in safely?"

"You'd be a lot better taking your chances with me than some of those other guys, I'll tell you that."

"Get out of here, Steve. I don't want to see your face anymore."

The sorrow was once again in his eyes and she felt a moment of guilt for putting it there. When you loved somebody the crazy way she loved Richie—or Steve loved her—it was hard to act sane around them. Steve was trying to win her over, was all. He might even believe what he was saying—at least for now—but the moment he set eyes on Richie . . .

Softly, she said, "C'mon, Steve. This isn't easy for either of us. Why don't you just go?"

He ran a hand through his hair. "I don't know what the hell you see in him, Susan. He's never done one damned thing for you."

"Just go, Steve, all right?"

He studied her awhile, as if trying to read her innermost thoughts, and then, with his sorrow and his rifle, he turned around and walked back to his car.

After Arnette started his engine, Susan said, "Come in the house, Jimmy. I want to talk to you."

Right away, she could see he was scared.

"Talk to me about what, Susan?"

"You acted very odd when Richie asked you about last night. I got the feeling there's something you weren't telling us. And I want to know the truth."

"I'm scared, Susan."

"I know you're scared."

"They'll hurt me again."

"Who'll hurt you again?"

"The people. The bad people."

She was angry, thinking that Jimmy might be withholding information from her.

But then she saw that Jimmy was crying, and she slid her arm around his shoulder and hugged him to her.

"Nobody'll hurt you, Jimmy. I promise."

"I'm scared of them, Susan. I'm real scared."

And indeed he was. He was trembling and clinging to her like a child.

"Come on inside, Jimmy. And I'll make you some hot chocolate."

She had said exactly the right thing. His mind flitted instantly from his fear to the hot chocolate.

"Can I have white bread with lots of butter on it, too?"

She smiled. "I guess I could arrange that."

"Arnette's a bad man, isn't he, Susan?"

"Yeah," she said, wondering where Arnette would go now. "Yeah, he is."

4

What happened was, one of the more eager searchers saw something moving in a stand of trees and blasted away at it, leaving a sweet little doe with a considerable amount of buckshot in her sweet little bottom. Fortunately, most of the men there were farmers—responsible men who knew and loved all God's creatures—and so two of them bundled up the doe and drove her ass over appetite to the vet's, which was about six miles away.

Right after hearing the gunshots, David and Helen got into Helen's Land Rover and drove to the approximate vicinity of the echoes that caromed around the valley.

Seeing a group of men standing on a hill, they raced up there, visions of a dead Richie lying on the ground filling their heads. . . .

Then they saw the doe. Saw all the blood. And heard all the terrible, sickening, frantic noises made by the soft-eyed creature . . .

*   *   *

They joined up with some of the merchants who were out here now in the posse.

They swung west, along cornfields that ran right up to tall red clay hills.

The men were distracted by their presence, of course. They had a lot of questions about how things were going in Washington, D.C. And what better time to ask those questions than now, when they were isolated on posse duty?

When they came to a road, Helen saw a Channel 3 station wagon, and a plump woman in too-tight jeans videotaping the valley below, where a few dozen men were still searching the cornfields. The woman swung her camera up to the sky a couple of times to catch some crows arcing down the air currents.

When the camerawoman looked in her direction, Helen waved. At first, the woman didn't seem to know who she was . . . and waved back . . . but without much interest or enthusiasm.

But then when David came along and stood next to his sister . . . the camerawoman trotted over right away.

Helen said, "Have you heard anything new?"

The woman shook her head. "Afraid not. Nobody's spotted him."

Then, "You think I could get some shots of you two walking past me up this hill—you know, like you might have seen something up there and were suddenly hurrying. Be pretty dramatic with your rifles and everything."

"Shotguns," Helen said.

"Oh, yeah, right, shotguns."

Helen almost said something snide: You'd think a woman as butch as you would know the difference between a rifle and a shotgun.

Helen hated butch women. She always felt them watching her, probing her.

But she needed to be cooperative.

She had instructed David's local office to make sure that they got on all *three* stations when a story was breaking.

And God help the office person who didn't *get* them on all three.

"We'll be happy to," David said.

"You think he'll do it?" he said as they jogged past the camera.

On screen, this would look like they were just having a nice, normal conversation.

The camera wasn't rigged up for sound.

"Think who'll do what?"

She knew what he was talking about but she never liked to make things easy for him. He'd had way too many things easy for him already.

"Think Steven Arnette will shoot Richie?"

"Of course he will."

"You said he seemed a little reluctant."

"He needed to think about it a little is all. That's a lot of money I offered him."

They trotted on, winded by now, both of them, passing a stand of fir pines that smelled sweet on the autumn air.

"You know what?" he said.

"What?"

"I think we've jogged far enough. I'm getting winded." Then, a note of panic in his voice. "You think that means anything?"

"Does what mean anything?"

But of course, she again knew what he was talking about.

"You know, is it a *sign* of anything? A symptom?"

"Oh, God."

"What?"

"You're worrying about your doctor's appointment tomorrow again, aren't you?"

They were walking back down the hill, toward the camerawoman.

"I guess I kind of am."

"I suppose it could be," she said.

"Could be *a sign of something?*"

"Yes, but they're good doctors—even if there is a little
something there, they can take care of it."

"A little something," he muttered, sounding absolutely terrified. "A little something. Oh my God."

He didn't see his sister smile.

She was very good at keeping things from him. And always
had been.

5

"God, Jimmy," Susan said. "You should've told me this this
morning."

Jimmy had a chocolate-milk mustache. His lips were slick
from all the butter she'd slathered on his toast.

"I was scared."

She wanted to be angry with him but couldn't be. Several
years earlier, Jimmy had gone through a period of depression.
Not even drugs seemed to help him all that much. Even with
his medication, Jimmy could still get in trouble from time to
time.

Helen had known exactly what threat to use with Jimmy.
Locking him away again.

Susan couldn't blame Jimmy for not telling her.

And even though he *had* told her, she knew that this didn't
necessarily mean that the authorities would believe him. Jimmy
had his flights of fancy. He had told people about trips to Mars
he'd taken. He had told people that he had been invited to appear on the Grand Ole Opry—after watching the Opry faith-

fully for years. And he had told people that President Clinton called him sometimes and said hello.

Now he was saying that he had seen Senator Cummings and his sister dump Darcy's body behind Richie's cottage last night. But Jimmy had started to hyperventilate a little—something he never did when telling one of his "stories." Jimmy was telling the truth.

Who else would believe him?

"Jimmy."

"Uh-huh."

"I want you to think carefully now."

"All right."

"You know how you make up stories sometimes."

"Uh-huh."

"Are you making this one up?"

"Huh-uh."

"Think hard, Jimmy."

He closed his eyes to show her how hard he was thinking.

"Are you sure you didn't dream this?"

"Huh-uh. I know I didn't."

"How do you know?"

" 'Cause I found this when I was up on the hill behind Richie's last night."

He dug in his pocket and came up with a brass button.

"What is it?"

"Miss Cummings' button. From her coat. Last night."

Susan held the button between finger and thumb.

"This should be helpful, Jimmy. Thank you." She reached across the table and touched his hand. "Now I need you to think real hard."

"All right."

"Is there anything else you need to tell me?"

"I don't think so."

She saw that evasive look in his eyes.

"Are you hiding something, Jimmy?"

"Hiding something?"

He had begun to lick his lips nervously, and look around the kitchen, as if for an escape route.

"Is there something else you should tell me?"

Just then, she heard a vehicle in her driveway.

She got up and walked to the window.

Amy and Sam were just now pulling in.

She turned away from the window just as Jimmy bolted from the table and fled to the back door.

"Jimmy! Stop!"

But Jimmy didn't even slow down. "They'll put me in that hospital again!" he shouted over his shoulder.

"Jimmy!" she shouted again.

But he was out the door before she could reach him.

She didn't bother to chase him. He probably wouldn't go far. Not with Amy here. He always wanted to see Amy.

The poor guy, Susan thought as she walked out to greet Amy and Sam.

That's why he ran. . . .

Then Amy and Sam were coming up the walk. . . .

6

Just as she was leaving Sam's car, Amy saw Jimmy dash from the farmhouse and run between some of the outbuildings.

"Where was Jimmy off to?" Amy said.

Susan looked excited. "I think I can prove that Richie didn't kill that girl."

Amy had been so worried about Richie that she couldn't quite believe what she'd heard.

"What're you talking about?" Amy said, obviously stunned by the words.

Susan grabbed her arm. "Jimmy said he saw Senator Cummings and his sister put the body behind Richie's last night."

"Senator Cummings?" Amy said. "God, are you serious?"

"He tell you this just now?" Sam said.

"Yes."

"Why was he running away?"

"I'm not sure. He just seemed spooked suddenly. I guess I scared him off a little. I asked him if there was anything else he wanted to tell me—and he looked . . . guilty or something."

"You know Jimmy and his stories," Sam said. "We'd need more than his word." Then, "You know, though, that's funny. I did see Senator Cummings and Helen last night. I had to help push their car out of the mud."

"He said that Helen Cummings dropped this on the hill last night."

She handed him the button.

"Then Richie's going to be free!" Amy said, feeling some hope again.

For as much as Jimmy liked to talk out his fantasies, everybody in town knew that because of the way he moved around the town, Jimmy picked up all sorts of stray information.

"I don't know how else he would've come by a button belonging to Helen Cummings, do you?" Susan said to Sam.

"No, I can't either, actually. But we're not sure it *is* her button."

"I'm going to go see if I can find him," Amy said.

She spent the next ten minutes walking between the outbuildings. Looking in the new barn. Looking in the old barn. Seeing if he might be hiding in the silo.

Not a sign of him.

Then, when she was about to give up, she walked past an

old storage shed . . . and heard something moving around inside.

She paused outside the door . . . listened.

Something moving around in there. . . .

Only one way to find out.

She reached out and gripped the door handle.

She could envision Jimmy crouched down in there, just hoping she'd go away.

All she had to do was open the door and—

She jerked the door open, flung it backward, and then peered inside to the dusty darkness.

She heard a growl and saw a flash of white-and-brown fur . . .

. . . and then she was very painfully knocked to the ground.

Susan's dog Andy probably weighed ninety pounds. Or more, given the way Susan felt as she picked herself up from the ground.

She dusted herself off and peered once again into the darkness of the shed.

Empty.

She started walking around the outbuildings again, calling his name.

Maybe she'd missed him the first time she'd checked out the farmyard here.

Maybe the barns would be worth another walk through. . . .

And that was when she saw him.

Her vantage point was between two outbuildings where she saw Jimmy out in the field. . . .

He'd been crouching out there, hiding. . . .

And now he was up and running away from the farm . . . toward the woods.

Why is he running? she wondered.

He only fled like this when he was scared.

What had scared him so badly?

*   *   *

When she got back to Sam and Susan, Sam said, "The Chief is around here somewhere. I've got a call in to him. I asked him to stop out here."

They were still in the yard by the back porch.

"You think he'll believe Jimmy?" Amy said.

"I hope so."

"I knew he couldn't have done it," Amy said. "I knew it."

"I just can't figure out what Senator Cummings would have to do with any of this," Susan said.

"Yeah," Sam said. "Hard to believe a politician would be involved in something illegal."

Then he smiled.

"God, for a minute there, I thought you were serious."

"Yeah, my high regard for politicians and all," Sam said. Then he told them about helping the Senator and his sister extricate themselves from the mud last night.

"Maybe the body was in the trunk," Amy said.

"That's what I was thinking," Sam said.

"C'mon," Susan said to Amy. "I've got some fresh coffee made. Might as well relax while we can."

7

It was kind of strange . . . but as he ran . . . instead of thinking of all the people pursuing him . . . Richie looked around him and thought of all the things he *should* have done with his life. . . .

He should have spent time in the woods . . . like this. . . .

He should have gone fishing and hunting, the way he had when he was a boy. . . .

He should have bought himself an acreage and lived on what he grew in the good Iowa soil. . . .

The harder and longer he ran, the more his life came into focus . . . and the less appealing it became.

Drink and drugs and women he didn't care about . . . with Susan there all the time . . . waiting for him. With his sister Amy urging him to finally grow up and be a man and take responsibility for himself.

He looked up and saw a hawk soar skyward . . . and almost cried at the thought of that kind of freedom . . . to rise above . . . to transcend the earth that way. . . .

Maybe he could still pull it off. . . .

If he could just prove that he didn't kill Darcy . . .

God, getting involved with Darcy had been so stupid. . . .

He ran on, a lone and desperate man . . . through woods and clearings and then woods again . . . intoxicated with the smells of the forest . . . of mold . . . of damp, rich earth . . . of leaves and foliage . . . of pine and mint. . . .

If he ever managed to extricate himself from this murder charge . . . he was going to live a very different life.

A very different one.

The old line shack.

That's where Richie had said he was going.

So that's where Jimmy was going, too.

He wanted to see Richie before Susan did. Because when Susan told Richie that Jimmy had kept a secret from them . . . Richie was going to be awfully mad.

And then maybe he'd never speak to Jimmy again.

And the one friend whom Jimmy treasured more than all the others in the world . . . would be his friend no more.

He ran on . . . through woods and clearings . . . clearings and then woods again . . . running . . . looking for his very best friend in all the world.

❖   ❖   ❖

Steve Arnette had guessed correctly. After leaving Susan's place, he'd parked his car in a copse of trees and then walked back to the field that ran right up to the farmhouse.

He crouched there, with his rifle, for the next twenty-one minutes.

A couple of times, he almost gave up. Maybe Jimmy didn't know where Richie was, after all.

Arnette still wasn't sure of his plans.

The reward money was damn tempting . . . but the biggest share of it could only be won if he actually *killed* Richie.

The funny thing was, as much as he hated the guy, and as much as he enjoyed stomping the hell out of him that drunken night not long ago . . . actually killing Richie was another matter.

And then he realized why.

Because Susan would never forgive him.

He'd have all this money to buy a divorce with . . . and it wouldn't matter.

Because Susan wouldn't have anything to do with him.

Jimmy appeared.

Just like that. No warning whatsoever.

Came flying out the back door of the farmhouse. Raced to the outbuildings and hid behind the grain bin . . . then hid behind the old barn . . . then hid inside the new barn.

All Arnette could do was hold his position . . . and wait . . . trying to figure out what the crazy bastard was doing.

Susan called out for him. But Jimmy didn't answer.

Sam and Amy came. Amy called out for him, too, even went looking for him.

By now, Jimmy was over in the bushes on the edge of the alfalfa.

Amy couldn't see him.

And then Jimmy was up. And running.

Arnette couldn't afford to run straight across the field to catch up with Jimmy. If he did, Amy would see him.

He had to run wide, into the woods themselves, and then run between the pines to find out where Jimmy was in all the trees.

Luckily, Jimmy wasn't what you'd call a skilled tracker.

For one thing, he made these really eerie humming sounds as he ran. And for another, he was wearing an orange shirt, which wasn't exactly a great trick for hiding.

Arnette lay back, played it easy.

All he had to do was keep at a half-ass run and he'd keep Jimmy in sight.

Arnette ran on . . . through woods and clearings . . . and woods again.

Ran on. With his rifle.

Ran on. Right to Richie.

SIXTEEN

1

Amy watched Chief Hadley's car pull into the driveway and stop. Hadley usually kept his car clean and shiny. Traveling these gravel roads today made that impossible.

He got out of the car and walked up to the backyard, where Amy stood with Sam and Susan.

"How you doing, Amy?" he said.

He had his enemies in town—he was way too political a being to ever be a truly competent lawman—but he was decent to most people. And he'd always been more than decent to Amy. Hard as she sometimes tried, she couldn't dislike him.

Before Hadley could even speak, he had to deal with Susan's frisky collie. The dog mounted Hadley's left leg, slurped his hand, and then aimed its nose directly at Hadley's crotch. You could see the khaki-clad lawman wince.

"Git, git," Susan said, pushing the dog away.

"Sam's got something you should listen to, Chief," Amy said.

"You sounded pretty damned mysterious on the cell phone," Hadley said to Sam.

Sam held up the button and handed it over to Hadley.

"This supposed to mean something to me?"

"Jimmy found it last night," Sam said. "By Darcy's body."

"What the hell was Jimmy doing with Darcy's body?"

"He was going to Richie's cottage," Amy said. "I'd made some homemade bread and asked him to give it to Richie."

"That's when he found this," Sam said.

"It's a button." Hadley turned the thing over and over in his fingers, assessing it. "Just a button."

"Not 'just' a button, Chief," Sam said. "It belongs to Helen Cummings."

At the mention of Helen's name, Hadley looked up sharply.

"What the hell's that supposed to mean?" he said.

"It means that Jimmy saw something last night," Amy said.

"Oh? And what was that?"

Chief Hadley's jaw muscles were already bunched. His eyes were narrowed, angry.

Amy said, "He saw Senator Cummings and Helen putting the body on the hill behind Richie's."

Hadley surprised her. Though he looked as if he were about to start shouting at her, he paused a moment and then broke into a grin. He looked fifteen years younger, wearing that grin.

"Well, I saw something last night, too, Amy. And you know what it was?"

He didn't wait for her to acknowledge his question.

"I saw the pope put a body behind *my* house."

"This is true, Chief," Amy said.

He scowled. "Is it?"

"Yes."

"Because Jimmy said he saw it?"

She hesitated. "Yes."

"Jimmy ever tell you about the time he was watching TV and one of the *Sesame Street* characters came right out of the screen and sat on the couch with him?"

"No, but—"

"Or about the time he was riding his bike in the woods and he saw Santa Claus sitting up on a tree limb playing cards with a squirrel?"

Sam said, "Chief, we know how Jimmy can get sometimes. He likes to fabricate things. But this is different."

"How is this different?"

"The button," Amy said. "You've got the button."

"What the hell good is a button, Amy?" Hadley said. "He could've gotten this button anywhere."

"Why don't you show it to Helen?" Amy said. "See if she recognizes it."

Hadley's jaw muscles were bunched again.

He glanced around the farm, settling his eyes on the new John Deere tractor down by the new barn.

Susan said, "I think Amy's right, Chief. I think you should show the button to Helen Cummings."

Hadley looked back to Amy. "You happen to remember how you got through college and law school, Amy?"

"This isn't easy for me, Chief," Amy said.

"You didn't answer my question."

"I got through on a scholarship that Senator Cummings got for me."

She was ten again, and being chastised by the principal.

"You know how many other people in this town got through college on scholarships that Cummings got for them?" Hadley said. "You have any idea how many businesses he's brought to this town?"

"I didn't say he wasn't a great man," Amy said.

"No, you didn't say he wasn't a great man. You just said that he and his sister are murderers."

"Jimmy saw them," Amy said.

"Yes," Susan said. "And not only saw them. She came to his cabin and threatened him."

"Helen Cummings did?"

"Yes, Chief," Susan said. "Helen Cummings did."

Hadley's mouth twisted into a sour expression. "Two of the finest people I've ever known. And you three are trying to get me to believe that they killed a young girl."

"All we're saying is show her the button, Chief," Sam said. "And ask her about it."

"You know what she'd think of me if I asked her about it, Sam? She'd think I was the most ungrateful son of a bitch in the whole state. And you know what? I wouldn't blame her. I wouldn't blame her at all. Whenever anybody in this town needed anything, the Senator and his sister were there. And now we're going to repay them by accusing them of murder because some crazy bastard like Jimmy said he saw them?"

He paused and looked at Sam. "You remember what I told you yesterday? I said never make me choose between you and the Cummingses. You remember that, Sam?"

"I remember."

"Well, that's the position you're putting me in. You're making me choose. And you know who I'm going to choose, Sam?"

"My brother didn't kill that girl," Amy said.

"He did, Amy. Of course he did. I know that's a terrible thing for me to say but it also happens to be the truth. He did kill her, Amy. He was drunk and he was pissed off that she'd followed him into the bar and he got carried away and he killed her. He'll get second-degree . . . maybe even manslaughter . . . but he did kill her. He really did."

He put the gold button on his thumb, then flipped it back to Amy.

"I don't have time for this bullshit," he said. "I need to stop that brother of yours before he kills somebody else." His jaw muscles were once again massive lumps. "Now tell me where he is."

"I don't know where he is."

"How about you, Susan?"

"I don't know, either, Chief."

"You know, Sam, you'd be out of a job if you had anything to do with hiding Richie."

"I'm not hiding him, Chief. And I don't know where he is."

Chief Hadley was just about to speak again when he was interrupted by the sound of a vehicle in the farm driveway.

"I'll be damned," he said.

The Land Rover belonging to Senator Cummings was just now being parked next to Hadley's car.

"You don't say a damned word to them," Hadley said. "You understand me?"

As soon as Helen stepped down from the Land Rover, Amy looked at her jacket, seeing if it had brass buttons.

"Afternoon, folks," David said in his best amiable aw-shucks voice.

Everybody nodded as David and Helen reached them.

"We were just over the hill," Helen said. "We saw you pulling in, so we thought we'd see what was going on."

Helen was speaking only to Hadley. That was a trick of hers, Amy had long ago noted. She always addressed her remarks to the person in charge. Never any of the lessers.

"Any word yet on Richie?" she said.

Hadley shook his head. "Afraid not."

Helen surprised Amy by reaching over and touching her gently on the arm. "I'm sorry about this, dear. We'll help you in any way you want us to."

"That's why we're here," Senator Cummings said. "To help." Once again, he was doing folksy to the max.

Amy watched them and almost smiled. They were damned good, no doubt about that.

Just last night they'd killed a girl. But you'd never know it now.

"I appreciate that," Amy said, almost gagging on her words.

She scanned Helen's coat again. Wrong color, wrong style for buttons like the brass one now in Amy's pocket.

Then she noticed the Land Rover that sat in the driveway. She should look in there, too. A lot of people left jackets in their vehicles.

"I need a drink of water," Amy said. "I'll be right back."

"We're sorry about all this," Helen said again.

"We certainly are," David said.

Amy nodded her thanks and then started walking to the house, moving at an angle that would bring her within inches of the Land Rover.

They started talking again, behind her, about how the search was going.

Amy didn't listen. She knew she would have only a few seconds to look inside the windows of the vehicle. Any more time, and she'd look suspicious.

She reached the front fender and began peering inside as she slowly walked toward the house.

Nothing in the front seat.

Slowly . . . slowly . . .

The backseat was cluttered with a couple of seat cushions with Hawkeye black and gold . . . with a number of paperback political thrillers . . . with a small picnic basket.

But no jacket.

She knew she'd never have the simple good luck to just *find* the jacket. . . .

One last chance.

But as she saw the back cargo area, she saw no jacket there, either . . . just a spare tire, a couple of sun-faded copies of *People,* a gold-and-black Hawkeye football blanket that covered about a third of the storage area, and a cloth carrying bag that read Carry Me to Kenwood Cleaners.

No jacket . . .

She had just given up, just started to walk directly to the farmhouse, where she'd play out the charade of getting a drink of water . . . when she saw the edge of a sleeve peeking out from the mouth of the bag. She hadn't been able to see the sleeve, because of the way the bag was angled, until she reached the rear bumper.

She saw a brass button identical to the one she held in her hand.

Excitement raced through her. She felt she'd just been given a shot of pure adrenaline.

She could barely control herself. She wanted to open the hatch and reach in and grab the bag and then hold the jacket up for inspection.

She looked back to Sam and the others.

Helen was watching her suspiciously.

Amy felt great frustration. This was the perfect moment. . . . Sam was here and so was Chief Hadley.

But how was she ever going to get the jacket out of the back?

2

The line shack dated back to the time of the flappers, when rural areas were finally getting electricity. In those days, the shack was a good, clean place to sleep and eat evenings when you couldn't get back home. The electrical company used the shack for various purposes until the late sixties, when a new power substation was built sixteen miles to the east. Then ownership of the shack changed hands . . . the raccoons and badgers and snakes and occasional wrens and ravens took over . . . and inside the cabin young boys and girls still in the experimental stage struggled with awkward kisses and vastly misunderstood urges . . . and some tried out cigarettes for the first time, and then marijuana . . . and drifters driven here in rain sometimes cowered in the rotting corners overnight . . . one hobo from Ruiz, Oklahoma, being found dead and decomposed by two sixth-grade girls picking mushrooms for a class science project.

The thing was . . . for all the kids that had played in and around the shack for three generations . . . only a few of them knew about the root cellar. The man who'd designed the cabin thought that the root cellar would be a great idea because, just as the pioneers had used such cellars to store produce and vegetables, the linemen could do the same thing . . . until power was strung all the way out here. And after the shack had power, the root cellar could be used for additional storage space.

Steve Arnette knew about the cellar because he and Susan and Richie used to play up here . . . and because one day Susan found the trapdoor and wondered if it led anywhere . . . and then they found the cellar.

He was crouched behind an oak on top of the grassy hill overlooking the shack.

He had caught up with Jimmy ten minutes ago and had simply followed him here.

Jimmy was now at the shack door, calling out Richie's name. The only answer was the sound of some sheep in a nearby pasture.

Jimmy called his name a few more times, then pushed the door open and disappeared inside.

The first thing Arnette thought was: the root cellar. That's where the son of a bitch is hiding.

The searchers would certainly look in the cabin . . . but most of them wouldn't know about the cellar.

They'd be within a few feet of Richie . . . and walk right by him.

Arnette was still thinking about the money.

There were two considerations, the first being that he'd never killed a man before. Much as he got carried away sometimes with prisoners, breaking bones and sending some of them to the hospital, killing a man was another matter entirely. On TV, they made it look so easy. You just pulled the trigger a few times, and your man was dead. Then you just walked away and went on with your life.

But it never worked that way in reality. He knew only two cops who'd killed people. Their lives had been changed completely by the deaths. For one thing, unless it was a clear-cut case of self-defense, you got a reputation as a fast gun. This went on your record and stayed there. And people, particularly your superiors, remembered it for the rest of your career. Cops who killed people got promoted far fewer times. Cops who killed people had much higher incidence of divorce, alcoholism, and even impotence. There were statistics on all this. You didn't kill a man and then just walk away. That was TV bullshit.

The second consideration, of course, was Susan. After seeing her an hour ago at her farm, he'd come to understand clearly that she really didn't want anything to do with him. Whatever love they'd once had was gone. And gone forever.

Which was a kind of freedom.

Now that he wasn't going to be silly enough to worry about Susan anymore . . . Susan who would never be his under any circumstances . . . he felt free to think about himself.

The kind of jack he could get for killing Richie . . .

That kind of jack, he could leave Crystal Falls . . . maybe try Chicago. He'd have money to just take it easy for a while. Of course he'd have to make some kind of financial arrangement with his wife but . . .

He wanted a new life.

He wanted to wake up one morning and feel good about himself and his future.

He'd get tough again, youthful. Maybe get a personal trainer and get toned again. A new car, definitely. And some women. Emphasis on the plural. He wanted to stand at a bar, a few drinks in him, and test himself again, see if he could score with a beautiful woman.

A part of him knew he was being silly . . . this was high school stuff . . . but another part of him didn't give a damn.

In not too many years now, he'd have to start getting those annual checkups his older brothers were always bitching about. Heart. Prostate. Lungs. Digestive tract. Eyes. Reflexes.

. . . all the old-man shit that started about your thirty-fifth birthday.

. . . well, he had years before he reached that particular birthday . . . and he planned to raise a lot of hell in the interim. Someday, he wouldn't even give a damn about Susan anymore . . . wouldn't even think about her. . . . He was still in love with her and maybe always would be . . . but his one fine dream was dead and was never to be . . . so he might as well have himself a good time. . . .

His attention shifted back to the shack.

Ancillary noises. A state patrol chopper chugging through the air to the east. A yipping dog to the west. Hum and thrum of a bluebottle fly nearby.

No sound at all from the shack.

His palm was sweaty from holding the rifle so long. He wiped it off on the grass. Then sighted again.

All Richie had to do was walk out that door. . . .

His finger touched the trigger.

Bam bam.

He could hear the sound of the rifle.

See the bullets striking Richie in the chest, see the blood blooming on his shirt.

See Richie falling over backward . . .

The bluebottle fly buzzed even closer. Arnette tried to swat it away.

He looked back at the shack. He wondered what Jimmy was doing inside. . . .

There was one thing wrong with his fantasy of Richie walking out into the sunlight.

Richie wasn't going to do it. . . .

Why should he? For the time being at least, he was hiding in the root cellar, and there was a damned good chance none of the searchers would remember the cellar until it was too late. . . .

Nightfall, Richie would for sure start moving again. And escape wouldn't be all that difficult. There were trains he could hop, there were big eighteen-wheelers he could sneak aboard.

And then he'd be gone . . . and so would Arnette's money.

No . . . getting Richie would take some risk.

He'd have to get up and sneak down to the shack and then get inside without being heard.

Then he'd have to open the trapdoor fast and poke his rifle down into the darkness and start firing . . . scare the hell out of Richie . . . the surprise of it all forcing Richie into surrender.

And then as Richie came up the steps of the ladder . . .

Bam bam.

Swatting the annoying bluebottle again, Arnette slowly got to his feet, brushing grass and prairie dust from his shirt and trousers.

He was still hidden behind the oak, just in case Richie *wasn't* in the cellar . . . just in case Richie had the itch to do a little killing of his own. . . .

The thing he'd have to do, if he wanted to make it to the cabin without getting picked off, was swing to the north, and walk a ways along the creek bed, then come upon the shack. He could take the creek until he was directly behind the shack. He could then easily belly crawl up to the front door and burst inside.

The thing was . . .

. . . could he really kill Richie . . . even after hating him all these years?

He put the thought from his mind, and gave himself over to action. He did that sometimes when he wasn't sure of his feelings . . . just started *doing* things . . . almost as if his body was suddenly acting independent of his mind . . . just started *doing* things and watched him the way he'd watch some guy up on a movie screen.

He moved quickly through the dusty buffalo grass, down the sunbaked sand hill to the narrow but fast-moving creek.

A milk snake—pale and sickly white—lazed on a sun-drenched rock, paying him no attention whatsoever as he put his feet in the shallow water and broke into a crouch-run, barrel of his rifle gleaming in the sunlight.

3

Amy stood hesitantly at the rear door of Helen Cummings's Land Rover, the brown suede jacket sleeve with the brass buttons angled out of the laundry bag.

Helen must have sensed something wrong because she called to Amy, "Are you all right, dear?"

"Yes, I'm fine."

"I thought you were going into the house for a drink."

"I am, I—"

Amy placed her hand against the back door, as if she needed help standing up. "I just feel a little dizzy is all."

"Oh, I'm sorry," Helen said, already on her way back. "I'll walk inside with you."

Damn.

She'd come back here and there'd be no hope of ever getting that jacket.

All Amy could do was open the door right now and reach inside and—

But Helen was already standing in front of her.

"You do look a little pale, dear."

"Oh, I'm fine."

Helen noticed where Amy was staring.

Amy smiled nervously. "Oh, I was looking at your football blanket."

"Oh. It's a pretty one."

Helen took Amy by the arm and turned her away from the Land Rover. "Let's go get you that drink of water."

Playing out the rest of the charade, Amy pretended to be wobbly on her feet. She made her knees tremble as she walked. She'd learned how to do that in her senior-high drama class.

"I'm sorry you have to go through all this, Amy. It's just too bad that your brother didn't turn out the way you did."

"He didn't do it, Helen. He really didn't."

Helen patted her arm gently, reassuringly. "He couldn't ask for a more loyal sister than you, that's for sure."

Inside, Helen led Amy to a chair at the kitchen table and then sat her down, as if Amy were a very old and brittle lady.

A minute later, Helen placed a glass of water on the table in front of Amy.

"This should do the trick," Helen said. "Water always helps me when I feel a little woozy."

"I really appreciate this, Helen."

"My pleasure, dear. My pleasure."

Amy sipped her water. "This does make me feel better."

"I knew it would."

Thinking about the coat in the back of the Land Rover, Amy said, "I think I'm all right now, Helen. This is just what I needed."

Helen smiled. "Let's give it another minute or two. We want to make sure you're *really* all right." Her smile broadened. "At least, that's Dr. Helen's advice."

"Thanks again for everything, Helen."

"My pleasure, dear. My pleasure." Then, "I was thinking. Was there anyplace special that your brother played when he was a kid?"

"No place special that I can think of. I mean, he roamed all over the place. You know, the way most little boys do."

"But no one special place?"

"Not that I can think of. Why?"

But, of course, Amy knew why—so Helen could lead Chief Hadley to Richie, and Hadley would arrest Richie, and the verdict of the trial would be a foregone conclusion. And David and Helen Cummings could return to Washington with nothing to worry about.

"I was just thinking . . . if there was a special place where he used to hide . . . some secret place . . . you know the way boys are . . . David was always like that . . . always wanted to have hiding places that nobody else knew about . . . that maybe if Richie had had a place like that . . . maybe that's where he'd hide out now."

"There's no place I can think of."

"Are you sure?"

Amy shrugged. "Pretty sure. I mean, if I think of it, Helen, I'll tell you."

"That's very honorable of you, dear."

"Maybe we should get back."

"You sure you're feeling better now?"

"Positive."

Once again, Helen helped Amy to her feet. Amy might have been her ninety-three-year-old grandmother.

How am I going to do it? Amy thought. She and David are

going to get into their Land Rover and drive away and I'll never have a chance to get the jacket.

They went out the back door and down the walk to the farmyard.

Amy couldn't take her eyes off the back of the Land Rover.

Sitting in there was the evidence that might well begin to prove her brother's innocence.

Helen, seeming to sense Amy's interest in the vehicle, held tightly to Amy's arm and guided them wide of the Land Rover.

Amy realized that there was only one way she was ever going to get the jacket . . . and that was to take it. To bolt from Helen's arm . . . run to the Land Rover . . . throw open the back door . . . and take the coat out.

She prepared herself.

In eight or nine more steps, they'd draw even with the Land Rover. That would be Amy's last chance to bolt free.

Three steps . . . four steps . . . five steps.

"How's Amy doing?" David Cummings said, interrupting the conversation he was having with Sam and Hadley and Susan.

Six steps . . . seven steps . . . eight steps . . .

"Oh, fine," Helen said.

And in just that moment, her attention focused on her brother rather than Amy's arm . . . her grasp lightened . . . and Amy jerked away.

"What're you doing, dear?"

Helen, startled, tried to keep her tone sweet, but in her words you could hear a bit of confusion and panic . . . and certainly anger.

"Where are you going?" she snapped then.

Amy knew she didn't dare hesitate. Amy put her hand in her pocket and brought the button out as she ran toward the Cummingses' car.

She rushed over to the back of the Land Rover and grabbed the rear door handle and turned it and it was locked.

"Just a minute here!" Helen snapped, stepping over to where Amy stood. "Just what the hell do you think you're doing?"

Amy tried the handle again, giving it a savage turn to the right.

This time, the locking mechanism turned, and the handle went all the way down.

She hadn't turned it hard enough before.

Just as Amy was starting to open the door, Helen grabbed her arm.

This time it was not the loving touch of a nurse that Helen used. This time it was the death grip of an enemy.

With her other hand, Helen seized Amy's shoulder and pushed her back from the open door.

"Hey, what's going on there?" Chief Hadley said.

As Amy was pushed back from the vehicle, she felt her left hand open and the brass button fall from her grasp.

The button landed on the bare earth of the farmyard. It lay there like some gleaming artifact of cosmic importance.

Helen saw it, too, and instantly seemed to recognize what it was . . . and what it meant to her and her brother.

Amy bent to pick it up but Helen shoved her out of the way.

Amy, losing her balance, almost went over backward.

Helen bent down from the waist and started to pick up the button.

That was when Amy realized the opportunity Helen had given her.

While Helen was picking up the button, Amy would have time to—

She took three steps back to the open hatch door and groped inside and grabbed the carrying bag.

Helen had the brass button in her fingers before she saw what Amy had done.

"Give me that!" Helen said, trying to swipe the bag out of Amy's hand.

But Amy jerked it away, and then, seeing Sam, tossed it over to him.

"What the hell's going on with you two?" Chief Hadley said, looking from Helen to Amy.

Amy, breathless, said, "When David and Helen were putting Darcy's body in back of my brother's cabin last night, Helen lost the brass button I showed you, Chief. Sam can show you where it came off. It's a suede coat and got drenched last night, so Helen was taking it to the cleaner's this morning. I showed you the button." She nodded to Helen. "She has the button now. Ask her to give it to you."

"I don't have to tell you how ridiculous this all is, do I, Chief?"

But Hadley, surprisingly, looked as if he didn't consider this to be foolish at all.

Has he finally begun to believe me? Amy wondered. Is that possible?

Chief Hadley glanced at Sam a moment and then back at Helen. "You're one of the oldest friends I've got in this town, you and your brother. So I don't want anything to do with causing you trouble. I just couldn't bring myself to do it."

So I was wrong, Amy thought. Even though he knows that the button is worth pursuing as a piece of evidence, he is just going to let them walk away.

"So, Helen," he said, "I'm going to let Sam here handle this investigation."

Amy wondered who looked the most startled at that moment—Helen or Sam.

4

By the time Steve Arnette reached the back of the shack, his khaki clothes were soaked with sweat and creek water.

He came up from the creek bed with his rifle aimed directly at the back of the shack. He moved slowly, certainly, in a crouch.

But while his rifle was fixed on the shack, his mind was fixed on the reward money. By now, he'd pretty much decided he'd kill Richie McGuire. Helen Cummings could handle any legal hassles that might arise.

He came to a stand of jack pines and stopped, raising himself up. His bones cracked and his thigh muscles were sore from crouching so long. It had taken fifteen minutes of crouching to reach this point. Jimmy appeared briefly in the window—then vanished.

The day was beautiful as ever, the intoxicating smell of burning leaves making him melancholy for the better times of the past. The hoot of a distant train in the autumn-blazing hills filled him with an almost enjoyable loneliness. Maybe some long day from now, when the death of Richie McGuire was long behind him, when the town of Crystal Falls was also long behind him . . . he would call Susan and she would see, at long long last, that he was the person she should be with. And then she would join him. . . .

He inadvertently put his weight on the end of a small fallen branch. The snapping sound seemed as loud as a gunshot in the woodsy silence.

The thing to do now was to swing wide, get in position to charge the front door of the shack, kick it in, and then move quickly to the trapdoor and Richie.

Richie might think he was tough. But he wouldn't be tough after a minute or so of what Arnette had in mind. . . .

He circled wide, leaving the protection of the jack pines to arc about twenty yards directly in front of the shack.

Then, hefting his rifle, patting his holster to make sure that his magnum was still comfortably in place, he put his head down and began running straight for the cabin door.

Rotting wood gave beneath his shoulder, wood that ripped away from the doorframe with a nasty tearing sound.

The smells of the cabin rushed at him: decades-old water-soaked wood; dog shit and cat shit and squirrel shit and raccoon shit; the sweet-smelling soil beneath the floor where wood and linoleum alike had rotted through; and the ancient, shocking scent of death . . . so many, many creatures having died in here in the past eight decades.

The sights were no more pleasant, the floor littered with crumpled-up cigarette packs, McDonald's wrappers, Trojan packages, Hostess Twinkie wrappers, crushed Pepsi cans, stray pages torn from girlie magazines, and tin cans that had held everything from baked beans to SpaghettiOs, the cans being the sustenance of hobos and drifters and fugitives. . . .

The trapdoor was at the back of the cabin, concealed by an empty metal cabinet so rusty that it had rotted through in many places. You had to push the cabinet away to get to the trapdoor . . . and then pull it back in place when you were down on the ladder.

He had to work quickly now.

He tossed the once gray and now empty cabinet aside with no more effort than he would have a cardboard box.

Then he dropped to his knees, threw open the trapdoor.

The chill, fetid smell of grave-darkness . . .

He pushed the barrel of his rifle down there and opened fire. . . .

This was the only way he'd ever get Richie out of there . . . to scare him out so he could get a clean daylight shot at him. . . .

The gunfire was noisy in the old shack. Three . . . four . . .

five shots . . . the sound harsh and violent in the surrounding forest silence.

There were shouts, curses, cries, gunshots fired in response.

Arnette jumped back from the edge of the trapdoor while Richie fired off his rounds. . . .

Richie was an amateur. He wouldn't be carrying the extra rounds Arnette was . . . and he wasn't a marksman, either. Every summer in Des Moines, at the police academy where Hadley sent each of his officers for further study, Arnette took first place on the firing range.

Arnette waited for silence from below. Richie would quit firing for a time and then Arnette would shove his rifle down there and fire some more. He didn't especially give a damn if he killed Richie down there . . . but it would definitely look better if Richie died out in the sunlight with his weapon in his hand . . . making it look as if Arnette had had to fire in self-defense.

Then he heard, from below, Jimmy whimpering.

But Richie surprised him.

After a few moments of silence, Arnette leaned cautiously forward and poked his rifle in the trapdoor opening.

He was just about to squeeze off a few shots but Richie beat him to it, fired off three quick shots of his own.

This time, the cries and curses belonged to Arnette, who jerked back from the opening as the bullets tore into what was left of the roof.

The son of a bitch.

The thing was to move now. Not to give Richie any more time.

Arnette moved.

He squeezed off three shots.

This cry was different. This was not a cry of fear. This was a cry of pain.

But the voice—teary, horrified, frightened—didn't belong to Richie. It belonged to Jimmy.

There was some luck for you, hitting that crazy bastard.

Jimmy began sobbing.

"You asshole!" Richie shouted. "You hit Jimmy."

"Bring him up, then."

"Yeah, and have you shoot us both?"

By this time, Jimmy was wailing. "Am I gonna die, Richie?"

"You'll be fine, Jimmy."

"You got to get me to Doc Klever. You gotta, Richie, or I'll die."

Jimmy was getting more scared by the moment. This was actually to Arnette's advantage, of course. This just put additional pressure on Richie to come up from the cellar.

"C'mon up, Richie."

Jimmy was sobbing.

The sound aggravated Arnette. He hated this kind of weakness. It was his wife's kind of weakness. She had no reserve of strength to call on in times of crisis. At least Jimmy had the excuse of being retarded or whatever the hell he was.

"C'mon up, Richie," Arnette said again.

There was no response from Richie.

"It hurts real bad in my side, Richie," Jimmy said. "Real bad."

"You son of a bitch!" Richie shouted up.

His exasperated tone made Arnette smile. Richie would soon enough give in. Richie would soon enough come up from the cellar.

"Tell him to get you to Doc Klever, Jimmy," Arnette shouted down into the darkness.

Jimmy blubbered some more. "He's right, Richie. You gotta get me to Doc Klever."

Then there was a great cry of pain. Wherever he'd been hit,

Jimmy's wound was starting to take a major toll. Richie didn't know what he was going to do. Jimmy could very easily die down there.

"He'll kill us if we go up there, Jimmy," Richie said. "Don't you understand that?"

Arnette smiled again. Richie really was getting desperate. He was trying to reason with Jimmy, for God's sake. Who could reason with Jimmy?

"You're losing a lot of blood, Jimmy," Arnette said. "Ask Richie if he's just going to let you die down there."

"Richie, please!" Jimmy wailed. "Please help me!"

"You bastard!" Richie shouted up at Arnette.

"You're running out of time down there, Jimmy. You really are."

Jimmy fell to sobbing, then, a wretched, pathetic sound that spoke implicitly of how desperately human beings cling to life ... even human beings like Jimmy, who really didn't have much to live for. . . .

"Oh, Richie!" Jimmy cried. "It really hurts! It really hurts!"

This time, significantly, there was no epithet from Richie.

Just the echoes of Jimmy's painful scream.

Richie said, "We're coming up, Arnette."

Arnette didn't say anything.

Good psychology. Rattle Richie a little more. Why is Arnette so silent suddenly? Richie would be thinking.

"You hear me? I said we're coming up!"

Arnette didn't answer this time, either.

Jimmy started wailing again, screaming about how much it hurt.

"You cocksucker!" Richie shouted up. But there wasn't much passion in his words.

He was shouting just to relieve himself of anger and frustration.

"You'll have to help me, Jimmy," Richie said. "I'm going to

carry you over to the ladder and then you'll have to climb the steps. I'll be right behind you."

"I don't think I can, Richie."

"Goddamn it," Richie exploded. "It's the only way you're gonna get out of here!"

Jimmy started crying again, great gasping tears of fear and self-pity.

"Oh, shit, Jimmy. I'm sorry. I shouldn't have yelled at you. It's just—" He paused. "C'mon, Jimmy, I'll carry you over to the ladder. You ready?"

Then there were the sounds of grunting in the darkness below. Arnette could make out the indistinct shapes of two people moving toward the ladder.

Several times, Jimmy whimpered like a damaged animal. Several times, he started crying.

Bodies slammed hard against the ladder. Arnette saw the top of the ladder jostle.

"We're coming up," Richie said.

The anger was still there but now there was a hint of fear, too. He obviously didn't like handing himself over to Arnette this way. And wouldn't have if it hadn't been for Jimmy.

Arnette stood up, his long flanks painful once again from all the crouching.

He held his rifle at the ready, pointed directly at the trap-door.

He wasn't sure what was going to happen. He thought of just shooting the two as soon as they emerged from the cellar. He could then take the bodies back down and lay them on the floor. His story would be simple. Richie'd engaged him in a shoot-out and he'd been forced to kill him. Jimmy had been killed by getting in the way.

Jimmy moaned and whimpered all the way up.

Twice he screamed that he was falling over backward.

But somehow he made it.

Arnette waited. . . .

The hand-streaked blood was like a mask over Jimmy's face. He'd pawed the red stain from his wound all over his cheeks and forehead. He looked like some kind of crazed Indian warrior. Only his blue eyes shone brightly, and they shone with fever and delirium.

"You shouldn't've shot me, Steve," he sniffled when he saw Arnette standing there. "I wasn't hurtin' you or nothing."

He had never liked being called "Steve" by Jimmy. It implied an intimacy they didn't have. He called everybody by his first name. Most people thought it was cute.

"Just get up here, Jimmy."

Arnette couldn't see the wound until Jimmy stood on the floor.

He'd taken at least one bullet in the right side. His shirt and part of his jeans were soaked with blood. He smelled of sour piss.

"You go stand over there by the wall."

"You ain't gonna shoot us, are you?"

"You just go over there and stand and shut up. You understand?"

"You said you'd get me to Doc Klever, Steve."

Jimmy held his side. The wound was still leaking blood badly.

He went over and eased himself back against the wall. Under his blood mask, he was looking paler by the moment. He was crying again.

Darkness down the hole of the trapdoor.

Richie still had a handgun.

The son of a bitch wasn't going to make it easy.

"Get your ass up here, Richie."

Silence was the response.

"You hear me, Richie?"

Silence again.

He should have known it wouldn't be smooth, getting both of them up here. Nothing in his life had ever been easy, why should this be?

But he wasn't going to fuck around with cat and mouse.

Richie might think he could wait him out, but he was wrong.

"Richie, this is your last chance. You get your ass up here now or I'm going to change the fucking rules. You understand?"

Still, there was no response.

What he really wanted to do was kneel down at the trapdoor opening and fire blindly until he hit Richie. Like a shooting gallery. With the biggest prize ever won by anybody.

But that might not work.

Firing blind that way, Richie might be able to elude him for a long time. And Arnette didn't have all that many rounds left.

One thing was for sure. Richie was making this easy. Arnette was going to be so frustrated and so pissed off that he wouldn't have any trouble at all killing either one of them.

"Richie. You listening, Richie?"

No response.

No sense wasting any more time.

Arnette turned around and walked over to where Jimmy had slid down the wall to the floor.

Arnette pointed the tip of his rifle directly at Jimmy's head.

Jimmy looked up. He tried to scream but he didn't have the proper strength.

All he could do was blubber.

"I'm going to kill Jimmy in fifteen seconds, Richie. That's how much time you've got to get up here, you understand?"

Jimmy just blubbered some more.

As he stood there pointing the rifle, thinking of the reward money and how he was going to start a new life for himself, Arnette learned something about himself, learned he really could pull the trigger if he needed to.

"You've got twelve seconds, Richie," he said. "Twelve seconds."

This time, Jimmy was able to scream good and loud.

5

Amy saw right away that the Senator was going to be easier to deal with than his sister. The Senator looked anxious, even vaguely frightened after Sam took Helen inside the farmhouse and started asking her questions. Susan had gone back to the house with them. Chief Hadley, looking extremely uncomfortable, had left quickly. Amy had been surprised by the older man's sudden burst of integrity. She suspected that Hadley himself had been somewhat surprised by his own action. All these years as a lawman had taken their toll. Presented with a choice between right and wrong—even with powerful forces urging him to lean to the wrong—she sensed he would now do the honest thing. Knowing how difficult this had been for Hadley, Amy felt a new respect and affection for the man.

"This is crazy, Amy."

"Maybe it is, Senator."

"I don't have to tell you you won't be getting my support anymore."

She looked at him. "No, you don't have to tell me that, Senator. I figured it out on my own."

"We didn't have a damned thing to do with that girl's death."

"Then how did your sister's button get by the body?"

Senator Cummings shook his handsome, impressive head. "My God, Amy, listen to yourself. You're basing this whole thing on a story that Jimmy told you."

"He wouldn't have any reason to make it up."

"Oh? He wouldn't? How about saving the life of his hero? That seems like a pretty good reason to me."

Actually, Amy had thought of that herself.

Jimmy wasn't the most reliable witness. And there was no doubt that Richie was his hero.

She worried about how this slim piece of evidence would hold up in a murder trial.

But if the evidence was all that slim why was Cummings so nervous?

"I've done a lot for you, Amy."

"Believe me, Senator Cummings, I'm well aware of that."

"I've also helped your brother over the years."

"That's true, too."

She marveled again at how photo-op he always looked. She'd seen him swimming. Even dripping wet, hair plastered to his skull, he looked photo-op, like an aging Olympic diver.

She didn't have much time, she realized.

Sam probably wasn't getting much cooperation from Helen.

The Senator was Amy's only hope. . . .

"I want to say something to you, Senator."

The photo-op face scowled. "I'm not sure I want to hear it."

"One thing I've learned working in the district attorney's office is that . . . mistakes happen."

"Whatever the hell that means."

"It means that I doubt you meant to kill her," she said calmly, not taking her gaze from his. While she was fishing for a response, she believed what she was saying. The Senator's hankering for young women had long been an open secret.

But this one had gone wrong somehow . . . this one had ended in death. She didn't believe that the Senator would ever be capable of violence. But an accident, yes . . .

"I don't want to talk to you anymore, Amy," he said. "You're being ridiculous."

But Amy continued on. "We'll know a lot more when Doc Klever tells us how she died. But I'll bet you didn't mean to do it. I'll bet the worst thing you did in all this was trying to put the blame on Richie. That's probably your only real crime."

She heard the back door open and turned around to see Sam walking toward them. She wondered where Helen was, and what had happened.

"I'll have to ask you to stay here awhile, Senator," Sam said. He looked tense. He glanced only once at Amy. He was clearly trying hard to be professional about all this. He didn't want her feelings for Richie to influence him in any way.

"I'd also," Sam said, "suggest that you contact a lawyer."

"A lawyer?" the Senator said. "A lawyer? Sam, for God's sake. Do you know who you're talking to?"

"Yes," Sam said quietly, "yes I do, Senator. And I mean no disrespect. I'm just doing my job."

Now he looked at Amy. "I've called off the search. I don't want that posse looking for somebody who may be innocent. We'll find him some other way."

He nodded to the Senator's Land Rover. "And one of the state forensic men is on his way out here to go through the Rover."

That was when the Senator surprised them both by sinking back against his vehicle and hanging his head. "I have cancer. I'm a sick man. I can't deal with anything like this. One of the things the doctors warn you against is stress."

When his head came back up, he was smiling an eerie smile. "How's this for stress? Being accused of murder?"

He took a deep breath and sighed. "I've got a doctor's appointment tomorrow. I find out if everything's going to be all right. If I'm still in remission and everything. Wait till I tell my doctor that I'm a suspect in a murder investigation."

He looked at Amy when he spoke next. "You guessed right, Amy. It was an accident. A pure accident."

They didn't speak. He seemed to have more to say.

"I had a little thing with her. Just a little harmless thing was all. And then the accident happened and—you know what she did, she fell over backward and hit her head on the edge of the TV. God, who would've thought you could die from something like that? Think of how many times the average human being must hit his head. And nothing ever happens. But this one time—just my luck—this one time . . ."

This time when he shook his head, he was no longer the photo-op senator.

There were tears in his eyes now. "I've got my doctor's appointment tomorrow. My God, I didn't need this. I sure didn't."

"I need to talk to Susan," Amy said.

She wished she could feel more compassion for Senator Cummings—he looked so frail and old suddenly—but somehow she couldn't.

All she could think about was finding Richie . . . before the posse got him.

Maybe Susan knew where Richie had gone. . . .

She hurried back to the house.

SEVENTEEN

1

Once again, Richie McGuire felt an overwhelming sense of unreality . . . of moments that had the texture and feel of a bad dream.

Ever since Darcy had come to the bar last night . . .

Darcy . . . something he had to remember about Darcy. Closed his eyes. Concentrated as hard as he could. Darcy . . . what was he trying to remember, anyway? The whole damned night was lost to him . . . no solid memory of anything really . . . but a memory fragment lingered nonetheless . . . the hill behind his house . . . saw something out his back window . . . but what had he seen? Had somebody been up on his hill doing something he wasn't supposed to?

Had to think. Had to fight down the panic. Needed to think calmly, rationally. On the hill last night, in the slashing rain, on the hill last night, somebody had been doing something . . . but who . . . and what?

Then, up top, Steve Arnette was shouting again, warning

him that he had only twelve seconds to come up and hand himself over or he would kill poor Jimmy. . . .

What choice did he have?

Jimmy was alternately crying and screaming.

You never knew about Arnette. Maybe he really *would* kill Jimmy. There had always been that element of craziness in Arnette. Back when they'd been friends in high school, Richie had the reputation for being crazy . . . but it was Steve Arnette who deserved the title. Richie recalled one night especially . . . the night Arnette blindfolded himself and drove drunk out along the curvy river road at seventy miles an hour. . . .

"You hear me, Richie? Twelve seconds!"

What choice did he have?

The cold, decay-heavy air of the root cellar was getting to be too much for him anyway. Starting to make him nervous . . . starting to remind him of the final darkness. He needed sunshine and warmth now.

Who had been on the hill last night? What had he seen? Somebody had been up there. . . .

He put his hands on the ladder, took a final glance behind him at all the empty orange crates that had been used to store the various fruits and vegetables many decades ago. . . .

He started climbing the ladder, one careful rung at a time.

Up top, Jimmy was crying again, yelling for Arnette not to hurt Richie. The wound had looked pretty bad. He was surprised that Jimmy still had the stamina for so much howling. He felt guilty about Jimmy. This was all Richie's fault that Jimmy had been wounded. Hurting Jimmy was the same as hurting an innocent child.

Doc Klever was the first consideration. No matter what else Arnette had in mind, he had to get Jimmy to the Doc first.

Daylight and warmth came nearer as Richie neared the final rungs of the ladder. Dusty sunlight, slanting through the holes in the roof, fell on the floor around the opening. He could actually smell the sunlight.

Richie reached the final rung of the ladder and started to peer up through the trapdoor opening, like a hibernating animal taking its first peek at spring.

Arnette stood there waiting for him, legs spread wide, rifle aimed directly at Richie's head.

"Where's the gun?"

"Here," Richie said.

"Lay it down real easy on the floor."

"I've only got one shot left."

"I don't give a shit, Richie. I said lay the gun down on the floor."

Richie reached down to his belt and tugged the gun loose. Then he started to bring it up through the opening.

"Nice and easy so I can see what you're doing," Arnette said.

Richie laid the weapon down a foot from the opening.

"Now you come up real slow, too."

"How's Jimmy?"

"You don't worry about Jimmy. You just worry about getting your ass up here."

"I ain't doin' real good, Richie," Jimmy said. "I'm scared. I'm real scared."

"We'll get you to Doc Klever," Richie said.

"I hope it's real fast, Richie."

All the time he spoke, Richie was slowly emerging from the cellar.

Moments later, he stood on the floor of the cabin. For all its clutter, it looked a lot better than the gravelike darkness he had just come from.

"Get over there by Jimmy," Arnette said.

"We need to get out of here," Richie said. "Get him to the Doc."

"I'll worry about the Doc. You just worry about getting over there by Jimmy."

Richie didn't move. Just stared at his former friend in disbelief. "Shit, man, you're really gonna do it, aren't you? You're really gonna kill us."

"I'm scared, Richie," Jimmy said. His voice was losing power. His words were croaked out.

"Get over by him, Richie. Now."

Richie took two steps over to where Jimmy was propped up against the side wall.

"You're really going to kill us," Richie said.

"Just shut up," Arnette said.

"Is he gonna kill us, Richie? Is he really gonna kill us?" Jimmy didn't wait for an answer. He began crying sad, almost silent tears. Then, more to himself than to Richie, he moaned, "He's gonna kill us."

"You'll never be able to explain this, Steve," Richie said.

"Sure I will," Arnette said. He smiled. "I've got a good friend of mine helping me with this."

"I didn't kill her, Steve."

"Right."

"I didn't. Honest to God. I'm starting to remember seeing somebody on the hill last night . . . an hour or so more it'll come back to me, Steve. It really will. I'll be able to figure out who killed her."

"You better be quiet, Richie," Jimmy said. "You better be . . ."

Delirium must be setting in, Richie thought. The fever from the wound was making Jimmy babble nonsense sentences. It wasn't a good sign. Maybe it was already too late for Doc Klever.

Then Jimmy started sobbing again. Richie slid down the wall so he could reach over and give him a small hug.

"You'll be all right, Jimmy. We'll get Doc Klever."

But when he looked in Jimmy's eyes, he saw that the man was starting to withdraw from the cabin here. Pull deep into himself.

Jimmy wasn't going to be alive much longer.

Then he turned his attention to Arnette, and was startled to see that Arnette had put down his rifle and was holding Richie's handgun to his own forearm.

He held the weapon further away, now a full two, two and a half feet from his arm.

What he was doing was obvious: he was going to wound himself with Richie's gun.

A perfect setup.

What lawman wouldn't be justified in shooting, and fatally wounding, the man who had just shot him in the forearm?

Arnette looked at him and smiled. "This is where you can kiss your ass good-bye, Richie. Right here."

2

Susan was in the kitchen, talking on the phone to a neighbor who'd just called.

Amy walked up in front of her. Susan saw immediately that something was very wrong. She excused herself to the neighbor, then hung up.

"Senator Cummings just admitted that he accidentally killed Darcy," Amy said.

"Are you serious?" Susan said. "My God."

"The posse's being called back. But what I'm afraid of is that there will be a couple of gung ho types wandering around. They'll be all liquored up and if they see Richie, the first thing they'll do is fire at him."

Susan saw instantly what Amy was saying. "The old line shack. That's where he's hiding."

"God, I didn't think of that," Amy said.

She and Richie and Steve Arnette and Susan had played down there many, many hours.

"I know a shortcut from here," Amy said. "I can be there in fifteen minutes."

"That posse was pretty worked up," Susan said.

"Very worked up."

"I'll go with you."

Amy put out her hand and touched Susan's shoulder. "Thanks. I figured you might want to go along."

They hurried to find Sam and tell him where they were going.

"Richie'll be all right," he said, obviously concerned with Amy's fear and dread that it was too late to save her brother.

3

Sam was just coming out the back door of the farmhouse, Senator Cummings and his sister preceding him.

Cummings looked even sicker than he had ten minutes ago—pasty, sweaty, trembling.

Helen kept glancing at him and shaking her head. "I knew you were going to ruin it for me, David. I finally got my chance to be senator and now this happens. I knew you were going to ruin it for me."

But Cummings didn't seem to hear her. His eyes were fixed on some distant point up in the autumn-hazy hills.

"Letting Amy sweet-talk you like that," Helen went on angrily. "You could've kept your mouth shut for once, couldn't you?"

Sam led them over to his car and held the back door open for them.

David slid onto the backseat. Said nothing. Helen followed him into the car. She was muttering to herself.

After Sam closed the door, Amy rushed up to him and told him where Richie was.

"I can get there in fifteen minutes," she said. "I'm leaving right now."

Sam nodded. "That's probably a good idea. There may be a few people who haven't heard that the search has been called off."

"That's what I'm afraid of."

Amy glanced to the woods in the distance. "We have to go."

As they came to the first field, Amy held the strands of twisted wire apart so that Susan could slide through.

Then she climbed through herself, and they were off, jogging toward the woods and the shortcut that would lead them to the line shack.

4

Steve Arnette changed his mind, decided to kill Richie and Jimmy before wounding himself.

"You come over here near me," Arnette said to Richie.

"He's gonna kill you, Richie."

"It'll be all right, Jimmy."

"He's gonna kill us both."

Jimmy started crying again, then put his hand to the wound. "He's gonna kill us both is what he's gonna do. He honest to God is." He started breathing in spasms, then. Even talking wore him out now. The wound was bad.

Richie pushed himself to his feet.

He wondered if Arnette was going to be stupid enough to kill both of them in the shack.

Arnette would want to make it look as if Richie had been trying to escape.

"C'mon, Richie, let's go outside."

"What if I say no?"

Arnette spoke calmly. "I'm going to count to ten. If you're not outside, I'll kill Jimmy right now. And I think you know I'm not bullshitting you."

Richie stared at him. "You know the funny thing?"

"I don't have any time for funny things right now, Richie."

"The funny thing is that Susan *should* have picked you over me. You really loved her. You really wanted a life with her."

"Maybe it's not too late."

Richie felt a spasm of pity for his old friend. For all his "good sense," Arnette had always been as much of a dreamer as Richie was. He was just quieter about it was all.

"It was too late a long time ago," Richie said, not unkindly.

"Fuck this bullshit," Arnette said abruptly. "You just get your ass out the door. You hear me?"

"He's gonna kill you," Jimmy said.

"Shut up, asshole, or I'll come over there and kill *you.*"

Arnette was starting to come apart.

He glowered, waving his gun in the direction of the doorway.

Richie looked down at Jimmy. "Just stay there, Jimmy."

"He's gonna kill you, Richie."

Richie nodded and turned around and went out the door.

It was such a ridiculously beautiful day. The birds were singing their asses off, the sun was laying down dusty golden beams, the pine forest was almost overwhelming with sweet scents.

And he was going to die. Right here. Now.

But for all the terror of this moment—he just didn't want his bowels to let go, even now he still had a little sense of dignity left—he kept trying to put last night together in his mind.

What had he seen up there on the hill behind his cabin? He'd seen *somebody.* He was sure of it.

Arnette walked him out five yards in front of the cabin.

"Stop right there."

Richie stopped.

"Turn around and face me."

Richie turned around. "You really think you can do this, Steve?"

"Shut up."

"I don't think I could kill you unless I absolutely had to."

"Shut the fuck up. And I mean it."

"You don't have a lot of leverage here, Steve. You're already going to kill me, anyway. So what if I keep talking? I'm a dead man already."

Steve raised his weapon. Pointed it directly at Richie's chest. "I fucked her first. You didn't know that, did you? I'll bet she never told you that, did she? She was a virgin when I got her."

"You're a pretty pathetic son of a bitch, you know that?"

"Yeah. Look who's talking. The golden boy. The big-time pro football player. You didn't do so fucking good yourself, asshole."

Arnette steadied the rifle as much as he could. "You son of a bitch." He seemed to be responding to demons in his head rather than to anything he could actually see, cursing a lifetime of failures with Susan, the only person he'd ever truly cared about.

Richie knew that Arnette was ready now. Could actually do the deed.

Fragments of a prayer filled his mind. He felt his cold bowels slither. A deep shudder traveled the length of his body.

So this was how dying went. All his life he'd feared it and now it was here. And it was just as scary as he'd always feared.

He wanted to cry out, plead with Arnette. It wasn't pride that stopped him. It was simply that he couldn't make himself speak. Fear had paralyzed him completely.

And then, finally, it happened. His voice returned.

"I don't want to die, Steve. I'm asking you not to kill me, all right?"

There. The supplicant tone that Arnette had waited all his life to hear in Richie's voice.

Or had he?

Arnette didn't even seem to hear Richie speak now.

He simply raised the rifle again, resighted along the barrel, and then squinted one eye closed for a better shot.

Richie closed his eyes.

No macho bullshit now, man.

He was afraid to die.

He certainly wasn't going to watch Arnette fire.

He kept his eyes closed, trying to somehow *will* himself out of this situation.

But what he was really doing was waiting . . . for the crack of the rifle . . . for the explosion of the bullets inside him.

And then he remembered last night. . . . The memory that had eluded him all day today . . . suddenly came clear. . . .

Then the rifle barked a shot—but he felt nothing.

He heard the groan and opened his eyes.

Arnette was just now sinking to the ground. And then pitching forward, unconscious, on his face.

And, framed in the cabin door, was Jimmy.

"I got him with a rock," Jimmy said. "I got him real good, didn't I, Richie?"

5

The sound of the rifle shot reached Amy and Susan just as they were about to leave the woods and enter the small clearing surrounding the line shack.

Amy's pace slowed momentarily as a terrible image filled her mind—her brother lying mortally wounded on the ground.

"Hurry!" she said, trying to see through the last ten feet of trees that lay before her.

Susan started using a longer stride as they jogged down the narrow dirt trail that wound through these woods.

"God, I hope he's all right!" Amy said, realizing that she was about to give in to her worst panic.

Susan said nothing. Kept running. Amy could hear her friend's breath coming hard and harsh now.

They reached the clearing less than a minute later, and there—as if in a miraculous vision—stood Richie over the fallen body of a man in a khaki police uniform. Presumably, the body was that of Steve Arnette.

Another moment of panic—had Richie killed him? It would be so ironic to be falsely charged with one murder only to actually commit a second killing.

Richie looked up, saw them coming.

As she hastened toward him, she told him about David Cummings's confession.

"God, I was so worried about you," Amy said, rushing to him and taking him into her arms.

He grinned his best boyish Richie grin. "Yeah, so was I." Then he said, marveling at the words he spoke, "I can't believe it. He confessed."

Susan nodded to the unmoving form of Steve Arnette. "Is he dead?"

Richie shook his head. "He was going to kill me and then Jimmy threw one of his rocks at just the right minute." Then he said, "Where's Jimmy?"

He looked around, saw nothing.

"Damn it," he said, and started walking quickly back to the shack.

Amy saw him go inside, then heard him say, "Jimmy!"

Amy and Susan ran to the shack.

Richie was propping Jimmy up in the corner.

Jimmy's eyes were closed. The only evidence of life was the moaning sound that filled his chest and throat. Blood had completely saturated the right side of his shirt.

"Jimmy? Jimmy? Can you hear me?" Richie said.

Amy knelt down next to her brother. Touched Jimmy's sweaty face. Skin was cold, didn't feel like skin at all. His cheeks were especially pale.

"Poor Jimmy," she said.

Susan leaned out of the shack doorway. "Listen."

Amy heard nothing. At first. Then the sounds of choppers reached her.

"Two of them," Susan said.

"Let's get them to land," Amy said. To Richie, "We'll be right back."

"Fine. I'll stay with Jimmy here."

Amy and Susan went outside and started waving up to the state police choppers.

There was just enough room in the clearing for one but not two of the machines to set down.

One of the choppers arced away eastward while the other proceeded to ease its way down, churning up dirt and loose grass and sand as it did so.

Moments after the machine reached the ground, the khaki-clad trooper in the shotgun seat jumped down out of the chopper and ran over to the waving women.

"Do you have a stretcher on board?" Amy said, shouting above the tumult of the spidery, dirt-churning machine.

The trooper nodded and walked back to the chopper.

Moments later, he was back with a rolled-up canvas stretcher.

They went to the cabin.

"Thank God," Richie said. "He seems to be slipping pretty fast."

They got the stretcher laid out and then carefully placed Jimmy on it.

The two men carried Jimmy out of the cabin and to the chopper.

They made Jimmy as comfortable as possible in the back of the machine.

"Why don't one of you go along with us?" the trooper shouted as the rotors started moving again.

Richie shrugged. "I'm filthy and I've got to get out of these clothes." He was covered with sweat, dirt, and Jimmy's blood. "You want to ride along, Amy?"

"Sure. That's fine."

The trooper helped Amy climb aboard. There was enough room in the back end for Amy to sit next to Jimmy on his stretcher.

The machine smelled of heat and oil.

She waved to Richie and Susan, who stood side by side waving back.

Maybe after all these years, her brother and Susan would finally be getting together.

She hoped so . . . for Richie's sake. He needed a good strong woman like Susan if he was ever to grow up and take control of himself.

The machine started its ascension. For a rickety moment, she felt the chopper engine surge, as if it weren't quite getting sufficient power. The moment scared her. She wasn't crazy about flying. Then everything felt fine. The chopper rose above the forest and headed north, back toward town.

Jimmy's hands were folded on his chest. He would look this way in his coffin.

But that was such a terrible thought.

Jimmy was going to be fine. After all they'd been through, there just wasn't any way that Jimmy would die.

There just wasn't any way.

She put her hands on his, closed her eyes, and said a silent prayer.

6

"It's over," Susan said.

"Yeah," Richie said. "Yeah, it is."

She smiled. "You're a free man again. How does it feel?"

"I sure owe you one."

"You don't owe me anything." Then, "Well, let's say you owe a dinner. How's that?"

"That's great."

"I wear my best dress and you wear your best suit and we go in to Iowa City."

"The new Italian place?"

"I was thinking more of the old steak house."

"The old steak house it is," he said.

"And when will this great feast take place?"

He could see how happy she was, and he felt like shit. He was going to hurt her again.

"How about tomorrow night?"

"Fine by me."

"Then maybe we go back to my place afterward?"

"You have something against my cabin?" He smiled.

"My place is more comfortable."

"That it is, my lady. That it is."

He checked his wristwatch. "I guess I'd better get going."

"Richie."

"Yeah?"

She looked at him without fear. With great determination. "I want it to happen for us this time."

"Yeah, I know you do."

"I want us to be married and have children and the whole nine yards."

"The whole nine yards," he said. "That sounds good."

"Does it? Really? It never sounded good to you before."

The tenderness of his kiss startled her. Richie was usually after only one thing: sex. But this embrace was very, very different.

"You've been damned good to me my whole life, kiddo."

"I'll be even better to you after we're married."

He held her for a long moment, feeling like a shit all over again.

"It's going to happen for us this time, isn't it, Richie?"

"Yeah, it is."

"You promise?"

"I promise."

"I couldn't take it if you ran away again this time, Richie."

"I know."

"I wouldn't have a life left." She looked so sad. "I'm supposed to be this strong, independent woman. But I'm not where you're concerned, Richie. I hate myself for it but I can't help it. The only man I've ever been able to love is you." She smiled with great melancholy. "So I guess you've got me even if you don't want me."

"Yeah," he said. "Yeah, I guess it kind of looks that way, doesn't it?"

Then they set off through the woods to their respective residences.

7

The pilot set the helicopter down in the backyard of Doc Klever's small brick clinic. Doc Klever and two nurses were waiting to help bring Jimmy inside. Jimmy was taken to the largest of the rooms, where Doc Klever performed a variety of outpatient operations for local people. Klever wanted to examine Jimmy's wound. If it looked too much for him to handle here, the chopper would fly Jimmy on to Cedar Rapids.

A few minutes after Jimmy was put on a gurney and wheeled into the surgery, Sam came through the front door and sat next to Amy in the reception area.

"Now if Jimmy's all right," Amy said, "this'll all turn out all right." She shook her head. "Except for Senator Cummings, anyway. I can't help but feel sorry for him."

"Our little Darcy wasn't exactly a saint," Sam said, and told her some of the things Cummings and his sister had shared over at the police station.

Amy was especially surprised by the blackmail photos.

"She was really into games."

"She sure was," Sam said. "Dangerous games."

"Boy, you should've seen Richie's face when we told him that Senator Cummings had confessed."

"I'll bet," Sam said. He took her hand, held it gently. "Take this the right way, all right?"

"I think I know what you're going to say. You just hope that Richie turns his life around."

"Right."   -

"God, after this experience—"

The surgery door opened. Doc Klever stuck his head out the door. "I'll be able to take care of this right here."

"Then it's not life-threatening?" Amy said. She felt relieved.

"He's lost a lot of blood but I can get the bullet out clean," Doc Klever said. "So, no, I wouldn't say it's life-threatening."

The surgery took a little under an hour and a half. Sam read a Luke Short paperback that Klever kept on the magazine table. This was for older men who were raised reading westerns. Amy looked through magazines.

A few times, Jimmy bellowed, sounding in great pain. Every time he did, Doc Klever said, "Ah, hell, Jimmy, if this is the worst thing that ever happens to you, you'll have led a charmed life." Doc Klever had never been a past master of bedside manner. He loved telling stories about World War II, when he'd operated on men with no anesthetic but whiskey.

Sam's cell phone rang several times, mostly Chief Hadley telling him how the whole police station had gone crazy with reporters wanting to know the story about Senator Cummings's confession.

This was just the first wave of reporters, Hadley told Sam, the local and state boys and girls. Pretty soon, because Cummings was, after all, a United States senator, the national people would be descending on the station.

It wasn't every day that a United States senator got himself involved in the death of a fifteen-year-old girl. At least, that most folks knew about, anyway.

But, like Amy, Sam wanted to wait here and make sure that Jimmy was all right.

"Plus," Sam told Amy after the third call, "I sure don't want to deal with any more reporters than I have to."

Last summer he'd worked on a very sad case where two elderly people, both ill and both penniless, had made a suicide pact. They'd died, just as they'd hoped, but Sam had never seen the press more vicious or exploitative. They covered the story for nearly a week but never addressed the real issue of two lonely old people unable to survive in the world. Sam wasn't up for another round of shrieking headlines, though God knew, this story was every tabloid editor's wet dream.

One of the nurses came out.

"How's Jimmy?" Amy said, getting up from her chair.

"He's fine."

"He took the bullet out?"

She nodded. "Took the bullet out, cleaned the wound." She smiled. "And even handed him a can of Pepsi, which Jimmy really seemed to appreciate. But he wants Jimmy to lie down in

there for a while. Then we'll have to have somebody take care
of him for a few days."

"He can stay at my place," Amy said.

"Great," the nurse said. "I was hoping you'd say that."

She started walking over to her desk, then said, "Oh, Sam,
the doctor would like to see you a minute. Why don't you
go in?"

"Sure," Sam said.

"I transferred all the calls over to the answering service," the
nurse said. "I'd better check in."

While Sam went to see the doctor, and the nurse checked
her messages, Amy drifted over to the window and looked out
on the small town she loved so much.

Maybe now there was going to finally be a place here for
Richie.

Maybe he'd put away all his childish pleasures and find in
himself the desire to start living like a responsible adult.

She knew there wasn't any more she could do for him. It
would be up to him.

She started planning meals for Jimmy for the next few days.
She wanted to make him things that would be good for him—
he had an atrocious diet, running to chili dogs and Dinty
Moore beef stew—but she also wanted to make him meals he'd
be happy to have. She was grateful to him for saving Richie's
life.

She was still staring out the window five minutes later when
she heard the surgery door open.

She turned and saw Sam coming out. She wondered instantly what was wrong.

He did not look happy.

"Is everything all right?"

For one of the few times since she'd known him, Sam lied
to her.

"Everything's fine. There's just something I need to do."

"And you're not going to tell me what it is?"

"I'll tell you a little later."

Sam was having some trouble looking directly in her eyes. He nodded to the door.

"I really need to get going."

"Sam," she said. "Tell me what's going on."

From the doorway, Doc Klever said, "Jimmy's waiting to see you, Amy."

She sensed that he had chosen this moment to interrupt them so he could help Sam get out the door.

"C'mon in, Amy," Doc Klever said, trying to sound like a favorite uncle inviting a favorite niece inside for a treat. "Jimmy's been asking for you."

"I'll call you," Sam said, and walked straight over to the door, and out to the parking lot.

"Did something happen I don't know about, Doctor?" Amy said when she moved away from the window.

Doc Klever looked evasive, too. "Why don't you spend a few minutes with Jimmy? Then walk down the hall to my office. I'll be in there."

Jimmy was lying down on a bedlike cot. His arms were at his sides. A heavy pink blanket covered him.

He tilted his head up to see her. "Hi, Amy."

"Hi, Jimmy."

"Doc Klever says you're doing very well."

"It hurts, Amy."

"I'll bet it does."

She walked over to the cot. "You're going to stay at my place for a few days."

"I am?"

His excitement was clear. A bit of color returned to his cheeks. "That'll be great, Amy." Then he looked at her a long time. "I didn't mean to tell them, Amy. But when he saw my neck, he started asking me questions."

She felt alarm, panic, but without knowing why. "I guess I don't know what you're talking about, Jimmy."

"The bruises, Amy."

"Bruises?"

"Yeah, on my neck. And hers."

"Who's 'hers,' Jimmy?"

"You know, that girl's."

"Bruises on Darcy's neck?"

"Yeah," Jimmy said. "And bruises on my neck."

He stretched his neck so she could see what he was talking about.

"You see the bruises, Amy? Doc says they're all over my throat."

And indeed they were.

"I didn't want to tell them, Amy. I really didn't. I don't want Richie to hate me. But I'm scared he will, Amy. I'm scared he will."

Then he started crying.

"So that's where Sam went?" Amy said five minutes later, as she sat across from Doc Klever in his cluttered little office. His desktop was an explosion of papers of various sizes, shapes, and colors.

"Once I saw the similarities, I asked him to come in and take a look."

"I see."

"I'm sorry, Amy."

She was still numb from what she'd learned. Numb . . . and confused.

Just a few minutes ago, her world had been bright and shiny again.

But now—

"I'll talk to you later, Doctor," she said, rising from her chair and walking trancelike out the door.

"Amy? Amy, are you all right?" Doc Klever called.

EIGHTEEN

1

Sam's car was parked next to Richie's cottage.

Amy had just finished parking her own car when she heard the explosion from inside. The gunshot.

She hurried from the car to the front door of the cottage.

No sound whatsoever came from inside.

She tried the door handle. Locked. She pounded on the door several times, shouting, "Richie! Richie!" as she did so.

Still no response.

She walked over to the vine-entangled window and tried to peer inside.

Richie had a gun. Sam was lying in the corner, apparently wounded. Blood covered the left shoulder of his khaki uniform shirt.

Richie glanced up. Saw his sister in the window.

"Let me in!" she shouted.

"Go away, you don't want to get involved in this."

"Let me in right now, Richie! I think you owe me that much, anyway."

Richie looked at Sam. "You stay right where you are."

Sam glared at him. "You've got my gun, Richie. And I've got a bad wound. I don't think there's a whole hell of a lot I can do to you."

Amy had never heard Sam's voice so contemptuous before.

As she waited for Richie to open the door, the beauty of the day again seized her. She wanted to be walking through the woods, collecting the most beautiful of leaves to press between the pages of a cherished book. She wanted to be horseback riding up in the hills. She wanted to be watching a good movie on TV with a fireplace crackling nearby.

All the terrible nightmares had ended less than a few hours ago, it had seemed, with the confession of Senator Cummings.

Her hand slipped inside the purse that hung from her right shoulder.

But now . . .

Richie opened the door. "You shouldn't be here."

"I don't want anybody else to get hurt."

"Sam being shot wasn't my fault," Richie said. "I was just trying to get away and I shoved him into the wall. The gun misfired."

"That isn't true, Amy," Sam said, speaking through gritted teeth. The pain must have been pretty bad. "He jumped me as soon as I got inside. He got my gun from me and then he shot me. Point-blank."

She could see by Richie's expression that Sam's words were true.

Before her now stood a stranger. Though she'd known Richie her whole life, she knew Sam a lot better.

She said, "You were drunk when you strangled Darcy, Richie. You'd get second-degree at most. Diminished capacity. You don't want to run now."

"I don't, huh?" he snapped at her. "You really think I want to spend ten years in prison? There's no fucking way, Amy. No way. I'm heading for Mexico. I can be there in two days. I know people there. I can vanish for the rest of my life."

"And it'll be some life," Amy said.

"Better than life in prison." Then, "That fucking Jimmy. He had to go and tell everybody what he saw."

This is what he'd suddenly remembered about last night. . . .

Darcy hadn't been dead when David and Helen Cummings set her on the hill behind Richie's cottage. The blow to her head had knocked her unconscious, but in their panic they hadn't checked her carefully. Last night's hard, cold rain had awakened her and she'd gone down to Richie's cottage. She was angry, threatening to tell her father on him if he didn't let her spend the night there. Richie, blind drunk, strangled her to death and then put her back on the hill. Jimmy saw all this. He'd come to give Richie the bread from Amy. Then he saw Richie, still staggering drunk, take Darcy up on the hill again and cover her with leaves once more.

"I can barely remember it," Richie said, "and for that I'm going to prison? No fucking way."

"Your life won't be over if you turn yourself in now, Richie," she said. "But it will be if you run."

She watched as Sam tried to push himself to his feet. "Listen to your sister, Richie. She's right. I'll tell everybody that the gun discharged accidentally while you and I were wrestling for it. I'll make sure there aren't any charges."

"You could even be out in less than ten years," Amy said. "And you'd be free to do what you want."

"Oh, yeah, an ex-con has so many great choices in life."

Richie was facing her again, forgetting Sam momentarily. "I appreciate everything, Amy. But I've got to leave. I really do."

She watched as Sam leaned forward—his eyes never leaving

Richie's back—and began to slide his hand down his black boot.

His spare gun.

She'd forgotten about that.

This was the best she could hope for. Sam would take his spare gun and make Richie hand his gun to Amy. Then nobody would be hurt.

"I'm leaving now, Amy," Richie said. "I want you to stand over by Sam."

Was there going to be time for Sam to pull his gun? His hand was still in his boot.

"Go on," Richie said. "Stand over there now."

She felt the weapon in her own pocket. Moments before entering the cottage, she'd transferred the gun to the right-hand pocket of her jacket.

"Go on," Richie said.

She walked over to the wall where Sam sat. His hand was still in his boot.

When Richie saw the angle of Sam's arm in relationship to the boot, he smiled.

"Caught you, didn't I? You cops always carry guns in your boots, don't you? Hand it over."

He walked over, reached down, and put the tip of his gun barrel right against Sam's forehead.

"Give me the gun," Richie said.

Sam looked up bleakly at Amy and shook his head. They both knew what lay ahead. Richie was going to escape. There would be an even wider manhunt. And given Richie's temper, he'd be shot to death somewhere on the American side of the border.

Sam slid a blue snub-nosed .38 from inside his boot.

Richie held his hand out. Palm up.

Sam laid the .38 carefully across Richie's palm.

Richie hefted the gun momentarily and then shoved it into his back pocket.

He walked over to the telephone, bent down, found the cord connecting it to the jack, and then ripped the cord free.

"No phone," he said. "And no cars. I'm going to fix your engines so they won't start. And I'm going to take your cell phones. It'll be a while before you're able to contact anybody."

He was a stranger again to her. She'd never seen her little brother's face this hard, this angry. He showed no remorse at all. This terrified her. She remembered all the stories she'd heard about his hard, cold temper. All the years she'd refused to believe them . . . but now . . .

"Richie," she said, "you killed a girl last night. And it doesn't seem to matter to you."

"She was a bitch," he said. "I didn't have a hell of a lot of choice, did I?"

"Sure you did. You didn't have any right to kill her no matter *what* she said to you."

He walked up to her. Put his hand on her shoulder. "Amy, I really appreciate everything you've done for me all my life. But I'm not going to prison. And that's where she wanted to see me go. I was dumping her, so she was going to ruin me. I know you don't believe this but I didn't have any choice."

He walked over to the door. "You'll hear from me sometime. From Mexico."

"You won't get that far, Richie," Sam said. "They'll find you. And you'll have to kill them or they'll have to kill you. You don't want any more blood on your hands, do you?"

Richie smiled. "Thanks for the pretty speech, Sam. I need to hear things like that every once in a while."

He walked over to the table and picked up a small collection of money. Stuffed it in his pocket.

She wouldn't have many chances, she knew.

It had to be very soon.

He said, "I guess there isn't much more to say, Amy. I don't blame you for being pissed."

"Pissed? Richie. You killed somebody." She heard the whine in her voice but his words had stunned her. He was talking as if he'd committed some kind of social faux pas instead of murder. Now she had no doubt that he would also kill others when he felt he needed to. "Don't make this any harder than it has to be for us. Sam and I are sworn to uphold the law. We can't let you walk out of here."

The chill smile. "You can't, huh? How you going to stop me?"

"I have ways."

"I kind of like it when you're pissed like this, Amy. Shows me a side of you I never saw before."

"I'm telling you, Richie. You're not going to walk out that door."

He glanced at them both and then walked to the door.

He turned his back to them to open it, and that was when she took her gun out and said, "Stop right there, Richie."

He turned around to see that she was holding a gun on him just as he was holding a gun on her.

He said, "I don't want to have to kill you, Amy."

"I don't want to have to kill you, either."

"Put your gun down."

"It's too late, Richie. I have to turn you over to the law."

"I'm afraid I can't let you do that, Amy." To Sam he said, "Sam, tell her. You know people like me. Tell her that I'll kill her if I need to."

"I think she already knows that, Richie," Sam said softly. "I think she realized that a few minutes ago."

Richie laughed. "Another one of your nice little speeches, huh, Sam?"

"Put your gun down on the table," Amy said.

"It's not going to happen, Amy. I'm going to walk out that door and you're not going to stop me."

"But I am, Richie. That's what you don't realize. I can't let you go on and kill somebody else. I've got a duty to stop you."

He stared at her gun for a long moment, then raised his gaze to hers. "You're not going to kill anybody, Amy, and you know it." He spoke in a curiously gentle way. Then he said, "I love you, Amy. I really do."

He glanced around the cottage one final time and then put his hand on the door again.

"Don't walk out the door," Amy said.

But he did, of course. That was *exactly* what he did. Walked out the door.

Or started to, anyway.

He had two more steps left to cross the threshold when Amy said, "Stop right there, Richie. I mean it."

And that was when he turned around and crouched down and fired.

Amy returned fire immediately.

She saw a bright blooming red flower on her brother's chest. His arms being flung wide. His weapon fly clattering against the wall. And him fall over backward, half in, half out of the cottage door.

He was crying. Sobbing.

She ran to him, knelt down next to him.

She could see that at least two of her bullets had done enormous damage. One to his chest. One to his stomach.

"I wanted you to kill me, Amy," he said, his voice husky but faint. "I didn't have nerve enough to do it myself."

He squeezed her hand with the last of his strength. "I love you, Amy. I'm sorry I made my life so miserable for you."

He was looking up at her with eyes so forlorn she could barely stand to see them.

He looked so young. He looked so scared.

She leaned down and kissed him tenderly on the cheek and then took his bloody hand and held it.

"I'm sorry, sis," he said.

And then he died.

She took his hand and pressed it tenderly to her cheek. Her eyes shone with tears. She looked up at Sam. "I didn't have any choice, did I, Sam?"

He came over and put his hand gently on her shoulder. "No," he said. "You didn't have any choice at all."

EPILOGUE

The minister did a damned good job.

She never got sappy. She talked about the good things Richie had done, yet she also talked about the bad things as well.

And she talked about how difficult it is to know somebody else, to truly *know* him, because we are all prisoners of our own needs and desires and demons.

Richie had his demons, she said, and not one of us here, not even his beloved sister, ever had any real insight into those demons. They were locked inside Richie. He took them with him to his grave.

She ended by saying that the town would always remember what had happened here this week. And rightly so.

But she hoped that, in time, the life of Richie McGuire could be put into some kind of perspective. That the town could forgive and love him again . . . as they had loved him one time long ago, on the autumn afternoons when college football was played . . . for that had been part of Richie, too . . . his great skills as a player . . . and the thrills he had inspired as a hero.

Driving out to the cemetery, Sam next to her in the backseat of the funeral-home limousine, Amy looked out the window at the warm fall day and said, "I keep trying to think I did him a favor, Sam. I keep trying to think that he really wanted to die."

"I think he did," Sam said.

"Yes," she said, beginning to cry, looking out at the country-side where Richie Douglas McGuire had played as a boy. "Yes, I guess he did."

Then Sam took her in his arms and held her as the limousine climbed the steep road to the cemetery.